Before You Sleep
A Novel
Amy Martin

Before You Sleep
Copyright © 2014
Amy Martin

Cover design by ninjaMel Designs

CHAPTER 1

I'm pretty sure Brenner Fieldhouse at Sumner College is climate-controlled, but right now, I can't really tell. I'm currently in the middle of an intense fourth quarter in the county summer basketball league's final game, and my team—the Pacers—is down by four points to the Bulls. So, while anyone sitting in the stands is probably cool and comfortable, down on the court the atmosphere is all heat, sweat, and adrenaline.

Brynne Lostrand, who plays forward for the Sumner Township Lady Panthers during the regular high school season, inbounds the ball to me under the Bulls' basket and I dribble up court, my left hand raised in the air and fingers flexing in order to signal what play we're going to run for this offensive set. Plays never come naturally to me during summer season, since I can't use the same set of signals I use when I lead the offense for the Titusville Lady Titans. Summer league teams are chosen by a random drawing of players from the county's four high schools, so if I used the same signals I use during our official high school games, I'd basically be giving our strategies away to our rivals. So, each team devises a set of plays during the four weeks of the league, which means the sets are never quite as automatic as the ones we use with our respective school teams during the regular season.

But, for now, they're automatic enough. Geri Anne Mason, a guard from Tusculum, calls out "Zip!" using the nickname even cross-county rivals know after all these years fits me better than my real name of Zara thanks to my speed on the basketball court. I don't throw the ball to her, however, because her yelling out to me is part of the plan. Two members of the Bulls' defense rush over to guard her under the assumption I'm going to pass to her. Instead, I shake my defender and drive the lane for a layup, but when I come down, I land on someone's foot in the chaos under the basket and my left ankle turns, leaving me in a heap on the floor.

Please, no, I think as I lie on my back and stare up at the fieldhouse ceiling. *Nooooooooo…*

Coach Dawson, who during the regular season coaches the River Run Lady Waves, kneels down next to me after running over from the bench.

"You okay?"

I rub my lips together and nod, pain shooting through my left ankle.

"Did it go in?" I mumble.

He leans down closer to my mouth and asks, "What?"

"The ball. Did I score?"

"Not that you should be worried about it at a time like this, but, yes—you scored," he says with a sigh.

"Good," I breathe.

Coach Dawson pushes a shock of sandy hair out of his eyes and removes my shoe and sock, a flash of embarrassment gripping me for a second over the fact my foot probably smells pretty rank after four quarters of basketball.

"There doesn't seem to be any swelling," he tells me, and I exhale with relief. "Do you think you can put pressure on it?"

"Maybe."

Coach jerks his head at someone, and Geri Anne appears at my side as I sit up. With their help, I get to my feet to discover I can put some slight pressure on my left foot. I drape my arms across their shoulders and hobble off the court with their support. They deposit me on the bench, and I elevate my foot on the seat next to me. One of the assistant coaches brings me an ice pack to guard against swelling, and I'm relegated to the position of spectator for the remaining few minutes of my summer league career.

4

Not like I needed the reminder, but the thought of how quickly what matters to me can disappear floats through my mind. If I'd landed just a little more awkwardly, any chance at a state championship or a basketball scholarship would have faded away as I'd need to spend months on crutches and might not be ready to play in November. I lift the ice off my ankle and flex my foot, letting out another relieved breath that my basketball career will live on.

I replace the ice pack and look up into the stands to find something—some*one*—else who also matters a great deal to me. My boyfriend, Kieran Lanier, sits flanked by his adoptive father, Jim Lanier, and his birth father, Morgan Levert, who recently started working on the Sumner grounds crew. Since the action's starting back up on the court, I don't have time at the moment to think about the weird set of circumstances that have transpired over the last seven months to lead Kieran to be sitting between his dads. I give him a thumbs-up sign to let him know I'm okay and turn my attention to my teammates who, thanks to my bucket, are now down by only two.

Back on the floor, the action progresses at lightening speed. Taylor Berend, a Sumner Township forward, blocks a shot from the Bulls and the rest of my teammates are off and running. Taylor passes the ball to Brynne Lostrand after they cross midcourt. Stopping behind the three-point line, Brynne's open enough to square her shoulders and put up a shot that clunks off the back of the rim but falls through the hoop, giving us a one-point lead.

The Bulls inbound the ball and their point guard, my Titusville teammate Tori Sandowsky, is immediately hampered by a full court press, a smothering form of defense designed to keep her near the baseline. She's eventually able to pass to Ashley Keep, one of my good friends and, during the regular season, a guard on the Titusville team, but too much time has run off the clock, and once

5

Ashley gets to midcourt, she puts up a desperation shot that falls a few feet short of the basket—Pacers win.

Confident I can put weight on my ankle, I slide back into my shoe and hobble from the bench to the court for the traditional high-fiving of the other team and saying "Good game," after which the Pacers, Bulls, and the rest of the NBA-named teams—the Heat, the Sixers, the Celtics, and the Mavericks—gather at midcourt for the awards presentations. After accepting my team championship trophy along with a smaller one as the summer league's Most Outstanding Player, I say goodbye to my teammates and head toward the doors to the lobby, where Jim, Morgan, and Kieran are waiting. But Cassie Newbaum, a fellow Titusville rising senior and one of my closest female friends, stops me at midcourt before I can take a step.

"How's your ankle?" she asks, sliding a caring arm around my shoulders.

"Fine. Just tweaked it a little."

"That's a relief. It'd be a long season without our star player."

I roll my eyes because Cassie knows she's just as important to our success on the court as I am, and as Ashley and our fellow senior Lauren Pipher are as well. After so many years of playing together, the four of us are a well-oiled machine and without one of the components, the whole mechanism would probably fall apart.

"Well, at least you didn't get stuck on the Heat this summer," she grumbles, her team having shamed their NBA counterparts by putting up the summer league's worst record. I give her a playful elbow to the ribs before she changes the subject. "Don't worry about giving me a ride home, by the way—I see you've got company." Cassie nods toward the Laniers and Morgan.

"You're sure? What about Ashley and Lauren?" I ask. I'd driven all of Titusville's rising seniors to Sumner this morning after dropping my mom off at her arts and crafts store.

6

"Ash is getting a ride from her mom." Cassie nods down court where Ashley's talking to her mother, an administrative assistant for Sumner's psychology department. "Lauren and I are going to the mall with Brynne after we shower up."

"You're hanging out with Brynne Lostrand?" I don't bother to mask my surprise. After summer league, we're all supposed to go back to being rivals. "Traitor."

"I know, I know. But have you met her brother? He goes to Northern and he's totally hot," Cassie gushes, and now, of course, I understand her sudden urge to hang out with Brynne. Cassie and Cody Hull, her off-and-on-but-mostly-off boyfriend since eighth grade, shifted their relationship back into the "off" position about three weeks ago for reasons I'm too bored after all these years to care about.

"And I'm guessing Brynne's brother is home for the summer?"

"And working at the Pretzel Hut in the Food Court," Cass confirms. "He's only here for another two weeks but there's nobody in Titusville left to date."

Cassie's pointing out a sad fact about our tiny hometown—in her case, most of the guys around our age are in the "Friends of Cody" category and, therefore, not dateable unless she wants to cause a fight at River Bend Park, where Titusville's "no-dude-she's-my-girl-not-yours" boxing/wrestling matches tend to take place. Any older guys in Titusville are undateable because if they haven't figured out a way to get out of town after graduation they must be slackers, drug dealers, meth addicts, or some combination of all three. And most younger guys are out of the question because usually, they're someone's brother and we've known them since they were in diapers—and have possibly seen them in those diapers, which is kind of creepy.

"Well, enjoy stalking Brynne's brother, then," I tell her, feeling sorry for Lauren over getting dragged along on Cassie's manhunt.

She gives me a little laugh.

"Have fun with your lover boy and his fam," she says, and bounces off toward the locker room.

Morgan is part of Kieran's "fam," of course, only not in the way Cassie—or anyone else around here—thinks he is. Everyone in Titusville already believes the Laniers are weird. I mean, sure—Jim being the head of the Counseling Center at Sumner College and his wife Carlie being a physician-turned-stay-at-home-mom, people can relate to. They can even kind of understand Kayla, Kieran's moody, standoffish sister, because what teenager isn't kind of moody and standoffish sometimes? But Kieran's sleeping disorder, which everyone outside my family and his believes is narcolepsy—but is really something much, much more complicated—is a little harder for folks in town to comprehend.

Ever since Kieran passed out on my desk in English class on his first day of school, most people around Titusville have steered clear of him. Now that Kieran and I have been a couple for a while, my friends, at least, are starting to warm up to him. And Kayla's boyfriend, recent Titusville graduate Brad Wallace, always accepted Kieran, which didn't change once Kayla leveled with him that Kieran's sleeping disorder isn't narcolepsy, but something caused by a drug Morgan cooked up with Kieran's birth mother when they were living a life of crime in New York City.

Brad, however, is an awesome person, and he's so out of his mind over Kayla that she could have told him Kieran was a scaly lizard creature from another planet masquerading as a human being and he would have figured out a way to deal and keep the secret. Telling everyone else in Titusville how Morgan did time as an accessory to armed robbery, a robbery in which Kieran's mother was killed in a police shootout, would be complicated to say the least. And then there's the whole matter of Morgan's memory loss—caused by the drug—and the fact that Kieran used to dream glimpses of future events thanks to the drug, which he ingested while still in his mother's womb. These are the kinds of secrets families want to keep secret, not to mention the fact that Morgan's former partner in crime, Frank Dozier, was at one time trolling around town and had lured Morgan to Titusville by threatening Kieran's life. But instead of learning the formula for the drug, which had fallen into one of the empty pockets in Morgan's memory, Frank ended up drowning in the Wyatt River after Morgan tricked him into believing they should kidnap Kieran and get both Kieran and the formula out of town. So they stole Cody Hull's car and chased Kieran and me to the river on Prom night, where I wrecked my mom's vintage Camaro to avoid going into the water. Morgan and Frank, however, launched off a rut in the gravel and their stolen car ended up submerged in the murky waters. Morgan escaped, but Frank's body was eventually discovered downriver near Sumner.

So, yeah—revealing too much truthful information about Morgan to people around town wouldn't be the best idea.

As far as everyone's concerned, Morgan is Carlie's cousin from New York who came to Titusville after he lost his job and fell on hard times, and he's now renting out one of the extra rooms in my grandparents' house until he can get back on his feet. No one knows Kieran's adopted, but he and Morgan look scarily alike and they both bear enough of a resemblance to Carlie and Kayla—blue eyes, inky-black hair, fair skin—that passing Morgan off as a cousin is plausible. Only the Sumner College Employment Office and Dewayne Masters, who owns Titusville's Downtown Diner where Morgan works a second job on weekends as a cook, are aware of Morgan's status as a convicted felon, and Dewayne knows enough about how people are not to spread the word around.

With Cassie gone, I half-hobble, half-stroll over to Kieran, Jim, and "Cousin" Morgan, who's clad in a maroon Sumner College polo shirt and dirt-stained jeans.

"You look like you've been working hard," I point out to him as Kieran slides an arm around my shoulders.

"Weeding flower beds. And congratulations, by the way." He nods at my two trophies. "Too bad you almost had to sacrifice life and limb to get those."

I glance down at my ankle. "It just hurts a little right now, but it's not swollen," I assure everyone. "I'll be good as new by tomorrow."

"Good," Kieran comments, flashing me a loopy grin that always makes my stomach turn back-flips. He leans in to kiss me, but I whisper, "I'm all sweaty," as he gets closer.

"Like I care," he whispers back, before planting a chaste, closed-mouth kiss on my lips in the presence of his dads. "I'm proud of you. You were awesome out there, Most Outstanding Player. You and your mom might need to build a trophy room onto your house."

I shrug as if my awards are no big deal, but on the inside, I'm thrilled that I've had such a productive summer season. Between the county league and a few exhibition games I've played in around the state in front of scouts, I'm hoping my recruitment profile's gone up enough that some colleges might be interested in me.

"Yeah, you know how it is. I was thinking I could just store my trophies in a closet for now." I fight to keep my expression earnest. "I mean, I'll probably go on to win more awards in college, and then there's all the accolades I'll rack up during my sports broadcasting career. If Mom and I add an addition to the house now, we'll just need to expand later, so we might as well wait."

10

"Or you could build a museum," he suggests, also deadly serious. "You know—kind of a presidential library-type deal. A monument to the greatness that is Zip McKee."

"Now, *there's* an idea."

Jim breaks into a wide smile, wrinkles in his forehead straightening out as he does. "You two never fail to entertain," he comments, shaking his head.

"Thanks, Dad," Kieran answers for both of us before I change the subject.

"So, what are you guys doing here? This is a nice surprise."

"Kieran wanted to watch your game, so he came to campus with us this morning," Jim explains.

"The Counseling Center is full of couches," Kieran begins. "It's very convenient for me."

"And I'm on my lunch hour. I caught most of the fourth quarter," Morgan adds, before glancing at the clock above the doors to the lobby. "Speaking of my lunch hour, I need to grab a sandwich or something at the Union and head back out. Those flower beds aren't going to weed themselves." Morgan gives me a slight pat on the shoulder before congratulating me again, and he and Jim arrange to meet at Jim's car at five o'clock for the drive to Titusville. As Morgan disappears through the gym doors, Jim says to us, "I should probably be getting back to the office as well."

"Would you be able to give me a ride home?" Kieran asks me. "I'm not sure I can take the non-stop excitement of the Sumner Counseling Center all afternoon."

"Thanks," Jim says, but he's smiling, and I tell them both "Sure—no problem. I just need to shower first so I don't stink up the car."

"I'll stay with Kieran until you get back," Jim offers, turning to his son. "I'll show you the new pool while we're waiting. Apparently they just finished it last week."

"Awesome," Kieran grumbles. "I love looking at things I'd never be allowed to use in a million years."

Jim sighs at Kieran's sarcasm before turning to me. "We'll meet you out front when you're done?" he asks.

"Sure thing," I reply, giving Kieran a tiny sympathy smile and wishing I could kiss away his anger over his limitations. I smooch him on the cheek and trot off to the locker room, the pain in my ankle nearly gone. After a quick shower, I change from my summer league uniform into a pair of cutoff jean shorts and a plain gray t-shirt, combing my wet hair back into a messy bun at the nape of my neck. Before I leave, I place my silver charm bracelet—a gift from Kieran on our mutual April first birthday—around my left wrist. By the time I've gathered up my stuff to meet them outside, Jim and Kieran have finished their tour of Sumner's new, state-of-the-art natatorium and are waiting for me on the front steps of the fieldhouse.

"I'll be home a little before six," Jim tells Kieran, as if we don't already know the drive from Sumner to Titusville takes about forty-five minutes.

"Got it."

"If you get hungry before then, there's some leftover Paulie's in the fridge from the other night."

"Okay." Kieran nods and Jim says goodbye to both of us before walking down the stairs and over to the intersection of College Avenue and Second Street to cross back over to the main part of campus.

"Paulie's Pizza?" I say to Kieran as we watch his father walk away.

"Yeah. What?" he responds to my smirk.

12

"Well, Kayla's been spending every waking minute with Brad, and your mom's out of town. Sounds like you guys are living the ultimate bachelor life now without a regular female presence in the house." I take Kieran's hand and we head down the stairs to the parking lot at the other side of the fieldhouse, where I'd parked my mom's Chevy Cobalt in one of the spaces near the entrance to Panther Stadium.

"We ordered pizza sometimes when Mom was here, too," he reminds me. "But for your information, we got Paulie's the other night when Kayla brought Brad over to hang out while you were at your grandparents'. And you're forgetting—I *have* a regular female presence in my life." Kieran drops my hand and puts his arm around my shoulder, pulling me close as we walk. "But, yeah—I think I'm finding out Mom's the one who was behind the 'law and order' in our house all these years, and Dad just went along with things. Life's been *a lot* more relaxed since Mom's been gone."

Carlie's been in New York for the past three weeks, working with scientists at Halloran Industries to develop a treatment to counter the effects of the one that caused Kieran's sleeping disorder. This latest trip is just one in a series of excursions the Laniers have taken to the city this summer. Back in June, we met Frank Dozier's illegitimate son Cooper Halloran, who had discovered the formula for the original drug on a piece of paper Morgan had buried on a Halloran family farm when he was evading the cops years ago. While the page was too damaged to be able to make out the details of the formula, seeing an artifact from his past helped jar some of Morgan's returning memories loose to the point he was able to recall the formula down to the last detail.

Once Morgan remembered, we called Cooper, whose mother had married Ben Halloran, CEO of Halloran Industries, when Cooper was still a toddler. Not only was Cooper adopted into the Halloran

13

family, but he was also granted lifelong access to more money than a person could ever want along with a stable of companies. Two of those companies—Malsun Foods and Deelite Cosmetics—have complexes full of labs and scientists desperate enough to keep their jobs they'll do, or make, whatever Ben and Cooper Halloran command. Reconstituting the original drug had been easy enough for the Halloran team, but making a substance to counter the sleeping disorder it induced in Cooper and Kieran was proving to be a more difficult challenge. Both Kieran and Morgan, accompanied by Jim, Carlie, and occasionally, Kayla and Brad, made several trips to New York over the summer where both they and Cooper were run through a battery of physical and physiological tests in order to determine what alteration of the original formula might cure—or, at the very least, *help*—Cooper and Kieran. Knowing Carlie's background as a physician, in addition to her personal stake in wanting to find an antidote to the original drug, Ben Halloran invited Carlie to join the research team. And while reluctant to leave her family for so long, Carlie wanted to help in whatever way she could. So, with the blessing of the rest of the Laniers, she stayed in New York after their last trip.

"Has there been any news?" I ask Kieran, knowing he'll understand what I mean. We're almost at the car, so I press the door unlock button on my keychain.

"No," Kieran says after we're in and buckled up. "Mom called last night like she does every night, and it was the same old, same old—she works with the research team every day, they think they have some ideas but they're limited in what they can come up with since only two people on the planet have my condition, and so on, and so on. And then the whole conversation kind of turns into one of those science specials on public television and I tune out like always and hand the phone to Dad."

I nod in understanding as I start the car and ease out of the parking space. I'm a good student, but math and science are my weak spots and I've always had to work a little harder in those classes. And given that Kieran's interests tend more to art than to science, I have no doubt of his zoning out whenever his mom starts describing the details of life in the Halloran labs.

"I think she's starting to feel more comfortable hanging out at the Hallorans', though," Kieran continues. "And he'd never admit it in a zillion years, but I think from some things he's said that Cooper's kind of enjoying having a pseudo-mom around. Although, if she hovers over him all the time like she hovers over me, he's due to get sick of her any day now."

I shake my head as I pull out onto College Avenue and steer us toward Main Street.

"I still can't believe your dad's okay with your mom staying with some strange man and his kid," I say.

Kieran lifts his shoulders to his ears as if he thinks Carlie's temporary living arrangement is weird and not so weird all at the same time.

"It's not like Mr. Halloran's ever around. According to Coop, he's off being 'Mr. Corporate' most days, so whenever Mom's not at the lab—which isn't very often, from what it sounds like—it's basically just the two of them at the apartment. And the place is so big, they probably don't run into each other much."

Kieran and his family had stayed with the Hallorans during their New York trips, and his descriptions of the Hallorans' "apartment" made their home sound totally unlike the run-down Sumner student apartments out past the football field. The Hallorans' New York City residence is basically a multi-million dollar palace contained within a high-rise on the Upper West Side. During the day, an army of servants attend to the "apartment's" upkeep, but only

Victor Loughlin, Cooper's driver, all-purpose general employee, and big brother figure whom we first met in June, is on the premises around the clock.

"Dad and I aren't too worried about Mom. I mean, sure, Dad wants her home because he misses her, but he understands her need to do everything she can to help Cooper and me. And she can stay away as long as she needs to if it means she and the Halloran lab rats will come up with something that isn't going to kill me."

"Kieran," I warn, pressing down on the accelerator now that the speed limit's picked up on our approach to the highway.

"I know," he says, sighing. Kieran's always believed his dreams about the future have mysteriously stopped because he's going to die, and not because his mother and the Halloran researchers will be able to devise a substance to cure his sleeping disorder—and the flashes of the future that had always accompanied it—forever.

"I'm sorry," Kieran continues. "It's just scary, you know? Drugs have side effects. The one Morgan and my birth mother messed around and came up with had some pretty wicked side effects, so it's hard for me to accept that any kind of a cure won't be worse than the disorder somehow."

I can't convince Kieran of anything other than gloom-and-doom in his future—I've tried for almost two months now. So, the best I can do is be mildly contradictory whenever he does start talking this way.

"Maybe death won't be a side effect," I begin, numbed into total calm over discussing my boyfriend's potential demise because I'm doing so for the millionth time. "Maybe what they come up with will have the same side effects normal drugs do—you know, like on those commercials on TV." I lower my voice in a not-too-accurate impersonation of an announcer. "Side effects include nausea, vomiting, diarrhea…"

16

Kieran snorts and starts giggling like a little kid on my mention of "diarrhea."

"Death might not be so bad, then," he jokes, before completely sobering up. "Seriously, though. They always list 'death' as a possible side effect on those commercials. It happens."

"Only in extreme circumstances." I gun the engine as we exit onto the state highway. "You've got to believe that, Kieran."

Out of the corner of my eye, I catch him shooting me a dialed-down version of the loopy grin that's one of my favorite things about him.

"I shouldn't keep bringing this up. And I'm trying to be positive, but—"

"I get it." I cut him off. "I can't imagine what it's like for you to live with so much uncertainty. But I'm here for you, no matter what, or no matter how negative you feel you need to be."

I shift my eyes from the road ever so slightly to see his grin widen.

"Nice dig, there, McKee," he says as I match his grin with one of my own. "I'll shut up about it now—I promise, okay?"

"Okay."

"And, anyway, I guess I need to assume I'll still be alive in September when the college tests roll around again, or I'm going to be totally screwed, right?"

"Right," I say with enthusiasm, hoping to encourage Kieran's focus on his immediate future. We're both retaking our college entrance exams in early September so we can bring our scores up— me, in the hopes that higher scores will equal more academic scholarship offers in case basketball scholarships don't come through, and Kieran, in the hopes that new and improved scores will increase his chances he'll be accepted somewhere, assuming his parents would let him go away to college to begin with given the nature of his

17

disorder. But *that* family squabble is a whole other story, and since Kieran's being positive at the moment, I don't bring it up.

"What do you say we spend the afternoon studying at my house?" he offers, his hand caressing my knee telling me he may have other ideas.

"You're sure 'studying' isn't code for something else?"

And there goes the grin. "I'll be good. I promise."

"Suure you will," I tease, pressing down on the accelerator a little more and speeding us toward Titusville.

Chapter 2

When we walk into the Laniers' sprawling house located on the old McCaffery farm, Kieran immediately heads for the stairs.

"Where are you going?" I ask.

"My room. My study guides are in my room."

"Of course they are," I say, folding my arms over my torso.

"If you don't trust me to behave, I'll bring the stuff down here and we can study in the kitchen or the living room." His lips curl into a mock-pout once he's done speaking.

"It's not you I don't trust," I point out, shaking my head. "It's me. It's *both* of us."

"You don't think we can be alone in my room for ten minutes without being all over each other?"

I join him at the base of the stairs, sighing. "I guess we can try. It'll be a good test of our self-control."

In seconds, I'm in Kieran's unusually messy room, an explosion of sketch pads and dirty clothes littering the floor and his bed rumpled and unmade, the untidiness a by-product of his mom and dad having mellowed out since learning of Frank Dozier's death and Morgan's lack of desire to do Kieran harm. The first time I was in here back in March, everything seemed way too neat and orderly for a teenage boy's room—no posters on the walls, no mess, and no dust sheen covering the surfaces of his desk or nightstand—and I later learned that the bizarre cleanliness of Kieran's supposed private space was merely scratching the surface of his parents' desire to control his life. At least now, they seem to have backed off controlling his room, if not much else.

Kieran grabs the study guides from his desk and flops down on the bed in front of me.

"Vocab?" he asks.

"It's as good a place to start as any, I guess. Want me to quiz you?"

"I've been studying," he says, sitting up straight with pride. "Bring it on."

"Okay." I flip to a page with vocabulary words and randomly pick the first one my eye lands upon. "Perspicacious."

"Um…possessing keen vision and understanding?" He narrows his eyes with his question.

"Impressive, Mr. Lanier," I compliment him, and he flashes me that grin.

Oh, that grin.

"Um…okay," I mumble, composing myself. "Next word. How about 'loquacious'?"

I look up from the book to find him staring at me, his amazing grin still on his face as if it's permanent, like a tattoo.

"Kieran?"

"I can't imagine a moment when I won't want you," he says, his expression shifting to something more serious.

"That's not the definition of 'loquacious'," I fire back, trying to be smooth and probably failing.

"No, it's not, and I kind of don't care. I'm just being honest about how I feel. I don't think I can sit here and spit out definitions when you're right in front me, being you."

And…that's it. I toss the book to the floor and push him back on the bed, kissing him with all the strength I can muster.

"Incorrigible," I whisper against his mouth. His hands move to my head, releasing my knot of hair from the ponytail holder, his fingers finding their way to my cheeks and on up into my now loose and still damp strands.

"Impertinent," I say, kissing him again. "Impetuous," I mutter as my mouth pulls away from his only far enough to still feel the surface tension between our lips.

"Okay—are you quizzing me or insulting me? I'm confused."

I smile before lowering my mouth to his once again. When we finally come up for air, I pant, "So much for lasting ten minutes, huh?"

"No kidding. Who knew you were such a harlot?"

I let out a hearty laugh on his use of such an old-fashioned term.

"*Harlot*? Where'd you come up with that?"

"I told you—I've been studying my vocabulary. And I'm just kidding about the harlot thing, by the way. This is totally my fault. I'm irresistible."

"Oh, you are," I assure him. "In fact, I think I'm kind of in love with you, Kieran Lanier."

"And I think I might be in love with you, too, Zip McKee. Just maybe."

He sits up, forcing me to sit up with him, and after a few minutes of kissing, tugging, pulling, and groping, we're under the covers, our breathing so heavy together it almost seems to fill the room with sound. But before we can make any further moves, before we can stop to discuss protection or positions or any other possibilities, Kieran's eyes droop and I surrender to the inevitable. As he collapses onto his elbow and then onto his side, I roll over to face him, pulling him against me as he drifts off to sleep.

This has more or less been the story of our summer when Kieran hasn't been in New York. With the adults in our lives being at work every day and now with Carlie out of town as well, Kieran and I have been enjoying more alone time recently than we've ever had since we've been a couple.

And I don't think I'm speaking only for myself when I say our alone time has been pretty awesome—incredibly awesome, in fact.

But while we've rounded every single base in the metaphorical baseball game people use to describe physical affection, we haven't yet managed to cross home plate. Kieran's inability to stay awake in situations of heightened emotion always kicks in, and while we love each other enough to keep hitting triples for the rest of our lives and be fine, just once, we'd both like to knock one out of the ballpark.

I stroke his cheek, my forehead touching his, until he gradually wakes up. He pulls back enough to look into my eyes, his puzzled expression telling me he's trying to piece together what's happened, an act that isn't always successful. His eyes widen slightly and he lifts up the covers enough to take in our rather…um…*natural* state, and this time, at least, things come back to him…to a point.

"No?" he asks.

"No."

He rolls over onto his back and lets out a frustrated breath.

"Kieran, come here." I whisper, and he rolls over to face me once again. I gather his hands in mine and rest them together between us against our chests. "Let's talk for a minute."

"You're not going to start quizzing me on vocabulary, are you? Because I'm not sure *now* is the time. I might not be able to concentrate with you next to me like this."

"Very funny. But I think we need to talk about the whole sex thing."

"Awesome." And there's that grin again. "I happen to be really good at *talking* about sex. Doing it? Not so much."

"And that's what I want to talk about."

He frowns. "The fact that I suck at sex? Can we talk about something else?"

I untangle one of my hands from against our chests and run it through his hair.

"I love you so much, you know? Sometimes, though, I think maybe we're trying too hard. Or, maybe we're trying for the wrong reasons. I just want to make sure we want this because we really want to be together, and not because we want to see if we can get it done." My mouth twists up in frustration. "I'm not making sense."

Kieran takes his free hand and smoothes my dirty blonde bangs off my face.

"No—I understand. You don't want us to get so caught up in seeing if I can stay awake long enough to do it that it ends up overshadowing the actual, you know, *doing* it."

I can't help but smile at his always interesting way of getting a point across.

"Pretty much. I just don't want us to forget that we love each other, and that's the most important thing. Sex shouldn't be something we're trying to cross off our 'to do' lists."

Kieran holds his hand in the air, his fingers ticking off "to do" items as he talks.

"Sure. Graduate from high school, get into college, lose our virginity. Yeah—it does seem kind of unromantic in that context, doesn't it?"

"Exactly."

"Zip, don't worry, okay?" He rests his hand on my shoulder, his touch feather-light. "I promise, I want you for the right reasons. And I know you want me for the right reasons. I'm not going to lie and say conquering my super-special variety of sexual dysfunction isn't a big deal for me, but that would be icing on the cake compared to finally being with you."

"So, would I be the cake in this scenario?" I squint at him.

23

"Yeah. I guess so." He laughs. "You're a big awesome slice of red velvet cake. I need to brush up on my analogies, or I'm never getting into college."

Kieran knows red velvet cake is my absolute favorite dessert.

"Okay," I say, sighing. "Now I'm hungry. Thanks to you, I just realized I haven't eaten since before the game."

"Well, we don't have any red velvet cake, but there's that leftover pizza," he reminds me, rolling over. "Race you to the kitchen." He jumps out of bed ahead of me to get dressed and head downstairs, beating me by only a few seconds thanks to my bum ankle. I'm in the middle of heating up Paulie's deluxe slices in the microwave when we hear the front door open, voices floating back to us from the hall.

"Seriously—you need to call or text or email this guy or *something*." Kayla's breathy voice is clearly exasperated. "He's going to be your roommate for a year, you know."

"I have," Brad insists over the sound of the door shutting. "We email and text all the time."

"Well, not about anything important, obviously. If you two don't have a serious conversation about who's bringing what stuff for your dorm room, you're going to blow a lot of money you can't afford and end up with two TVs and two microwaves."

"We can rent microwaves and fridges from the school," he fires back as they approach the kitchen, stopping in the entryway once they see Kieran and I are already there.

"And you say *we* act like an old married couple," Kieran says to his sister, tilting his head toward me from his perch at the far end of the kitchen table. I snort as the microwave beeps and Kayla raises both middle fingers, extending them in her brother's direction. The plate's too hot for me to grab with my bare hand, so I open the drawer to my left and grab a potholder. That's how frequently I'm over here

24

now—I know where Carlie keeps the potholders. And Kieran's probably spent enough time at my house at this point he would know we keep the potholders in a drawer next to our fridge, which would almost put him ahead of my mom, who doesn't exactly consider the kitchen her favorite room of the house.

Brad slides into a chair as I deliver a steaming plate of pizza to the placemat in front of Kieran.

"Oooh…is that leftover Paulie's from the other night?" he asks Kieran, eyes widening.

"Yup."

"Can I have some?" He slides his seat back, the chair legs squeaking on the hardwood floor. "I skipped lunch at work today."

"Work" for Brad this summer means volunteering at Med-West Health Center in Sumner, another experience line for his future medical school applications. He moves toward the counter, and I turn to grab two plates from the cabinet, one of which I hand to him and the other I use after I take one of the already-heated slices from Kieran's plate.

Kayla, meanwhile, sits down opposite her brother. "So, what are you two up to this afternoon?" she asks him.

"Vocabulary review," Kieran answers through a mouthful of pizza.

Kayla shoots Kieran a look. "Oh, is *that* what we're calling it now?" She raises her hands and makes scare quotes in the air with her fingers. "'Vocabulary review.'"

"Better than 'Going bowling'." Kieran makes scare quotes of his own and matches his sister's mocking tone note for note. She only smirks at his reference to Kayla and Brad's most recent Saturday night date, bowling at Starlight Lanes on the state highway near the mall.

"Sad thing is, we *actually* went bowling," Brad comments.

25

"My condolences," Kieran mutters after swallowing a bite of pizza. Kayla tosses her long, black braid off her shoulder and leans in toward Brad.

"Wait—I thought you liked bowling," she protests.

"And I thought *you* liked bowling," he mumbles back.

"Awesome communication skills you guys have there," Kieran says, as the microwave beeps.

"I didn't say anything when you suggested it because you seemed so excited," Kayla explains to Brad, ignoring her brother's dig at them.

Brad laughs as he gets up to grab his meal from the microwave. "I was excited because I thought you really wanted to go bowling." He leans forward and kisses her on the forehead. "But thanks for liking something because you thought I liked it."

Kayla reaches for his hand before he can turn away from the table, and she rubs her thumb back and forth across his wrist. "Thanks for wanting to go somewhere just because you thought I was into it."

Kieran pretends to gag on a bite of pizza at their display of affection, while I just laugh. This summer has been a long road for Brad and Kayla, so a little misunderstanding about bowling is nothing. Once we learned Frank Dozier was dead and the Laniers were no longer in danger, Kayla, who had successfully pushed Brad away to protect her family secrets, vowed to level with him about everything rather than risk losing him forever. Brad, who is pretty much Titusville's Mr. Upstanding, naturally had a little trouble absorbing the fact that the girl he'd fallen for had been lying to him for months about nearly every aspect of her life. But after a few awkward reunion dates—not to mention more than a few conversations with me in which I assured him Kayla's parents hadn't given her much choice about leading a double life—the two have settled back into a relationship, one that they've vowed to continue even after Brad leaves for Northwestern in two weeks.

Brad breaks away from Kayla, but before he can grab his food the doorbell rings, prompting all of us to glance toward the hallway.

"You expecting someone?" Kayla asks Kieran, who shakes his head.

"Well, maybe Dad ordered something and it's being delivered." Kayla shrugs and rises from her seat, as she's sitting closer to the hall than any of us. Her flip-flops flip flop against the wood as she makes her way to the front of the house and opens the door, shocking all of us by shrieking at someone who apparently isn't a delivery driver—

"Oh, my God. What are *you* doing here?"

CHAPTER 3

On cue, Brad, Kieran, and I stand up from the table and start for the hall, even Brad primed for danger now that he's aware of the Laniers' past.

"What?" A familiar voice drifts back to me. "I can't fly in to visit my favorite niece for no reason?"

"I'm your *only* niece, Jilly," Kayla points out as we all gather behind her to find Jillian Lanier, Jim's older sister from North Carolina, standing in the doorway. Much like her niece, Jillian sports a long braid slung over her shoulder, only hers is rust-red, the same color as her brother's hair. Her plain gray t-shirt and cargo shorts are rumpled from a plane trip and subsequent drive from the airport, and she rubs her eyes as if she's tired from catching an early flight. Kayla throws her arms around her aunt for a hug, which she only breaks in order to drag Jillian inside to stand before Brad. "This is Brad Wallace," she says by way of introduction. "Brad, this is my Aunt Jilly."

Jillian extends a hand. "I've heard a lot about you. And you're every bit as good-looking as Kayla's told me—*repeatedly*, I might add."

Brad shakes Jillian's hand and blushes all the way up to the dark bangs flopping over his forehead. "Nice to meet you, Dr. Lanier," he responds, using the appropriate title for her given her Ph.D. in English.

"He's polite, too," Jilly says to Kayla as she gives Brad his hand back. "Good work, Kay."

Brad continues to redden as Jilly gathers Kieran first and then me into crushing hugs. "Good to see you again, Jillian," I say, this being the first time I've seen her since both my family and the Laniers crashed at her house back when we all believed Frank Dozier was still alive and we had reason to be in danger.

"Good lord, child." She holds me at arm's length, studying my face. "You're practically family, as far as I'm concerned. It's *Jilly*." She turns to Brad. "That goes for you, too. None of this 'Dr. Lanier' business. That's for my students."

Brad and I both nod at her as Kayla, ever suspicious, asks once again "So, what are you doing here?"

"Just thought I'd visit for a few days," she responds airily, but Kieran's not buying.

"After Mom asked if you'd come, right?"

Busted, Jillian sighs and reaches out to rumple his hair.

"And you think you're not smart enough to get into college," she chides. "But, yes—Carlie called me and asked if I'd come here and play secret agent spy for her while she plays mad scientist in New York. Oddly enough, something about your repeated insistence that you're all doing fine without her didn't sit well, so she's convinced your dad must not be feeding and clothing you properly and the house is a mess. And for God knows what reason, she thought I might have enough of a maternal streak to come down here and straighten all of you out. Silly woman." Jilly raises her nose into the air. "Do I smell pizza? All I've eaten today are airline pretzels."

In a flash, we're back in the kitchen and devouring what's left of the pepperoni and deluxe pizzas. Brad stands near the sink after politely giving up his seat to Jilly, who sits next to me at the table and amuses us with stories about students in her summer class. Once we're finished eating, Kayla and Brad head upstairs so Brad can download some software onto Kayla's new laptop—Kayla and Kieran each getting their own computer being another sign of Jim and Carlie easing up on hovering over their children. Jilly and I rinse the dishes and straighten up while Kieran falls asleep at the table practically on cue, his body conditioned to take an early afternoon nap because doing so lessens the possibility of his falling asleep out of the blue before bedtime. This reflex is particularly useful during the school year when he needs to stay awake for afternoon classes, and it's a reflex that doesn't always kick in because the universe likes nothing more than throw off his best laid plans. And as soon as Kieran's schedule gets out of whack or something else stressful happens, his brain shuts his body down when he doesn't intend it to happen.

"Kid'll do anything to get out of chores," Jilly jokes, wiping her hands on a dishtowel as she nods at Kieran snoozing away, his folded arms cradling his head on the placemat. She tilts her head toward the hallway, and I follow her out of the kitchen to the spotless living room, where the two of us flop down on either end of the Laniers' overstuffed moss green couch opposite the fireplace.

"How long are you going to be in town?" I ask. "My mom'll want to hang out, and I'm sure my grandparents will want to meet you. We told them all about you after we got back from North Carolina so, naturally, they're curious."

Jilly's eyes give off a little twinkle. "I'll bet. But, unfortunately, I can't stay long. School starts in two weeks and I'm not even close to ready yet. Carlie was so insistent, though…"

Her voice trails off as if she'd rather me push her for information instead of volunteering it, and so I start nudging.

"Is Carlie okay?"

Jilly kicks off her sandals and tucks her feet up under her.

"She's fine. She's just going through some guilt over leaving her family for so long, even though everyone understands the situation. And, like I said before, she's a little worried about how Jim and the kids are getting along." She raises her eyebrows, obviously fishing for information I'm not sure I want to give. "Zip, it's fine," she assures me, sensing my discomfort. "You're not telling tales, and I'm

30

not going to go running to Carlie with details. Besides, if things still aren't straight with Kayla and Kieran and their parents, I won't be able to perform miracles in a weekend."

Jilly makes a good point.

"I think things are still sort of awkward," I admit, my diagnosis based on nearly two months of being over here all the time and observing Kieran's interactions with his parents. "I mean, Jim and Carlie have obviously loosened up since the whole Frank thing went away, but Kieran may never trust them again after everything they kept from him for so long. And I get that. For eighteen years, he believed a set of facts about his life, and his parents sat him down one night and wiped everything out. Now, Morgan's in the picture, too, and that's weird for everyone."

"Understandable." Jilly glances out into the hallway and lowers her voice. "How's Kayla adjusting?"

"To Morgan?" I ask, and Jilly nods. "I think she's accepted he's a permanent part of the family, although it probably helps that he doesn't live here. She doesn't snipe at him anymore like she used to, at least, not when I'm around. And she's with Brad practically twenty-four hours a day anyway…"

I don't finish my sentence, and Jilly seems to understand my implication that Kayla's head is filled with other, more pleasant things beyond worrying about the ex-con living down the road.

"I like Brad," Jilly informs me, glancing out into the hall once again. "He seems like a good kid."

"Oh, he totally is. I've known him all my life."

"Kayla needs something positive in her life, something that doesn't revolve around the family." Jilly sighs. "She deserves it. She's had too much responsibility for too long."

I nod in agreement. Kayla was eleven when her parents told her the truth about Kieran's parentage and how his birth parents'

31

crimes could come back to haunt them all. And until Kieran's eighteenth birthday, she'd carried that burden, along with the burden of looking out for Kieran when his parents weren't around, all by herself.

"And Carlie tells me she and Jim are going to look into Kieran taking classes online if he gets accepted to college." Jilly says, moving the focus away from Kayla.

"Assuming Carlie and the Halloran people can't come through with something to change his condition."

Jilly ignores my hopeful sentiment and focuses on the present, pointing out, "You know going off to school the way things stand without someone looking after him would be pretty difficult."

"I know. And he's probably not going to get into the same schools Kayla and I are looking at."

Kieran should have graduated already, but he's a year behind in school thanks to his disorder and the fact he never quite caught up, even with Carlie homeschooling the siblings for years. Although he's a talented artist and loves to read, he's not exactly a standout student in subjects other than art and English. Kayla, meanwhile, even with her home school credits, is sitting along with me atop the incoming senior class with a perfect grade-point average. We've already talked about applying to the same schools and rooming together, our excitement over the future completely separate from any guilt we might share over the possibility of having to leave Kieran behind in Titusville, as if the two concepts aren't connected at all.

Jilly leans forward, her freckled and weathered face serious as she stares at me. Putting her hand over mine on the couch cushion between us, she says, "I wasn't kidding earlier when I said you're practically a part of this family. After all that's happened, I feel it, and I'm sure Jim and Carlie would agree."

I'm at a loss for words, so I just bob my head and hope she interprets my action as gratitude.

"You're good for Kieran, and even Kayla seems less angry somehow when you're around, which is quite the achievement."

"I think that has to do more with Brad than with me."

Jilly squeezes my hand. "Regardless, you've been a good friend to her and to this family as well. I hope that doesn't change."

Her eyes flick away from me for the briefest second, and I can't help but be a little suspicious.

"Why would it change?" I ask, eyes narrowing.

"This family needs you, Zip. And they're going to need you in a way I don't think even *they* understand if anything can be done about Kieran's condition."

I wonder if I'm talking to a psychic or an oracle all of a sudden.

"Has Carlie said something about the research?" I ask. Kieran never understands enough about his mother's work with the Halloran researchers in order to relay that information to me, and while I spend a ton of free time at his house, my relationship with Jim Lanier isn't familiar or comfortable enough for me to ask him to explain the details of what's going on in New York. Jilly, who double-majored in English and chemistry and wrote a book on potions in Shakespeare's works, would have more than a passing interest in Carlie's work with the Halloran team, and since we seem to be sharing things at the moment, I'm comfortable enough to press her about what, if anything, Carlie's told her.

"They're getting close to something." She shakes her head and presses her lips together. "I can't say anything more. Carlie doesn't want Kieran to find out in case things don't work, and I don't want to put you in the position of having to keep this from him."

"I appreciate that."

Jilly takes her hand from mine and adjusts her sitting position, moving her legs out from under her and drawing her knees to her chin.

"But if they're able to treat him—*when* they're able to treat him—and the treatment works, then everything changes."

"Well, changing things is kind of the point, right?"

"True," Jilly says, cocking her head. "And I want him to have a normal life as much as anyone. But Kieran's been the way he is his whole life, and both he and his family…they don't understand anything else." Jilly's eyes are riveted on me so intensely that I don't dare look away. "And things could get…strange. Kieran will need support, but so will the entire family. You and Brad…I hope you're here for them. I obviously don't know Brad as well as I know you, so I'm telling you. This family's going to need you around."

Jilly's not making much sense, but the alternative—having her reveal everything she's learned from Carlie when I can't tell Kieran—is unacceptable. I sigh inwardly at yet more evidence that the Laniers are always keeping secrets, and usually, they're keeping them from each other.

"I'm not going anywhere," I assure her. "No matter what happens, I love Kieran. Kayla's my friend. And the rest of you crazy people have kind of grown on me, too."

Jilly tilts her head back and roars with laughter. "See? *That's* what I mean. This family needs you because you're smart as a whip and funny, and Kieran couldn't possibly do better than a girl like you."

I hitch my shoulders up to my ears.

"Well, I don't know about all that, but thanks."

"No problem." She checks the slender silver watch on her wrist, and apparently determines Kieran's been asleep long enough to ward off any episodes later in the afternoon. "Let's go wake our boy

34

up, shall we? I get the feeling we're going to have to make a grocery store run so y'all don't have to keep ordering pizza." She squints, thinking. "This town has a grocery store, right?" Since this is Jilly's first time in Titusville, she honestly wouldn't know.

"Yeah. Out by the highway. You probably passed it on the way in, but you might not have noticed it if you were trying to pay attention to the road."

Jilly nods, seeming to remember the cluster of gas stations, convenience stores, and local restaurants just off the exit from the interstate that obscure Foxworth's Grocery, which sits back from the road a bit.

"Well, Marta sent me here armed with a bunch of recipes she claims aren't too hard to make if I can just follow directions," she says, referring to her girlfriend.

"Oh, *now* we're in trouble. You and following directions don't exactly mix."

Jilly and I both look out to find Kieran standing in the hallway, still heavy-lidded from sleep but texting someone on his phone, his thumb moving at warp speed as if it's detached from the rest of his sluggish body. "It's Cooper," he informs us, still stabbing the screen.

"Ah, the mysterious Mr. Halloran," Jilly sings, standing up from her perch on the couch and looking down at me. "What's your assessment of the Laniers' newest family friend?"

"He's sort of an asshat," I tell her, and Kieran chuckles at my description. "But he and Kieran have this whole 'brother from another mother' thing going on, so I'm trying to look past it."

"I just told Coop you called him an 'asshat,' by the way," Kieran says, not taking his eyes from his screen.

"Oh, my God, Kieran. You did *not*."

He looks at me sideways and grins.

"I'm just kidding. And I don't need to tell him because I think he's already well aware of what you think about him."

"Well, anyway, let him know I said 'hello.'"

Kieran taps out my message to Cooper, relaying words aloud as he types each word:

"'Hello…Cooper…You…Are…An…Asshat.'"

I heave an audible sigh, but I'm smiling because I know he's just messing around. Jilly, however, steps in to scold him for me.

"Kieran, stop teasing this poor girl or she won't be your girlfriend much longer."

Kieran rounds the couch to give me a kiss on the forehead and to offer a hand to help me up from the couch.

"That's more like it." Jilly voices her approval of the chivalrous version of her nephew.

"Did I hear something about a grocery store run?" Kieran asks, putting his phone in the pocket of his khaki cargo shorts and ending any further texting with Cooper for the moment. "Because you don't even want to see what the pantry and the fridge look like right now. Those leftover pizzas were about the last of the food."

"That's what I thought." Jilly smirks "I'll text your dad to tell him he'll be coming home to a well-stocked house." She takes her phone from her pocket and heads out into the hall, stopping at the base of the stairs once she's finished firing off a message to Jim. "Now the real question is, do we make those two up there come with us, or do we leave them here to do whatever they're probably already doing?"

"You mean, 'installing software'?" Kieran makes scare quotes in the air as he and Kayla had been doing to each other earlier in the kitchen, and his implication is enough for Jilly to yell up the stairs.

36

"Kayla? We're going to the grocery store. Do you two want to come with us, or do you want us to leave you here so you can keep making out?"

Kieran and I both fall out with silent laughter as Kayla yells down from her room "Jilly! Oh, my God. We'll be down in a minute, okay?"

Jilly turns to us as we struggle to control ourselves. "Well, she answered right away, so they couldn't have been doing anything *too* involved."

Seconds later, Kayla and Brad come barreling down the stairs, Brad blushing once again, and I wonder if he'll be able to have a moment with normal skin tone so long as Jillian Lanier's in town. Feeling sorry for him, I pat him on the back as we gather at the front door. "Welcome to the family," I whisper.

"Awesome," he mumbles, and Kieran, catching our conversation, breaks into a smile.

CHAPTER 4

Even though I sweat all the time on the basketball court, I'm not a big fan of doing so in non-athletic situations, such as the one I'm in right now. I'm sitting at a computer in my journalism elective on the first day of senior year, the heat from the motherboards combined with both the ninety-two degree heat outside and the interior of the ancient, un-airconditioned Titusville Junior/Senior High building making me wonder if the actual temperature inside the classroom isn't hovering somewhere around the boiling point for liquids. Looking around the room at the dopey, glazed-over looks of my classmates, I note that the temperature definitely seems to have passed the boiling point for teenagers.

Kayla, at the computer next to me, fans herself with a spiral notebook. Meanwhile, Doug Callahan struggles to keep his eyes open on my other side while Mr. Murphy, one of the youngest teachers in school and the newly-anointed coach of the boys' basketball team after Coach Ferlinberg's retirement in May, drones on about article assignments for the first edition of the *Titan Times* as we all creep closer to certain death. Ashley Keep, who is sitting at a computer across from me, raises her hand—the one not currently resting on her cheek to keep her head from collapsing on her desk—and slowly waves it back and forth in order to get Mr. Murphy's attention.

"Ashley?" he says, pointing at her. "You had a question?"

"Sort of. I mean, it's reeeeallly hot in here. Could we put our heads down or something until the bell rings?"

The class mumbles its assent as Mr. Murphy runs a hand through his dark hair and smiles, the prominent dimples standing out in either cheek not doing much to dissuade every unattached girl in the room—and more than a few with boyfriends—from falling further in lust with him.

"So, you guys think you're in Kindergarten, I take it? You don't get naptime in high school, and you're already getting out early for the day," he reminds us, referring to the fact that when the temperature hits ninety, the school district lets us out at noon so we don't spend the afternoon roasting like chickens in the deli department at Foxworth's.

"Come on, Murph," Doug grumbles, employing the nickname Mr. Murphy's never scolded anyone for using, although he probably should. "We're dying here."

"Any more complaining, and I'm making you all stay after school," Mr. Murphy threatens, but he's still smiling and so no one takes him seriously, the class letting out a collective whine of "Mururph!"

"Okay, okay." He relents. "You win. Turn off your computers and put your heads down until the bell."

We all mumble variations on "Thanks, Murph" as he sinks down into the chair at his teacher's desk and removes his glasses, wiping sweat from the bridge of his nose. I shut down my computer and push the keyboard out of the way so I can rest my head on the table. Kayla follows suit, her face turned toward me.

"Asheville was never this hot," she mumbles. "I don't get how you and your mom stand it."

"We're staying with Gram and Gramps until the heat wave breaks," I tell her. My grandparents' house has central air while my house, which my dad and Gramps built with limited professional help on a piece of my grandparents' property not long after my parents married, is a tiny sweat lodge in this weather, even with all the windows open and fans going.

"You should hang out at our house after school," she suggests, because the Laniers also have central air. She turns in her seat and glances at the clock over the classroom door. "Brad doesn't have class between twelve-thirty and two on Mondays, so I'm going to see if he can video chat. That should give you and Kieran plenty of alone time if you wanted to, you know, *whatever*."

"*Whatever*." I mimic her suggestive tone and roll my eyes at her teasing. Out of respect for Kieran—out of respect for both of us, really—I've tried to keep the gory details of our relationship as private as possible. Kayla knows that Kieran and I were in the middle of hooking up on Prom night when we were so rudely interrupted by Frank Dozier executing his kidnapping plot, but I haven't told her anything else. Although, since she's more than familiar with Kieran's propensity for passing out in heated situations, I'm sure she's aware we're having some issues.

Neither of us can muster up the energy to keep a conversation going in the last few minutes of class, choosing instead to rest our heads on the relatively cool surface of the long computer table. The bell finally rings, and we drag ourselves from the lab at the back of the school to the main hallway, where the seniors are shuffling like a ragged zombie nation to their lockers. My locker is only a few feet from Kayla's, so I catch up to her quickly after putting away my new textbooks, and the two of us continue on down the hall to where Kieran's sitting on the floor in front of his locker, his flushed cheek pressed against the cool metal and his knees drawn up to his chest so he doesn't get trampled by the slowly moving herd of our classmates.

"It's way too hot in here," he says wearily.

I crouch down next to him, Brittany Solomon accidentally pinging me in the head with her backpack as she brushes by Kayla.

"Oh, shit—sorry, Zip," Brittany eeks out, tossing her blonde highlighted curls before scrunching her shoulders up to her ears in embarrassment.

"No big deal." I wave her off, and she gives me a smile before rushing off down the hall. I turn back to Kieran. "Can you get up?"

"I think so. Just a little...drowsy."

Kayla loops her arms through her backpack handles and crouches down on Kieran's other side so we can pull him up, each of us holding him under an arm.

"Sorry," he whispers, mostly to me, the one who doesn't have as many years of experience dealing with him under her belt. I kiss him on the cheek as we begin stumbling down the hall, the three of us attached to each other like we're doing some expanded version of the three-legged race at the county fair. Once we reach the school lobby, Kieran begins to feel less heavy against us, and Kayla and I tentatively loosen our grip, the two of us nervous parents watching our baby prepare to walk on his own for the first time. Kieran seems steady enough after a few more steps so we let him go completely, and he stays upright rather than butt-planting on the floor like an unstable toddler, allowing the three of us to walk at normal speed to the parking lot.

The heat bubbling up from the asphalt gives the illusion that the cars in front of us are swimming in the late afternoon haze, and Kayla can't turn the air on in her Jeep quickly enough once we crawl inside, our bodies immediately stuck to the black leather seats. But since the Laniers and I only live about five minutes from school, the car hasn't even begun to cool off by the time we pull into their driveway. Inside, Kieran and I head straight for the kitchen to find some lunch, but Kayla bounds upstairs without a word.

"How's she doing with the whole Brad thing?" I ask Kieran over my shoulder, hearing her footsteps heavy on the stairs.

"Pretty good, all things considered. I mean, he's been gone less than two weeks, so we'll see how she holds up, but they've been talking every day and she's making plans to go to Evanston for a visit sometime soon..." Kieran's voice trails off and he shrugs, entering the kitchen and beating a path to the fridge.

"She'd mentioned going to visit him," I share. "And it didn't really hit me until this morning at school, but not having him around is a little weird for me, too."

Joining Kieran at the fridge after dropping my backpack in a chair, I survey the miscellaneous compilation of condiments and not much else in the way of food.

"I mean, Brad wasn't there, but neither was Marcy, Candace, Marissa, Kelsey ..." I stop ticking off names of last year's seniors, even though I could name each member of their class of ninety-two graduates if I wanted to, and could probably name them in alphabetical order if I concentrated long enough. "This is the first day I haven't been in school with those guys, like, ever. It's kind of bizarre to think about them moving on while we're still here."

Kieran shrugs. He's lived in Titusville less than a year, and so he doesn't have the attachments to people in town that I do.

"Well, I guess we'll get used to it and by the time we do, we'll be the ones moving on." He pauses. "Or *you'll* move on, anyway. And Kayla. Meanwhile, I'll be upstairs experiencing college via laptop. I wonder if online programs host virtual frat parties on weekends?" Kieran shuts the fridge, biting his lip. "Maybe we should order pizza. I don't think we have anything edible here."

"Frat parties are kind of overrated and stupid," I point out, trying to lighten the darkness settling over the room. "That's what I've heard, anyway. Never actually been to one. And I'll bet most college classrooms are crowded and smelly and the dorms are old and gross."

Kieran cracks the tiniest hint of a smile and says "Yeah. I don't understand why anyone would want to go away to college."

I step to him, putting my arms around him as he leans back against the refrigerator door.

"Maybe Kayla and I will stay here and go to school online with you."

"Sure—you, me, and Kayla, all rotting away here in Titusville for the rest of our lives. Our families would *love* that." His smile twists into something warm and bitter all at the same time. "No. I may not be getting glimpses of the future anymore, but I'm sure of this—you and Kayla are going off somewhere to Awesome State University and I'm going to stay here, sitting up in my room and preparing for a career Mom and Dad won't let me leave the house to pursue anyway, so what's the freaking point? This is all assuming, of course, that I don't end up dead sometime in the next few months."

I sigh, choosing not to engage in the "I'm going to die" discussion for the millionth time.

"You can come to school with Kayla and me," I say, my voice small and my sentiments stupid. Kieran and I have had different versions of this talk all summer, but we always end up in the same impossible place—in a year, I'm leaving and he's not. The conversation never progresses beyond the point of next August, as if not talking about the fact we're going to be in a long-distance relationship means we won't ever actually be in one. And I think we're both observing Kayla and Brad's situation with more than mild curiosity right now, as if they're running some science experiment we hope to replicate so long as theirs is successful.

Kieran pulls me close and presses his lips to my forehead, his breath hot against my temple.

"We've been through this," he begins. "I won't have the grades or the test scores to even *think* about going anywhere you two

43

would. And you and Kayla choosing a school just because it might be somewhere I can get in is unacceptable. Our parents won't stand for it, and neither will I."

I lift my head so my lips can meet his for a brief kiss.

"You should talk to your parents again about going away, though," I suggest when we part. "I've been looking at all the stuff I've gotten from different schools and I think every place has offices and programs for people with—" I realize what I'm about to say, and I stop myself. "You know," I mumble instead.

"Limitations," Kieran fills in for me, stroking my hair, and I can almost feel the restrained rage at his disorder flowing through his body. "I get it."

"Or maybe you could hire someone to follow you around all the time at school," I say, my voice a little too chipper. "You know— someone to drive you places and go to class with you and stuff. Kind of like the deal Cooper has with Victor."

"I've always kind of wanted my own personal assistant. Wonder if ol' Vic could refer somebody to me?" He winds his arms around me tightly, his voice in my ear. "For once, I wish I was still dreaming the future. I'd give anything for a clue as to how this all ends."

"Me, too," I mumble into his shoulder.

"But I do know that I love you, okay? And whatever happens, happens, and we'll figure out how to deal." He pulls back from me, his face settling into a smile. "Now let's order some food. I'm starving."

He reaches to his pocket for his phone, but I'm quicker to break away from him and move to my phone in my backpack. "I've got this," I tell him, feeling the need to make up for leading us into the "college conversation" again. "Mom finally paid me my sweat-shop wages for working at the store last week." I hit the number for Paulie's Pizza on my speed dial. "A large deluxe?"

"As always," he says. I give our order to Paulie himself and am finishing up when Kieran's phone buzzes.

"Hey."

I put my phone back in the outer pocket of my backpack and study Kieran's face for signs as to who's calling him, but I get my answer soon enough.

"Hey, Coop? I'm going to put you on speaker, okay? Zip's here." Kieran nods as Cooper says something to him, then he hits the speaker button and places the phone on the kitchen table.

"Hey, Cooper," I call out.

"Hey, Zip," he says, his normally husky voice sounding as far away over the phone as it is in reality. "Keeping our boy in line?"

"As much as possible."

"So, you said you had some news," Kieran says.

"Yeah," Cooper rasps back. "Have you talked to your mom lately?"

"Every night."

"But you haven't talked to her yet today?"

Kieran shoots me a look. Something's up, and he doesn't take his eyes from mine when he answers "No. Should I?"

"The research team had some kind of a breakthrough or whatever, I guess. They think they've got something that will work." Cooper's speaking quickly, his voice anxious. "I can't believe she didn't tell you about this."

Kieran's still staring at me, and I give him a shrug because I don't really know what to say. Of course, Jilly had hinted something like this might be coming when she was here a few weeks ago, but I can't break her confidence and tell Kieran.

"Well, Mom usually waits to call until she's sure we're all going to be home," Kieran tells Cooper. "But, they really think they've got something?"

"Yeah." Cooper's tone switches from excited to irritated. "But when I tried to talk to one of the guys on the research team I'm kind of cool with, he fed me all this 'We'll need to do more tests and run some more panels from the blood samples and test tube this and extract that and whatever.' Like the two of us aren't pissing our lives away waiting for them to figure out what the hell they're doing." He snorts in a disgust that's obvious even over the phone. "I almost wish they hadn't told me. I don't like getting my hopes up."

Jilly's voice rings in my ears, telling me about how Carlie didn't want Kieran to find out about how close they were to a treatment so he wouldn't get his hopes up. Kieran's eyes had shifted to the table on Cooper's mention of them wasting their lives, and I can only imagine his mind is drifting back to his theory that whatever the Halloran researchers are devising will end up killing him rather than treating him. "Yeah," he says, just loudly enough for Cooper to hear him.

"So, anyway," Cooper begins, switching topics as if the cure for his condition doesn't matter and we're just chatting as if we're all old friends, "that's that. What's new with you guys out in flyover country?"

"Not much." I hitch my shoulders, forgetting that Cooper can't see me. "First day of school. We got out early because of the heat, so we're just hanging out."

As I'm trying to make small talk with Cooper, Kieran's eyes have moved from the table to me and then to the phone.

"Hey, Coop? Since Zip's here, there's something I've been meaning to ask you. I didn't want to have this conversation without her being here."

46

I have no idea where this is headed.

"Yeah? What's up?" Cooper responds.

"Okay," Kieran pauses as if he's searching for the right words to begin whatever discussion he wants to have. "So...stuff with girls...how do you *do* that?"

Cooper asks, "What are you talking about?" but I immediately read what Kieran's trying to get across.

"Kieran, no!" I practically screech, putting my hands to my ears as if I can stop myself from hearing the rest of the conversation I'm sure is coming.

"Zip, you okay?" Cooper doesn't wait for an answer, instead directing his attention to Kieran. "Dude, seriously—what are you asking me?"

"Well, you kept talking when we first met about how you'd been with a lot of girls. And...just...I mean...how do you do that without...I mean, you fall asleep when things get tense, too, and..."

Cooper bursts out laughing.

"Wait—you're asking me about *sex*? Oh, my God. You're kidding me, right? You don't ask about this stuff in front of your girlfriend, dude."

"Or, ever," I chime in, knowing full well guys do the whole "locker room talk" thing—and knowing girls do it, too, for that matter—but knowing doesn't mean I have to stand for this gross amount of over-sharing happening right in front of me. "And you definitely don't ask *Cooper Halloran*, of all people."

"Hey, why not?" Cooper fires back, his voice indignant. "I'm an expert."

I groan loudly enough for him to hear, which provokes another laugh from across our fiber-optic distance.

"So, guys really don't talk about this stuff?" Kieran asks, and I put my head in my hands and don't look at him. This conversation isn't going to end well for me, I'm afraid.

"God, you really are clueless, aren't you?" Cooper snaps. "That's not what I said. Of course, guys talk about this stuff—but not in front of girls, and definitely not in front of *your* girl. This is something you do over beer and cigarettes, or before, during, or after a sporting event. Or after watching porn."

I risk looking up. Kieran's nodding at his phone, smiling with wonder as if he's Luke Skywalker and Yoda's just finished instructing him on proper use of The Force.

"*Please* tell me you're not taking him seriously," I beg, which produces a breathy laugh from Cooper. I can just picture his usual lizard-like grin taking over his face.

"Zip, you know I'm the only real guy friend he has," Cooper points out. "He's got to learn the finer points of being with girls *somewhere*. Let me do him a favor here. Hell, let me do *you* a favor here."

"We watch a lot of movies," I fire back. "We'll pick things up. We'll pick things up anywhere but from you."

Kieran waves at the phone as if Cooper can see him. "Um…guys. I'm right here." And to me: "Sorry. I thought he might be able to help and I didn't want to talk to him about it without you here because I thought that would be really rude and—"

I cover his hand, cutting him off with a smile to tell him everything's okay—or, as okay as things can be when your boyfriend wants to talk about your sex problems with a total tool who's probably slept with most of Manhattan's Upper West Side. Since I'm already embarrassed, I'm positive this situation can't get much worse.

And then Cooper starts speaking again.

"So, do you guys want my advice or would you rather give up and die pure and virginal?"

Yeah. I was wrong—this could get *so* much worse.

I look at Kieran, he looks at me, and we pause just long enough for Cooper to plow on ahead without waiting to find out if we're ready.

"So, first, I need to know what you guys have accomplished already in the hooking-up department."

"No," I mouth at Kieran, because I definitely don't want Cooper walking around with *those* images in his head.

Kieran nods at me and says to Cooper "You know. Stuff."

"Okay." I can read the snarkiness in Cooper's voice. "No details. I get it. I guess what I should have asked was, did your condition mess with you at all during this 'stuff'?"

"Not much," Kieran begins, keeping his eyes on me and probably waiting for my inevitable freak-out the second he strays into Too Much Information territory. "Usually only the first time we tried something. Eventually I'd relax and things were okay."

"Sounds familiar. If you're anything like me—and, of course, *you are*—it'll take you more than a few trips up to bat to hit a home run, if you get what I'm saying. The first few times I tried, things didn't go well. Like, I mean, things didn't go *at all*. After a while, I thought I was just going to have to face facts. I said to myself, 'Self, you're amazing, and girls will always want to get with you—'"

An audible groan escapes me at Cooper's extreme confidence. While he's not my favorite person, I can admit Cooper's a reasonably good-looking guy—sandy brown hair flopping over his forehead and into soft brown eyes, muscular build, strong jawline...

And then he opens his mouth and ruins everything—at least for me, anyway. Apparently, if Cooper's to be believed, other girls aren't at all immune to his charms in the way I am.

49

"'But maybe actual, real-live, full-on sex is never going to happen for you.'" Cooper continues quoting his previous thoughts aloud right over my groan. "And, of course, once I was okay with being the way I am and I stopped caring, it happened."

"So, you gave up and you stopped caring," Kieran paraphrases, glancing at me. "I don't think I can do that. I love Zip. I'm not giving up."

I smile in spite of myself. Hearing Kieran tell someone else that he loves me can't help but melt my heart.

"I didn't stop caring about the *girl*," Cooper insists. "I really, really cared about the girl, if you want the truth. What I stopped caring about was the sex." He pauses and backtracks a bit. "I mean, I didn't stop caring about the sex exactly…you always *care*…but I guess what I'm saying is, once I stopped worrying about whether or not it was going to happen, I wasn't under any pressure anymore, and everything fell into place."

"Makes sense, I guess," Kieran mumbles, looking at me.

"So, in other words, focus on the process and the end product will eventually take care of itself," I rephrase.

"Something like that. I mean, don't get me wrong—there have been plenty of times since when I didn't care about the girl much at all, and that made things a whole lot easier."

"Charming," I mutter under my breath, and Cooper must not hear because he continues right over my comment.

"But with this first girl, I think I got so caught up in trying to do the deed that for a long time, I couldn't. Once I kind of let go, I calmed down."

"So, who was the girl?" I ask, giving Cooper an amused smile, although he can't see it.

"What?"

"The girl you lost your virginity to. I'm amazed a girl exists who could bring the great Cooper Halloran to his knees."

Cooper snickers and says "Trust me—you don't know her." And then, before I can say anything else, he asks Kieran "So, K-Man—any other issues I can enlighten you on today? Threesomes? Bondage?"

I sigh and pick the phone up from the table.

"We're hanging up on you now," I say directly into the speaker. "Go terrorize someone else."

My thumb hovers over the disconnect button as Kieran leans in and says, "Thanks, Coop, but I think we've done enough damage for one day."

"Okay, then. Zip, go easy on him, okay? He's still learning how to be a guy's guy."

"That's what I'm afraid of," I tell Cooper as Kieran calls out "Bye" and Cooper says "Later" right before I end the call.

Kieran takes the phone from me and slides it back into his pocket.

"I'm such an idiot. I shouldn't have brought this up with him, but he's the only person in the world who would understand exactly what we're going through. I'm so sorry."

I step forward and wind my arms around him.

"I get that. It's just embarrassing is all, and then Cooper's douchebag attitude about everything just makes it worse."

"Looks like you were right, though," Kieran says. "We just need to stop trying so hard."

"Guess so," I whisper, as his lips move just inches from mine. "He didn't say we had to stop trying altogether, though."

The ache that rises in my stomach whenever we're close like this starts to overwhelm me, and I close my eyes.

51

"No, he didn't," Kieran says against my mouth before we meld together, all thoughts of Cooper Halloran, of my embarrassment, of anything at all breaking apart and dissolving into nothing. But we only kiss for a few seconds before Kieran pulls back from me slightly. "I knew the research team was getting close, by the way."

He's obviously—and understandably—too preoccupied with this big news to continue making out, so I back up against the sink.

"How?" I ask.

"The day Jilly showed up, I woke up while you two were talking in the living room. I was about to walk in on you when I heard her say Mom had told her they were close to something, but she didn't want me to find out. I didn't say anything because I didn't want to put Jilly in a bad position with Mom, and I didn't want to put you in a weird position with Jilly. And I didn't tell Coop because I didn't want to kill his buzz over telling me the big news. He's got all of those Halloran people wound around his finger so tight that I knew someone would say something to him if they were really getting close." Kieran pushes his hair out of his face and avoids my eyes, but I step into him, wrapping my arms around his neck again.

"Why does your family feel the need to keep secrets to spare everyone's feelings?" I say, smiling.

"We're just special, I guess." He sighs, the smile he returns to me sadder than the one I'm giving him.

"I feel bad you've had to carry that around for the last few weeks." I tell him, brushing his cheek with my hand. He angles his face to drop a kiss into my palm.

"I needed some time to think before I said anything anyway," he explains. "I figured they'd hit on something eventually, but I just didn't think it would be so fast."

The distant look in his eyes tips me off enough that I can guess at what he's thinking to some extent.

"You're scared."

"I wouldn't admit it to anyone but you, of course, but yeah," he says, a tiny version of his grin settling on his lips. "How I am is all I've ever been. This life is all I've ever known. If they've come up with a treatment, everything changes...for better or worse."

I know what the "worse" is for Kieran—death. And I don't want to go down that conversational road again.

"For better," I insist. "Your mom wouldn't let you go through with a treatment with that big of a risk. And think about what happens if—*when*—the treatment works. You could go away to school, do things by yourself..."

"That all sounds great," he says in a tone of voice that makes me wonder if he thinks it all doesn't sound so great. "But I've never known how to be anything other than who I am. I can't even get my head around being...*normal*."

I rise on my toes so I can kiss him on the forehead before telling him "You, Kieran Lanier, will never be *normal*—and I mean that as the highest compliment in the world. No matter what happens, you'll always be..." I pause, wracking my brain for the right word to convey what I believe about him, not quite sure the appropriate term even exists. But I hit upon something that works for now, and I go with it. "You'll always be *extraordinary*. Trust me. And your family and I will help you with all the boring regular human stuff you'll need to get used to."

He stares into my eyes, his grin undoing me as he slides his arms around my waist.

"What would I do without you in my life?" he says, sighing.

I lean in to kiss him, promising, "You'll never have to know."

CHAPTER 5

Just after school starts, my grandparents take pity on the Lanier household and invite Jim, Kayla, and Kieran over for dinner. As my mom and I set the dining room table before our guests arrive, I can't help but be reminded of the time the Laniers had dinner over here back in March, one of the initial tentative steps Jim and Carlie took toward lowering the wall they'd built around their family. That night was the first time Kayla had ever dropped her icy demeanor around me and started treating me as something halfway resembling a human being. It's kind of amazing to think about how close Kayla and I have become over the last six months considering where we started. As much as she infuriates me sometimes, I can't imagine life without her now, and I definitely can't imagine life without her brother.

"So, any news about when Carlie's coming home?" Mom asks, following along behind me with a fistful of silverware from which she doles out utensils after I put plates at each seat.

"No. And don't bring it up, either," I warn, knowing my mother is just the type to slip up and do so. "It's kind of a sore subject. Everyone understands what Carlie's doing is important, but from what Kieran's telling me, I think Jim's getting a little fed up over her not being here."

"Well, it's been a long time. Can't say I blame him."

Mom puts a fork, spoon, and knife at the last place setting and tucks a loose blonde lock from her messy ponytail behind her ear. I'm sporting a messy ponytail myself, as usual, and other than the fact that I'm a good two or three inches taller and don't have age lines near my eyes like Mom does, we could be mistaken for twins.

Our brief conversation about Carlie grinds to a halt as the side door to the house in the kitchen slams shut. I'm immediately hit with the intoxicating smell of steak seasoned with Gramps' secret dry rub, prepared on the grill by Gramps and Morgan. Mom and I slip from the dining room into the kitchen just as Gramps removes his glasses from his round face and wipes them on the shirttail of a gray Titusville Athletic Boosters shirt.

"Morgan's a natural, I tell you. Look at these steaks," Gramps booms, sweeping his hand toward the platter on the kitchen table. "He's a regular grill master."

"Congratulations," my mom says to Morgan, giggling. "Bet you've waited your whole life to hear *that*."

"Well, I've definitely been called worse," he replies, running a hand through his thatch of dark hair that's shorter than Kieran's and pretty much the only thing, other than the lines in his face and the always scruffy facial hair, distinguishing him from his son. "I don't remember grilling out much when I was a kid."

When Morgan was growing up, he was too busy getting bounced from foster home to foster home to experience many, if any, family cookouts. Once he and his girlfriend Jenna Bradley, Kieran's birth mother, aged out of the foster care system, they lived hand-to-mouth in a tenement in New York City, so opportunities for grilling out would have been pretty low then, too. And Morgan was barely out of his teens when he went to prison, where I'm guessing the only things resembling a grill were the steel bars of a cell.

My grandmother, a few inches shorter than Gramps and a little thicker around the middle, but with identical wire frame glasses and the same loveable demeanor, wipes her hands on a towel and walks over from the counter to Morgan where he stands near the side door.

"Now that we have a master griller in the house, we might need to break the grill out more often," she says, placing a kind hand on Morgan's arm.

"Careful," Mom warns him. "You're going to have a third job before you know what hit you. Sumner College landscaper, Downtown Diner cook, and grill servant to the Shipman family. The last one will be unpaid, I'm sure."

"I'm glad to help out however I can," Morgan says, darting his eyes to the floor as he turns my mom's teasing into something serious. "You've all been so good to me. Most guys who get out of prison aren't so lucky."

Gramps leans over to me and puts a hand on the back of my head.

"You took care of our Zipperino," he says to Morgan, employing his penchant for making my unusual nickname even more unusual. "You're welcome in this house for as long as you like."

Morgan and I glance at each other and share awkward smiles over the reference to Prom night, when Morgan called for an ambulance after I crashed my mom's car and suffered a concussion.

We don't get to dwell on Morgan's grilling skills or guardian angel abilities any further as the doorbell rings, sending Gram speeding down the hall to greet the Laniers. The rest of us move to the dining room, and I peer out at everyone, noting how different the greetings are this time as opposed to six months ago—rather than tentative handshakes and introductions, Gram and the Laniers all exchange hugs, Gram taking Kieran's and Kayla's faces in her hands before she lets them go.

"Everything smells great, Mrs. Shipman," Kayla gushes, taking a seat at the far end of the table with her back to the hallway. Kieran sits down next to her and I take the seat on his other side as

Kayla corrects herself with Gram's given name before Gram can. "Sorry—'Barbara'."

"Thank you, Kayla. I hope it tastes just as good." Gram smiles and slides into her seat at the head of the table nearest the kitchen. Mom sits on the other side of the table flanked by Jim and Morgan while Gramps, at the opposite head of the table, remains standing, reaching for his wine glass and raising it to eye level.

"I'd like to propose a toast if I could," he says after clearing his throat.

Gram gives him a warm smile and scolds "Don't go on too long, Larry. The food will get cold."

"Not to worry, dear. I just want to toast the members of our family. And by 'family,' I mean everyone sitting here right now. We've all been through a great deal together the last few months, and I think it's brought us closer together than some people who share the same last name. Being family doesn't always mean you share the same bloodline. It means you share unbreakable bonds, and I for one am honored to share unbreakable bonds with everyone sitting here, whether those bonds are new—" Gramps glances to his right at Morgan—"or not so new, but are still just as strong as the day I asked her to be my bride." He tilts his head toward Gram, whose cheeks flush with emotion.

"So, here's to our family and the unbreakable bonds we share," Gramps concludes, lifting his glass just a bit higher. "I can't think of a better group of people to call my kin."

We all rise from our seats so we can clink glasses, my mom saying "Aww, Dad. You're going to make us all cry," as she taps her wine glass to his. When we sit back down, Kieran grabs my hand under the table and gives it a little squeeze, and I can't help but wonder if someday, in the far, far away future after college and after we're settled into something resembling a stable life, Kieran and I

57

actually *will* become family, further uniting everyone at the table. But given that we can't even get our lives beyond next August sorted out, I don't dare dream for longer than a second, and Gram nudges my arm so she can pass me the salad bowl, so I'm brought back to the present pretty quickly anyway.

As the food bowls and platters make their way around the table, I catch my mother glancing at Jim and I can tell she's restraining herself from bringing Carlie into the conversation. I flash wide eyes at her and, once she's seen me, she quickly shifts her attention to Kayla.

"Kayla, how's Brad? Doreen came into the store the other day and said he seemed to be doing well, but I thought you might have a different take on things."

"Doreen" is Brad's mom, and while I know Brad gets along pretty well with his parents, Mom's right—he's probably sharing aspects of life at Northwestern with Kayla that he may not be mentioning to his parents, which doesn't necessarily mean Kayla's going to be willing to share those things with a roomful of adults who *aren't* his parents.

"I think he's adjusting. He likes his roommate and he says most of his classes are pretty manageable, but his bio class is kind of hard. I'm hoping to go up there next weekend if *someone* ever gets around to giving me permission." Kayla glances in her father's direction and purses her lips while Jim shifts his eyes to his plate.

"Not now. We're guests in someone else's home," he tells her quietly.

"But we're all family, right? So, I should be able to speak freely." Kayla looks to Gramps for confirmation as she carves up her steak. Gramps gives her the slightest nod, and I feel bad for him that thanks to Kayla and her ability to make any situation awkward, his toast about our extended family bonds is probably about to blow up in his face.

"Kayla, I'm warning you," Jim says through gritted teeth, but Kayla continues undeterred as the rest of us focus on eating our food.

"No—seriously, Dad. You need to make the decision yourself about whether or not I can go visit Brad. No more of this 'Well, your mother and I didn't get around to talking about it.'" She says this last sentence in a fairly accurate imitation of Jim's baritone. "Mom's not here, and we don't know when she's going to be. *Somebody* in our house needs to put on some grown-up pants and do some parenting."

Jim opens his mouth to say something, but before he can, Kayla glances past me to Kieran.

"Hey, you're eighteen," she points out. "Maybe you can be the grown-up in the house. What do you say? Can I go to Northwestern next weekend?"

Kieran gives his sister a sugary smile.

"Sure, Kay—anything to get your crabby ass out of the house for a few days."

Jim's fork drops to his plate, the sharp clatter of silver meeting china raising the hairs on the back of my neck.

"Kieran, your language is completely inappropriate." He shifts his gaze to his daughter. "And your behavior is inexcusable. Absolutely inexcusable."

Kieran mumbles a "sorry," but Kayla sets her mouth in a tight line and doesn't say a word, apologetic or otherwise.

Jim rises from his chair and sets his napkin next to his plate, saying, "Barbara…Larry…I'd like to apologize on behalf of my children. Apparently, their mother and I failed to teach them to appreciate others' hospitality. And as much as I hate to ruin this dinner, I'd like to talk to my children on the front porch if you don't mind."

"Of course," Gram tells him. "I'll put your plates in the kitchen and we'll warm up your food when you come back inside."

59

"Thank you."

Jim rounds the table and ventures out into the hall. Kayla and Kieran don't follow, but instead give each other confused glances, which causes Jim to double back once he realizes his children aren't following him to the front door.

"*Now*, you two," he booms from just a few feet behind me, and Kieran's shoulders rise at the sound of his father's voice. He and Kayla get up and shuffle after Jim into the front hall and out onto the porch. Gram, as promised, takes Jim's plate to the kitchen, and I follow along behind her with the siblings' partially eaten meals. After we place them on the counter next to the stove, Gram puts a hand on my arm and gives me kiss on the forehead, and I thank her with a sad smile. While the tensions in the Lanier family have a long history, I don't think any of us quite know how to handle their latest struggles.

Back in the dining room, my grandparents, Mom, Morgan, and I resume eating in a tense silence made even more uncomfortable by the muffled sounds of the discussion on the front porch. Thankfully, the window behind my grandfather is closed, so I can't make out anything the Laniers are saying to each other, and I'm not sure I'd want to. After about a minute or so of all of us pretending nothing strange is going on, my mom decides to strike up a conversation in a way only she could.

"So, Morgan," she begins, "ever thought about settling down and having more kids once you get on your feet?"

Morgan coughs down some salad at Mom's untimely suggestion.

"No," he says once his throat is clear. "And even if I had, I think Kieran and Kayla just cured me."

"April," Gramps warns, but Mom continues.

"Well, you know, parenting isn't all bad." She nods across the table at me. "My Zip is a perfect little angel—when she's not mixed-up with ex-cons, that is."

"So, I've heard."

"Very funny," I say, smirking at both of them. "Really. You two should take your act on the road."

Mom and Morgan snicker at me, and all I can do is sigh. With Morgan living in my grandparents' house and hanging out with my mom whenever we're over here, my mom now has another friend in town close to her age, which is never a bad thing considering most other adults around here in their late thirties and early forties are too preoccupied with their out-of-town jobs and families to socialize much. And while I'm unsure about Morgan's long-term plans, I do know that I worry about what's going to happen to my mom when I leave for college. She's admitted to me that she gets pretty lonely when I go visit my dad, and I've never been away from home for more than a month at a time. Maybe having Morgan to hang out with will kind of lessen the blow of my leaving town.

"Our perfect little angel isn't always so perfect, either," Gramps points out, looking at Gram and Mom in turn. "In fact, Morgan, let me tell you about this time when April was about six…"

Gramps doesn't get the chance to embarrass Mom and she doesn't get the chance to protest as Gramps twists in his chair to glance out the window.

"I heard a car," he explains, rising so he can peek through the opaque window shades to get a better view of the driveway.

"Can you see who it is?" Gram asks, clearly confused. My grandparents don't get a ton of visitors to begin with, and they definitely wouldn't at dinnertime on a Friday night, when half the town's probably headed to the varsity football game in Brownsville.

"No…wait…someone's getting out…"

61

I glance across the table at Mom and Morgan and they, like me, appear to be sitting on the edge of their seats because unknown cars and their drivers are the kinds of unusual things that would excite people around this town.

"It's Carlie," Gramps says, turning away from the window, his expression a mix of confusion and happiness. Without a word, I'm up from my chair and out on the front porch in seconds to find Carlie exchanging hugs with her husband and kids. She's in the middle of hugging Kieran when she spies me over his shoulder.

"Zip," she breathes, and Kieran turns in her arms. With her arm around his shoulder, the two of them walk over to join me on the porch, Jim and Kayla following behind. "How are you?" She gathers me to her with her free arm.

"I'm good, thanks. You're home," I reply, so surprised that I can't do more than point out the obvious.

"It was time." She gazes up at Kieran. "I missed my family."

Kieran wriggles out of her grasp and faces us, saying, "And you're close to something—you and the research team, I mean."

Morgan and my family slip out onto the front porch as Carlie nods and says, "You must have spoken to Cooper today."

"Yeah," Kieran mumbles, not bothering to reveal Cooper had called several days ago, and not revealing that thanks to Jillian, he and I already knew a treatment was near.

"I thought he might call." She glances past Kieran to the rest of the gathering assembled behind him. "Hello, everyone."

Over mumbled greetings from Morgan and my family, Carlie continues, "They think they're close to something usable. But there's still a lot of testing that needs to happen. They don't know when they'll have something safe for use. With such an indeterminate timetable, I didn't think I could stay any longer. I spoke with Ben and Cooper late this morning, and Ben arranged for the Halloran jet to fly me to O'Hare, where I rented a car—which we need to drop off in Sumner tomorrow, by the way." She directs this last statement at Jim, who narrows his eyes and nods as if making a mental note, and then she continues addressing Kieran. "I noticed you and Kayla and your dad out here on the porch as I was driving by, so I turned around in our driveway and came back." I feel her shrug against me and glance over at Jim, who's moved over next to Kieran. "I wanted to surprise you, so I didn't call. But I can't believe Cooper didn't say anything."

She directs her last statement at Kieran, and once again, Kieran declines to tell her he spoke with Cooper earlier in the week rather than today.

"What were the three of you doing out on the front porch by yourselves to begin with?" Carlie asks, apparently just now realizing their behavior would be out of the ordinary. Her eyes dart from Kieran to Jim to Kayla, none of whom immediately speak up.

"Dad was just giving us some pointers on how to behave when you're a guest in someone's house," Kayla finally volunteers with a tight smile. "We've gotten a little rusty in that department since you've been gone."

"Do I want to know what she's talking about?" Carlie asks Jim, sighing.

"No," he replies. "Let's just say we're happy you're home and leave it at that."

"And we've got plenty of food," Gram chimes in from behind Kieran. "And now, we've got something to celebrate, too. Everybody come on inside—we'll reheat things and move the kids into the kitchen to eat."

On Gram's invitation, everyone starts to file into the house. Carlie lets me go, and Jim sidles up on her other side, his hand on her back guiding her through the door ahead of him. Kayla, Kieran, and I move out of the way so the adults can enter before us, and Kieran pulls me to him, prompting Kayla to give us a knowing look before disappearing through the front door, leaving us alone. But as I wind my arms around him, I can feel a tremor moving through his body.

"What's wrong?" I whisper in his ear.

"I'm not sure," he says into my hair. "It's all…*real* now, I guess. Hearing from Jilly and Cooper that something was close was one thing. But hearing it from Mom…and now she's back…I know she said they were still a ways off from a treatment they can use, but either way, it's sinking in that my time's almost up."

I step back and take his face in my hands.

"Your mom knows what they're working with as far as the treatment's concerned," I assure him. "She can tell you what the risks are, and she's not going to let you take something if she thinks it's dangerous. Talk to her, Kieran. Tell her what you're afraid of. You don't need to live in fear like this."

Kieran reaches up to grab my hands and pulls them down in front of us, linking his fingers with mine as my charm bracelet bumps up against his wrist.

"I don't know if I can tell her," he whispers. "It was hard enough telling you and Kayla. I'm not sure I can look at my mother and tell her I'm afraid my dreams ending might mean I'm going to die. She's spent almost my whole life worried that something bad's going to happen to me."

"Exactly—so she knows how to deal with that worry. I think it's part of the 'mom' job description. Maybe not to this extreme, but worrying to some extent is probably always there."

He gives me a weak smile.

"It just doesn't seem right to keep your mom in the dark about your fears when she might be able to put them to rest," I continue. "I know you've had a hard time connecting with your parents after finding out they lied to you for so long, but look at what your mom's been doing for you—she left town for weeks because she's so desperate to help you. Regardless of everything that's happened, they love you more than anything. You get that, right?"

Kieran sighs and looks away from me.

"I know. And maybe you're right. You've said all along the reason I've stopped dreaming is because something's coming that will help Cooper and me."

"So, you'll talk to her?" I prod.

"I'll talk to her." He smiles. "Promise."

Kieran's pressing his lips to my forehead when Gram pops her head out the front door.

"You two can kiss around on each other later," she whispers, causing me to blush. "Come inside and eat before your food cools off—it's not going to stand being reheated again."

Kieran and I exchange smiles and part, him hanging behind me as we enter the house to join our combined families, now complete once again.

Chapter 6

Late Saturday morning, I'm at the kitchen table struggling through my physics homework and am on the verge of cursing out my textbook and throwing it across the room when my phone buzzes.

"Oh, thank you," I mutter, activating the home screen to find a text from Kieran:

"Lunch?"

"Ur place or mine?" I text back.

"I want 2 take u out."

I decide this conversation will be easier if we're talking rather than typing, so I hit Kieran's number on my speed dial.

"Hey," he says once he's picked up. "I need to get out of the house. Kayla and the parentals have been going at it about her wanting to visit Brad next weekend ever since they got back from the car rental place in Sumner. And I'm hungry, but they've commandeered the kitchen for this particular battle. No way I'm interrupting."

"What did you have in mind?" I ask, shutting my evil physics textbook and pushing it away to the other side of the table before it can steal any more of my soul.

"I'm thinking cheese fries at the Downtown Diner. Morgan's working today, and I don't want to pass up an opportunity to see him in an apron."

I snort. Morgan's second job resulted from an amazing case of serendipity. Eric Hollander, who had been the Diner's weekend cook for two years after he graduated from Titusville High, finished his associate's degree at Wyatt County Community College this spring and quit in July so he could move across the state to go to school. Morgan happened to have cooking experience from a stint working his prison's kitchen, so Dewayne Masters hired him as the Downtown Diner's latest employee. And while Dewayne's okay with the Lanier "cousin's" felony history, he has no idea of the connection Morgan shares with one of Dewayne's other former employees, Danny Dubrow, better known to my family and Kieran's as Frank Dozier. And none of us plan on setting Dewayne straight as to "Danny's" true identity.

"Make those cheese fries *chili* cheese fries and I'm in," I tell him, licking my lips. Other than the occasional deluxe pizza, I've kept to a strict training diet all summer, trying to get my body in the best shape possible before basketball season. But I'm a teenager, after all, and I've just spent the last hour wrestling with Demon Physics, so I'm totally in the mood to drown myself in chili, processed cheese sauce, and fried potatoes right now.

"Chili cheese fries, it is," he promises. "See you in a few?"

"Mom took the car to the store this morning, but I should be able to get the truck from Gramps," I say, looking out the window and over to my grandparents' house at the dirty white Ford parked in their driveway. "I'll text you if I can't borrow it for some reason."

About fifteen minutes later, I pull the truck into the Laniers' driveway behind Kayla's Jeep and don't get the chance to turn off the engine and go inside because Kieran's already waiting for me on the front porch. He walks over as I'm putting the truck into "park," and climbs up into the cab on the passenger side.

"Things must be bad if I can't even meet you inside," I say, leaning over to give him a kiss.

"Oh, it's World War Three in there right now," he tells me when we part. "Mom and Dad are convinced if Kayla spends the weekend on a college campus without any adult supervision, all she's going to do is get drunk and have sex the whole time."

"I'm sure she'll fit in some other activities while she's there," I joke, putting the truck in reverse so I can pull around to the other side of the driveway.

"Oh, I'm sure." Kieran laughs as we rumble back down the long gravel driveway to the county road. "But, seriously, though—it's like my parents have never even *met* Brad before. He'll probably spend the whole weekend studying and Kayla will spend the whole weekend staring at him like a dopey, lovesick puppy. I don't get what they're so worried about."

"I think they're just worried because Kayla has a boyfriend, and that boyfriend now lives far away. It's one thing to adjust to your daughter having a boyfriend who lives across town, but it's probably something else to let your kid go off to visit said boyfriend when he's a hundred miles away. I mean, our parents had to take some time to get used to the idea of us being together, so this whole long-distance thing with Kayla and Brad is probably an adjustment for your parents, too."

I'm teetering dangerously close to the always-awful subject of our possible separation next year, and so I'm desperate to change the subject as I make the left turn off the county road onto Main Street.

"So, did you talk to your mom like we talked about last night?"

Way to go, Zip. I think to myself as I cringe. *Go right from one bad subject into another. Nice work.*

"I did, actually." Kieran surprises me with his bright tone. "And you were right. I feel a lot better."

"Yeah. One of these days, you'll get used to me being right all the time," I tell him with a smile. "Eventually you won't even question me anymore."

Kieran laughs, and I'm glad he's taking my statements as the joke they're meant to be.

68

"Sounds like she told you what you wanted to hear?" I ask.

He nods as we make the right turn from Titusville's decrepit Main Street, with its mostly empty storefronts, onto River Avenue, which over the years has become Titusville's main business district save for the cluster of stores, restaurants, and gas stations out by the interstate.

"Uh huh. Mom said they can't be sure of all the side effects of the treatment, of course, but she doesn't think death is even a possibility. She said they're thinking side effects like headaches, occasional blurred vision…"

I pull into a parking space as Kieran continues ticking off a list of minor side effects. And although I'm bobbing my head at him as he speaks, I'm really lost in my own thoughts. I'm no science expert—the fact that I'm already struggling with physics after one week of school is proof enough—but I can't help but wonder if Carlie isn't painting a rosier picture of the treatment for Kieran than what's actually true. The combination of Kieran's wanting to believe something positive about his future and Carlie's history of lying to Kieran to protect him might not lead to the happy ending Kieran wants—and it might not lead to his death, either—but when he's in such a good mood, I don't want to say anything to bring him down.

Shaking off my negative thoughts, I turn off the truck's engine and Kieran and I get out to head for the Diner's entrance. I'm so hungry I have visions of chili cheese fries dancing in my head, but those visions are quickly replaced by something a little more bizarre once we're inside. My mom is sitting on a stool at the end of the counter furthest from the door, which isn't unusual in and of itself. But what strikes me as odd about this scene is Morgan, standing behind the counter clad in a grease-stained white t-shirt and an apron. He's leaning in toward my mother and saying something, their faces only a few inches apart. And Mom's laughing, a really goofy, high-

69

pitched laugh that doesn't sound like her regular one at all, but at the same time sounds like a laugh I know from somewhere. Kieran and I both wave at them and are sliding into our favorite booth next to the door when it hits me where I've heard that laugh before.

Mom used to act like that around my dad. The memories are hazy and far away because my parents split up so long ago, but they're still there in the back of my mind. Her laugh is like an audible tether back to those times.

I tilt my head at Mom and Morgan and shoot Kieran a "What do you think that's all about?" look, which he answers with an "I don't know" heave of his shoulders. We watch, my body turned in the booth so I can see behind me, as Morgan ducks back into the kitchen and my mom slides off the stool and walks over next to our table.

"Hi, guys," she chirps, shaking the plastic to-go cup she's holding, ice cubes clunking against the sides. "Taking a study break?" She fiddles with some strands of the loose bun at the nape of her neck, something she always does when she's not sure what to say or what to do.

"Something like that," I tell her. "Who's watching the store?"

"Things are pretty slow today," she says. Her arts and crafts store across the street, Doodles, doesn't always do a brisk business, which means her small business is no different than any other in Titusville. "Thought I'd pop across the street and grab some lunch to go."

One of the few nice things about Titusville being a small town is that my mom can leave her store unattended for a few minutes on a slow Saturday and not have to worry about returning to find half her inventory has been wiped out. The flip side, of course, is that she doesn't have to worry too much about missing out on any customers.

70

Dewayne Masters slides up next to Mom so he can take our order for chili cheese fries and sodas. He exchanges some pleasantries with Mom before disappearing down the aisle and through the swinging doors for the kitchen. When the doors swing again a second later, Morgan walks out, slipping behind the counter to grab a paper bag into which he slides the Styrofoam container he's carrying, and then he joins my mother next to our table.

"Here you go, April," he says, handing her the bag. I catch him touching the small of her back for a split second, but he quickly drops his hand to his apron, wiping his palm down the front.

"Thanks." She smiles at him and turns her attention to me. "Well, I should be getting back over to the store, I guess. Are you going to be at home the rest of the afternoon?"

"I don't know." I shrug, trying not to glare at her as she fiddles with her loose hair. "Hadn't planned out my day."

"I'm hoping I can get her to take a break from studying for a while," Kieran chimes in. "Maybe we can use the net at Gram and Gramps' house so she can teach me some more basketball moves."

"Oh, that sounds fun," Mom says, her voice a little too chipper. "And, Morgan, thanks again for the food." She raises the bag at him in salute.

"No problem. See you soon," he replies, as Mom walks to the door and says "'Bye" at all of us before venturing out onto the sidewalk. Morgan watches her go and then, getting his bearings, turns to Kieran and me.

"Did Dewayne take care of you guys already?"

"Yeah," Kieran says, smiling. "We're great."

"Okay, then." He's practically moving away from us already. "I should head back to the kitchen. Tell Dewayne to let me know when you're getting ready to leave and I'll pop back out to say goodbye."

71

Morgan speeds down the aisle and I twist around in the booth to face Kieran, who's leaning back in his seat, arms folded over his chest and his usual loopy grin on his face.

"So, clear this up for me," he starts. "If *your* mom starts dating *my* dad, do we have to break up?"

"Not even funny. And, legally, Morgan isn't your dad, anyway—Jim Lanier is. Plus, if they got married, we'd only be step-siblings and not blood-siblings, and…" I realize what I'm saying and I shake my head so hard I can almost hear my brain rattle. "Oh, my God. Why are we even talking about this? They're not dating."

"Maybe not. But unless I was imagining things, *something* seemed to be going on." Kieran pauses as Dewayne delivers our sodas. "And you have to admit, they make sense together," he continues, ripping the paper wrapper from his straw.

"How so?"

"Well, think about it. It's pure biology. I'm attracted to you and you're attracted to me, so it's totally logical that my dad would be attracted to your mom."

"I think my brain just exploded," I grumble. "Let's not talk about this any more."

"Deal," he says, putting the straw into his drink and taking a sip. "And I wasn't kidding when I told your mom I was hoping you'd teach me some more basketball stuff today. It's either that or go home to my war zone of a house." He narrows his eyes, thinking. "Or we could go to your house and watch movies and make out."

"How about we do the basketball stuff first so we can work off our lunch, and *then* we'll go to my house and watch movies and make out?" I suggest, mock-seriously.

"Good idea. I don't want to make out on a full stomach. I might get a cramp."

"Okay," I say, laughing, before I rip off the edge of my straw's paper wrapper and blow it at him. He takes the paper from where it lands on the edge of the table, crumples it up, and throws it at me, but it lands next to my cup.

"We need to work on your aim," I tell him.

"Which is why I need more expert Zip McKee Basketball Instruction," he points out as Dewayne brings our fries. We load up on food and when we're done, we ask Dewayne to call Morgan out from the kitchen so we can tell him a quick goodbye before heading back to my grandparents' house, where, unlike my house, there's a hoop and a paved driveway.

Right on schedule, Kieran's fully immersed in his afternoon nap by the time I pull the truck off into the grass next to the driveway. The passenger window's rolled down and the weather isn't too warm today, so I decide to leave Kieran in the truck until he wakes up, closing the driver's door softly when I get out so I don't wake him.

Gram comes out on the front porch, likely having heard the truck pull up. "Kieran with you?" she calls to me as I round the truck and jog up to her. She squints in my direction, obviously not able to see whether or not Kieran's still in the truck.

I kiss her on the cheek and say "He's sleeping. We're going to shoot some hoops, but he needs his nap first." I tilt my head back toward the truck to indicate that Kieran's snoozing inside the cab. "Is Gramps out in the studio?"

"He'd probably appreciate the company," Gram says, nodding. "He always likes it when you come out and ask him questions about what he's working on."

I don't need any further invitation. After squeezing her hand, I leave her and walk around to the tool shed at the back of the house, which Gramps converted into an art studio for himself and my mom years ago, choosing to keep the actual gardening tools in the basement of the house.

The shed is usually a mess of various projects that Mom and Gramps are working on. Mom's been into making jewelry and other accessories for the past few months, and the workbench on the left side of the studio is covered with sheets of copper, tiny wires, and small square boxes of beads. And at the moment, Gramps is sitting on a stool in the back corner, carving away on a tree stump he's been gradually trying to transform into a bear since last winter. I love that bear as I love everything about this art studio, especially since Kieran and I had our first kiss here in the corner behind the lithography press on our mutual April first birthday.

"Zipperoo," Gramps says with his usual toothy smile once he notices me in the doorway.

"I don't want to bother you if you're busy."

"Nonsense." He waves me inside. "I was just working on old Norbert here."

I laugh as I glide over behind him and put my hands on his shoulders.

"You named the bear?"

"I thought he looked like a 'Norbert.' Kind of distinguished."

Tilting my head to the side, I give Norbert a once over.

"Okay, Gramps. I'll go with it."

Gramps reaches up and pats my hand with his free one.

"So, did you and Kieran have a good lunch?"

"Yeah," I say, contemplating whether or not to mention to Gramps the possible romantic entanglement between his daughter and his renter and deciding not to. "Kieran's having his after-lunch nap in the truck. We're probably going to shoot some hoops after he wakes up."

74

Gramps slides out from under my hands and stands up to take the carving knife he's working with over to the workbench.

"And how's the basketball tutelage coming along?"

"We shoot a lot of free throws. The whole 'running, dribbling, and making layups' business is kind of too much for Kieran."

"That's a little too much for most people. You've been so good at basketball since you were a little girl, I think you forget sometimes how much coordination you need to play a sport."

I hitch my shoulders up and slide down on the stool next to my new buddy Norbert, who has ears and a pretty well-defined face at this point, but still needs about half a body and legs.

"I know it all comes pretty easy for me," I tell Gramps. "But sometimes, I hurt for Kieran that he can't even do a small portion of what I can do. And I know it's frustrating for him, too."

Gramps squints and purses his lips for a second, thinking.

"Zip, do me a favor," he says at last, nodding toward an easel with a large sketch pad resting on it sitting near the end of the workbench. "Drag that stool over here and draw me something."

"Um, what?" My head jerks back at his request. Gramps knows that he has more artistic talent in his little finger than I have in my entire body.

"You heard me."

He turns back to the bench and, with no further instructions, I carry the stool over to the easel and sit down, staring at the blank page in front of me."

"Draw anything?" I ask Gramps.

He doesn't look up from his tools when he says, "Anything. But don't over-think it. Do it as fast as you can."

With that information to go on, I pick up a piece of charcoal from the easel rest and get to work drawing one of the few things I know how—a tree. I make two broad strokes a few inches apart in the

75

middle of the sheet for a trunk and draw a bunch of spindly-looking lines snaking out with smaller straight ones attached to indicate branches. I'm in the middle of sketching parabola-shaped leaves when we hear a knock on the open door, and I look over at Kieran standing just inside the studio, still looking a little sleepy as he rubs his eyes.

"Hey. Did you get enough sleep?" I ask, walking over to give him a hug.

"Yeah, I think so. When I woke up, I didn't know where I was for a minute, but then I recognized the house. Gram told me you were back here." He looks over my shoulder at the easel. "Were you drawing?"

"Uh huh."

"I'd asked Zip to draw me something," Gramps explains, turning away from the workbench. "Now it's your turn, if you're up to it."

"Sure." Kieran shrugs and walks over to the easel, taking in my work. "Is this a tree?" he says to me as I stand next to him.

I bite my lip.

"It's not obvious?"

He slides an arm around my shoulder and says, "No, no. It's really good."

"No, it's not," I grumble.

Kieran cocks his head, as if looking at the tree sideways will make it more tree-like.

"It's really good," he says again. "I can make out the trunk and the leaves and—"

"Okay," Gramps says, stepping in to save us both. "Why don't we let Kieran draw something for us."

"Anything?" he asks.

"Anything. The only catch is, you have to be quick about it. I think Zip took about three or four minutes."

Kieran hitches up his shoulders as if to say, "No big deal," and he sits down at the easel, tearing off the sheet with my tree to reveal another blank page. I take my sad tree from him and he thinks for a second, grabs the charcoal, and starts making broad strokes that at first don't seem to be part of a coherent whole. But after two minutes, he's managed to marry the lines and shadows together into a basic sketch of Gramps from the neck up.

"Amazing," I say, resting my chin on his shoulder after he puts the charcoal down. "How did you do that so fast?" I slide my arms around his waist as he stares at his work.

"I don't know," he mumbles. "I always wanted to get my dreams recorded as soon as possible after I woke up, and sometimes I'd only have a few minutes before school or before I had to go do something else. If I could remember seeing something I thought I could draw, I tried to get it down as fast as I could. So, I guess I just adapted."

"When did you first learn to draw, Kieran?" Gramps asks, leaning up against the edge of the workbench.

"I'm not sure I really *learned*, you know? I've always doodled stuff. I think maybe it helped me stay awake sometimes if I kept my hands busy. And then I always got good grades in art classes. I guess it's always been easy for me."

I lift my head and glare at Gramps behind Kieran's back.

"Kind of like basketball is for me," I say to Gramps. "Way to make a point."

Gramps gives me a self-satisfied smile and says, "We all have our strengths and weaknesses."

"Do I even want to ask what's going on with you two?" Kieran asks.

77

"I'll fill you in later," I whisper.

"Kieran, have you thought about what you'd do with your future if you could do anything you wanted?" Gramps asks, changing the subject.

"Well, something dealing with art, obviously." Kieran twists in my grasp so he can face Gramps. "It'd be cool to be an art teacher or an art therapist, maybe work with kids."

Gramps nods slowly.

"Are you thinking about applying anywhere?"

"I've thought about it," he says. "Mom and Dad aren't exactly on board. They want me to stay home and do a degree online."

"Well, there are some decent programs online," Gramps says, stroking his chin and putting his retired art professor knowledge to good use. "And, of course, Sumner College has an excellent art and design program."

"Not that he's biased or anything," I mumble at Kieran.

"Of course not," Kieran says, and Gramps chuckles.

"My bias aside, I'd be happy to help you put a portfolio together if you wanted to apply to Sumner. Since your father works there, maybe it would be an option for you."

"He can drive me to school, but he can't go to class with me," Kieran points out.

"He can't go to class with you now," Gramps says. "You can alert your professors to your condition just as you have with the teachers at the high school. Wouldn't hurt to at least put together a portfolio and see what happens. If you get in and your parents decide they don't want you to go, then no harm, no foul."

"You'd help me do that?" Kieran's voice sounds small, yet grateful.

"Of course. Do you have copies of things you did in art class last semester?"

"Yeah. I've got tons of drawings I've done on my own, too, and stuff from my journals."

"Bring them over sometime," Gramps tells him. "We'll go through what you have, take some pictures. I could even teach you some basic carving and sculpting techniques if you wanted, and work on some other things if you wanted as well. If you pick up things quickly enough and finish some projects, we'll take pictures of those for your portfolio, too."

Kieran give Gramps a wide-eyed expression that looks as though Gramps just handed him a license to run the world.

"That...that sounds great."

"And if you're able to take the treatment at some point and it works, you might as well have some applications out there," I tell him. "Just because you apply to some schools doesn't mean you have to go if you get in."

"That's true, I guess," Kieran says, and then gets a strange look on his face. He reaches into his pocket and pulls out his buzzing phone. "Hello?" he answers. "Yeah...we're over at the Shipmans'...Uh huh...Yeah...We'll be there in a few."

"Everything okay?" I ask as he stands and puts his phone back in his pocket.

"I don't know. That was Mom. She said she wants me home right now."

I'm trying not to be concerned, but I can't help but feel a creeping dread—it's a sensation I get a lot where the Laniers are concerned.

"I'll walk you back—or, I'll drive you, if I can borrow the truck again." I look back at Gramps and he nods his approval.

"Hope everything's okay," Gramps says, laying a wrinkled hand on Kieran's shoulder. "Tell your parents if they need anything..."

Gramps lets his voice trail off, and Kieran gives him a nervous smile.

"Thanks," he mumbles, locking hands with me. We turn and leave the studio, and I can feel the electric pulse of fear in him as if it's coursing through his body and shooting into me through our joined hands.

"Any idea what might be up?" I ask him as we round the house.

"No. I mean, Mom just came home, she and Dad are fighting with Kayla...things seem pretty normal in the Lanier household for once. Or, normal by our standards, anyway." He shakes his head. "Either something's wrong with Jilly, or something's wrong in New York—that's all I can think of. Maybe somebody called and told her the formula's a total bust."

I know Kieran well enough to read the sadness in his icy blue eyes.

"I'm sure that's not it," I try to reassure him, although I have no grounds for doing so. He's pinning so much on the treatment eventually working that I want to help him keep a positive attitude.

"You're probably right," he says, playing along as we reach the passenger side of the truck. "I'm guessing Mom wants me home for dinner so she can rope me into this whole fight over Kayla going to Northwestern. I'm sure whatever it is, it's nothing major."

"Yeah," I say, standing on my tiptoes to kiss him on the forehead before heading to the driver's side, trying to shake any nagging doubts out of my head.

Because with the Laniers, it's *always* something major.

CHAPTER 7

Despite his attempt to stay positive, Kieran must be fearing the worst because he's asleep from anxiety almost as soon as he buckles himself into the passenger side of the truck cab. But the gentle jarring from the Laniers' gravel driveway as we travel up the slight hill is enough to bring him back.

"Wha?" He opens his eyes and sits up, and my sideways glance at his twisted expression confirms that even after only a few minutes, where we are and what we're doing is a little hazy.

"Your mom called," I prompt him. "She wanted you home immediately but didn't say why."

He nods, remembering.

"Got it—another Lanier family crisis. Must be Saturday."

Grateful for his sense of humor breaking up the tension, I shoot Kieran a half-smile as I park the truck and we head for the house.

"Hello?" Kieran says loudly once we're through the front door.

"In here," Kayla calls out from the living room when she hears Kieran shut the front door behind us.

"What's wrong?" Kieran asks, holding my hand and pulling me into the room behind him. The two of us stop on the other side of the glass coffee table from his parents, unwilling in this tense moment to let go of each other—or, at least *I'm* not anyway. Carlie, not the most relaxed person on the planet under normal circumstances, seems especially wound up, sitting forward on the couch, elbows on her knees and her hands on either side of her head as if she's trying to push something out of her brain. Her look doesn't make me feel any better about what she's going to say.

"Honey," Jim says, rubbing a hand up and down his wife's back. Carlie sighs deeply as if she's attempting to expel the fear from her body.

"Ben Halloran called," she begins, folding and unfolding her hands, something Kieran does when he's nervous, and I can't help but be amused about her sharing a habit with her adopted son. A long minute passes, and Kayla, who's sitting in the far corner of the room in an overstuffed chair with her legs tucked under her, shoots her mother an angry look.

"Oh, *please*, Mom," she says, tilting her head at Carlie's nervous display. "Cut it out and tell him."

Carlie's hands stop moving, folded together on her lap as if in prayer.

"Cooper...Cooper's in a coma—an *induced* coma, for his own safety."

Kieran's hand goes slack in mine, and I instinctively step in front of him and put my free hand to his side, guiding him toward the room's other easy chair before he can collapse into a sleep brought on by shock. I slide onto the edge of the chair and lean into him, rubbing my fingers up and down his arm in a desperate attempt to keep him awake because I'm sure none of us will want to explain Cooper's situation to him later.

"Ben was still trying to piece things together, but he wanted to tell us what was going on," Carlie continues, her gaze focused on the mobile phone lying atop the coffee table rather than her son. "He's supposed to call when there's more news." Her eyes gloss over as if she's somewhere far away.

"Mom," Kayla hisses, and Carlie snaps back to the living room from wherever she'd gone inside her mind. She casts a brief confused glance at Jim, almost as if she doesn't remember where she left off, almost as if she's Kieran and she's regained consciousness after a waking blackout.

Jim covers her hand with his and tells her "It's okay," in the voice of a parent reassuring a young child. "Just tell them what Ben said."

Kieran's trying to regulate his breathing, fighting to stay awake, the tiny tremors pulsing in his skin as I caress his arm matching the fear staining his face.

"Ben left for a business trip this morning and had just landed when Victor called him. Cooper talked someone on the research team into administering the treatment."

Carlie pauses to moisten her lips and, not wanting to lose her to whatever headspace she withdrew into before, I blurt out, "But the treatment didn't cause the coma, right? You said it was an induced coma."

Luckily, Carlie doesn't disappear into her previous hazy state.

"There's a high risk of injury or brain swelling with the treatment," she begins, "and they would need to—"

"*Brain swelling*?" Kieran interrupts her, wide awake now and his skin burning with fear.

Carlie holds out a hand as if trying to push back on Kieran's anxiety.

"It's something we were prepared for, but it was one of the possible temporary effects of the treatment the team was looking for a way to minimize. You can induce a coma as a means for the brain to protect itself. Once the risk passes, you bring the patient out of the comatose state. The process is very controlled, very safe."

"You normally don't hear 'coma' and 'safe' in the same set of sentences," Kieran points out.

"No, you don't." Carlie gives him a tiny smile, and calm, in-control Carlie seems to have returned to the Lanier house. "But even in the most traumatic situations, a coma can protect the brain. With an induced coma, doctors not only insure the brain is protected, but they're also able to perform other tests while minimizing brain injury. Of course, risks are always present." She looks away from Kieran to Jim as if she's afraid of Kieran's reaction. "If we could eliminate the possibility of brain swelling or other injury altogether, then we—the research team, I mean—wanted to find it."

"So, they'll definitely be able to bring him back." I'm less asking so much as I'm thinking out loud through everything Carlie's said.

"Yes," she tells me, still the Carlie I'm used to, and I'm struck with the thought that when translating medical information into language and concepts regular people can understand, she's in her element. When she lets her mind wander to what that medical information can do to her son and Cooper, then she becomes the distracted Carlie from earlier.

"Of course, the longer he's under, the worse the situation can be, so the sooner they're able bring him out, the better," Carlie continues.

"So, Cooper isn't going to die?" Kieran asks, his voice small as a scared little boy who wants his mommy to tell him the monsters under the bed aren't real, which, unfortunately, Carlie can't quite do.

"Not if anyone can help it." Carlie stands up from the couch and crosses the room, stopping in front of us. She holds out her hands, and Kieran rises to take them. "I'm sorry I can't give you one-hundred percent guarantees on anything," she says, pulling Kieran into a hug. "But let's put it this way—I'm ninety-nine-point-nine percent sure they'll be able to wake Cooper up when the time comes. He's in good hands."

I note that while Carlie's fairly certain Cooper can be brought out of the comatose state, she's not saying anything about what shape he's going to be in once he's awake, and I'm certainly not going to ask in this moment when she's trying to comfort Kieran.

"I can't help worrying," Kieran says, and his body slackens a bit in his mother's arms.

"You should go upstairs and rest," she points out, straining to hold up her much larger son. I rise to help her, but Jim gets to her side first, sliding one of Kieran's arms around his shoulders.

"Hearing this must be stressful," Jim begins, "but a nap might help." He and the barely-awake Kieran shuffle out of the room and into the hallway as Jim continues with "If we have any more news from Ben, we'll fill you in after you wake up."

Once I hear their footsteps on the stairs and am sure Kieran's safely out of earshot, I slide off the chair arm into the seat and ask Carlie, "So, what happens after they bring Cooper out of the coma? Is he cured?"

Carlie takes her gaze from the hallway and trains it on me.

"In a perfect world, he'll make a complete recovery. The team will need to run some tests, of course, to make sure there aren't any aftereffects from the treatment or the coma, and they'll observe him for a few days to see if the narcolepsy-like symptoms have disappeared." She moves back to the couch and sits down, tucking her feet up under her in a near mirroring of Kayla's posture in the easy chair. "The dreams…" She shakes her head. "I don't know about the dreams. I realize Kieran and Cooper have both said they aren't dreaming anymore, and they—or, Cooper, at least—believe that's supposed to be some kind of a sign the treatment will work." Carlie looks from Kayla to me and gives us a wan smile. "I don't deal in signs. I deal in science. So, I can't be sure whether or not the dreams will really go away, because the fact those dreams existed was never something I could explain to begin with."

"You said 'aftereffects,'" Kayla begins. "Like, what kind of aftereffects are we talking about here?" She glances out into the hall as if she's expecting Jim and Kieran to reappear any second, and then she lowers her voice. "Level with us, Mom. What shape is Cooper *really* going to be in when he wakes up?"

"He'll likely experience some confusion," Carlie answers, playing with a loose thread at the edge of a couch cushion. "Probably an extreme version of what people experience when they wake up from anesthesia—sort of a cloudy 'Where am I and what happened?' sensation. But that should be temporary." Carlie swings her legs out from under her to the floor, her gaze on the phone lying on the coffee table. "We were so close to something usable when I left…Cooper should be fine." Her eyes are glazing over again, and she's talking to neither of us in particular—in fact, it's almost like she's talking to someone who's not in the room right now. "We just wanted to address every possible side effect, but we were almost there…Cooper should be fine."

Kayla and I exchange glances, and I'm guessing from her narrowed eyes that she doesn't believe her mother any more than I do.

"Zip, you want to hang out upstairs in my room for a while?" Kayla asks, slowly shifting her eyes from me to her mom and back again. "I got these new earrings at the mall before Brad left, but I'm not sure what to wear them with. I need a second opinion."

I see right through Kayla's paper-thin ruse because she'd never ask for my feedback on anything involving fashion, but I say, "Yeah, no problem. Let's go."

Carlie snaps back to reality and says, "You girls have fun picking out outfits. I'll come upstairs if I hear anything more from Ben."

"Sure thing, Mom."

Kayla practically leaps from her chair and into the hall, while I follow at a much slower pace, my body weighed down by a sense of anxiety I don't quite understand. I want to ask Kayla what she's thinking as soon as we're halfway upstairs and out of Carlie's earshot, but we meet Jim on the landing as he's going back downstairs. "Kieran's sound asleep, so try to keep it down," he says gently, although he has no idea what "it" is Kayla and I might be discussing once we reach her room—and, for that matter, neither do I. We both nod at Jim and continue on up the stairs, past the half-closed door to Kieran's room and into Kayla's room at the end of the hall.

"You don't believe your mom for a second, do you?" I ask as Kayla shuts the door behind us.

"No. I've watched that woman lie for too many years not to know it when I see it." She flops down on top of her lavender comforter and reaches behind her for one of the pillows swathed in a dark purple pillowcase. Clutching the pillow to her chest and staring at the ceiling, she continues with, "But this time, she was acting hella weird. Like, weirder than usual, I mean. Cooper's not my favorite person on the planet, but I'm kind of scared for him."

"Me, too," I say, lying down on my stomach next to her and folding my arms under my chin. "I don't want anything bad to happen to him, even if he is a giant tool." Kayla giggles and I keep talking. "I'm sure your mom was just trying not to scare Kieran—or us."

Kayla rolls over on her side, propping her head up with an arm while keeping a death grip on her pillow with the other.

"Well, she needs to learn. Kieran's an adult, for crap's sake, and so are we, for all practical purposes. And it's not exactly like she avoided scaring us."

"True."

My phone buzzes in my front shorts pocket, the sound seeming unnaturally loud until I realize Kayla's phone is buzzing as well. We both sit up to check our messages, and I find with some surprise I don't have a text or a voicemail, but an email, which I rarely get unless the message is from school or from some website that has my address. But this email is from victor.loughlin@halloran.net, which I'm guessing is the email address for Cooper's assistant, assuming my morning bout with physics problems didn't damage my logical thinking abilities beyond repair.

"I think Victor Loughlin just sent me an email," I tell Kayla, scrunching up my face as I look at her examining her phone screen.

"Weird," she says, her expression when she turns to me every bit as confused as I feel. "I think I just got one from him, too. And Kieran's copied on it."

Examining my phone once again, I see that both Kayla and Kieran have been copied on the message, which reads:

Hello,

Mr. Cooper Halloran asked me to forward this video to you.

Sincerely,

Victor Loughlin

Below the email is an icon for a video file that I'm careful not to tap. I don't want to watch what Cooper's sent without Kayla seeing it, too—and Kieran.

"Man of few words, that Vic," Kayla says, and I look up at her staring at her phone screen. She gives me a sideways glance and I ask, "Should we—"

"Wake up Kieran?" she finishes for me. "Absolutely. I'll boot up my computer so we can watch whatever this is on a bigger screen."

I head down the hall to Kieran's room, pushing the door open to find him curled up in the fetal position and sound asleep atop his comforter, facing me. He looks so peaceful, his wispy eyelashes fluttering and his lips parted just enough to release raspy sleep breaths, and I almost feel guilty for waking him up. But I'd feel guiltier if I didn't wake him up and we learn Kayla watched the video without us.

"Hey," I whisper, leaning across the bed and gently shaking his shoulder. "Hey, Kieran."

His eyes pop open and then shut again as he struggles to return to waking life. I lie down next to him on the comforter so I don't have to stretch so far to shake him, and after a few seconds, his eyes open once more and stay open this time.

"Hey," he mumbles.

"Hey."

His face settles into that familiar grin.

"Someday, I want to wake up like this every day. I want your face to be the first thing I see in the morning."

"You know why I love you?" I smile. "Because you always say the perfect thing."

"That's because I'm so smooth," he deadpans, reaching out to tuck a hair that's come loose from my ponytail behind my ear.

"So, you're not going to ask why I'm here on your bed even though your parents are downstairs and your sister's down the hall?"

"I just woke up to a beautiful girl lying next me," he says. "I'm not dumb enough to ruin things by asking a bunch of questions."

I sit up so I don't get caught in Kieran's web of charm and forget what I'm supposed to be doing here.

"Victor sent all of us an email with a video attached. Cooper told him to send it to us."

On my news, Kieran shakes off any remaining grogginess and reaches behind him to his phone on the nightstand.

"Kayla's pulling the video up on her computer right now," I tell him as he glances at Victor's message. Leaving his phone on the bed, Kieran grabs my hand and we speed down the hall to Kayla's room where she's sitting at a mahogany desk in the far corner, Cooper's frozen face staring at us from her laptop screen. She twists to us when she hears me close the door.

"Ready to watch this—whatever it is?" she asks.

"I guess," Kieran says, sighing and trying to flatten some sleep-wayward strands of hair on the right side of his head.

Kayla hits "play" and Cooper springs to life and sits back.

"Hey, Kieran—and Zip and Kayla, too, if you're watching. This little public service announcement is mostly for Kieran, but I thought I'd send it to everyone just in case. Safety in numbers, or something."

Cooper fidgets in his chair, his eyes darting around. He's so nervous and twitchy, I'm having a hard time standing still just out of sympathy.

"So, if you're watching this, several things have happened. First of all, Victor followed my instructions, which were to send this a few hours after I'd undergone the treatment. So, props to him for doing his job, like always—if something happens to me, tell him I always appreciated that about him, would you?"

Next to me, Kieran breathes an impatient sigh.

"But, yeah—if you're watching this right now, it means I'm in a coma, which is kind of scary but kind of cool at the same time, right? I mean, it's like I'm speaking to you from *beyond the grave* or something."

Cooper takes a moment to indulge in his nervous habit of holding his hand out before him and curling his fingers toward him over his palm as if he's looking for dirt under his nails.

"Well, not really from beyond the grave because I'm still alive, but whatever. You get what I mean. It's weird."

"I so want to punch my screen right now," Kayla mumbles and Kieran shushes her so we don't miss anything.

"You're probably asking, 'Cooper, why did you do this, especially when the research team said they were close but still had some work to do?'" He reaches off camera and pulls a glass of water into frame. After taking a drink, he sets the glass out of view and wipes condensation down the sleeve of his gray, long sleeved t-shirt. "Well, as you know, I'm impatient, and I'm used to getting what I want when I want it. And I what I want right now is for my life to change. I've spent my whole life stuck with this brain that doesn't exactly work the way it should. I've been labeled a drug addict and a drunk by the press because my dad doesn't want anyone to think I'm defective in a way that can't be fixed by a weekend in an overpriced rehab. But I want to go away to college. I want to get out of this house." Cooper's eyes flit around, taking in his surroundings. "And, I mean, it's a nice house—you've been here—but it's not *mine*. I want my own space, something that's not controlled by Ben Halloran. And as much of a dude as Victor is, I don't want him following me around for the rest of my life. And you know as well as I do, nothing changes without the treatment."

I glance at Kieran out of the corner of my eye. He's riveted to the screen, his lips parted slightly as if he's breathing in every word Cooper says.

"So, I met with a couple of the guys on the research team and had them give it to me straight—what were the risks to undergoing the treatment as it stands right now. And they said the risks were minimal, but they'd have to induce a coma. Wild, right?"

I love how Cooper's describing this whole thing as if he's a little kid going to an amusement park for the first time and not as someone about to undergo a procedure that could radically alter the makeup of his brain.

"And it sounds kind of scary, too, but I figured, hey—I've already got a big head anyway. So, if my brain swells a little, there should be plenty of room."

Cooper flicks his hand in the air as if to say "no big deal," and I can't help but smile.

"They also mentioned something about temporary memory loss when I wake up, like kind of a haze. And I'm like 'Whatever, dudes. Do you know what my life has been like?'" Cooper points to his forehead. "It's already a big haze up in here half the time. I know you feel me on this one, Kieran."

Kieran nods although Cooper obviously can't see.

"Those were acceptable risks as far as I was concerned, and since I'm the boss' kid and these guys will do whatever I want, I waited until Big Ben was going to be out of town and I said 'Let's do this. Shoot me up, guys.' And right now, assuming nothing's gone wrong, I'm in a makeshift hospital room at Halloran headquarters, with medical personnel from the research team on stand-by in case this all goes to shit." He takes another pause for a drink of water. "And I'm guessing Ben's flown back by now and is by my bedside, holding vigil." Cooper sits back in his chair, his lizard grin spreading across his face. "Nah—who am I kidding? He's probably through the roof, cursing and firing people. I promise, I'll straighten everything out when they wake me up."

Cooper's world is so foreign to me. I can't imagine people being willing to do my bidding just because of who I am, and I can't imagine having enough wealth and influence to just throw money at something and fix it.

But all of Cooper's—or, rather, his father's—riches and power won't save him if something goes wrong while he's in the coma, or if something goes wrong afterwards.

"And I'm doing this for another reason," Cooper continues as I shake any tragic thoughts out of my head. "Kieran, unless we don't know something, we're the only two people on the planet who are the way we are. There are no guinea pigs for this stuff, no tests they can do other than injecting the treatment into a bunch of lab mice. And I've talked to the research team enough to know lab mice are great and all, but nothing's going to get you the results you want like testing on a real live human being."

Cooper's eyes dart to the surface of the desk, and he examines his fingernails almost as if he can see our gazes on him and he doesn't want to look back.

"Sure, I want to do stuff, and I want the treatment to work so I have the freedom to do whatever I can't do now. But, the thing is, in spite of everything, I'm well aware I've lived a pretty good life, better than what most people get. My grandfather hooked my mom up with Ben Halloran and I won the adoption lottery. And even if Mom and Big Ben hadn't married, my grandparents weren't exactly poor. Despite how messed up I am, I've been able to do almost anything simply because my dad is who he is and because we have the money we have. I've bought and sold my way through my entire life. I've used people because I can—hell, I'm doing that right now. At the moment, my dad is probably firing people for going through with what I threatened to fire them for if they *didn't* do, and when I wake up, I'll fight with him until he hires them back, and we'll pay them off so they won't say anything." He shakes his head. "It's messed up, but this is how life works when you're a Halloran. For the most part, people are just pawns, tools to be used for our personal and professional gain. Dad's practically drilled that into me in one way or another since I was a little kid. So, I decided for once in my life, I wanted someone to use me, because using me in this case might turn out to be something good. For once, I wanted to be the pawn. I wanted to be the tool."

Kayla snickers as Cooper continues, "Of course, if Kayla and Zip are watching this, they're probably saying, 'Hey, Coop, you're already a tool.'"

I smile, and Kayla turns around to roll her eyes at me.

"But you get what I mean," Cooper says. "Everything's been handed to me my whole life, and for once, I wanted to do something for someone else, something that didn't involve writing a check to a charity and patting myself on the back. Kieran, I know a lot of people and I hang with a lot of people, but you're the only person in the world I can really call my friend. You're the only one who truly understands what I go through on a daily basis. And I know your life hasn't been all smiley faces and rainbows and shit. But despite how they've kept you on lockdown for so long, your parents love you. Your sister loves you, too, not to mention the fact that she's totally hot, even if she's borderline insane."

Kayla sticks her finger in her mouth and pretends to gag.

"And you've got an amazing girl who loves you, which means your lame ass might actually get laid someday and so I owe it to you to help out in any way I can. I really worry about your ability to handle this one on your own."

Kieran and I both sigh in unison.

"Plus, you've got your art and stuff. You should be able to go to school and do something with that, you know—figure out what you want from your future. My future's already planned out. Business school, an MBA, and one day assuming my rightful place at the helm of Halloran Industries when my dad's too bored or senile to run the place anymore."

94

Once again, Cooper examines his nails, pursing his lips as he does.

"A coma and memory loss doesn't sound so bad in comparison," he continues. "Might open up more possibilities in my life than I have now, ironically."

Cooper's being sarcastic, but a hint of sadness in his voice almost makes me feel sorry for him.

"Anyway, dude, it's about t-minus twelve hours until I get shot up with the magic stuff," he continues, back to his confident self. "I need some sleep. Or, maybe I don't, considering I'm going to be in a coma for a few days." He shrugs. "At any rate, I've probably been rambling for too long. I'm leaving word with Vic that if anything happens to me, you should get all my stuff. I have some vintage dirty magazines that are worth *a lot* of money."

A smile's spreading across Kieran's face, so I elbow him in the ribs, and the two of us laugh silently as Cooper signs off.

"So, I'll see you on the other side, man. Hope to talk to you soon."

He reaches forward and the video stops, the Cooper of yesterday frozen in place on the screen. Kieran, a little shaky, moves quickly to sit on the edge of Kayla's bed where I join him, taking his hand in mine.

"How are you doing after that?" I ask, and I'm not just asking if he's about to pass out from anxiety.

Kieran reads what I'm getting at and tells me "I'm...I'm okay. And kind of blown away, actually. I mean, I knew Cooper and I were friends, but this is really above and beyond. How do you repay someone for doing something like this?"

Kayla turns around and rests her chin on the top of the chair back and mumbles "Well, if he never wakes up, guess you won't have to."

95

"Oh, my God, Kayla," I breathe, and she rolls her eyes.

"I'm totally kidding. I don't want anything bad to happen to the guy." She glances back at Cooper's image on the screen. "So the Evil Prince of the Upper West Side actually has a heart. Who knew?" Kieran and I shrug, and Kayla continues with "I don't think paying him back is the point. He's going out on a limb because he weighed the pros and cons and he thinks the risks are worth it—for both of you."

"Makes sense," Kieran says, looking down at our joined hands. "I'd like to think if the choice had been mine, I would have done the same thing. Coop's the only real friend I've ever had, too." He bumps his elbow against mine. "Except for you. But that's different."

"I hope so."

Kayla clears her throat and glares at her brother.

"That's different, too, Kay. You're my sister. You *have* to be my friend."

"Good point."

"So, what do we do about that video?" I ask, titling my head toward the screen. "Is this going to be another one of our secrets, or…"

I let my voice fade away, and Kieran jumps in to settle the question.

"No. I don't think we have the greatest history with keeping stuff from our parents. It always manages to go wrong somehow."

Kayla and I nod at each other.

"True," she says.

"And you need to be building up cred with the parental units right now," Kieran says to Kayla. "Getting caught in a lie isn't going to convince them that you're mature enough to visit your boyfriend at college for a weekend without ruining your life."

"Also true," Kayla grumbles. "And Ben Halloran's kind of done a lot for us, so I'd feel pretty bad about knowing why Cooper did this when he's probably going crazy trying to figure it out. I'd be honest with him just for the chance to stay at his house again." She glances at me. "The apartment in Manhattan, I mean. We haven't seen the beach house in the Hamptons yet, of course."

"Of course," I say, matching her smirk with one of my own.

"And Cooper didn't say we *couldn't* tell anyone about this." She tilts her head back at Cooper's image.

"Then that's it." Kieran glances back and forth between us, his gaze finally settling on his sister. "Feels kind of good to be honest with the parentals every once in a while, doesn't it?"

"Depends." Kayla shrugs. "If they start returning the favor on a regular basis, then—yes."

Kieran gives my hand a squeeze and lets go, getting up and heading for the door, which he opens to stick his head out into the hall. "Hey, guys?" he yells out to his parents. "Come here. We've got something we need to show you."

Chapter 8

Cooper Halloran may not be my favorite person, but over the past few days, he's become the center of my universe, even from nearly a thousand miles away. Every morning, I wake up and check my phone for a message from Kieran telling me the doctors have brought Cooper out of the coma and he's fine, but that message doesn't come. And every day after school, as soon as we're out of the building and in the parking lot where we're allowed to use our phones, Kieran checks for news. But Cooper's been in an induced coma for almost a week, with no indication from anyone as to when it might be safe to bring him back out.

Unfortunately, stagnant Titusville offers little in the way of distraction. The only recent change is that this school year, all first-period courses are specific to a single class year of students--meaning only seniors can be enrolled in a certain class, and only juniors, and so on—in order for the first period course to double as a homeroom where teachers can take attendance. Last year, the homeroom period was at the end of the day, but first period teachers were responsible for getting accurate attendance records to the front office, which the school board finally realized was stealing too much time from two different class periods.

So, like I said, Titusville isn't offering much in the way of distraction from the Cooper situation.

My first period course this semester is U.S. Government and Politics, and the class always ends five minutes earlier than our other classes so we can listen to announcements and so Coach Denton— *Mrs.* Denton when she's not on the court—can conduct any homeroom business. Today, she's in the middle of a lecture on Executive Branch powers when the speaker above the door crackles and Mrs. Gillette starts delivering the day's announcements, which range from telling us the special in the cafeteria today is fish sticks and French fries to reminding us of the football game tonight—not exactly earth-shattering stuff. Most of us are putting our books in our backpacks and readying for the bell to signal our movement to our next class rather than paying close attention.

"And, finally, I'm pleased to announce the nominees for this year's Homecoming Court," Mrs. Gillette chirps.

Okay—now I *really* won't need to pay attention. Mrs. Gillette runs through the three nominees each for Freshman, Sophomore, and Junior Princess, all of whom are the names I would expect. When you've been in school with pretty much the same people since Kindergarten, by the time you've reached junior high, you're almost certain which girls are going to be the eternal candidates for any title ending in the words "Princess" or "Queen."

"And finally," Mrs. Gillette sings, "here are the four seniors who have been nominated for Homecoming Queen, in alphabetical order."

I recite the names in my head as Mrs. Gillette says them aloud, but on the third name, she trips me up—

"Zara McKee..."

"Wait. What?" I say after whipping my head toward the speaker, my voice loud enough Mrs. Denton can hear me even though I'm sitting in the back of the room.

"Congratulations," she tells me, and most of my classmates turn to me, giggling in a half-congratulatory, half-amused manner at my obvious state of confusion. Considering I'm sitting here in track pants and a Chicago Bulls t-shirt, looking anything but regal, I'm guessing they're more than a little confused as well.

Kayla, however, doesn't seem confused at all. I turn to look at her sitting next to me, the sly grin she's wearing suspicious enough to mean only one thing.

"I'm going to kill you," I hiss at her.

The bell rings and Kayla shoots out of her desk as if someone's just lit her butt on fire.

"Kayla!" I call after her, but she's out the door before I can catch up to her, and even though we're in the next three classes together, she manages to avoid speaking to me by sliding into a seat as far away from me as possible just before the bell rings each time.

I lose Kayla in the hall after journalism class but assume I'll run into her at lunch, unless she plans on eating alone in the bathroom. Rather than heading directly to the cafeteria, I make my way back to the main hall so I can catch up with Kieran at his locker.

"Congratulations," he says as I approach. "Homecoming Queen—that's a big deal around here, I'm guessing?"

I scrunch up my face. At least three people have to submit your name for you to make the ballot for queen, and so I just assumed Kieran was one of them and Kayla probably strong-armed him into doing so.

"You didn't nominate me?"

"I didn't know I could. I had no idea all that stuff was going on. Sorry."

Breaking Titusville's "No PDA in the halls" rule just slightly, I reach out and squeeze his hand.

"Don't apologize. It's not like I've ever said anything about being Homecoming Queen."

As we start making our way down the hall toward the cafeteria, he asks, "Do you *want* to be Homecoming Queen?"

"No," I answer immediately, and then surprise myself by backing down a little. "I mean, I guess not. I've never thought it was a

100

possibility. There's a strictly defined set of girls who always win those things around here."

"Well, no matter what happens, you're already the Queen of My Heart," Kieran says, giving me an outsized version of his usual grin, and I burst out laughing.

"Oh, my God. Did you really just say that?"

"Yeah. Not one of my better moments, huh?"

"Well, it was definitely one of your *cheesier* moments," I tell him. "Even so, if we weren't in school, I'd push you up against the wall over there and kiss the crap out of you."

"I plan on taking you up on that after school," he says as we enter the bustling cafeteria and head straight for one of the "Jock Tables" in the back corner by the soda machines, a table Kieran gets to sit at without any question or comment by virtue of his relationship with me. As we approach, Kayla, Cassie, and Lauren, who are all sitting next to each other, look up from their food and shoot me satisfied smiles revealing exactly who nominated me for Homecoming Queen.

"Check it out, Kieran," I say, not taking my eyes off them as I slam my backpack down in the chair next to Cassie's. "It's the unholy trinity."

"Zip, come on," Cassie says through a little laugh, as Kieran tugs at the sleeve of my t-shirt.

"Let's get some food first. I don't want you doing battle on an empty stomach," he whispers.

I shoot the girls a "We're not done here" glare before Kieran and I take off for the food line.

"At least this means Kayla's got friends, right?" Kieran points out as I pick up two trays and hand one back to him. I guess Kayla's full acceptance into my circle of friends is a happy by-product of whatever's going on with this Homecoming business. Being Brad

Wallace's girlfriend has helped melt Kayla's Ice Queen image a little, and Cassie and Kayla had gotten to know each other last spring since they were both on the track team. Cassie talked Kayla into joining the volleyball team with Lauren and her this fall, and given her nearly six foot tall frame and limitless supply of pent-up aggression, I'm sure Kayla's going to be a superb outside hitter.

Back at the table, Ashley, Rick Matthews, and Jake Tomlinson, who were several people ahead of us in the food line, have joined the group, and I've barely settled into my seat between Kieran and Cassie when I start making demands.

"Okay, someone better explain this insane Homecoming Queen business."

"It's not insane, first of all," Kayla begins. "And you got *five* nominations, by the way. Thought you might like to know."

Kayla, Cassie, and Lauren make a point of staring across at Rick and Ashley, both of whom appear to be very interested in their fish sticks all of a sudden.

"So, Ashley I can understand," I start, because Ashley, Cassie, Lauren, and Kayla are my four closest female friends, "but what's your excuse, Rick? Trying to get in Ashley's pants?"

Kieran bites back a laugh as Rick pushes some strands of white blond hair off his forehead.

"Correction," Rick mumbles through a mouthful of fish sticks before swallowing. "I've already *been* in Ashley's pants. Several times. Everybody knows that."

Ashley and Rick are Titusville's longest-running "Friends with Benefits" relationship, which is basically the school's worst kept secret. Still, Ashley gives Rick a hard punch in the shoulder for his comment, while I get off unscathed even though I brought the whole thing up in the first place.

"Ow," Rick says, rubbing his shoulder as he looks back to me. "But, seriously, Ash came to me and made the argument for nominating you, and I couldn't say no."

"And that argument would be?" I ask, glancing at each of my female friends. Lauren twirls the end of her ponytail around her index finger and takes the bullet for the group.

"The same people get nominated for Queen This and Princess That *every year*," she explains, her voice sounding as if she's physically exhausted by the prospect of watching the usual girls serve as Titusville royalty. "So, Cass and Kayla and I were talking at practice the other day about how cool it would be if there was someone different on the Homecoming Court for once. And none of us were into it, so we thought you'd be perfect."

"So, I'm the sacrificial lamb. Awesome." I snicker.

"Not at all," Cassie chimes in, shooting Lauren a look. "Zip, you're *gorgeous* when you make an effort. Everybody thought so on Prom night."

I generally try to push most memories of Prom night to the back of my brain given everything that went down afterwards with Morgan and Frank. But I remember sitting at the dressing table in my mom's room, fiddling with the curled hair lying at my collarbone and smoothing out the skirt of the emerald green halter dress Kayla had helped me pick out, and I felt pretty. And that night was one of the few times I can recall feeling that way, not so much because I think I should be walking around with a bag over my head most days in order to spare everyone, but because being pretty usually isn't too high on my list of concerns.

"And all the guys on the football team think you're cool," Cassie continues. Anyone in school can nominate girls for the Homecoming Court, but after the nomination process, the queen and princesses are determined by the fairly sexist method of having the football team vote for the winners. "You've got a real shot at this."

"Not to mention, you could use some more extra-curriculars for your college applications," Kayla points out, sounding like a mom who isn't mine. My mom's never pushed me to get involved in things, probably because she wasn't much interested in being involved herself when she was in school.

"Homecoming Court isn't an extra-curricular," I fire back. "It's a popularity contest. And besides basketball, I was on Student Council sophomore year, I was a seventh grade mentor when I was a freshman, and, assuming I survive physics and some stiff competition from *you*, I'll be valedictorian. I think I'm covered."

"But it never hurts to put more stuff on your applications," Kayla sings, checking to make sure no cafeteria monitors are looking our way before pulling the forbidden-during-school cell phone from her backpack and playing an abbreviated version of the Northwestern University fight song.

"You have the Northwestern fight song on your phone?" I say, squinting at her as she shuts off her phone and slides it back in her bag.

"You don't?" she asks in a challenging tone.

I shake my head at Kayla before turning to Cassie.

"Despite what you guys think, everyone knows girls like Brittany Solomon and Chelsea Copeland and McKenna Dantino are the standard Homecoming Queen-types around here," I point out. "The guys on the team will just vote for them regardless of how much they like me, so this whole argument is pointless anyway."

"Well, let's get an objective opinion." Cassie rises out of her seat a little. "Jake!" she yells across the table. Jake's leaning back in his chair and talking over his shoulder to Cody Hull, who's at the "Jock

Table" next to ours rather than sitting with us and enduring Cassie's sarcastic jabs at him for an entire lunch period.

"Jake!" Cassie tries again, and she gets his attention this time.

"Yeah?" he booms. Jake's a defensive lineman and, along with Cody, one of the biggest guys in school. I think speaking quietly under any circumstances would be impossible for him based on his sheer size and the deep tenor of his voice.

"Would you vote for Zip for Homecoming Queen?"

Jake regards me with eyes that seem to be struggling to stay open above the girth of his cheeks. He raises his thin, dark eyebrows and his eyes bulge out as if he's never seen me before.

"Yeah. Okay. Sure. Why not?" He shrugs, turning back to Cody at the other table.

"Note the overwhelming enthusiasm," I point out, rolling my eyes at Cassie. "And did anyone ever think to *ask* me if I wanted to do this?"

"We figured you'd say no," Lauren mumbles, scrunching up her nose.

"Well, there you go." I sit back in my chair and fold my arms over my stomach.

Kayla stares past me to Kieran, who's pushed his half-eaten lunch out of the way and is engrossed in a copy of *The Prince*, our current read in English class. "A little help here, big brother?" she asks.

Kieran glances up at everyone—including Jake, who's done with Cody for the moment—and dog-ears his page before placing the book next to his tray. He leans his left elbow on the table and rests his cheek on his fist, his eyelids fluttering in a way I recognize as exaggerated. He lets out a loud yawn, and I can't help but smile.

"Don't even think about it, Kieran Lanier," Kayla snaps, pointing at him. "You're faking. I can tell."

Kieran's eyes pop open to full size and he falls back in his chair, sighing.

"You know, what's the point of having a stupid sleeping disorder if I can't use it to my advantage every once in a while?" he grumbles.

Cassie leans forward to look beyond me to Kieran.

"Hey, could you tell your girlfriend to keep her name on the ballot for Homecoming Queen?" she commands.

"Yeah, here's the deal." He mirrors my posture by folding his arms across his stomach. "I don't tell Zip what to do, and if she wants my opinion on something, she'll ask for it. And if she wants to be Homecoming Queen? Then, fine—I'll support her, and I'm sure she'll be the best Homecoming Queen this school has ever seen, whatever that means. And if she decides she doesn't want her name on the ballot, I'll support her in that, too. That's kind of how this whole thing works—she makes the decisions about her own life, and I'm just her cheering section."

Kieran shrugs, and I take in the surprised expressions on the faces of everyone but Kayla. I think Kieran's just said more words to my friends with his little speech than he ever has at one time.

"Suck on *that*, people," I say, flattening my hand and flicking it outward at the wrist. Kieran shoots me a grin, and I tilt my head toward him and murmur "Thanks."

"Sure thing."

"Okay," Cassie whispers, bumping against me. "I think I might be a little in love with your boyfriend."

"Hands off," I whisper back as Kayla says "So, Zip, what's it going to be? Are you in or are you out?"

Surveying the looks of anticipation on everyone at the table—everyone but Kieran, that is—I have to admit to myself I'm more than a little flattered my friends think so much of me. And I'm not sure what happens if someone pulls her name out of the running because that's never happened before, and I don't know if I want to be famous at Titusville High for being the first girl to refuse a shot at Homecoming Queen. I'd rather my legacy be what I do on the basketball court.

"Oh, whatever," I say, sighing. "I'm in."

Everyone's faces relax with relief, and so I decide to kill their collective buzz a little.

"*For now*, I'm in. But the second this starts to seem like some weird reality show dress-up crap, I'm shutting it down, got it?"

They all nod, although I don't trust any of them to let me back out of this without a fight.

After lunch, Kayla and I make our way to the library for study hall. Mrs. Bochine, the school's librarian, is pretty tolerant of talking as long as we're quiet about it, and we're allowed to get up and move around so we can use the computers or search for books. Once the bell rings to signal the beginning of the period, I grab Kayla by the elbow and drag her to the biographies section at the back of the library.

"Here's the deal," Kayla begins, preempting me before I can start laying into her. "Cassie came up with the idea. I just went along with it."

"Which is ridiculous. Cassie's practically a supermodel. *She's* the one who should be doing this. Or you."

Kayla snorts at my suggestion, but I don't change my mind.

"Oh, come on," I say, tapping my foot against the tile. "Have you *seen* yourself? Brad Wallace's jaw fell on the floor the first time you walked into this school. And I have it on good authority from several guys on the football team that you are, and I quote, 'totally smokin' hot.' Those guys barely know you and you stand a better chance of them voting for you than I do."

"I told everybody you'd fight this." Kayla shakes her head, ignoring my comments about her looks. "But I've got my own reasons for putting you up for queen other than wanting someone different on the court. I mean, think about it—I hardly know anyone around here, so to me, it's *not* the same old people up for Homecoming Queen. And I was home schooled until we moved to Titusville, remember? This is all sort of a novelty for me."

I kick the toe of my Chuck Taylor against the floor tile.

"Those don't seem like the most solid motives for wanting me to be royalty," I point out.

"Okay, then, how about this? A little distraction is a good thing right now, Zip," she insists. "All this stuff with Cooper? You, me, and Kieran need something *very* stupid and *very* high school to keep us occupied. Trust me, if I could run Kieran for Homecoming Queen, I would."

"*That* would definitely make history around here."

Kayla huffs out a breath and says "Well, hopefully, Kieran will be so preoccupied with school and with supporting you through this that he won't be spending his time obsessing about Cooper. And I've got schoolwork and volleyball, plus being your stylist."

"My stylist?" I put a hand on my hip.

"Cassie told me how this works. You need to get dressed up for the photos that go along with your profile in the school paper, plus you're going to need dresses for the pep assembly, the parade, the game, and the dance. And you can't be trusted to handle those kinds of fashion demands on your own."

"I own *at least* ten different hoodies and probably fifteen pairs of sweatpants," I tell her with a wry smile. "I'll be fine."

"Not funny."

"I'm guessing this means a trip to the mall?" I sigh.

"Oh, yes," she says, her eyes lighting up. I let a groan escape, but she's quick to slide an arm around me. "Zip, come on. This will be fun, I promise. And I think the two of us need a little fun with everything going on right now."

"Your definition of 'fun' and my definition of 'fun' don't come from the same dictionary," I tell her, but her determined smile wins me at least part of the way. "Can I wear workout shorts under my dresses?"

I try to match her smile, but her expression collapses into a frown at my joke.

"You're impossible. So, when do you want to go shopping? I'm still hoping I can visit Brad this weekend, and I've got a match next Saturday but—"

"Kayla. There you are." Mrs. Bochine appears from the end of the row of books just behind us. "You're wanted in the front office. Your mother called."

We exchange worried glances before Kayla shifts her attention back to Mrs. Bochine.

"What's going on?"

"Mrs. Gillette didn't say. She'll fill you in when you get to the office, I suppose."

Mrs. Bochine turns to head back to the front of the library, and Kayla whispers, "I'll text you," before rushing off, leaving me standing in the biographies section by myself.

The remainder of study hall is torture. I'm too distracted to get any work done, so I sit down at one of the computers along the library's far wall and pretend to be doing research, when in reality, I'm just skimming headlines on the web. With five minutes left in the period, I risk detention by sliding my phone from the front pocket of my backpack. Glancing over my shoulder to make sure Mrs. Bochine isn't looking in my direction, I keep the phone on my lap underneath the table and check my messages, which include a text from Kayla:

"Cooper's awake."

CHAPTER 9

I think about playing sick so I can get sent home early, but I've never been good at faking. Plus, the school would call my mom, and she'd see right through any pretend illness as soon as she got home. Somehow, I survive my last two classes, and once the final bell rings, I'm barely out of the building before I take my phone from my backpack and am greeted by "Come over" texts from both Kayla and Kieran.

In minutes, I'm pressing the Laniers' doorbell. Even though we've all become pretty close over the summer, I'm still not comfortable enough to walk into their house unannounced, no matter the circumstances. Kayla throws open the door and, without greeting me, heads into the living room. I stumble after her, hearing Carlie's voice floating down to me from the kitchen. But she isn't talking to Jim, who's in the living room leaning forward on the couch as if he's going to spring up at any minute. And while Morgan's sitting in an easy chair on the far side of the room, also looking tense, Kieran's nowhere to be found.

I've been through this enough times now to know—something pretty intense has happened, so intense that it would have sent Kieran upstairs to sleep off the stress, and so I don't bother to wonder where he is.

"So, Cooper's awake?" I ask Jim, sliding into the chair opposite the one Morgan's in. Kayla sits down on the chair arm and leans against me.

"Someone on the research team called Carlie around noon. His brain swelling had gone down enough a couple of days ago that the time seemed right to bring him out, but now there appear to be...complications."

I don't get the chance to prod Jim as to what he means because Kayla, always the most direct person in her family, ends any mystery.

"Yeah. The temporary confusion thing Mom mentioned? The same one Cooper said the researchers told him about? It's looking a little less temporary and like a whole lot more than confusion. He's been awake for almost two days—which Mom *conveniently* decided not to mention—and he can't remember anything," she tells me.

"Like, he can't remember anything about undergoing the treatment, or—"

"Like, he can't remember the procedure or who his father is or that he's even Cooper Freaking Halloran," Kayla blurts out, getting up from her chair and stomping down the hall toward the kitchen. I glance at Jim, who's quick to explain what he can.

"We're not sure yet what Cooper remembers and doesn't remember. But he doesn't recognize his father and he doesn't seem to recall his own name." Jim tilts his head back at the hallway. "Carlie's been on the phone with people in New York trying to find out what she can, but, obviously this is a changeable situation."

Kayla stomps down the hall to the living room with her mother on her heels as Jim finishes his explanation. "Kayla…" Carlie whines, and Kayla whirls around on her.

"No, Mom. Stop it. Stop trying to make this situation anything besides what it is." She points an accusatory finger at her mother. "*You knew* this was going to happen. You just didn't want to tell Kieran it was possible. You've known for two days Cooper was awake, and you didn't say anything because you were just waiting for the phone call telling you he was messed up." Kayla drops her hand to her side and starts shaking, tears springing to her eyes. "You'll never stop lying to us, will you?"

"I was trying to protect Kieran," Carlie says, her voice so breathy and small I'm almost not sure she's said anything at all.

112

"That's always your excuse." Kayla's starting to cry, a single tear falling down one pale, flawless cheek. "We're not little kids anymore. We don't deserve to spend the rest of our lives having you lie to us to spare our feelings." She looks back and forth between her parents. "Well, I can't speak for Kieran, but I'm *done*. Understand? Done."

Kayla starts bawling—a full-on, big, ugly cry—and I'm a little freaked out. I've never seen Kayla so out of control. Even in her worst moments, even when she was carrying so much guilt over letting Kieran and me out of her sight after Prom, Kayla's always maintained a certain calm. But now, I worry I'm watching her unravel for good right in front of me.

"I'm going to visit Brad tomorrow," she continues, pulling herself together and putting her hands on her hips. "You can't stop me."

"Kayla," Jim begins with a weary sigh. "This is a discussion for another time."

"It's a discussion for right now, but there's no discussion." She wipes away a tear with the back of her hand. "I'm going to Evanston. I'm doing whatever the hell I want from now on."

"I'm warning you, Kayla," Carlie says, her voice feeble and not at all threatening.

"Oh, you're *warning* me? That's cute. You didn't feel like *warning* us Cooper might wake up like this. You didn't feel like *warning* Kieran about being in danger from his dear old dad over here until it was almost too late."

Kayla flicks a hand in Morgan's direction. Morgan doesn't say anything, but instead shifts his gaze to the floor, seemingly uncomfortable with the direction this conversation has taken as Kayla marches on.

"All you two ever do is lie. So, I've had it. Maybe I'll just hire a lawyer and get myself emancipated. I'll bet a judge would be *very* interested in hearing the story of this messed up family."

Kayla says her last sentence through gritted teeth, and the tears start flowing freely once again. She opens her mouth as if she's going to launch another verbal assault on her parents, but instead, she darts out of the room, her footsteps heavy as she runs up the stairs.

An awkward moment passes as I survey the three adults.

"Um...you know," I begin, pointing toward the hall and addressing no one in particular, "I think I'm going to go upstairs and—"

"Please—go to her," Jim cuts me off, nodding.

I speed-walk out of the room and head upstairs, peeking in on a sleeping Kieran before heading to Kayla's room. She's sitting on the edge of her bed, crying and rocking back and forth, one of her pillows clutched to her chest. I go to her, and she tosses the pillow aside, collapsing into my arms. She sobs deeply on my shoulder for a tiny eternity, my hand rubbing up and down her back the only thing I can do to comfort her.

Eventually, the crying subsides and Kayla pulls away from me, wiping her swollen eyes.

"Okay. Wow. I'm really sorry about that. I've never had a total meltdown before."

"You've had to keep it together for your family's sake—for Kieran's sake—for years," I point out, giving her a smile. "I think you were due to have a meltdown at some point." She nods, and I ask, "You're not serious about getting emancipated, are you?"

She snorts, still wiping wetness from her eyes.

"Like I could afford a lawyer. They know that. I *am* going to Brad's this weekend, though, unless Kieran wants me to stay here. My parents can't think they can lie to me one minute and then tell me what to do the next. They've lost any cred they've ever had with me at this point."

"So, you're sure your mom knew there was a chance Cooper might end up like this?"

Kayla nods, saying, "Remember how weird she was acting when we found out Cooper underwent the treatment? And then I overheard her in the kitchen saying as much to one of the researchers on the phone. That's when I lost it."

I narrow my eyes, thinking something through after Kayla mentions the researchers.

"Why wouldn't the people Cooper talked to from the research team have warned him about this? I mean, he said all they mentioned was he might be confused when he woke up. Why would they lie to him?"

"They were probably so scared of losing their jobs, they kept the truth from him." Kayla shrugs. "Or maybe they told him some memory loss was possible, and Cooper just heard what he wanted to hear."

"Or maybe Cooper was telling Kieran what he thought *Kieran* would want to hear," I suggest. "Maybe the researchers told him amnesia was a risk factor, and he didn't want to scare Kieran unnecessarily in case it didn't happen."

"Well, protecting Kieran's feelings *is* all the rage these days." Kayla gives me a bland smile.

"Kind of a burned-out trend, if you ask me." Kieran's leaning against the doorframe, his eyes still half-closed as he's obviously not fully awake yet.

"How long have you been standing there?" Kayla asks.

"Well, I was hanging out in the hall, mostly, but I've been in the general area long enough to listen to your total big ugly girl cry.

That was *awesome*." He enters the room and sits down on the floor in front of Kayla's dresser, directly opposite the bed.

"Shut up," Kayla fires back, but with affection.

Kieran pulls his legs to him, resting his chin on his knees. "So, I'm guessing Cooper's memory didn't magically return while I was out?"

"No. Unless Mom's not telling us something, which is always a possibility."

I slide off the bed and crawl the few inches I need to in order to be at Kieran's side. "You okay?" I ask, resting my cheek on his shoulder.

"Well, my only real guy friend in the world probably doesn't remember who I am anymore, so that's kind of a buzzkill." He's trying to be flippant, but I sense an angry undertone to his voice. "And who knows what happens to the treatment now. What good is something if it takes care of one disorder but leaves you with a side effect that's just as bad, if not worse? And we don't even know yet if Cooper's sleeping disorder symptoms are gone." Kieran shrugs, forgetting my head is on his shoulder, and so I sit up straight as he continues. "He might have a sleeping disorder *and* memory loss. Unbelievable."

I scoot forward on the rug so I can look into his eyes, and I see the fear glowing in their more intense icy blue. The treatment could be a failure, and he'll spend the rest of his life the way he is right now—the way he's always been.

Pulling him to me, I whisper in his ear, "Sweetie, it's okay. They'll keep working on the treatment. They'll learn from what happened to Cooper and they'll fix whatever's wrong."

I know my sentiments don't mean much, especially since we don't know if they *can* fix things.

"You know, I don't care anymore," Kieran says, sighing against me before expressing something even Kayla and I are probably feeling right now. "I don't give a crap about the treatment at all. I just want Cooper to be okay."

CHAPTER 10

About two weeks after Cooper Halloran returns to reality in New York, I'm in the journalism lab after school with Emma Eckberg, my classmate who's been given the unfortunate task of writing my Homecoming Queen Candidate profile for the *Titan Times*.

"So," Emma asks, pushing "play" on a voice recorder on her phone and pretending like nobody's business to be a serious journalist, "tell me a little bit about yourself."

"You've known me since Kindergarten," I say through a slight laugh.

"Well, yeah. But, I mean, we need some interesting stuff for the profile. Like, what are your hobbies?"

"You *know* what my hobbies are."

"Okay. But...well..." Emma chews on the end of the pencil she's using to take additional notes. "Tell me something that might surprise me. There's got to be something, right? I mean, sure— everyone knows you play basketball and you're dating Kieran Lanier and you're a really good student. But what are people totally clueless about?"

I shake off any momentary insult at being reduced to nothing more than the smart, basketball-playing girlfriend of the school's new guy because I'm private enough that people around here probably don't know much about me, even after all these years. By contrast, I could write Emma's biography. A petite brunette who's one of the sweetest girls in Titusville, Emma's not only a good student herself, but she's also captain of the dance squad and a four-year member of the school choir, a logical extra-curricular for her since she's been stunning the members of the First United Methodist Church with her soprano every Sunday since she was five years old. She's hoping for either a dance or voice scholarship to a state school, and although I haven't heard around if she's going out with anyone right now, I remember she and Doug Callahan went to Prom last spring.

I stop myself from mentally listing off Emma's brothers' and sisters' names, in addition to any other trivia I can think of about her, realizing I could take this opportunity to invent a new persona for myself around here:

Well, Emma, I'm into long walks by the river at sunset, studying Karate, and cooking gourmet meals for my family in my spare time. And were you aware that on Prom night, I wrecked my car because Kieran and I were being chased to the Wyatt River by two ex-cons, one of whom turned out to be not only a pretty nice guy, but also happens to be my boyfriend's real father? Oh—by the way, before the car chase, I punched the other ex-con in the nose. And did you know that Kayla Lanier kidnapped me and dragged me off to North Carolina back in June? And then there's the whole thing about how this guy from New York who I once thought was stalking me now has amnesia and doesn't even remember who I am. Now, that's a story, let me tell you...

I sigh and decide the world is going to be better off if I stick with discussing what parts of the real me I can without giving up all of the Lanier family secrets.

"Well, I guess a lot of people wouldn't know my dream job would be to work for ESPN..."

While I'm babbling on about my hopes and dreams to Emma Eckberg, Cooper's never too far from my thoughts. Although Kayla's barely speaking to her parents, Kieran's tried to put any frustrations with them aside for the sake of understanding what's going on with Cooper, and we've both talked with Carlie and Jim several times, getting updates and explanations.

As far as anyone can figure out, the treatment provoked a kind of situational amnesia in Cooper. Jim and Carlie explained that people

119

usually develop this type of memory loss after a traumatic life event, and so the origins of the condition are more psychological than biological. But, given the bizarre nature of Kieran and Cooper's condition to begin with, "usual" is sort of out the window at this point, and the assumption is that the treatment somehow caused the amnesia. While Cooper's forgotten every autobiographical detail about his life, he can remember facts and figures and things he's learned in school. For example, he's taken French and Spanish since he was a little kid, and is fluent in both. And even now, apparently, he's still fluent—only he doesn't remember how or why because his memory of sitting in classrooms or working with tutors to learn the languages is now gone.

The good news, according to Carlie and Jim, is the amnesia usually clears up on its own in a few weeks with repeated exposure to familiar people and places. So although Ben Halloran pulled Cooper out of school in favor of private tutors to spare everyone the difficult explanations about Cooper's current state, we can all rest assured the confusion and amnesia will eventually disappear.

"Okay," Emma says, looking over her notes. "Let me make sure everything's accurate. Name: Zara Elizabeth McKee. Birthday: April first…"

I nod as Emma lists off various vital statistics everyone in town should know by now until she gets to one that's a little complicated.

"…Parents: Mitch McKee and April Shipman." She pauses. "Yeah—that's something I wanted to double-check. So, your dad won't be escorting you at the game?"

While members of the football team serve as escorts for the Homecoming Court at the pep assembly and the dance, they're obviously a little busy during the game and so each girl's father serves as her escort at halftime, when the court goes out to the field and the queen is announced. Unfortunately for me, however, my father doesn't think he's going to be able to get away from work early enough to make the drive from Chicago in time for the game, and so after *that* letdown, Gramps stepped in to be my escort.

"Yeah," I tell Emma, trying to keep the eternal disappointment with my mostly absentee dad out of my voice. "My grandpa will be my escort. Larry Shipman."

"Yeah. Larry Shipman. That's the information I got from Mrs. Gillette, but I just wanted to make sure." Her eyes scan the rest of her notes. "Okay, I think I've got what I need. Looks like there's time before Zach will need you for photos if you want to go freshen up a little. You look really nice, by the way."

"Thanks, Emma," I say, her compliment stifling the groan working its way up my throat at the thought of having to get my picture taken with the rest of the court by the big oak tree on the school's front lawn. Photo shoots aren't my thing, and posing next to the most beautiful girls in Titusville is going to be downright surreal—it almost makes the bizarreness happening with Cooper in New York right now seem normal by comparison. But Emma's kind words fill me with warmth. She's probably about the tenth person who's told me I look nice today, which is sort of cool, I guess. And while I don't think I'll be getting dressed up for school on a regular basis once all this Homecoming crap is over, I can't say I've hated people taking notice of me for something other than basketball.

I hitch my backpack up on my shoulder and glance toward the back of the room, where Brittany Solomon is finishing up her interview with Kyle Leighton. We exchange smiles and she shifts her gaze to Kyle and back to me so quickly, I almost don't catch her rolling her eyes at me. I giggle and head out of the room, making a quick stop in the bathroom to make sure I look okay enough to be photographed—not that I know what "okay enough to be

121

photographed" is supposed to look like, but with Kayla's coaching over the last week, I'm hoping that I at least look presentable.

Standing in front of the nearly wall-length bathroom mirror, I pull a compact from my backpack and dab some powder on my nose before coating my lips with a light sheen of gloss—enough to give my lips a little color, but not enough to make them seem all slobbery and gross in the pictures, per Kayla's instructions. The members of the court were told to dress "fall casual" for the photos, so Kayla helped me pick out the khaki pants and cap-sleeved rust-colored blouse I'm wearing now, and she came over this morning with a flat iron to help me smooth my wayward hair into a sleek side ponytail at the nape of my neck. I grab a brush from my backpack—I'm carrying around more beauty supplies today than I ever have in my life—and run it through my strands a few times before moving it away from the end of the ponytail resting below my collarbone. After I turn and bend down to make sure no one's in the stalls, I stand up straight again, squaring my shoulders and positioning the brush in front of me just below chin level.

"This is Zara McKee for ESPN," I say into my hairbrush microphone, holding my best "serious sideline reporter" stare for a second before dissolving into laughter at the strange girl in the mirror, a girl I've actually grown more comfortable with as the day's worn on. And as Kayla's pointed out to me several times since our Homecoming shopping spree, sideline reporters don't wear sweatpants, so at some point in my future, I'll need to get used to dressing the way I am now on a regular basis. Might as well start easing into it now.

With all of my beauty supplies tucked into my backpack, I head outside to the school's front lawn, where the entire court with the exception of Brittany Solomon is gathered around the ancient oak tree. Zach Bochine, nephew of our school librarian and photographer for the *Titan Times*, glances in my direction.

"Brittany's finishing up her interview," I tell him, and he turns to the rest of the court as I stop next to McKenna Dantino, queen candidate and the daughter of Paulie Dantino, owner of Paulie's Pizza. The Dantinos also own the only house in Titusville with an in-ground pool, which puts them at the top of the social order around here. All McKenna needs to do is wake up in the morning, and she's already Titusville royalty.

Zach pushes his glasses up on his head, resting them in his unruly nest of brunet curls, and surveys the semi-circle of girls.

"Okay," he says. "I guess we can start with the Freshman Princess and work our way through, so, Shelby—you're first."

The football team voted on the princess nominees earlier in the week, so Shelby Sandowsky, younger sister of my teammate Tori, steps up to perform one of her first official duties as Freshman Princess. She stands in front of the tree and Zach snaps several pictures of her in relaxed poses before moving on to Sophomore Princess Whitney Tannen.

"Okay, Whit. Maybe turn to the right a little...a little more...okay, now there's a shadow so come back to the left..."

I'm so engrossed in watching Zach direct Whitney as if he's shooting a magazine spread that I don't hear Brittany come up behind me.

"Totally glam, huh?" she says, and once I shake off being startled by her voice, I follow her gaze to the tree, where Zach's putting his hands on Whitney's shoulders, trying to position her in the best possible pose. Whitney, meanwhile, frowns as if she's less than thrilled about the geeky photographer guy touching her.

"Oh, yeah," I say sarcastically. "So glam."

Zach snaps a few shots of Whitney once he has her in place and then turns around to us as Junior Princess Kara Martel positions herself in front of the tree trunk.

"Which one of you guys wants to go after Kara?" he asks, putting his glasses back on so he can see us clearly.

Might as well get this over with…

"I'll go," I volunteer before anyone else can say anything. Zach turns back to Kara, who proves to be a pretty good model and is done with her photos in seconds. I, on the other hand, am more than a little modeling-challenged, my awkwardness prompting Zach to come forward and arrange me as he did with Whitney Tannen. As he's positioning my shoulders, I gaze past the rest of the court to see a tiny crowd gathering on the lawn a few feet behind them in order to watch the action, which doesn't make me feel any better about getting my picture taken. But then I see Kieran on the fringe, sitting on a parking bumper block at the end of an empty space, his legs stretched out on the grass and his grin automatically putting me at ease. Looking back at the court, I catch Brittany making monkey faces at me while Chelsea Copeland gives me a thumbs-up. Even McKenna, who's not the warmest person in the world, shoots me a smile, and I feel both my body and face relax.

Since we still have a group picture to take after Zach photographs the other queen candidates, I don't immediately run to Kieran as instinct would tell me to, but I instead stand with the rest of the court, occasionally sending a smile and a wave in his direction. We take a set of group pictures under the tree with the hoots and yells of the assembled crowd as a soundtrack, and only afterwards do I go to Kieran.

"I thought you were going to wait for me in the library," I say, dropping a quick kiss on his lips.

"I went there at first," he begins when we part, "and then I remembered a group of hot girls was getting pictures taken on the front lawn, and I had to ask myself what I was doing hanging out with Mrs. Bochine. Or, I should say, a group of six kind of okay-looking girls and *one* really, really hot girl."

"Nice save, Lanier," I grumble through a laugh, giving him a joke punch in the shoulder. He kisses me on the forehead before stepping to my side, still keeping a hand on my waist.

"We've got about an hour before Kayla's match," he says as we start walking. "Want to go get some food or something?"

Since I knew I'd be staying after school for the interview and photo shoot, Kieran had decided to go with me to Kayla's volleyball match, which I have to report on for the *Titan Times*. Carlie's supposed to meet us here at school, and Jim and Morgan are also coming to the match once they get back into town from Sumner.

"Or we could go to your house so you can change if you want," Kieran suggests. "Up to you."

I stop walking, stare down at my outfit and shrug.

"You know what? I think I'm okay like this—unless you think I'm overdressed or something?"

"Not at all. I think you're beautiful. You look amazing today. Not sure if I'd mentioned that or not."

He's grinning, and I can't help but grin as well.

"You've mentioned it about forty times," I remind him.

"Good. Just wanted to make sure." His expression gets a little more serious. "But, just so you know, I love you no matter what. Don't let Kayla get into your head with all of this 'You need a stylist' crap. You could have come to school this morning in a towel and I would have thought you'd looked amazing."

"As would every other guy in school, probably, since I would have been almost naked," I say, elbowing him in the ribs.

125

"Yeah—good point. So, maybe not a towel, but you get what I mean. I'm in love with *you* and not your clothes. But today, the you I love happens to be wrapped in a particularly nice package."

"Eloquently put, Mr. Lanier."

Before he can thank me, his phone buzzes.

"It's Mom," he tells me after checking his texts. The phone buzzes again. "She's asking if you're done with the shoot because she wants to take us out for some food before the match."

"She must be reading our minds."

Kieran texts her back and nods toward the small set of stairs leading up to the school's front entrance. "I told her we'd wait here," he says, putting a hand on my back and guiding me to the lowest step, where we sit holding hands and talking in the few minutes until Carlie pulls up.

"Hey, Carlie," I say, piling in the backseat as Kieran gets in up front.

"Hi, Zip. How was the photo shoot?"

"Fine, I guess. I don't think I'm going to start a modeling career anytime soon."

Carlie glances at me in the rearview mirror as she pulls toward the parking lot's side entrance.

"Kayla will be so disappointed," she says, the lilt in her voice telling me she's not serious.

"Kayla will just have to get over it," I say back, and Carlie and Kieran both laugh before Carlie sobers up.

"I heard from Ben Halloran today." She tilts her head toward Kieran.

"Did something happen with Cooper?" Kieran's voice is a mixture of fear and hope, and Carlie quickly puts both to rest.

"No. He's frustrated, though—Ben, that is. Nothing seems to be jarring Cooper's memory. I told Ben things could take a while, but he's a very impatient man."

"Must run in the family," Kieran says, glancing at me.

Carlie ignores Kieran's comment and continues.

"So, we were thinking if Cooper's memory doesn't return in the next few days maybe he could come here next weekend and spend some time with you kids. Maybe being with you and Kayla—and Zip, too, although she hasn't been around him as much—might help him remember something." Carlie shakes her head. "It's as good an idea as any, I guess."

"Next weekend's Homecoming," Kieran points out, once again glancing back at me.

Carlie makes the right turn onto River Avenue and pulls into a parking space in front of the Downtown Diner.

"This okay for dinner?" she asks, not immediately addressing Kieran's statement about Homecoming. Kieran and I nod in unison because we don't have a ton of dining options in this town.

"So, is there a problem with next weekend being Homecoming?" Carlie asks as she shuts off the car.

"Probably not," I say, opening my door. "I mean, I'll have stupid Homecoming Court stuff going on, but…"

"But Kayla and I will be able to spend time with him," Kieran fills in once my voice fades away. Up on the sidewalk, he reaches out to hold the Diner's door open so Carlie and I can walk in ahead of him. Once we're settled into a booth at the back of the restaurant, Kieran continues with "Kayla's going to be pissed, though. Brad's supposed to be here, and I don't think she'll be too thrilled if Cooper's tagging along with us everywhere all weekend." He glances at me, narrowing his eyes. "Can Cooper even go to the Homecoming stuff?" he asks me. "I mean, since he doesn't go to school here and all?"

"Titusville's never had any rules about that kind of thing," I say, shaking my head. "I know some bigger schools upstate have had trouble when kids from rival schools try to go to their dances, but nothing like that's ever gone on here, so there will probably be some people from Sumner or other places around who will show up as someone's date." I look back and forth between Carlie and Kieran. "Of course, we'll need some kind of explanation as to who he is. People are going to ask."

"We'll think of something, I guess," Carlie says as Dewayne comes up to get our drink orders. Once he leaves, Carlie begins perusing the menu, almost as if she doesn't want to meet our eyes when she mumbles, "Kayla's going to be unhappy no matter what happens."

"Do you blame her?" Kieran asks after taking a sip of his soda. "I mean, I'm *trying* with you and Dad, Mom—I really am—but I'm not going to stick up for you guys with her. I can't. Eighteen years of trust down the drain is a lot to ask me to get over. I can't fix things with you guys and Kayla, too.

"I know," Carlie says quietly, placing the menu on the tabletop.

"You and Dad may have done too much damage in her eyes this time. She's going to have to come around on her own."

Carlie reaches out for Kieran's hand resting on the table, but he flinches and pulls it away, placing it over mine on the cracked Formica seat. As Kieran squeezes my fingers, I can't help but wonder if the Laniers will ever be able to put their family back together completely.

"Can you at least try to help her understand why Ben wants Cooper here next weekend? Please?" she pleads, clearly shaken by Kieran's rejection.

"I can try, but only because I want to help Cooper. I *want* Cooper here." Kieran gazes at me. "I mean, I don't want him to ruin our Homecoming weekend, either, but—"

"What's to ruin?" I shrug. "I'm already going to have to do stuff at the game Friday night, and I'll have to spend part of the dance with Cody Hull, anyway," I remind him, as Cody's my football team escort, so once I'm at school, he'll have to accompany me into the gym for the main ceremony and first dance. "If Cooper's here, you'll have somebody to hang with while I'm doing all of my stupid royal duties and Kayla can spend time with Brad. So, it kind of works, actually."

Carlie gives Kieran a slow nod, and Kieran looks away from me to her.

"Okay, then. If Kayla throws a fit about Cooper being here, I'll do what I can to calm her down. But that's it, Mom. Kayla and I are still trying to come to terms with everything, okay? I can't make any promises, and I definitely can't make any promises for her."

"Okay," Carlie breathes, and Dewayne cuts short any further conversation on the matter by coming to the table to take our order. And while I can't be sure if Kayla and Kieran will ever forgive their parents for their complicated family history, I am sure of one thing— our Homecoming weekend just got *a lot* more interesting.

CHAPTER 11

I have two hours between the end of the parade and the start of the football game to go home, rest, and change into my second non-Zip McKee-esque outfit of the day. But not even twenty minutes into the brief power nap I'm squeezing in before I'll need to re-curl my hair, touch up my makeup, and put on the dress I'm wearing tonight, the doorbells rings, waking me up.

"Zip," Mom calls from her bedroom. "Can you get the door?"

"I'm trying to take a nap."

"Well, I'm half out of my clothes. Are you dressed?"

"Yeah," I mumble.

"You lose. Answer the door."

I groan and get up from the bed, stalking down the hall and into the living room, my mood instantly brightening once I find out who's here.

"Dad!"

"Hey, Zip-o-rama," he booms, and I wonder for the millionth time why he and my grandfather always insist on corrupting my nickname. I step back so he can come inside and he gathers me in his arms.

"What are you doing here?" I ask into his shoulder.

"It's Homecoming, and fathers are supposed to escort the members of the Homecoming Court onto the field at halftime, right?"

I pull away so I can look at him.

"I thought you couldn't come."

"Well, then he told me he *could* come, and we decided to keep the whole thing a secret so you'd be surprised," my mom says from behind me. She's standing just inside the living room from the hallway, smiling to beat the sun while Dad explains, "I was able to rearrange some things at work so I could leave early and drive down."

"I told the school Gramps was going to be my escort," I point out, slightly panicked. "We need to call somebody."

"Already taken care of," Mom assures me. "I swore Mrs. Gillette to secrecy, too."

I turn back to Dad, whose smile forces the tiny creases at the corners of his eyes to burrow deeper into his face. He's lost his summer tan, which makes his dark brown hair and bushy eyebrows stand out more against his skin than they did the last time we were together, during our North Carolina misadventures back in June.

"I'm glad you're here," I tell him, reaching up to hug him once again.

"Me, too. And Kathy sends her love and apologies for not being able to come with me. Olivia's taking dance lessons after school on Fridays, and we're paying enough for those that we didn't want her to miss." He smiles as he talks about my stepmother and half-sister. "And trust me—she wanted to skip her lesson. When she heard you were up for Homecoming Queen, she nearly came out of her skin. She's apparently been telling everyone at school her big sister is a real live princess."

"That's adorable. And not even close to accurate."

"I'll never hear the end of it for not letting her come," Dad says, shaking her head. "I promised I'd get lots of pictures, which is going to be kind of hard if I'm supposed to be part of the ceremony." Dad glances past me to Mom.

"Got you covered, Mitch," she assures him. "Between my parents and me, I'm sure we'll be able to send you enough pictures to crash your hard drive."

"How are your parents?"

131

"Good. Same as always." Mom shrugs. "They're looking forward to seeing you—it's been too long."

I do the math in my head and realize Dad hasn't seen his former in-laws since I graduated from junior high.

"And how are the Laniers?" Dad asks me.

"They're good, all things considered," I say with a sigh, my mind having been temporarily taken off the Cooper situation by Dad's arrival. "I guess Mom told you Cooper Halloran's coming down for the weekend?"

"No." He slides an arm around me and arches a questioning eyebrow at my mother.

"I guess I forgot to mention that," she tells him by way of an excuse. "They've tried everything to help him get his memory back, so his father's sending him here for a few days, hoping if he spends time with the Laniers and Zip, it might jar something loose."

"Of course, he's never seen me in 'princess mode,' so I don't think spending time with *me* this weekend is going to bring anything back to him," I add.

Dad steps a couple of feet away from me so he can take in my full ensemble.

"You look beautiful, by the way. Whether you win or not, you'll be the prettiest girl on the Homecoming Court."

"Oh, this isn't my outfit for tonight," I correct him, with a hint of sarcasm in my voice. "This is my parade outfit."

"Her *parade* outfit?" he asks, casting a sideways glance at my mom.

"That's what she wore sitting in the back of a convertible and doing the 'princess wave' this afternoon." Mom cups her hand slightly and displays a controlled wave like the ones we've seen from the British Royal Family on TV, a wave nothing like the loose back-and-forth-in-the-air one I was doing this afternoon to the point my elbow kind of hurts. "Then there's the outfit she wore for the *Titan Times* Homecoming Court issue, the outfit for the spirit assembly yesterday, the game outfit, and the dress for the dance tomorrow night. You may need to up your child support payment this month."

Dad lets out a hearty laugh and says, "I don't think so."

Despite Mom's brief reminder of their divorce, I'm pretty happy they're getting along well enough right now to joke around.

"Speaking of outfits," I begin, "I need to scarf down some food and start getting ready for the game." I take in Dad's shorts and sweatshirt ensemble. "I hope Mom told you to bring a suit."

"Who knew you'd become so fashion-conscious all of a sudden?" Dad says, jerking his head back.

"I'm *not*, but—"

"Zip, I'm teasing you. Your mom took care of everything. My suit's in the car."

"Sorry," I grumble. "I promise I won't turn into a total girly girl. After this weekend, it's nothing but sweatpants for a month."

"Girly girl or no girly girl, you're *my* girl." Dad laughs. "Don't ever forget it, and make sure you remind young Mr. Lanier of that fact every once in a while."

Now it's *my* turn to roll my eyes.

"Dad," I whine.

"Quit teasing the poor girl, Mitch," Mom warns, walking over to grab his arm. "Let's go get your suit and leave Zip to changing and fixing you two some dinner." She turns to me. "There's leftover pizza in the fridge."

"Nice to know a gourmet meal is still what it always was around here," Dad cracks as Mom crosses her arms over her stomach and heaves a frustrated sigh. "Warm me up a couple of slices, okay?" he orders me.

133

"Okay, but only if you promise to be nice to Mom while you're here. No more cheap shots about her cooking or anything else."

I arch an eyebrow at him, and out of the corner of my eye, I catch Mom sneaking me a smile.

"Promise," he says, crossing his shirt over his heart with his index finger for emphasis.

My parents manage to behave through our leftover pizza dinner and remain cordial to each other as they hang out after he changes into his suit because it takes me a little longer to get into the flouncy black skirt and forest green silk blouse I'm wearing tonight. I re-curl my hair and touch up my makeup before fixing the "Queen Candidate" sash across my body and walking out to the living room, my black high heels in hand because I don't want to wear those evil things any longer than necessary.

"There's my princess," Dad says, rising from the couch to give me a kiss on the cheek.

"You mean *queen*, right?" I correct him, my voice oozing sarcasm.

"Of course."

I surrender and slide into my heels, and the three of us make our way to the game together in Dad's SUV, looking like the perfect portrait of a happy nuclear family that we've never been. We park in front of the school and walk around back to the football field, Mom leaving us once we're through the gate so she can sit in the special section of the home team bleachers reserved for the court and their families. Dad and I, meanwhile, join the rest of queen candidates, princesses, and their fathers over near the entrance to the cafeteria, where Mrs. Gillette runs through some instructions for the halftime ceremony.

"I had no idea all this Homecoming business was so involved," Dad mumbles to me once we've been set free to head to the family section.

"Neither did I." I reach up and straighten his tie. "I've only watched this from outside all these years."

We're about to walk off toward the bleachers when I gaze past Dad and notice Kieran, Kayla, and Brad ambling up to us. They stop behind my dad, and Kieran buries his hands in his jeans pockets, seeming a little uncomfortable.

"Hi, guys," I say to them, and Dad turns around. Kieran hunches up his shoulders, shy in a way he usually isn't, before he pulls himself together, offering his right hand to Dad.

"Pleasure to see you again, sir," he says and I smile, amused at how polite he is and how nervous my dad makes him.

"Same here, Kieran," Dad says, sounding like he means it. "Kayla. How are you?" He turns to her once he's done with Kieran.

"Good, thanks." She gives his hand a firm pump, and I realize my dad probably hasn't seen Brad since we were little kids.

"Dad, you probably don't remember, but this is Brad Wallace."

Brad offers Dad his hand as Dad files through his memories.

"I remember your parents, I think," Dad says, squinting. "You lived in that house on Dodge Avenue next to the Newbaums, and you kids all used to play together, right?"

"Good memory, sir." Brad smiles, while Kayla and I exchange knowing glances. I think it's kind of funny for both of us to watch our boyfriends be so polite and formal around my father.

"So, is Cooper in town yet?" I ask, getting to what I assume is the real reason they've waited for us rather than trying to find us in the crowd inside, and Kayla nods.

"I've been texting you, but when you didn't answer, we thought we'd try to track you down before the game," she says. "I know you've probably been busy with Homecoming stuff."

"Yeah," I respond, tilting my head over my shoulder at the members of the court and their dads still milling around in the general area and talking with people before the game starts. Once Kieran convinced her that I'd be preoccupied with my ridiculous royal duties for most of the weekend, Kayla quickly accepted Cooper's visit as a good thing—Kieran would have someone to hang out with, and she wouldn't need to sacrifice quality time with Brad to keep her brother company.

"Cooper got into town with Victor about an hour ago," Kieran continues. "Mom and Dad and Morgan are driving him around and they're going up to the Burger Barn for dinner, you know, to see if anything comes back to him."

The Burger Barn out by the interstate was the first place I encountered Cooper after he hit on me in North Carolina, and it was where I became convinced he was after me for some reason. Only later did we all find out he was really tailing Kieran, and my seeing him at the Burger Barn was a total coincidence—he and Victor had just happened to stop there for lunch after driving in from Chicago.

"They're planning to come by here before halftime so they can catch the ceremony," Kayla notes.

"And what's the story going to be if anyone asks who he and Victor are?" I ask, and Dad gives me a smirk and says, "Ah—there's always a story, isn't there?"

Kieran buries his hands back in his jeans pockets and hitches his shoulders, giving Dad a sad little smile as if to say "Yeah—but what are you going to do, right?"

"His parents and our parents were friends in New York before we were born," Kayla explains. "So, Cooper's an old family friend

136

who's staying with us for the weekend, basically. That story would work whether or not someone recognizes the Halloran name."

"And Victor?" I ask.

"Cooper's personal assistant. Mr. Halloran doesn't like to send his son anywhere without a personal assistant."

I bob my head slowly, taking everything in.

"Well, the stuff about Victor is actually true, so at least that part won't be a hard sell. And the rest of the story makes sense."

"Of course it does," Kayla says, standing up straight. "I came up with it. I told Mom and Dad if there's one thing I know how to do, it's make up a lie. I learned from the best."

Dad cocks an eyebrow and I mumble "Long story" at him.

A clatter of noise behind us in the parking lot catches our attention, and we angle our heads to see the marching band filing out of the school's side entrance like a horde of navy blue and gold ants with brass contraptions attached to their matching bodies.

"Guess the game's about to start," I say, turning back to the group before eyeing the bleachers. "Most of the town's here, so you guys might have trouble finding somewhere to sit at this point."

"I told Kristi to save us some seats near Mom and Dad," Brad tells me, referring to his little sister, a freshman this year.

I let go of Dad and slide an arm around Kieran's waist.

"I wish I could sit with you, but I'm supposed to go be royal and stuff," I tell him.

"I understand, Your Highness," Kieran says, stepping away from me so he can bow. Brad starts bowing as well, which produces a laugh from my dad and a deep eye-roll from Kayla.

"Our boyfriends are weirdoes," she says, sighing.

"They are. But they're *our* weirdoes."

I lean over to Kieran to put my arm around him again, and he gives me a chaste kiss on the cheek in the presence of my dad.

137

"We'll catch up with you after halftime," he says quietly. "And, good luck. The football team is pretty stupid if they didn't vote for you for queen."

Brad snorts as Kieran had said his last sentence loudly enough for him to hear.

"You guys have never been to a Titusville football game, have you?" he asks, looking back and forth between the siblings.

"No," they answer in unison.

"'Stupid' doesn't begin to describe it, and this is coming from someone who played varsity for three years."

Brad and I exchange knowing glances. Titusville's football team has had a losing record since we were little kids, thus guaranteeing that the ceremony at halftime will be the most exciting thing on the field tonight. And the team wastes no time living down to our low expectations as Emmetsburg scores two touchdowns practically before the marching band is done playing the National Anthem. Since I was the last of the court to take my seat in our designated row at the fifty-yard line, I'm stuck on the end next to Whitney Tannen, who ignores me in favor of gossiping with Shelby Sandowsky. Thankfully, Dad's sitting right behind me since the next two rows are reserved for family of the court, and I spend the first half engaging in the very un-queenly behavior of dissecting Titusville's miserable offensive plays and weak defense with him. With about five minutes left before halftime, Mrs. Gillette, looking rather regal herself in a navy blue silk dress and her short hair in big curls, hustles the girls and their fathers off to the opposing team's side of the field.

Halftime begins with the Titusville Titans down 24-7, the team shuffling off the field to the locker room with their heads down. But their impending defeat quickly takes a backseat to what nearly the entire town has turned out to see—the crowning of the Homecoming

Queen, the young woman who will not only preside over the dance tomorrow night but will also rule over the annual Fall Antiques Festival in three weeks. In past years, "ruling" has entailed such activities as posing with the winner of the apple pie-eating contest and getting her picture taken with the mayor, so the royal duties aren't exactly strenuous.

After the Marching Titans get everyone warmed up with their nearly unrecognizable version of Lady Gaga's "Bad Romance," Bubba Stocket, who's lived in Titusville his entire life and has been the public address announcer at most Titusville sporting events for over forty years, comes rasping over the press box microphone.

"Ladies and Gentlemen, it's time to announce your Titusville High School Homecoming Court."

Polite applause and cheers bubble up from the crowd.

Each princess walks out to the center of the field with her father after Bubba reads out their names. Mrs. Gillette hands the girls a bouquet of white roses in turn, and Mr. Rosner, the school principal, places a small tiara on each of their perfectly-coiffed heads before their fathers steer them off to the home team sideline.

Bubba clears his throat before he begins announcing the queen candidates.

"Our first queen candidate is Senior Chelsea Copeland, daughter of Cindy and Andrew Copeland. Chelsea is escorted tonight by her father, Andrew."

Chelsea reaches the middle of the field, gives the crowd a wave, and she and her dad move slightly to their left so McKenna and her dad can have the spotlight. McKenna repeats Chelsea's actions, only she and her dad move to the right of the fifty-yard line to make way for me.

"Our next queen candidate is Senior Zara McKee, daughter of April Shipman and Mitch McKee. Zara is escorted tonight by her father, Mitch."

Dad and I walk to the center of the field without a word, but I can feel my cheeks burning despite the probably plastic-looking grin plastered across my face. Shaking off any momentary panic over how ridiculous I'm going to look in all the pictures being snapped right now, I raise my arm and wave at the crowd before tugging my dad off to the left.

"Well, that wasn't so bad," Dad whispers to me as Bubba introduces Brittany and her father.

"You're not the one wearing high heels on grass," I hiss back, and he gives me a sly smile.

Brittany and her dad take their places next to my dad, and the eight of us stand at the center of the field, waiting for Bubba's voice to put us out of our misery as if we're old-time criminals facing a firing squad. I scan the crowd, looking for familiar faces, but the townspeople are so far away from me at this distance that they all appear to be a mass of indistinguishable heads on multi-colored, formless bodies. I can't make out anyone individually at all.

Anyone at all, that is, except for one person. Racial and ethnic diversity aren't exactly local strong points, and so Victor—who is, at the moment, the only Hispanic person in Titusville—stands out like an island in a sea of pale. And now that I can see Victor, I can definitely make out the husky form of Cooper standing next to him, arms down at his sides unlike everyone else in the crowd who is currently clapping for Brittany.

The public address system crackles, distracting me, and I blink. When I refocus, I scan the crowd for Victor and Cooper, but Victor must have his head down because now I can't find them. And I'm struck with the thought that somewhere up there in the crowd,

Cooper Halloran is just another person, just another face, indistinguishable from others not only to me, but also to himself.

I glance down at my outfit that's about as far away from sweatpants and a t-shirt as I can get, short of wearing a full-on ball gown—I guess I'm totally not myself right now, in a way, but at least I recognize who I am.

Cooper Halloran, on the other hand, doesn't even have the luxury of that knowledge at the moment.

CHAPTER 12

Bubba's waited long enough that his pause now seems more excruciating than dramatic. He clears his throat into the microphone, and the high-pitched whistle of feedback makes the hairs stand up on my neck.

"This year's Titusville High School Homecoming Queen is…"

I inhale the crisp fall air into my lungs. One way or another, this brief, bizarre chapter of my life is almost over.

"…Brittany Solomon."

I smile as Brittany and her dad walk forward to Principal Rosner, who's standing a few feet in front of them ready to crown Brit with a tiara of a slightly higher quality than the ones awarded to the princesses. Mrs. Gillette replaces Brittany's "Queen Candidate" sash with one reading "Homecoming Queen" and hands her a bouquet of red roses, and I can't help but feel a sense of order returning to the universe. Brittany waves as Chelsea, McKenna, and I stand with our dads and clap for her along with the rest of the crowd. Finally, Mrs. Gillette gives the signal for us to walk off the field and once we're on the sideline, she visits each of the candidates in turn, effectively demoting us by replacing our "Queen Candidate" sashes with "Senior Princess" ones. At least we also get plastic princess tiaras and bouquets of white roses, so it's not like we're walking away from the ceremony empty handed, and it's also not like I care whether or not I get anything at all. Right now, truthfully, the only thing I want is to get out of these uncomfortable shoes.

We take a few pictures as a group, both with our dads and without, before Mrs. Gillette reminds us not to linger too long before taking our roses inside to the cafeteria, where they'll live in a giant industrial cooler overnight so they can hopefully remain in bloom for the dance. Finally, we're free to go, and I link arms with my dad and sigh, both with exhaustion and relief.

"Sorry, honey," Dad whispers as we walk off behind Chelsea and her dad.

"I'm not. I don't think I'm cut out to be a queen. Too much responsibility."

Dad gives me a little laugh and says, "'Heavy is the head that wears the crown'?"

"Something along those lines," I tell him, smiling. "I think I'll be happier spending my remaining time in Titusville as a princess. Brittany's been doing this stuff her whole life. Things ended how they were supposed to."

Once we're off the field and in the asphalt area behind the bleachers, we're immediately greeted by Morgan, my family, and the Laniers along with Cooper and Victor. Dad steps aside as Kieran comes up to me, leaning in for a kiss while trying not to crush my roses.

"Sorry you didn't win," he whispers.

"I'll live."

"I know. And you'll still always be the Queen of My Heart."

"And that will still always be the cheesiest thing you've ever said to me." I smile. "And I will always love you for it."

He leans in to kiss me again, and after a few seconds, I hear my dad say, "Okay. Enough," but when I pull back from Kieran, I catch Dad grinning at us.

"Sorry, sir," Kieran says with a smile.

I'm quickly bombarded with hugs from everyone—everyone but Cooper and Victor, who hang back from the group a little bit, as if they don't quite belong. Our families talk amongst themselves, and I slip over to Kieran and tilt my head toward his houseguests. Kayla notices my signal to him and so she joins us as we move to speak to them.

"Hey, Coop?" Kieran starts quietly, as if he's afraid of startling Cooper by talking too loudly. "This is my girlfriend, Zip. I showed you pictures of her back at the house before the game."

Cooper nods slowly, presumably because he's remembering seeing the photos of me and not because he remembers actually *knowing* me.

"Hi, Cooper," I say warmly, but inside, I'm kind of freaking out. What am I supposed to say? *'Nice to meet you.'*?

"I'm glad you were able to visit this weekend," is what I settle on. Cooper gives me a vacant nod.

"You remember Zip," Victor prods in his lilting, slightly-Spanish accent. "You met her in North Carolina a few months ago, and then we were here for a few days and..."

Victor's voice fades out once he notices Cooper's expression is still a blank canvas. As much as I want Cooper's memory to come back, I'm kind of glad for both our sakes he doesn't remember hitting on me like a total asshat when he followed all of us to North Carolina earlier in the summer.

Cooper studies me for a few more seconds and then shakes his head.

"Sorry, Zip. I've got nothing. It's kind of a trend with me these days, from what people tell me." He pauses, looking me up and down, his lizard-like grin spreading across his face. "And it's too bad. You look like the kind of girl a guy would want to remember."

Well, at least *something* about Cooper is still the same as before.

"Thanks," I tell him, accepting the compliment and dismissing the lecherous gaze that came with it.

Cooper shrugs, and from the corner of my eye, I catch sight of the rest of the Homecoming Court entering the school by a back door leading to the cafeteria.

"I need to go inside for a few minutes," I say to Kieran, weirdly grateful to get away from Cooper, who's staring at me so intensely I can almost see his brain working behind his eyes, trying desperately to call forth some memory of who I am.

"More royal stuff?" he asks, giving me a teasing elbow to the ribs.

"We have to put our flowers in the cafeteria kitchen." I look past Kieran to Kayla, making sure I have her attention. "Wait here for me? We can sit together and watch the second half. I don't think I have to be with the court at this point."

They both nod and I sidestep Cooper's stare, walking over to the back door and into the cafeteria. The other members of the court have already surrendered their flowers to Mrs. Gillette and are gathered around Brittany, doling out hugs and congratulations and fawning over her crown. I hand my bouquet over to Mrs. Gillette and hang outside the circle of girls until it breaks up, the others either leaving or talking amongst themselves as Brittany and I stand face to face.

"Congratulations," I say, stepping forward to hug her. She gives me a little squeeze before letting go.

"Thanks," she says, and drops her voice to a conspiratorial whisper. "I was actually pulling for you to win. You've always been really nice to me, Zip. You're nice to everybody, no matter who they are and whether they deserve it or not. I thought it was so cool when you got nominated because you're the kind of person who *should* be queen. And it would have been awesome to see something out of the ordinary happen around here for once, you know?"

145

I gaze at her and I can't picture myself with that crown on my head or imagine hearing people refer to me as "Queen Zara" tomorrow night. But I just nod at her and say, "Yeah. That's really nice of you to say, Brit. Thanks."

"Guess I could always, like, resign or whatever from being Homecoming Queen," Brit jokes. "'Resign' isn't the right word—"

"You mean 'abdicate'?"

"That's it. I could abdicate." She puts an arm around me and walks us toward the door.

"I don't think that's ever happened before," I say, reaching for the handle and motioning for her to step outside ahead of me. "And I don't think I'd automatically be Homecoming Queen. We'd have to go through the whole ordeal of finding out who got the second-most votes and feelings would get hurt—not mine—and then you'd be the biggest scandal around here until I could come up with a better one to cause a diversion."

"Okay, then." Brittany laughs. "Maybe I'll keep the crown after all." She looks off toward the fence separating the bleacher area from where we are, and I follow her gaze to find Kayla, Kieran, and Brad waiting for me. "You know, I've only talked to him a few times, but Kieran seems awesome. Not bad looking, either. You're pretty lucky to get both in one guy," she tells me.

"Thanks," I say. Kieran gives me a wave, which I return. I wish people would try to get to know Kieran so they could see him as more than the "hot new guy with the weird sleeping thing," but like Brittany suggested, around here, once people decide you are what they think you are, you're kind of stuck unless you can do something out of the ordinary to prove them wrong.

"Speaking of hot guys, I noticed two guys with your family and Kieran's earlier, and the one who was around our age was, like, *wow*. I'd never seen him in town before."

146

I lick my lips, ready to put the lie in motion as my stomach works itself into knots.

"He's the son of an old friend of the Laniers," I start, watching Brit's face for any signs of doubt—which there probably wouldn't be. "Cooper. He'll be around all weekend."

"Cool."

She doesn't press me for further details and I don't volunteer any, and my stomach knot unties itself.

"Well, I'm going to go find my parents. Talk to you tomorrow night." Brit's hazel eyes twinkle as she walks off toward the gate to the bleacher area. "Can't wait to see your dress."

"'Bye, Brit," is all I say in return, still not able to muster up much enthusiasm for what I'll be wearing, much less what she'll be wearing.

I head over to the Brad and siblings, who scramble to their feet as I approach, Kayla curtseying and Kieran and Brad bowing as Kieran says, "Here approacheth Princess Zip. All hail Princess Zip."

"All hail Princess Zip," Brad and Kayla yell, and I turn beet red as a crowd of people at the concession stand turns around and starts clapping for me. I give them a polite little wave and they all return to ordering popcorn and sodas.

"Oh, my God. 'Princess Zip' sounds so weird," I grumble.

"So, what—we're supposed to call you 'Princess Zara' now?" Kayla says, rising back up to full height.

"I think plain old 'Zip' will work, thanks." I glance beyond the fence as if I could actually make out our families, Cooper, and Victor sitting among the assembled townsfolk. "Where is everybody?"

"Mom and Dad took Victor and Coop back to the house," Kieran explains. "Coop seemed kind of overwhelmed and worn out."

147

I nod, the tiara slipping from my head. Kieran reaches out to catch it and hands the tiara to me, and I promptly put the tiny row of fake plastic diamonds on his head.

"That's a good look for you," Brad teases as Kieran places a hand on his hip and tries to strike a supermodel pose. The tiara immediately slides from his head, and this time, Brad saves it from hitting the pavement.

"Be careful," Kayla scolds as Brad hands the tiara to me. "Zip has to wear the tiara tomorrow night, too, you know."

"And it would be the perfect end to this whole thing if I showed up to the dance with a super-glued tiara," I point out, but I'm not able to put thoughts of Cooper aside completely in favor of joking around. "Do you think Cooper's going to be okay tomorrow night? He seemed really out of it earlier, like he was looking right through me."

"Everyone's telling him he's supposed to know you, but he doesn't," Brad explains. "Everybody's telling him he's supposed to recognize this thing or that thing, and he can't. He's lost."

"Yeah, I don't think being at the dance will bother him too much," Kayla chimes in. "He's probably not going to be any more confused and messed up than he already is. And he'll get to spend time with Kieran and me, which might pry something loose in his brain, and maybe he'll even have some fun, which he seems in dire need of right now."

"And we've already had our first questions about who he is," I tell them, relaying my brief conversation with Brittany a few minutes ago. "She didn't seem suspicious. You guys are still new enough in town I think anything's believable as far as you're concerned."

"Well, let's hope Ashley and Cassie feel that way," Kayla says, lowering her voice as if our friends are near enough to hear us, although they're likely somewhere in the stands at the moment cheering in vain for the Titans to pull out a come-from-behind victory. "They saw him when he was here back in June, remember? They're the ones I'm worried about."

"Lauren, too," I remind her, since Lauren was the waitress Ashley, Cassie, and I were visiting at the Burger Barn the day Victor and Cooper rolled into town and happened to eat lunch at the same place we were. "All they know right now is that Cooper's some hot stranger who was staring at me at the Burger Barn. Convincing them Cooper was here to visit your family but I hadn't met him yet and that's why I didn't know who he was should be pretty easy."

Kieran and Kayla shrug at my theory, as Brad asks none of us in particular "Do you guys ever get sick of this?"

"Sick of what, sweetie?" Kayla takes his hand in hers and looks up at him.

"Always having to make up cover stories. Always worrying somebody's going to find out things aren't the way you say they are."

Kayla purses her lips for a moment, thinking.

"I've been sick of it for years," she breathes. "But it's what we do."

Brad looks down on her with a sad smile and they kiss, their gazes locked on each other when they part, the moment broken by a roar rising up from the crowd. We turn toward the bleachers as Bubba yells over the PA system "Touchdown Titans!"

"How about that?" Brad says as we all face each other. "They make the extra point and this might actually be a game worth watching."

"There should still be some seats near my family, assuming the entire court didn't go back to the center section," I point out. "Maybe we should go inside and pretend to be normal Titusville citizens for once."

149

We all exchange nods as Kayla says, "Normal. What a concept."

Brad puts an arm around her and guides her toward the gate as Kieran does the same to me, stopping me for a brief kiss before we join the crowd of Titusville townsfolk, who are oblivious to the Laniers' secrets and to the identity of the rich stranger in their house a few miles away.

CHAPTER 13

If I never wear a tiara again, it'll be too soon—these things are a total pain in the ass. At least Kayla's here to help me arrange my hair.

"Ladies, your escorts are getting antsy," Mom says, poking her head into her bedroom where Kayla and I are using her dressing table. Kayla's trying to set the tiara on my head so it doesn't push my bangs forward into my eyes, but we've already learned if she angles it back too far, the too-small-to-be-useful combs won't stay in my hair and the tiara slides when I walk.

"We'll be out in two minutes. I promise," Kayla says, to which my mother replies "Well, Zip's going to be late for her own ceremony if you're not."

"No big deal." I shrug, and the tiara falls off my head. Kayla lets out a groan, and Mom can't help but snicker at our predicament.

"Good luck, you two. I'm leaving so your grandparents and I can get seats in the gym. See you in a little bit, I hope."

I wave a goodbye at my mom as Kayla surveys the mess of makeup, hair accessories, and styling tools on Mom's dressing table.

"Okay, I've got it," she says, her eyes wide like a mad scientist who's figured out a plan for world domination. "Turn toward me."

I swivel to my left as she grabs a flat iron and runs it through my bangs. Next, she pulls my bangs off to the side, far above my eyebrow, and secures them behind my ear with a bobby pin. When she sets the plastic monstrosity on my head, the arm of the tiara obscures the pin, and my bangs are high enough on my forehead the tiara forces them down slightly, but I can still see. And being able to see where I'm going is going to be important, considering I have to

151

walk into a almost dark gym with a spotlight shining on me and nothing but Cody Hull's arm to keep me upright if I trip.

"Thanks," I tell Kayla, giving myself one last glance in the mirror. My dress is the same emerald green as my Prom dress, but it's a little shorter with a full skirt and spaghetti straps because I don't have the goods up top to pull off a strapless. The silver beading at the waistline is barely visible after I drape my "Senior Princess" sash across me. Kayla, meanwhile, is gorgeous as usual in a royal purple dress in a similar style, only she can pull off a strapless with little effort.

"Okay," she says, her final primping done. "Let's go dazzle the men."

And the men are appropriately dazzled. Brad twirls Kayla around and Kieran, in a dark gray suit with a tie that matches my dress—Kayla's doing, I imagine—gathers me into his arms.

"You're beautiful," he whispers.

"You know, I don't think I'll ever get tired of hearing you say that."

He gives me his familiar grin, and my insides turn to mush.

"Good. I don't plan on ever getting tired of saying it."

Over Kieran's shoulder, my gaze falls on Cooper and Victor milling around by the front door. I slip out of Kieran's arms and walk over to them, taking Cooper's hands in mine.

"You look wonderful, Ms. McKee," Victor says.

"Thank you. And you need to start calling me Zip."

Victor tilts his head at me in agreement, although I know he probably won't ever call me by my first name.

"You look great, Cooper," I tell him, taking in his tailored black suit and red tie. Kieran comes up behind me and puts his hands on my shoulders as Cooper gives us a crooked smile.

"Thanks. I feel a little awkward, though—I mean, more awkward than I should considering I don't, you know, *remember* anything." He casts a glance at Victor. "I understand I'm usually not without a date to such things."

Victor nods, and I can almost feel Kayla rolling her eyes behind me.

"Don't worry, Cooper," she says. "Zip and I have a couple of sad-ass friends with crappy ex-boyfriends. Once they get a look at you, you won't be without a dance partner for long."

"Are they as hot as you and Zip?" Cooper asks, his voice sounding a little too innocent.

"Down, boy," Kieran says with a laugh. "Brad and I don't want to hear that stuff. And you know I'm not going to say anyone's hotter than Zip because that's just impossible."

"Unless we're talking about Kayla, of course," Brad interjects and Kieran shrugs.

"Well, before we all puke from the overwhelming display of chivalry," I start, raising my hand to my shoulder to pat Kieran's wrist, "I'm supposed to be at school and on the arm of one of our friend's crappy ex-boyfriends in exactly seven minutes. So, we need to get a move-on."

We head out of the house and pile into Victor and Cooper's rented Escalade for the five-minute drive to school. Victor drops us off at the front steps, intending to park in the far corner of the lot and watch a college football game on his phone rather than coming to the dance—we figured showing up with the Laniers' obnoxiously wealthy "family friend" would be enough to explain to people without having the weirdness of his personal assistant and driver lurking around the gym as well. And while I'm all for avoiding weirdness, I can't help but feel a bit bad that Victor has to amuse himself for hours while we're inside. Once we're all out of the

153

Escalade, I turn back and signal for him to roll down the passenger window.

"Are you sure you're going to be okay out here?"

"I appreciate your concern, Ms. McKee, but I'll be fine. Go be the princess that you are."

I give him a warm smile that's shattered by Kayla's sniping.

"Zip! You've got one minute to get inside. No one wants Mrs. Gillette going ballistic on you."

Turning around, I take Kieran's hand and we trot up the stairs behind Kayla, Brad, and Cooper. They deposit me at the cafeteria doors, Kieran giving me a kiss near the ear and whispering "Good luck," before I bound inside past Mrs. Gillette's disappointed glare.

"Sorry," I mumble, grabbing the remaining set of white roses from the table next to her and taking my place in the line of royalty next to Cody Hull.

"Thought you weren't going to make it, Princess," he teases.

"Shut up," I say back, my voice full of snark.

Mrs. Gillette gives us final instructions on how to curtsey and bow when the time comes, which leads to a lot of snickering among the court. I don't know if Mrs. Gillette learned all of this royalty stuff to make up for birthing a punishing bruiser of a daughter—my former basketball teammate and Titusville graduate Marcy—but I don't think I'm alone in wishing I had a video of her stout frame simulating a ladylike curtsey and manly bow. Although apparently I might get one, as I hear Doug Callahan say, "Oh, this is *so* going on the web tomorrow," and I turn to catch him fiddling with his phone as Brittany giggles.

After an eternity of waiting in the school lobby for the other princesses to be introduced and escorted into the gym, it's finally my turn as I'm the last of the Senior Princesses alphabetically. Cody and I step out of the harsh brightness and into the gym, the soft lights up on

154

stage where the rest of the court is waiting for us all that guide our way. The sudden contrast of stark fluorescence with near dark, combined with the spotlight trained on us so the crowd can see—not to mention the flashes from the crowd's cameras—nearly blinds me, and now I understand why Mrs. Gillette's command to walk slowly was less of an order and more of a necessity.

"I can't see shit right now," Cody whispers.

"That makes two of us."

"Maybe we should get on our hands and knees and crawl."

"We'd probably get there faster. And stop trying to make me laugh," I hiss.

"Sorry," he mumbles.

Once we pass half court, my eyes adjust and I can make out the stairs leading to the stage in front of us. Eventually, our long journey comes to an end, and we take our places next to McKenna Dantino and Jake Tomlinson and await the arrival of Queen Brittany and Doug Callahan.

Once Brit is safely on her throne—which is actually a chair from the music room swathed in a purple sheet—Doug and the rest of the court stand before her, the girls curtseying and the guys bowing behind us. Our backs are to the assembled crowd and I hear giggles up and down the royal line, telling me I'm not the only one who counts this moment among the ridiculous things she's done in her life. After the curtseying embarrassment, I take my throne—also a chair from the music room, but mine's draped in a navy sheet and isn't elevated on a purple painted crate as Brittany's is.

Zach Bochine snaps pictures as the crowd breaks into thunderous applause, and a few parents—not mine, thankfully—make their way to the floor to get photos, only to be shooed away by Mrs. Gillette and the other chaperones so Queen Brittany can have her dance. Brit and Doug make their way to midcourt and everyone watches the two of them sway together, both of them probably wishing they could be dancing with their actual dates. The entire court takes the floor for the next song, everyone dancing as robotically as Brit and Doug. I spend the opening notes searching for Kieran, but I can't find him in the darkened gym. About halfway through the song, however, the lights come up a bit more as the rest of the crowd is invited to dance along with the court, and I spy Kieran sitting at the end of a bleacher seat with my mom and dad. Glancing around at the couples on the dance floor, I find Kayla and Brad swaying in rhythm next to Cassie and Cooper. Cass seems pretty comfortable in Cooper's arms, so I'm guessing he was introduced to her as someone other than "the hot guy who was staring at Zip at the Burger Barn in June."

"So, who's the dude with Cassie?" Cody asks me, following my gaze. I swivel my head back to him to find his expression is full of "I'm so going to kick that guy's ass" intentions, his eyes glowing and his jaw set in a tight line.

"He's a friend of the Laniers' who's visiting for the weekend, so we thought we'd bring him along," I explain, and before Cody can ask me anything else, I say, "Why are you looking at Cassie like you're going to beat the hell out of anyone who comes near her? *You* broke up with her this time, remember?"

Cody doesn't answer me, but keeps his focus on the mystery guy slow dancing with his ex. The song can't end soon enough, and when it does, my obligations to Cody—and to the Homecoming Court—are done. I step back from him and watch as his gaze locks with Cassie's across the gym. Cooper's giving her a confused look, so I dart over to him and link arms, steering him off toward my parents and Kieran as Cassie and Cody exchange a few words and start dancing together.

"Girlfriend's a little weird," Cooper informs me, glancing back at Cassie over his shoulder.

156

"You have no idea," I tell him.

My parents and Kieran rise from their bleacher seats as we approach, and my dad steps forward to gather me into a hug.

"You look great, honey. Really proud of you."

"Save your pride for when basketball season starts," I say. "Then I'll give you something to be proud of."

He steps back and squeezes my shoulder, saying "I'll hold you to that."

"I'll go onstage and get your roses and take them home," Mom says, pulling me into a hug. "I don't have the best record with plants, but maybe I can keep those alive for a few more days."

"Thanks, Mom."

She lets me go, and Kieran slides an arm around my waist as they start walking off toward the stage.

"Have fun tonight, guys," Dad says as he turns to wave at us.

Kieran, Cooper, and I call out "Thanks" at their backs, and then the three of us sit down on the bleachers to stare at people flailing around to the beat pulsing through the speakers. A slow song starts up and Kieran and I exchange glances before looking at Cooper.

"Coop? You okay if I dance with my girl? We won't go too far from the bleachers in case I have a moment, so we'll be right here if you need anything," Kieran tells him.

"Oh, yeah. I'm good." Cooper leans back, resting his elbows on the bleacher seat behind him. "I'll just sit here and take everything in. This is all kind of fascinating."

I give a little snort at the idea of anything about Titusville fascinating Cooper Halloran, but given his lack of memories, I guess life in general is fascinating to him right now.

Kieran and I fall into each other's arms a few feet from the bleachers, and out of the corner of my eye, I notice Cassie and Cody rocking back and forth together across the gym.

157

"You have no idea how happy I am we're together," I say, and Kieran follows my gaze and instantly understands.

"Me, too. I can't imagine not being with you."

We forget where we are and press against each other, kissing until Mrs. Gillette comes up and taps me on the shoulder. She shoots each of us a sharp look and walks away, and when we glance over at Cooper, he's laughing hysterically and pointing at us.

"Coop seems like he's doing okay," I say, giggling as Kieran makes an obscene hand gesture in Mrs. Gillette's general direction that she thankfully doesn't catch.

"Yeah. I mean, in a lot of ways, he's the same old Cooper. He just doesn't *remember* he's the same old Cooper."

"So, nothing at all's come back to him?"

Kieran shakes his head.

"I'm glad he's here and everything, and I'd never say it to Ben Halloran's face, but Coop's visit is kind of a waste. His life is in New York, and, I mean, I don't understand how this is all supposed to work, but it doesn't seem like he would have known us long enough for being here to make a difference."

We rock together until the song ends, and the hired DJ puts on another slow song. Kieran and I pull back from each other, both of us glancing over at Cooper, whose attention is fixated on the colored lights of the DJ booth at the far end of the gym.

"I feel kind of bad that he's sitting there all by himself," Kieran says.

"Me, too."

I survey the dance floor. Cassie is still pressed against Cody, and Lauren—dateless thanks to her recent breakup with Bill Burcheron, who admitted to her he spent the first quarter of his freshman year at Illinois sleeping around—is nowhere around at the moment. Everyone else I'd be comfortable introducing to Cooper is already paired up with someone.

Kieran and I stop dancing and face Cooper.

"Are you thinking what I'm thinking?" Kieran asks me.

"Probably."

We walk over to Cooper and he stands up.

"Want to dance?" I ask him.

"With you?"

Kieran rolls his eyes and says, "No. With me."

"Thanks, but I'm guessing you're not my usual type." Cooper laughs before looking at me for a second and shifting his gaze back to Kieran. "You're really okay with this?"

"As long as you return her to me," Kieran tells him.

"Oh, trust me," I say. "I'll make sure of that."

Cooper puts an arm around my waist and leads me to the spot on the floor where Kieran and I were a few seconds earlier. And he behaves like a perfect gentleman, keeping his hands in the appropriate places and not saying a word—snarky or otherwise—until the song is about half over.

"What is this?" he says, grimacing almost as if he's in pain, which is understandable because this song, whatever it is, totally sucks. The singer sounds like Maisie Baker, Cooper's publicity-stunt girlfriend from a couple years ago, and the lyrics are some simplistically rhyming stuff about a relationship gone wrong:

It was all just pretend
Should have known it had to end
Shouldn't be a big mystery
Why we could never be
We were lying from the start
But the truth is, you broke my heart
So why won't my heart mend

If it was all just pretend?

"Sounds like Maisie Baker," I tell him, cringing. "I'm not a fan so I wouldn't know, but maybe this one is new or something. It's not familiar at all."

Maisie Baker is one of those artists whose songs are hard to avoid even if you don't consciously seek them out. Shopping at the mall? Maisie Baker's probably playing in the store. Flipping through radio stations? Pause for a second, and you'll probably stop on a Maisie Baker song. Watching TV? One of her songs will be the soundtrack to at least one commercial per show. Even though I don't like her music, it's inescapable enough that I can guess right now we're listening to a just-released tune.

Cooper stops swaying and stares up at the ceiling as if Maisie's voice is coming from the rafters before he darts his gaze to the floor and begins blinking.

"I...I know these lyrics." He squeezes his eyes shut. "She said those things to me...when we broke up."

My mouth falls open, while at the same time, Cooper leans forward, resting his forehead on my shoulder.

"Wow. I have the most amazing headache all of a sudden," he tells me, his voice almost a whimper.

Having witnessed the weirdness that just took place on the dance floor, Kieran's at my side in seconds.

"What's happening?"

I lean into Kieran as much as I can with Cooper's girth holding down my other side.

"I think his memory's coming back," I yell over the music.

Kieran's eyes widen, and his shoulders lurch in a telltale sign of weakness. I don't know how much longer I can support Cooper leaning against me with his full weight, so I can't deal with Kieran passing out on me, too.

160

"Kieran," I snap, and his drooping eyes pop back open to full size. "I need you to find Kayla and Brad. I don't think I can hold Cooper up for long, and if any of the chaperones look over here right now, they're probably going to think either one or both of you is trying to grope me."

"I might need to get some air," Cooper mumbles against my shoulder.

Kieran takes a few deep breaths, his expression wild as he surveys the crowd. I can't see much beyond Cooper's shoulder, his bulk weighing me down, but from the corner of my eye I catch Kieran raise his arm and wave, and seconds later, Brad is at my side, lifting Cooper off me.

"Can you walk?" Brad says to him.

Cooper lifts his head and nods.

"I think so. My head hurts *so bad*."

Brad's status as an ex-football player is coming in handy right now as he's able to half-drag Cooper from the gym by himself with the rest of us flanking them. Luckily, we're close enough to the gym doors that we don't have to walk through the crowd, and as I turn back, I notice only a few people at the edge of the dance floor staring at us, the rest of the attendees jumping around behind them to the song now pulsing through the speakers. And I'm guessing anyone watching assumes Cooper's either drunk or high because that would be my best guess if I were standing where they are right now. Unfortunately, Principal Rosner definitely thinks Cooper's messed up as we step into the brightly-lit lobby.

"What's going on with that young man?" he asks, rising from his seat behind the ticket table as we shuffle Cooper past him.

"Keep moving," Kayla hisses at Brad.

"Stop," Rosner commands. "Is he drunk?"

161

I'm gripping Kieran's hand with all my might, hoping the anxiety flowing through my body is electric enough to keep him from toppling over right now.

"He's not drunk," I snap at Rosner, a little testier than I should be with the person who holds my permanent academic and behavioral record under his command. "He's *sick*. He has a migraine. We're taking him home."

Rosner sits back down, looking almost disappointed to be missing out on a chance at busting an underage drinker.

"Oh. Oh. I'm sorry, Zara. I hope your friend is okay."

I nod and guide Kieran outside, grateful at the moment for my reputation around school as an upstanding citizen. Kayla and Brad are already in the parking lot, practically dragging Cooper off toward the far spaces where Victor's parked.

"Victor!" Brad yells, when they're a few feet behind the Escalade, and Victor must either hear or see them or both because he opens the driver's side door and steps out onto the pavement, his movements jumping into hyper-speed once he finds all of us hobbling toward him.

"Mr. Halloran?" Victor asks after he rounds the Escalade and opens the passenger door. When Cooper doesn't answer, Victor's mouth drops open. "What happened?"

He and Brad get a passed-out Cooper into the front seat as Kieran and I, finally caught up, stop behind Kayla.

"He remembered something while we were dancing," I explain. "The DJ was playing some Maisie Baker song, and Cooper said something about her saying the words in the lyrics to him. Then he started talking about how he had a massive headache."

"But the elder Mr. Halloran and I have been playing Ms. Baker's songs ever since Mr. Halloran was brought out of the coma. Nothing's worked." Victor shakes his head. "Ms. Baker's on tour at

162

the moment or we would have invited her to the residence as well. I don't understand why this is happening now."

"I think that song might be new," Kayla says, confirming my earlier hypothesis. "I read something about it on the web the other day."

"Regardless, we need to get Cooper back to your house," Brad says to her, leaning inside to glance at Cooper before sticking his head back out. "Your mom will know what to do."

Kieran grows weaker and heavier against me, and Kayla moves to help me get him in the car.

"Oh, yes—Mom *always* knows what to do," Kayla spits as we buckle Kieran in and slide into our own seats for the ride home.

Chapter 14

By the time we park in the Laniers' driveway, Kieran's fast asleep and Cooper's still passed out. The rest of us proceed to spend what to any outsider would look like a comical few minutes attempting to wake them. Victor gets out and walks over to the passenger side of the vehicle, opening the door and slapping Cooper solidly on both cheeks as Kayla and I each shake one of Kieran's shoulders, me from behind in the second back seat and Kayla from the bucket seat next to him. Kieran wakes up first, his grogginess more pronounced than usual because we're no longer where we were when he fell asleep.

"What's going on?" he asks, staring over at his sister.

"Cooper's memory's coming back," Kayla says, opening her door and not waiting to find out if Kieran remembers anything from when we were still at school. We all pile out of the Escalade, Victor—not a small guy himself, by any means—half-dragging a barely lucid Cooper down the path to the house. Victor had called ahead as soon as we pulled out of the school parking lot, and so Carlie and Jim are outside on the front porch before Victor's even halfway down the walk.

"Oh, my God. Cooper," Carlie says, barreling down the few stairs from the porch to the walk and taking Cooper's face in her hands.

"Hey, Carlie," he mumbles, still not fully with us.

With Jim's help, Victor gets Cooper inside to the living room couch and, ever the assistant, removes Cooper's shoes so he can lie down and put his feet up. Carlie places a throw pillow behind Cooper's head while the siblings, Brad, and I stand behind the couch, waiting for whatever's going to happen next.

Carlie sits on the edge of the coffee table and leans down to Cooper's ear as if he would have trouble hearing her. "Cooper, can you tell us what happened at the dance?" she prompts in a comforting voice.

I'm a little confused as to why Carlie's asking this because Victor already gave her the play-by-play on the way home. But then the reason hits me—she wants to hear the details from Cooper himself because she wants to know what he remembers.

"Zip and I were dancing to this song, and as I started listening to the lyrics, I realized they sounded a lot like all this stuff Maisie said to me when we broke up." He blinks rapidly and glances around. "And that's when I got the headache and then I woke up here."

Victor, who has been tapping around on his phone, asks, "Was this the song?" He presses his thumb against the screen and the awful song from the dance fills the living room, sounding even more crappy thanks to the tin-can quality of Victor's phone speakers. We all listen for a minute, Cooper's face contorted as if he's trying to concentrate. Once Maisie returns to the chorus for a second time, Cooper bolts upright on the couch and puts his head in his hands. Carlie stands and places a shaking hand on his shoulder.

"Cooper?"

Cooper drops his hands and glances around at all of us, smiling.

"I remember...God, it's so vivid. Like everything just happened." He stares forward at nothing in particular. "She came over and we were sitting in my room, and she's telling me her handlers want her to break up with me." He looks around at each of us. "I don't know why, though."

"I think I can clear things up for you, Mr. Halloran," Victor starts, nodding, "but tell us what you remember first."

"Okay." Cooper shuts his eyes again and doesn't open them as he speaks. "She was saying she didn't really want to break up, but I'd ruined everything and there was no way her people were going to let us keep seeing each other, and she was disappointed enough in me she wasn't sure she *wanted* to keep seeing me." He opens his eyes and pulls his knees up under his chin. "She said she couldn't understand why it hurt so much to have to break up with me because the whole thing was for show. And I said something like, 'Right. It was all just pretend, so eventually the relationship was going to end anyway.' I was trying to be all cool and stuff, but I remember feeling really, really bad for some reason. Then she was crying and stuff, and saying things didn't seem pretend to her after a while but after what happened, we couldn't have a real relationship." Cooper looks up at Victor standing at the end of the couch. "Jesus, Vic—what did I do to this girl?"

Victor fills in the missing pieces that Cooper had told us about when we first met him. Ben Halloran had cooked up a scheme with Maisie Baker's management to have Cooper and Maisie pretend to be dating because Cooper had been photographed passed out in a restaurant due to his sleeping disorder. With the tabloids screaming about how the future CEO of Halloran Industries was likely either a drunk or a drug addict, and with Maisie Baker's career having been built around sappy love songs about a boyfriend who didn't exist in real life, Ben Halloran and Maisie Baker's people pushed the two kids into a fake relationship to help everyone's images. But when Cooper fell asleep on Maisie at a restaurant and paparazzi captured the incident, Maisie had to break up with Cooper or risk the press tormenting her for being the good girl who couldn't tame the bad boy after all.

"I don't remember any of that. I guess I just remember the aftermath," Cooper says sadly, still staring at Victor. After a long minute, he cocks his head to his side and then straightens up again. "Victor Loughlin," he announces, his eyes boring into his assistant. "Your mother, Carmen, came with her family from Puerto Rico as a child and settled in Jersey City. Your father, Peter, was a bricklayer and your mother worked as a custodian at Halloran's Midtown office building for years. Since your parents were working all the time, you were raised mostly by your grandmother, who never learned to speak English, and so you're bilingual. Your mother helped you get a job as one of our family drivers, and my dad was so impressed with your professionalism and work ethic, he assigned you to be my driver and personal assistant when I was twelve. Dad always said to us he hoped some of your good qualities would rub off on me."

We're all taken by surprise by Cooper's speech, none of us more so than Cooper himself, who glances back and forth between Victor and Carlie with wild eyes as if someone else had inhabited his body and was speaking through him.

"Correct, sir," Victor says smiling.

Kieran's holding my hand so tightly as we watch this scene unfold that it's starting to go numb, while Cooper takes his eyes from Victor and turns once again to Carlie.

"So, I can remember details from *Victor's* life, but I can't remember anything from mine, except for Maisie Baker crying her eyes out in my bedroom after she dumped me?"

Carlie reaches out and places a comforting hand on Cooper's shoulder.

"Things will probably come back in bits and pieces for a while." She pauses. "Do you remember anything about anyone else?"

Cooper fixes his gaze on each of us in turn and shakes his head, saying "Sorry."

"It's okay," Carlie assures him, before looking over to Jim, who is at the end of the couch near Victor. "Honey, can you get my

167

medical bag from the bedroom, please? And can you call Ben Halloran as well? He'll want to know what's going on."

Jim nods and leaves the room as Carlie keeps her hand on Cooper's shoulder as if she's anchoring him to the couch. She angles her arm so she can check the time on her watch. "Zip," she starts, glancing up at me, "could you call over to your grandparents' house and ask if Morgan's home yet, please? I think he should come over. He used to get headaches like this, too, when he first started remembering things. Maybe he and Cooper should have a talk."

"Sure thing," I say, pulling Kieran out into the hall with me as I dig in my tiny bag for my phone. Kieran, breathing heavily and obviously a bit overcome with all of the excitement, sits on the stairs as I stand above him and explain the situation to Gram, who informs me Morgan's just come home from work and she'll send him over in a few minutes. I'm hanging up just as Jim bounds down the stairs past us, holding his mobile phone out and away from him in one hand and carrying a black medical bag in the other.

"Carlie," he begins, looking at his wife from the hallway, "it's Ben."

Carlie rounds the couch and takes the phone from Jim.

"Ben...Ben...yes," she starts, walking down the hall to the kitchen.

I sink to the stairs next to Kieran, studying his drained expression.

"You're exhausted," I tell him, reaching out to stoke his hair.

"I am, but I don't want to miss anything." He tilts his head toward the living room, where we can see the backs of Cooper's and Victor's heads as they sit next to each other on the couch. Jim walks into the room and sits down in one of the easy chairs, saying nothing, while Kayla and Brad hang awkwardly on the perimeter of the room, bit players in the drama unfolding before them. "Story of my life," Kieran mumbles. "I'm always missing something."

I slide my arm around Kieran as he rests his head on my shoulder. He's about to drift off to sleep, Carlie's voice floating to us from the kitchen not loud enough to keep him awake, when the sound of the doorbell forces his head to dart upright. Since I'm sitting closer than anyone else at the moment, I get up and open the door for Morgan, still in his grease-stained t-shirt and jeans after a shift at the Diner.

"Gram said Cooper's memory's coming back?" he asks, stuffing his hands in his pockets. I motion him inside as Carlie speeds down the hall, the phone still to her ear.

"Ben? Can I call you back? Morgan's here. I'll examine Cooper as best I can and get back to you. Yes? Okay...'Bye." Carlie taps the phone screen while putting an arm around Morgan, guiding him to the living room. I lean up against the door frame as Morgan rounds the couch, crouching next to the coffee table just a few inches in front of Cooper.

"Hey, kid," Morgan starts. "Remember me?"

Cooper moves his head back and forth slowly.

"That's okay," Morgan assures him. "I didn't remember anything about your mom for a long, long time, and I had no idea you existed until we met," he reminds Cooper.

Cooper's mother, a Connecticut socialite with a craving for any drug she could get her hands on, had been mixed up with Morgan, his girlfriend Jenna, and Frank Dozier when they were younger. Frank's relationship with Cooper's mother led to her pregnancy with Cooper, which she didn't discover until after her parents had brought her home to get straightened out. Frank and Morgan went to jail for the armed robbery that resulted in Jenna's death during a police shootout, and Morgan never knew Frank had a son—at least, not until that son showed up here in Titusville earlier in the summer with a faded piece of paper containing the remnants of the drug formula that made Kieran and Cooper the way they are—or *were*, in Cooper's case.

Morgan had buried the formula on a farm that had been in Cooper's mother's family for generations, information that had been lost somewhere inside Morgan's brain for years. But after meeting Cooper and seeing the paper with what was left of the original formula, Morgan's long buried memories—a side effect from using the original drug—began to return. Over the last few months, he's recalled knowing Virgina Malsun, Cooper's mother, and eventually, he remembered one time in particular when he, Frank, Virginia, and Jenna had traveled to the upstate New York farm for a weekend-long drug binge, which is how Morgan knew of the farm and chose it as his hiding place after the armed robbery went south.

Carlie walks over and, bending slightly at the waist, puts her hand on Morgan's shoulder. "Morgan's memory loss was even more pronounced than yours," she tells Cooper. "After I give you a brief exam, I'm going to compare your symptoms." She nods across the coffee table at the doctor's bag Jim placed on the edge when he walked into the room.

Cooper eyes Morgan with suspicion and mumbles, "So, how long did you go before you started remembering things?"

I draw in a breath as a momentary flash of panic crosses Morgan's face.

"Not long," he lies, obviously not wanting to crush Cooper by admitting the original drug had caused pockets of memory loss that afflicted him for nearly twenty years. He gets to his feet and steps aside, saying, "I'm going to let Carlie get started with checking you out."

Carlie moves for her bag, Morgan shuffles to the easy chair in the corner, and I glance over my shoulder to find Kieran snoozing away on the bottom stair, his head against the wall.

"Kayla," I hiss, jerking my head toward the hallway. She leans forward and gazes past me to her sleeping brother. We walk out into the hall with Brad following, and Kayla sinks down on the step next to Kieran.

"We should get him to bed," she suggests. "I don't think anything else shocking's going to happen tonight that we can't fill him in on tomorrow."

"You got this?" Brad says to Kayla, nodding down at Kieran before he bumps my elbow and shifts his eyes to me. "I don't know about you, but I'm sensing we're a little unnecessary right now."

Kayla nods and leans forward, assessing what's going on in the other room.

"Yeah. You two might as well go," she says. "I'll call if anything earth shattering happens, but like I said, I think the big shockers are over for tonight. I can get Kieran upstairs."

Brad leans down to kiss Kayla, and he and I slip out of the house unnoticed thanks to the activity in the living room. Out on the front porch, the night air prompts my skin to break out in goose bumps, and I must be shivering since Brad takes off his suit jacket and hands it to me.

"Here. This should keep you warm enough until we get to your house."

"Thanks," I say, slipping the jacket on and taking off my shoes, dangling them from my left hand as we descend the stairs to the Laniers' front walk. We stroll in silence until we're past the garage and out into the scrubby grass and dirt separating the Lanier house from mine.

"Some night, huh?" I mumble at last.

"You could say that." Brad laughs at first, but his pleasant expression fades almost immediately. "How do you do this, Zip?"

"This?"

He sighs, hair falling back off his forehead as he studies the sky almost as if searching for the right words.

"Being in love with a Lanier."

Now it's my turn to laugh.

"Not the easiest thing in the world, is it?"

"Not at all." Brad shakes his head and jams his hands into the pockets of his dress pants. "The first time I met Kayla, I was like, 'Wow—she's amazing.' And as long as I was talking to her about regular stuff—you know, school and sports and music and things like that—everything was great. She was this smart, funny girl I loved hanging out with. But every time I tried to get to know *her*, this wall went up."

"Sounds familiar."

"She pushed me so far away after Prom I didn't think we'd ever put things back together. And after she finally leveled with me about her family, I wasn't sure I *wanted* to. But now that I know what she's been through all these years, I have such an amazing respect for her. You were a big part of helping me realize that, Zip."

After Kayla revealed her past and the Lanier secrets to Brad, I'd spent some time talking things out with him, trying to help him understand that much like everything else in her life, lying to him was just another thing Kayla felt she had to do. But, obviously, Brad still struggles with being part of the Laniers' inner circle, and he's evidently struggling right now.

"It just seems like it never ends," he continues. "There's always some secret, some drama. At least I'm away from it sometimes now that I'm at school. You're around this *every day*, and you've been around it every day for months. I don't understand how you don't go

172

crazy sometimes." Brad glances over his shoulder at the Laniers' house, all lit up against the inky black of the rural Illinois sky. "I mean, Carlie's back there right now giving Cooper a physical, which, technically, she shouldn't be able to do unless she's licensed to practice medicine in Illinois. And the whole 'secret research' thing with this formula? I want to be a doctor someday, and this is all pretty shady. Sometimes, I wonder if I should be around any of it."

I merely hitch my shoulders up because I'm not sure what to say. I've spent a while now trying to push the shadiness of the Lanier/Levert/Malsun/Halloran family dealings to the back of my mind in favor of focusing on Kieran and the hope of an eventual remedy for his condition. But sometimes, the moral ambiguities bubble to the surface for me in a way that they apparently do more often for Brad. Morgan saved Kieran and me on Prom night, but he had to steal a car to do it, a crime that's gone unpunished. Ben Halloran is pouring time and money into developing a treatment for his son and Kieran, but he's using Halloran employees and Halloran resources to do it in secret. And I hadn't even thought about Carlie until Brad brought it up just now. She hasn't practiced medicine—in Illinois or anywhere else—for years, yet she was, to my understanding, a vital part of the research team developing the formula.

We descend into silence again until we've reached Brad's truck, which is parked in the grass next to my driveway so my mom would be able to pull her car back under the carport when she arrived home from the Homecoming ceremony.

"Brad," I say, turning to face him. "You love Kayla, right?"

"Of course."

"Well, first of all, good luck with that," I start, and he gives me a little laugh. "But if you love her, you'll stick by her, no matter how messy this gets," I tell him, and I have a brief memory flash of Jilly saying something similar to me when she was here in July. "And if Kayla loves you, which I know she does, then she'll understand if you need to distance yourself from all of this craziness every once in a while. Just be open with her about it, okay? If you start pulling back and you're not honest about why, she'll freak out and bolt. It took a lot of work and some changes in circumstances for her to be able to tell you everything. Now isn't the time for you two to stop being real with each other about stuff."

Brad nods at me as if what I'm saying makes sense, and I follow his gaze back across the field to the Lanier house.

"Wonder what's going on over there right now?" he muses, almost to himself.

"No clue. My heart's breaking for Cooper, though. I can't imagine feeling as lost as he does."

"No kidding." Brad pauses for a beat before asking me. "So, not that this is going to happen, but what would you do if what happened to Cooper happened to Kieran? I mean, what if he'd taken the treatment and woke up and didn't remember who you were?"

I can't bring myself to meet Brad's stare, but instead keep my eyes riveted on the house in the distance, recalling Cooper's vacant stare last night at the game when we were introduced to each other, the way he seemed to be, at first, looking *through* me and not *at* me. And I remember the confusion in his face as he appeared to be trying so desperately to remember who I was, this person everyone was telling him he'd already met.

I don't want to imagine having to be re-introduced to my own boyfriend.

Kicking at the grass with my bare foot, I continue to avoid Brad's gaze.

"I don't know 'what if,'" I tell him finally. "Hopefully, I'll never have to."

174

CHAPTER 15

After all these months, nothing about Cooper Halloran should surprise me. And, yet, I'm still shocked when he and Victor show up at my door the Saturday evening of the Fall Antiques Festival, three weeks to the day after his memories started resurfacing on the dance floor at Titusville's Homecoming.

"Coop?" I squint at him standing on my front step, Victor lurking around on the lawn behind him.

"In the flesh," he says, spreading his arms out before him, his flesh in reality hidden from me by jeans, boots, and a navy t-shirt under a distressed leather jacket. Fresh from a shower, my damp hair dripping down my back, I'm wearing only a thin Wyatt County-Sumner College Summer Basketball League shirt and plaid sleep pants, and I hug my arms around myself to ward off the chill entering the house through the open door.

"You're freezing," Coop says, taking note of my behavior. "Can Vic and I come in?"

I shake off my surprise at seeing him and step back. "Of course," I tell him, sweeping my arm out to invite them inside.

Cooper bounds into the living room and makes himself at home on the couch while Victor, ever formal, stands next to me as I close the front door.

"Sorry to disturb you like this, Ms. McKee," he says sheepishly. "We wouldn't normally barge in on you like this, but Mr. Halloran insisted on surprising you."

"Because I love nothing more than a good surprise from Cooper Halloran," I say with obvious snarkiness, staring at Cooper rather than at Victor and Cooper just laughs at me.

"Oh, come on, Zip. Surprising you is priceless." He reclines, stretching his arm across the back of the couch and looking me up and down. "Although, this would have been more fun if you'd been wearing a bathrobe. Seriously—who doesn't wear a bathrobe when she gets out of the shower?"

I exhale and tap my bare foot against the carpet.

"What are you doing here, Coop?"

He indulges in his lizard grin before answering.

"I heard this was the weekend of the Fall Antiques Festival."

"You don't strike me as being the 'antiques' type."

Cooper pouts and grabs his chest as if I've mortally insulted him while Victor leans toward me and says, "I love antiques, actually."

"Really?"

He gives me a broad smile and responds, "No, not really. I'm just kidding."

"I've been working with Vic on his sense of humor. I'm trying to get him to loosen up a bit," Cooper explains.

I pat Victor on the back and say to Cooper, "Keep working on it."

"We will, Ms. McKee," Victor says, returning to his serious self. "Mr. Halloran wanted to speak with Mr. Lanier in person about his experiences since the treatment, and Mr. Lanier had mentioned this was weekend was a special weekend in Titusville."

"So was Homecoming," I point out, my eyes still fixed on Cooper. "You know, the Christmas Parade is right before we get out of school for the holidays in case you wanted to mark your calendar."

Cooper shakes his head and gives me a sad smile.

"He won't listen to me, Zip," Cooper points out in reference to Kieran. "I thought maybe if he could see me in person—"

"It won't work."

I fold my arms over my chest. Once Cooper went back to New York after Homecoming, his memory began to return in tiny trickles at first and then, after about a week, in a flood of recollections. Although some of his childhood memories are still a mystery, he remembers everything that's happened to him over the last few years and, if today is any indication, he's returned to being the same old Cooper we all know and love...or, well, *like*, anyway. He's spent the previous week calling and texting Kieran repeatedly, trying to get him to undergo the treatment. But after watching Cooper walk around like a hollow-eyed version of himself, Kieran has no interest in taking something that will cause memory loss, no matter how temporary.

"He hasn't seen me like *this*," Cooper insists. "The last time, I didn't have any of the sleeping disorder symptoms, but I was kind of...*blank*, I guess."

Blank is a pretty accurate descriptor, and Victor must think so, too, because I catch him nodding along with me.

"But now, I'm my old self, but without the sleeping disorder. My memory's mostly back, and I'm totally fine. Hell, I'm better than fine. I'm *perfect*."

I can't help but snicker at Cooper assessment of himself.

"Don't push your luck, Coop."

He drags his arm from the back of the couch and leans forward, elbows on his knees.

"You get what I mean. I want to show him what he can do, what his life can be like."

"So, you're surprising him, too, I take it?"

"The Laniers' house is the next stop on our 'Surprise Tour.' Want to join us?" Cooper grins and I shake my head.

"They won't be home. Jim and Carlie took him to the festival and I'm supposed to be meeting them in a little while."

"Guess we're going straight to the festivities, then," Cooper pronounces. "How about if Vic and I give you a ride?"

"Might as well," I say, hitching my shoulders. "I need a few minutes to get dressed. You guys want anything to drink while you're waiting? Soda? Tea?" I offer since I've been ambushed into being a hostess for the time being.

Victor shakes his head and Cooper says, "Nah, I'm good." I nod toward a worn easy chair, and Victor reads my silent invitation and sits down. "I'll be ready in a few minutes," I assure them, starting for the hall.

"I'd be glad to help," Cooper offers, rising from the couch. He's obviously joking, but I put Victor on alert regardless.

"Victor, if he takes one step down this hallway, I'll scream so loud they'll hear me all the way in New York."

"I won't let him out of my sight, Ms. McKee."

In my room, I take a few minutes to blow dry my hair and get dressed in jeans and a thick cable sweater, fastening my charm bracelet around my left wrist before slipping into my Chucks and rejoining my surprise guests in the living room. They both stand, Cooper stepping to me and offering his arm. "You look really nice," he says.

I don't take his arm, but I bump my shoulder against his. "Thanks."

"You're welcome."

Cooper and I exchange warm smiles. Sometimes, when he's not being a total creeper, he's kind of okay.

Less than five minutes later, Victor pulls us into one of the few remaining parking spaces on Main Street, nearly a block away from River Bend Park. Most people who live in Titusville can walk to the festival, considering most of the town's population lives within a four-block radius of the park. But anyone who lives "out in the country," like I do, where no sidewalks line the roads into town, or anyone from "*way* out in the country," like some of the families in the Titusville School District who live out in Rainey or on farms in the general area, would need to drive to the festival, creating Titusville's annual version of a traffic jam and parking mess.

"So, this thing must be a pretty big deal around here," Cooper notes, looking around at some of the other people making their way down the sidewalk toward River Avenue and the park.

"Other than Homecoming and the Christmas Parade, this is the *only* deal around here," I confirm, as a strange but intoxicating mix of food scents wafts toward us. Cooper angles his nose up slightly, breathing in the night air thick with kettle corn, caramel apples, bratwurst, and ketchup.

"Everything smells really good and really weird all at the same time," he says to me. "How is that?"

I laugh at his alien behavior and ask, "The Prince of the Upper West Side has never been to a festival, has he?"

"I don't think so."

"The San Gennaro Festival in Little Italy, sir," Victor says suddenly. "You'd seen something about it on television, and your father asked me to take you. That wasn't too long after I started working for you, so you were about twelve. I don't know why we never went back after that." He tilts his head toward the lights and commotion ahead of us. "This reminds me a little of that night. Mix in some Italian food, and it would be just about the same."

Something tells me a street festival in New York City would probably be a lot different than Titusville's dinky Antiques Festival, but Victor's just too polite to say so.

"I don't remember that at all," Cooper says, shaking his head at Victor's story before glancing at me. "Some things are still kind of fuzzy. It's frustrating."

179

"Patience, sir. Everything will come back eventually," Victor assures him.

We've reached the edge of the park, and Victor and Cooper look to me for guidance on which way we should go. Music carries over to us from a grandstand at the south end, and directly in front of us is a line of booths with various carnival games. At the end of the park near the Downtown Diner are the antiques and craft booths that give the festival its name, and knowing my mom has a booth set up, I decide the antiques and craft booths would be as good a place as any to start our exploration. I text Kieran to tell him I'm headed to Mom's booth and lead my guests off toward the line of tents near the Diner.

Kieran and his parents must have been in the vicinity because they're already waiting for us when we arrive a minute or so later, everyone's eyes widening on seeing who's with me.

"Coop!" Kieran says, stepping out into the grassy path in front of a large open tent my mom's set up to display arts and crafts from her store. He and Cooper exchange one of those brief, slap-on-the-back hugs guys always seem to engage in when they know each other too well just to say "hi," and Kieran glances back and forth between Victor and Cooper. "What are you guys doing here?"

"Uh…antiquing, I guess?" Cooper mumbles, picking up the first object on the table lining the front of Mom's booth, which happens to be a copper earring holder my mom's fashioned into the shape of a tree.

"That's not an antique," Mom corrects him from behind the table. "That's an April Shipman original. All the antiques tents are further down, closer to the river." She waves her arm in the general direction of the river bank.

Cooper turns the earring tree over in his hands as if he's trying to examine it from all angles.

"I'll take it," he says, looking up at Mom. "I think I know someone who might appreciate this."

Behind Cooper's back, Kieran and I exchange glances, and I'm pretty sure we're both making a mental note to ask Cooper about his strange purchase at some point when we're alone. My mom wraps the earring tree in tissue paper and puts it in a plastic bag while Carlie moves next to Cooper, gathering him in a warm embrace. "How are you?" she asks, pressing her cheek against his hair.

"I'm great, thanks. Never better," he says pointedly, glancing beyond Carlie to Kieran. "My short-term memory is back completely, and every day I remember something else from my past." He nods toward Victor, who's milling around on the far side of Mom's booth, checking out some beaded earrings that are also April Shipman originals. "We wanted to come back this weekend because I felt a little bad about all the commotion I caused when I was here over Homecoming. Wasn't exactly the ideal visit."

"Feeling bad isn't necessary," Jim points out, shaking Cooper's hand. "We were just happy your memory started to come back."

Cooper moves from Carlie's embrace and shrugs.

"Well, I also wanted to come here and spend some quality time with Kieran as 'New and Improved Cooper,' since I was so out of it before."

Kieran lets out a laugh and walks over next to me, reaching for my hand.

"'New and Improved Cooper'?" he parrots. "I can only imagine what *that* means."

"It means I'm doing everything I've ever wanted to do and more," Cooper says with a knowing smile, handing some money over to my mother for the earring tree.

"I can hold this for you here if you kids want to walk around the festival for a while," she offers.

"Thanks," Cooper says as she puts the bag under the table.

"Where are Gram and Gramps, by the way?" I ask, knowing that an annual eleven o'clock ritual during the festival is the three of us helping Mom pack up her wares to cart them across the street to the store for the night before bringing them back over Sunday afternoon.

"Dad went off in search of funnel cake and Mom went after him to complain about his cholesterol levels and try to talk him out of it," Mom explains with a smile. "You know—just an average Saturday night at the Titusville Fall Antiques Festival."

Laughing, Jim and Carlie excuse themselves to leave but not before reminding Kieran he needs to be home in plenty of time to be in bed by eleven, which is the strict bedtime he keeps in order to hold his sleeping episodes at bay. He accepts their reminder with a sugary smile as Cooper raises his eyebrows at him.

"April, tell Barbara and Larry we'll talk to them tomorrow," Carlie says, reaching out to squeeze my mother's hand. "There were a few antique booths I didn't get to tonight."

Mom looks past Carlie to Jim and says, "Don't forget your credit cards," which produces a hearty guffaw from Jim before the two of them walk off toward River Avenue, leaving Victor and the three of us kids alone with my mom.

"The midway's open 'til eleven, too," Mom says to the males, who wouldn't know since they've never been here before. "You guys should battle it out at the ring toss to see which one of you can win a stuffed animal for my daughter."

"Aaaand...we're leaving now, Mom," I say, turning Kieran around to face the midway and its commotion of lights and noise as Cooper laughs and falls in next to us on my other side with Victor following behind us as we walk away. "I own enough stuffed animals from this thing for one lifetime," I tell them. "No competition necessary."

We stroll down the midway, watching Titusville's kids try their luck at the carnival games. I see Brittany Solomon, all dressed up with her tiara on her head and her "Homecoming Queen" sash draped across her, standing in front of the squirt gun game getting her picture taken with some little girls. When I wave to her, she shoots me a quick, goofy grimace before relaxing her mouth into a smile more befitting her beauty queen status, and I continue heading toward the end of the midway with the guys.

"So," Kieran starts, glancing across me to Cooper. "I'm assuming 'new and improved' doesn't mean you've developed a love for antiques."

"No." He laughs, running a hand through his hair. "I definitely wouldn't recommend taking the treatment if *that* were one of the side effects."

"Cooper—" Kieran begins, sighing, but Cooper doesn't let him get anything else out.

"Every time we talk on the phone or text, you blow me off. I wanted to come here so you'd have to pay attention to what your life could be like."

Kieran cocks his head at his friend.

"And what am I supposed to be seeing?"

"A guy who doesn't have to go to bed at eleven o' clock, for one thing," Cooper fires back as Kieran purses his lips. "And a guy who doesn't have to worry about falling asleep at the slightest bit of physical exertion. Like, I don't have to limit myself to push ups and sit ups and crunches anymore."

For emphasis, Cooper takes off his jacket and hands it to Victor so he can roll the sleeve of his t-shirt up over his shoulder, revealing an arm that doesn't appear to be any more muscular than it did three weeks ago.

"I can lift actual weights, instead of Vic here spotting me when I work out with dinky hand weights. Do you know how humiliating that was?"

Victor returns Cooper's jacket to him as Kieran says, "I can only imagine," with a flatness to his voice. Kieran's never shown much desire to be the athletic type, outside an interest in basketball that's mostly about me. So, trying to convince Kieran the treatment is worth it just so he can lift weights isn't going to work.

"My whole life, we've had a weight room in the house, and I've never been able to use it until now. And I'm going to learn how to swim, finally. I live in a house with an indoor pool, and I've never learned to swim. And this summer, I'm getting my driver's license."

"You live in New York City *and* you have your own driver," I say to him, glancing behind us at Victor. "Why do you need to learn to drive?"

"I don't *need* to. I *want* to, because now I can. Besides, we have a house in the Hamptons, and I want to be able to go places by myself when we're there. Nobody uses a driver out there if they're old enough," he informs us, the "duh" tone to his voice suggesting we should have already known how life in the Hamptons is supposed to work.

"Sounds like he's trying to make you obsolete, Vic," Kieran says.

"It would be my pleasure to be obsolete where Mr. Halloran is concerned. I always knew the day would come eventually, perhaps when he married and established his own household. But I'd rather he be independent sooner than later. And the elder Mr. Halloran has assured me I will always have a place at Halloran Industries."

"Not to mention I still need someone to spot me when I lift," Cooper chimes in.

"Of course." Kieran rolls his eyes at me, and I do the same back to him.

"And I'll always need Victor to some extent," Cooper continues. "I mean, I'm rich, for God's sake. I shouldn't have to do *everything* for myself."

"You're not really making your case, Coop," Kieran says with a smile.

Cooper stops walking and turns to face Kieran, right in front of the Funhouse. But we don't need to go in and view ourselves in the distortion mirrors because we're experiencing enough distortion out here on the midway right now.

"Look, Kieran, here's the deal. I sleep when I want to now. I go to bed when I decide I want to go to bed—none of this staying on a rigid sleep schedule crap. Two nights ago, I stayed up all night watching movies, just because I could. I watched the sun rise, and it was awesome." Cooper's eyes flick away for a moment as he remembers, and I can only imagine that watching the sun come up over Central Park *would* be kind of awesome. "And I don't see things before they happen anymore—"

"Neither do I—anymore. Neither one of us has had that problem for months."

"Keep your voices down," I warn in a loud whisper, not wanting anyone in the crowd to hear the two of them arguing over the weirder aspects of a disorder everyone in town believes to be narcolepsy. We're almost at the end of the midway, so I tug Kieran's sweatshirt sleeve and walk us off into the shadows behind the Funhouse, with Victor and Cooper following.

"And you know why we're not dreaming things anymore," Cooper says, lowering his voice even though now we have a small

185

measure of privacy. "This is how everything's supposed to work. I stopped dreaming first, I took the treatment, and now I'm *fine*. I'm better than fine."

"You're 'new and improved,'" Kieran points out, crossing his arms over his chest.

"And you will be, too. Look—the timeline makes total sense. You stopped dreaming a few months after I did. So, I took the treatment first—no more dreams, no more sleeping disorder. Now it's your turn. There's almost no risk of death from the treatment, so that theory's out the window. You're going to take the treatment, and you're going to live a whole new life, just like me."

"You left out the part about the amnesia, not to mention the hollow-eyed 'wandering' thing," Kieran points out. "And your memory's still not back completely."

Cooper makes a "pfft" sound with his lips.

"So, I can't remember some stupid stuff from my childhood. Big deal."

"Well, I don't want that. And I don't want to be in a coma and I don't want to wake up and not know myself or anyone else."

Kieran almost sounds like a stubborn child and, in a reaction that makes sense give Kieran's demeanor, Cooper reaches out and grabs his shoulders.

"That was *temporary*. A few weeks of weird for a lifetime of wonderful—think about it, K-Man."

Kieran shrugs out of his grasp, and as Cooper shakes his head, his attention catches on something just beyond the end of the midway.

"Now, what in the hillbilly hell is going on here?" he almost shrieks, strolling away from us toward two walls of hay bales joined together by a sign outlined in tiny while lights announcing "Hay Bale Maze."

"It's a hay bale maze," I tell him, pointing up at the sign.

"So, once again, I ask—what in the hillbilly hell is a hay bale maze?"

Kieran puts a hand on Cooper's shoulder.

"I think it's a maze. Kind of looks like it's made out of hay bales."

"Thanks," Cooper snaps at Kieran and then turns his attention to me. "So, like, it's an *actual* maze? With, like, dead ends and stuff and then you come out the other end like you're a lab rat or something?"

I look to Victor for assistance, asking him "What's so hard to understand about this? Do they not have hay bale mazes in New York?"

Victor shakes his head, and Cooper says, "Maybe upstate. Not in Manhattan."

He walks a few feet forward to Leonard Marsh, who's the local farmer tasked with manning the entrance at the moment. "How much to go through this thing?" Cooper asks him.

"Totally free." Leonard takes off his Chicago Cubs hat and scratches his head.

Cooper turns to us and sweeps a hand toward the entrance.

"Guys. Come on. We *have* to do this. I'm not leaving until we do."

Still holding Kieran's hand, I start pulling us forward, but Kieran doesn't move with me and I snap back into place next to him.

"You know," he begins, speaking more to Cooper than to anyone else, "you guys should go. I'll just go hang out with Zip's mom at her booth."

Cooper shoves his hands in his jacket pockets.

"Dude, come on."

"No. Seriously," Kieran continues, engaging in my nervous habit of kicking at the ground with the toe of his shoe. "I had a bad experience with one of these things in North Carolina when I was little. Kayla and I went in by ourselves and we kept hitting dead ends and I got all worked up and passed out. Kayla wasn't used to taking care of me as much yet, and so she freaked out and started screaming and they had to get someone to find my mom and send her in after us. When I woke up, I was embarrassed and Kayla was embarrassed..." His voice trails off and he darts his eyes down at his foot kicking up tufts of grass. "Just go without me. I'll be fine. I wanted to see if Gramps was back at the booth anyway. There's some stuff about my art portfolio I was hoping to talk to him about."

I shoot Cooper a pained look.

"You and Victor should go," I tell him. "I'll walk Kieran back."

Kieran stops kicking at the ground and fixes his eyes on me.

"You shouldn't have to do that. You guys go through the maze, and I'll just walk back by myself."

I glance at the midway, which is long enough that I can't even make out the craft booths at the other end. And I think we all know, given Kieran's condition, that his walking even a short distance alone might not be the best idea considering the crowd and the noise and the electric activity that would be swirling all around him.

"Mr. Lanier, I can walk you back if you like," Victor offers, scratching the dark stubble on top of his dome-like head. "I noticed some earrings I might like to buy for my mother. And I'm betting Mr. Halloran would appreciate going through the maze without an adult chaperone."

"Thanks, Vic," Cooper says, holding his hand out toward me. "Come on, Zip."

I glance back and forth between Cooper and Kieran, biting my lip. This situation is more than a little uncomfortable.

"Look, Kieran. I'll go back to the booth with you."

Kieran pulls me into an embrace.

"Go," he whispers in my ear. "I'm always holding you back."

"But—"

"I'll be fine," he says, pulling away a little so he can look at me. "Victor will walk with me. And Cooper needs someone to hang out with." Kieran raises his voice. "I don't trust him to be smart enough to make it through that thing alone without your help."

"Hey now," Cooper warns, dropping his hand to his side, and Kieran laughs.

"Are you sure about this?" I whisper.

"Positive." He glances past me to Cooper. "Bring my girl back to me safe and sound. Okay, Coop?"

"Sure thing."

"And if you guys aren't at your mom's booth in an hour, I'm sending a search party in after you," Kieran warns him, putting an arm around me to walk us forward toward Cooper.

"Got it," Cooper tells him.

"Have fun."

Kieran waves and backs away until he's standing next to Victor, and the two of them turn and head down the midway side by side. Cooper and I watch them walk off, two almost matching figures in jeans and black clothing—Victor with a black leather jacket and Kieran in a black hoodie—standing out against the bright lights of the carnival booths. I stare at Kieran's back, watching him lope along lazily next to Victor until they're swallowed up by the crowd.

CHAPTER 16

I can't help but feel as though Kieran has sort of handed me over to Cooper like I'm a stuffed animal prize from one of the carnival games. And the feeling isn't awesome at all.

"Ready?" Cooper asks, holding his hand out to me once again.

"Touch me and you're dead, Halloran," I snap. "I've punched a guy in the face before, remember?"

Cooper jams his hand into his jacket pocket.

"You're making me think twice about wanting to get trapped in a maze with you, you know," he says.

I groan and walk ahead of him to the entrance, the sweet smell of hay tickling my nose as I start down the main passageway. Just a few feet in front of us, the path forks in three directions. I turn right and a wall forces me to make an immediate left, which leads straight into a dead end.

Turning around to retrace my steps, I run smack into Cooper's chest as he was following just a few paces behind me. He puts a hand on each of my shoulders and backs me up until I'm against the hay bale wall.

"What part of 'Touch me and you're dead' did you not understand?" I snap.

Cooper jerks his hands away as if my shoulders have sprouted razor blades.

"Sorry. I just want to talk to you for a minute."

"We can't talk and walk at the same time?" I try to look around him, but his closeness combined with his girth won't let me. He's like a giant wall made out of t-shirt and leather jacket. "Back off me and we can talk, okay?" I tell him, sighing.

Cooper slides to my right and leans up against the hay. He opens his mouth to say something, but I preempt him.

"You know, a simple, 'Hey, let's talk' would have worked just fine. No need to get all Neanderthal Man on me. Hope you don't use those tactics with the girl you're dating."

"What girl?" He narrows his eyes.

"Whatever girl's going to be the proud owner of the earring tree you bought from my mom." I decide to venture out on a limb I'm not sure is strong enough to hold me. "It's Maisie Baker, isn't it?"

A tiny smile tugs at Cooper's mouth.

"What makes you say that?"

"Just a guess. Her lyrics are what brought your memory back. Sounds like your pretend relationship wasn't pretend to her, and I'm betting it wasn't for you, either. You seemed genuinely upset that night at the Laniers' thinking you'd really hurt her in some way. You wouldn't have had that reaction if deep down you didn't care about her."

Cooper shifts his eyes to the ground for a second before returning my stare, telling me I'm right.

"The whole thing started out fake, but after a while, it was real for both of us," he says, his focus trained on the hay-littered path rather than meeting my gaze. "But my condition screwed everything up, and her people and my dad would never let us stay together—not when there was a story that needed to be spun for the press. So, I acted like I never cared about her to begin with. I hated hurting her, but I figured if she thought I was a prick, she'd move on faster. And pretending like I didn't care kind of made things easier on me, too." He looks at me. "Remember when I was here the first time and I was talking all kinds of smack about her?"

"Yeah."

"That's just how I'd always dealt with the situation. After a couple years of telling myself I didn't care about her, I'd almost started to believe it." He lowers his voice because we can hear the raised tones of little kids approaching. "She was my first—she was the girl I was so worked up over I couldn't sleep with her at first."

Two little kids I recognize as Jimmy McCaffery's eight-year old twins emerge from the other side of a hay bale wall and stop giggling on seeing the two of us. "Dead end," one of them says, and the giggling starts up again as they turn around and run back in the direction from which they came.

"So, after I started remembering things, I took a chance and called her to tell her what had happened," Cooper continues. "She never knew the details of my condition. She always thought I had narcolepsy because Dad never wanted me to trust her with the reality. I was almost, like, relieved to tell someone the truth."

"And she was cool with everything?"

"Once we talked for a while, yeah," he says, nodding. "So we've been talking and texting off and on—she's touring in Japan right now—and we're thinking about getting together when she's back in the States after the new year."

"That's great," I tell him, my body relaxing now that I know he doesn't have any designs on me—or, at least I hope he doesn't, anyway. January is still over two months away.

"Yeah," Cooper says, his eyes glossing over for a second as if he's far off somewhere. Then he shakes his head a little and refocuses. "Okay—we're supposed to be talking about our boy Kieran here."

"We are?"

A boy and a girl I recognize from the junior high come up on us, both giggling and saying "Sorry," before locking their hands together and shuffling away.

192

"Maybe we should keep moving after all," Cooper suggests. "Wouldn't want any of your friends to find us hanging out back here and get the wrong idea."

"Good plan," I say, walking out of the dead end ahead of him. We make our way back to the main path and take one of the other directions, which also leads to a dead end. After winding our way back out and taking the only remaining path, we find ourselves at another fork after only a few feet.

"You decide this time," I tell Cooper, and he steers us to the left, then to the right, and straight into a dead end.

"Remind me again why I thought this was going to be fun?" he says. I grab his arm and yank us back to the fork, where the McCaffery twins come up behind us.

"Weren't you guys ahead of us just a second ago?" I ask Brian McCaffery. Or maybe it's Bailey—I'm not sure. Never could tell those kids apart.

"We made it all the way out and came back in," the twin I'm speaking to informs me, wiping a hand across his snotty nose. "This is our fourth time through."

"Yeah, we're trying to time ourselves and you're holding us up," the other twin practically shrieks, prompting Cooper to step aside.

"By all means…" he says, sweeping his hand out into the path, and the little McCafferys take off running ahead of us, darting down a path to our left.

"Follow them?" Cooper asks me.

"You know it," I say, and we trot off after the boys to find out they weren't kidding around—we're at the end of the maze in seconds.

"So, we don't get a piece of cheese after beating the maze?" Cooper says to me as the McCafferys round the maze, probably headed back to the entrance for another go.

I smile and nod toward a spot in the grass on the river bank, where a small opening in the trees allows for a clear view of the water floating by.

"You said you wanted to talk about Kieran?" I remind him.

Cooper reads me, and we head toward the river bank and sit down a few feet from the water's edge.

"You have to talk him into taking the treatment, Zip," he says, pulling his knees to his chin and wrapping his arms around his legs.

I'm immediately taken back to the day I'd found out my friends had nominated me for Homecoming Queen, and Cassie told Kieran to talk me into keeping my name on the ballot.

"I can't tell him what to do. He makes his own decisions, and my job is to support him after he does."

"But he's making the wrong decision." Cooper lowers a hand and begins picking at a tuft of grass. "I can't sit by knowing how great my life is—how great it's *going* to be—and not want the same thing for him." He tosses some grass out in front of us and turns to me. "I'm going away to Harvard in the fall. Dad went there, and that's where he's always wanted me to go, but we weren't sure I could—*physically* could, I mean. Dad's been talking to people there for years about me doing a degree online or having Victor go to class with me or something. They were going to work things out, but now, we don't have anything to work out anymore."

I love how for Cooper, attending one of the best universities in the country is a foregone conclusion because of his father's name, and not something he needs to work for like the rest of us. Cooper's pretty smart and everything, and he'd probably have no trouble getting into most places. But I'm guessing that even if his academics didn't quite

194

measure up, the best schools would still fall all over themselves to admit the scion of one of the world's most prestigious families.

"I might put Harvard off until the spring, though," he continues. "The treatment kind of set me back school-wise, and even with private tutoring, I might not be able to graduate on time. So, Dad and I are talking about how I could finish over the summer and go to Europe for a semester to study the operations at some of the Halloran subsidiaries over there."

"That's great, Cooper, but I don't get what any of this means for Kieran."

Cooper lies down in the grass and props himself up on his side, facing me.

"Kieran won't be able to do any of these things if he doesn't take the treatment."

I cock an eyebrow at him.

"Most of us can't go to Harvard. So what?"

"I'm not talking about Harvard. He can't go away to school where he wants. He could never travel to Europe by himself. He can't drive, he can't swim—"

"And he can't bench press. Got it, Coop."

"And I've always been able to do things to some extent because of Victor," he says, smiling at my annoyance. "But Kieran doesn't have Victor. He's had his parents and Kayla, and now you. But his relationship with his parents is iffy on a good day, and you and Kayla are going away to school eventually. When that happens, where does that leave Kieran?"

I don't like having this conversation with Cooper any more than I like having it with Kieran, but I don't get the chance to say so as Cooper continues.

"He'll listen to you, Zip. You're the only one he'll take seriously besides me, and I'm obviously not getting the job done. I

195

don't know how his parents feel about him taking the treatment, but his relationship with them is pretty much trashed anyway. And Kayla's too busy spending time with Mr. All-American to be much of a help." He glances around as if he's looking for something. "Where is the Beautiful Ms. Lanier tonight, anyway?"

"In Evanston with Mr. All-American," I grumble, and Cooper gives me a "There? See?" arching of his eyebrows.

"Kieran will take things seriously if *you* outline all the reasons why he should do this," he goes on. "He could have everything he's ever wanted. *Both of you* could have everything you've ever wanted. You could both go to school in Chicago, or wherever, so you wouldn't have to be apart. He could pursue his art. You two could have a life together—*a normal life*—someday. Don't you want that?"

"I do. I want *him* to have a normal life, and if I get to be a part of that, then fine. But his happiness is what's most important."

"I know," Cooper murmurs. "But it's like I said before—a few weeks of weird for a lifetime of wonderful. Convince him. Let him know that while he's trapped in here—" Cooper points to his forehead—"you'll still be waiting for him out here. If I were him and I had a girl like you, even amnesia wouldn't be enough to keep me away."

I sidestep Cooper's compliment.

"I don't think that's exactly how it works."

"Whatever. But you're the key to getting him to do this. I meant what I said in that video I sent you guys. I wanted to be the guinea pig so Kieran could have the life he's always deserved. Don't let what everyone tells me I went through for all those weeks be in vain, okay?"

I heave a deep sigh and tell him "You know, despite the fact that you come off like a raging douchebag most of the time, deep down, you're a pretty nice guy."

196

"Thanks," he says through a laugh as he stands and offers me his hands to pull me up. "We should probably get back before Kieran thinks I've run off with you."

I take his hands in mine and dart up to my full height, giving his left hand a little squeeze before I let go. He must read something in the gesture because he asks "You'll talk to him about the treatment?"

"I'll try. But I won't make any promises about how things are going to turn out."

"That's all I can ask," he says, and we start making our way along the river bank past the antiques tents. "If you can get him to do this, it'll change his life. It'll change *your* life. Trust me—it's all good."

I give Cooper a weak smile.

"I hope so."

CHAPTER 17

Cooper and Victor have to go back to New York on Sunday, so Kieran and I had planned to meet up with them for breakfast at the Burger Barn on their way from their hotel in Sumner to the airport. I pull into the Laniers' driveway a little early, hoping I can talk to Kieran about taking the treatment before we leave for the restaurant. But I'm stopped from entering the house by the sight of Carlie sitting alone on the front porch swing, her feet up on the seat and her hands curled around a cup of coffee. The morning's chilly and overcast— we're only a few days away from Halloween—but even though Carlie's wearing only a gray sweatshirt and navy sweat pants, she doesn't seem to be cold.

"Hey, Carlie," I greet her, standing in front of the door and looking down the porch at her.

"Hi. Kieran was about to get in the shower when I came out, so he should be ready in a few minutes."

"Thanks."

My hand's on the front door knob, but before I can twist it and go in, I hear Cooper's voice in my head, practically begging me to talk Kieran into taking the treatment. And I realize there's one bit of knowledge about the treatment I don't yet possess.

"Zip? You okay?" Carlie asks after I've hesitated long enough I must look like I've forgotten how to open a door.

"Can we talk for a few minutes?" I walk down the porch toward her. "I mean, if Kieran won't be ready for a while anyway."

She pats the seat next to her with her foot.

"Of course. Sit down."

I grab the chain connecting the porch swing to the ceiling and lower myself carefully, not wanting to rock the swing and cause Carlie to spill her coffee.

"Has Kieran talked to you at all about taking the treatment?"

Carlie's face falls.

"Some. Especially right after Cooper started getting his memory back. He wanted to know if the treatment was safe."

Kieran's question is my question as well, and it's the one thing Cooper had neglected to mention during our discussion last night that I had also neglected to ask. I can only assume that since Cooper came out of the amnesia with no lingering side effects, then the amnesia itself must be the only side effect. But I'd like to do more than assume.

"And I told him the truth," Carlie continues before I can ask. "Other than the memory loss and any potential complications implicit with brain swelling and an induced coma, the treatment is probably as safe as it's going to get."

"Those are some pretty big exceptions."

She nods, and I think I see a flicker of sadness in her eyes.

"You'll never get rid of side effects completely. We were hoping to eliminate the possibility of brain swelling from the equation entirely, but we realized that might not be possible for a long time, or maybe ever. As much as I wish Cooper hadn't appointed himself a lab rat, he took a risk and it paid off. After he came through the treatment with just temporary memory loss, we thought maybe we'd hit upon something."

Carlie glances down into her coffee cup, and I sense there's a 'but…' she's not adding onto her previous sentence.

"But you're worried the treatment might not work on Kieran in the same way?" I ask.

She rubs her lips together.

"Situational amnesia doesn't manifest itself identically in everyone. Cooper's memory came back after only a few weeks. Assuming the treatment causes amnesia in Kieran as well, his condition could last for a few days, weeks, months…we don't know. We just know the condition usually clears up on its own after repeated exposure to familiar stimuli. But, then again, this type of amnesia is usually psychogenic rather than organic, so in some ways, we don't really understand what we're dealing with."

I listen in amazement at how effortlessly Carlie can take a conversation about her son and lace it with scientific terms to the point she almost seems to be talking about some random, anonymous patient. But I look past the science to the fact that to some extent, she has no idea what the treatment will do to Kieran.

"But you didn't tell him whether or not to go through with the treatment," I say rather than ask because I know that if his mother had told him to take the treatment, he would have shared that information with me.

Carlie gives me a wan smile.

"You know, I've spent a large portion of my life controlling *his* entire life, telling him what to do and when to do it. And I did everything for his protection—or, that's what I told myself. But Jim and I should have been honest with him about everything—who his real parents were, what the real nature of his condition was— as soon as he was old enough to understand because now, our opinions mean nothing to him, whether those opinions are expert or not."

"If Kieran didn't trust you at least a little, though, he wouldn't have asked you if you thought the treatment was safe."

"True," she says, and takes a sip of her coffee. "But I think he was asking more for medical, informational purposes." I watch her eyes glaze over in the same way they did that day we found out Cooper had taken the treatment. "He was asking me as a patient asks

200

a doctor, not as a son talks to his mother. So, I'm sure he won't bother to ask me what I think about him taking the treatment."

"And what *do* you think?"

Carlie swivels until she's sitting next to me with her feet on the porch.

"Nice try," she says, patting my leg. "If I tell you what I think he should do, then you'll tell him what I think he should do."

"No, Carlie, I wouldn't—" But even though I'm protesting, I know she's right. I'd tell him—I wouldn't be able to walk around with that knowledge on my conscience.

"Zip, it's okay. I'm glad Kieran can confide in you and vice versa. And that's how things should work. He's eighteen—nineteen in a few months. He's *supposed* to be pulling away from his parents at this point in his life." A tiny smile pulls at the corner of her mouth. "In a way, this is what I've always wanted for him—independence."

I glance at her quickly and then stare down into my lap.

"So, even if I wanted to tell you—or tell him—I wouldn't," she continues. "What I think doesn't matter anymore. Kieran's an adult, and I've given him all the information he needs to make an informed decision. Now he has to make that decision, one way or the other. But I do know this much—"

She pauses long enough I have to prompt her to continue by asking "What?"

"As a parent, I'd give up anything for Kieran to have a normal life. And if I were him?" Her mouth twists up for a second. "I'd take any acceptable risk to be able to live my life."

I nod at her, understanding.

"I think I should probably go check on Kieran," I say, standing up from the swing, once again careful not to sway the seat too much. "Thanks for talking with me."

"Anytime, Zip."

I cross the porch, but before I can put my hand on the doorknob, Kieran opens the door and steps to me, gathering me in his arms.

"Hey. Did you just get here?"

"I've been here for a few minutes," I tell him. "Your mom and I have been hanging out."

"Sounds like trouble," he comments as he waves down at her and she waves back.

"You guys have fun," she calls out to us. "Tell Cooper and Victor it was nice seeing them again."

Kieran lifts his chin at his mother in an affirmative and guides me down the front step.

"So what were you and my mom talking about?"

Since we're going to be at the restaurant in a few minutes, I don't want to start a discussion about the treatment now.

"We were just talking about the future," I hedge.

"My favorite topic," he says, his voice tinged with sarcasm.

"Well, how about we talk about the very near future instead? Have you picked out our movies for Halloween yet?"

Trick or Treating would be kind of difficult for Kieran—not to mention we're getting too old for that anyway—so we've scheduled a scary movie night at my house instead, even going so far as to invite Kayla so she doesn't have to sit around all night moping about whatever fun college Halloween events Brad's engaging in without her.

"Well, I did some searching online the other day, and *Killer Zombies from the Deep 3* is out."

"They made another one?" I spit in disbelief. Kieran and I watched the second *Killer Zombies from the Deep* movie at my house back in June on a night that ended up being memorable not so much because the movie was one of the worst horror films I've ever seen,

202

but because that night was when Morgan finally remembered the formula for the original drug that caused Kieran's condition.

"Went straight to DVD, so we're talking about some high quality stuff. Since we never saw the first one, I'm thinking we should have a *Killer Zombies from the Deep* marathon."

"Sounds good. Kayla should be thrilled," I note, knowing Kayla's not really a horror fan at all and will probably spend the evening sinking even further into the bad mood she's going to be in to begin with.

"Kayla can suck it. We're doing her a favor allowing her mopey butt to hang out with us in the first place. If she doesn't like the movies, she can go home and read or pine for Brad or something."

Rather than driving through town and having to deal with vendors heading to the park as they set up for the festival's last day, I make a right turn instead of a left at the intersection of the county road and Main Street and, once I'm past the high school and a few houses, I take the exit ramp to the county highway that connects with the interstate. We'll have to get on the interstate and double-back to the Burger Barn at the Titusville exit, but on a day like today, one of the few busy ones in Titusville, taking the highway and interstate is a much quicker route. By the time we pull into the Burger Barn parking lot, Cooper and Victor have already arrived and are leaning against the back bumper of their rented SUV.

"Morning, Sunshine." Cooper beams at Kieran.

"Hey, yourself, Handsome," Kieran fires back.

"You two are so weird," I mutter at them, and Victor chuckles, stepping ahead to open the restaurant's door for us. As usual, on hearing the bell over the door, the restaurant patrons jerk their heads towards the front to see if they recognize who's joining them. The Burger Barn clientele is a mix of townies and people passing by Titusville on the interstate, so the Titusville residents eating here right

203

now would be curious about, but not surprised by, any strangers in their midst. And since I'm already going out with the mysterious Lanier boy, adding two more people no one knows into the equation doesn't provoke too many weird looks from the Titusville folks in the middle of their breakfasts. And given that it's Sunday morning and most of Titusville is either at church or helping to set up for the festival right now, a quick glance around the nearly full restaurant tells me out-of-towners passing through outnumber town residents two to one.

We head for the one remaining booth along the opposite side of the restaurant, and Cooper, Kieran, and Victor take menus from the little metal holder against the wall and start surveying the Burger Barn's breakfast offerings. I've been eating here practically since birth—and before, if you count my mother's penchant for takeout over home-cooking—so I've already decided on ordering a veggie omelet, hash browns, bacon, and coffee.

"What's good here, Ms. McKee?" Victor asks, not taking his eyes from the menu.

"Everything, so long as you're not watching your diet."

Victor bobs his head and keeps surveying his choices as Lauren strolls toward us, removing her order pad from the front pocket of her apron.

"Hi, guys," she says, stopping at the table. She points her pencil at Cooper. "You're Cooper, right?"

"Yeah. Good memory…Lauren?"

"Yeah." Lauren flashes him a toothy smile and blushes, blotchy red patches breaking out on her neck. The Laniers and Brad must have introduced Lauren and Coop at the dance while I was busy being royal. And, of course, she's probably also remembering him as the hot guy who came into the restaurant back in June.

204

"I don't think we've met," she says, gathering herself and looking at Victor. Victor places the menu on the table and stands up next to the booth.

"Victor Loughlin." He holds out his hand, and Lauren puts her pencil back into her apron so she can accept his handshake offer. "I'm Mr. Halloran's driver and assistant."

"Nice to meet you," she says politely, but she flashes me a split-second "What the hell?" wide-eyed expression that I meet with a hitch of my shoulders. When she and Victor are done shaking hands, she asks "Coffee for everyone?"

We all murmur affirmatives at her except for Kieran, who mumbles "Orange juice, please." Lauren takes note of our drink orders and heads back to the kitchen.

"Your friends are all hot," Cooper says to me. "Must be something in the water around here. I may need to visit you guys *a lot* more often."

"I thought you were all about Maisie Baker?" I note, smirking.

He picks up the salt shaker and starts sliding it back and forth on the table next to his paper placemat.

"Maisie's on tour, and there are no guarantees we're getting back together. I can shop around all I want."

Cooper Halloran would be a dream come true for most girls in this town, a knight in shining armor riding in with a black SUV instead of a white horse, bringing with him enough money to take care of them and their families for the rest of their lives. The trade off, of course, would be being stuck with Cooper and his smarmy attitude forever, but I'm guessing at least a few girls around here might be willing to take that deal.

We make meaningless conversation about what we're going to eat until Lauren brings our coffees and takes our food orders. Cooper

205

leans over the back of the booth to watch her walk away before turning to Kieran.

"You know what else I've done since taking the treatment?" Cooper pauses to grab some sugar packets, but doesn't wait for a response. "Went up in the Statue of Liberty. Raised in New York City and never able to do the whole Statue of Liberty tour until now. Oh, and you know what else? Zip-lining." He stirs his sugar into his coffee and puts his spoon on the placemat, raising both hands in the air as if he plans to paint Kieran a visual picture. "Oh, my God. It was so amazing—a total rush. If I end up going to Europe this fall, I'm going to do a few over there." He pauses again, glancing at me as if he's just realized something. "*Zip*-lining. Huh—that's funny."

"Yeah. Hysterical," I say, in a tone of voice that clearly implies his statement is anything but.

"Oh, and I did a rock wall last week." He plows on ahead, his lack of focus rivaling that of a hyper little kid. "First time, I went all the way to the top of this twelve foot thing with no help whatsoever. I felt like I could conquer the freaking world."

Kieran takes a sip of his juice and grumbles, "You about done?" to Cooper, who jerks his head around as if to say "What? Me?"

"Yeah," he says aloud, once no one else speaks up. "What's wrong, K-Man?"

Cooper's so disingenuous I almost want to punch him in the face.

"Coop, come on," Kieran starts, his voice full of frustration. "You know what's wrong. Just cut it out, okay?"

I glance at Victor, surprised he hasn't taken his usual borderline paternal role and scolded Cooper for passive-aggressively badgering Kieran. But Victor merely sips his coffee and glances around at the restaurant patrons as if he's completely disconnected from the conversation.

Cooper sits back against the booth, his arms folded.

"Okay, dude," he starts. "I've been trying for weeks to give you examples of what your life could be like if you, you know." He glances around, not saying "the treatment" aloud because doing so might get awkward in a restaurant full of people. "But, obviously, that's not working. And I hate having to get all mushy, but you leave me no choice." Cooper clears his throat and leans forward. "I care about you. You're, like, the closest thing I've ever had to a brother. All that time we spent together this summer getting blood drawn and having the research team poke around on us, I felt like we really bonded, you know? And all of our talks and stuff...other than maybe Vic here, I've never had that kind of relationship with anyone else."

Kieran's expression remains neutral as he says, "So, are you proposing to me here, or what's the deal? Because I don't know if I'm ready for that kind of commitment."

I nearly spit coffee out my nose at Kieran's teasing statement, and I see Victor's trying to hold back a laugh. Cooper, meanwhile, finds Kieran's comments less than funny.

"Whatever, dude," he grumbles, collapsing against the booth again. "I don't know why I'm even trying." Shaking his head, he looks at me, and I try to sober up.

"You know what though?" Cooper starts again, turning his gaze back on Kieran, "I *do* know why I'm trying. I'm trying for you, and I'm trying for her."

I sit up straight in my seat as Cooper nods toward me before darting his eyes back to Kieran.

"I'm not proposing to you, smart ass, but one day, you might want to propose to this girl over here. And one day, you two might want a life where she doesn't have to look after your sorry butt all the time."

Kieran purses his lips but doesn't say anything in response, and, thankfully, Lauren comes out from the kitchen with our food. She places a plate in front of each of us and refills the coffee cups before asking, "Can I get you all anything else?"

I'm tempted to ask for some extra knives we can use to cut through the tension, but I don't think anyone would find that funny at the moment.

We eat mostly in silence, only exchanging a few comments to each other about the excellent quality of our respective dishes. Cooper leaves Lauren a sizable tip under the pepper shaker and pays our bill at the front on the way out, waving off Kieran's offer to pick up the tab. Out in the parking lot, Kieran grabs Cooper's arm before he can open the door to the SUV.

"Sorry I got a little testy in there," he says. "I just...I've made up my mind, I think."

The "I think" from Kieran makes me wonder if Cooper hasn't shaken his resolve a little.

"I'm sorry, too," Cooper says back. "I just get so excited when I think about how things could be for you, and I—"

"I know." Kieran cuts him off and waves across the SUV to Victor. "Victor. Nice seeing you again."

"Likewise, Mr. Lanier."

As Cooper and Kieran say their final goodbyes, I walk over to the driver's side of the SUV. Victor's about to get in, but I hold out my hand for him to shake.

"'Bye, Victor. Drive safely."

A hint of a smile crosses his lips, and he surprises me by enveloping me in a hug, crushing my outstretched hand against us.

"Change his life, Ms. McKee," Victor whispers in my ear. "You know it's in your hands."

Stunned, I step back and tilt my head at him slightly as he gets in the car. Victor rolls down the window, and I gaze across him.

"'Bye, Cooper," I say as Cooper buckles himself in.

"Later, Princess."

Kieran comes up next to me, and we watch them pull out of the parking space and drive off, the chill from Victor's words almost enough to keep me from feeling Kieran's hand slide around my waist.

CHAPTER 18

We stare in silence at the black SUV until it turns down the exit ramp to head to the interstate.

"So, what now?" Kieran asks, putting his arms all the way around me. "A fun afternoon at the antiques festival?"

"I was thinking we could hang out somewhere quiet and talk for a while."

"Your house?" he suggests, knowing my mom would already be at the park for the festival. But I know better—if we go to my house, we won't talk. We need to go somewhere private, but not somewhere too comfortable.

"I've got another idea."

I don't tell him where we're headed and he, trusting me, doesn't ask, and so I almost feel guilty about not revealing our destination given its significance. As we drive through town, I turn on the radio as a distraction, and the station's in the middle of a Maisie Baker track. Kieran and I spend the ride trying to crack each other up by making up goofy fake lyrics, but Kieran's good mood fades once he realizes we're on the county road to our respective houses. His mood sours completely after we pass his house.

"Where are we going?" he asks, his voice low with suspicion.

I take a deep breath.

"I thought we might go to the river."

"The river." He echoes, and from the corner of my eye, I glimpse him staring out the window. "Okay."

He knows what conversation I'm going to start with him once we get there—I can sense it in the flatness of his voice. I turn left down the path, and as soon as the car hits the gravel, the jolt feels like traveling downhill into the heart of our relationship and everything that's happened to us over the last nine months. Kieran first told me about his dreams here at the river, back when we were still just friends. And, of course, our Prom night misadventures ended here as well, with a follow up visit to the boat launch a week later so Morgan could explain how he wasn't the bad guy everyone assumed he was.

This is our first trip to the boat launch since the night we met up with Morgan, and as I slow and roll over the rut in the gravel that was ultimately Frank's undoing, I see that thanks to two trucks parked on the left side—people down here fishing, most likely—I'm going to have to park on the right side of the gravel near the woods. And as I pull over to the same side of the boat launch area I did on Prom night—*without* skidding into a tree this time—I'm struck with how different everything appears in the tepid daylight of a gray fall morning. The trees, bare of leaves, seem less like threatening black snakes when they're not backed by a purple night sky, and the river itself rolls along, the water sloshing against the rocks loud and hypnotic enough through my open window I'm almost able to forget about Frank Dozier's body floating downstream and ending up on a grassy bank near Sumner.

Almost. Things always *seem* less depressing in the daylight, whether or not they actually are.

I shut off the engine and Kieran meets my intentions for coming here head on.

"Cooper convinced you to talk to me, didn't he?" he asks, untangling himself from his seat belt and turning to face me.

"Pretty much. And I talked to your mom for a while, too, and that got me all the way there."

"I knew I should have showered faster," he grumbles, but the wisp of a smile playing about his lips tells me he's not angry with Carlie or with me.

"Kieran, you heard Cooper last night and this morning. He's been practically taunting you for weeks with everything he can do now. And your mom—"

Kieran holds up a hand to stop me.

"I've kind of already put together what she and my dad think. But I'm not changing my mind. I won't take the treatment. I don't want to wake up and not know who I am, or who anyone is." He glances down into his lap. "I guess Mom told you there's not exactly a firm time limit on the whole amnesia thing."

I wriggle out of my seat belt and squirm in my seat to face him.

"She mentioned it."

"That's a deal breaker for me. What if my memory never comes back?"

I don't say anything because doing so might keep me from saying what I'm certain I'll need to later.

"Zip, I don't want to live in a world where I don't recognize you. I don't want to wake up every day and not be in love with you." He puts a hand to my cheek, his flesh warm and comforting against the fall air. "I was practically in love with you before I met you, when you were just some pretty girl running around my dreams. A future where I can't remember you isn't a future to me. It's death."

I cover his hand with mine.

"But it won't be death because you won't know. You won't remember being in love with me. It'll be like we never happened."

My words shatter my confidence, chipping away at my heart like an ice pick. I draw in a breath at the empty chill of what I've just said, and Kieran gives me a sad smile, his hand against my face the only heat I feel right now.

"And that's another reason I won't do this. I could never hurt you like that.

212

"But, again, you won't remember."

I inhale once more, taking his hand from my face but keeping his fingers laced with mine against the cloth seat.

Here goes nothing.

"You're not going to hurt me," I start, staring into his eyes and speaking slowly so I can ensure he takes in every word, "because I'm letting you go."

He slumps, eyelids fluttering.

"You're breaking up with me?" he whispers.

His eyelids flutter again, and he's out like an extinguished candle, his body crumpled against the seat. I reach out and brush some hair off his forehead, almost meanly grateful for the chance to collect my thoughts for a moment.

I'm not breaking up with Kieran—I can't even get my head around the concept. But, somehow, I have to make us both okay with the possibility he could wake up and not remember that he loves me, whether his lack of memory lasts for a few weeks or forever.

Not having the heart to wake him up, I sit and stroke his hair, watching the river flow by and losing myself in the thought of how the ripples in front of me right now will be in Sumner in less than an hour. Later this afternoon, those same ripples will empty into the Mississippi at St. Louis, and by tomorrow, the stretch of water I'm looking at will pour into the gulf at New Orleans and flow out to the ocean. I'm reminded of the old saying about how one never steps into the same river twice, and I realize if I came down here at the same time tomorrow, the water would still be flowing by, but it wouldn't be the same water I'm staring at now—the ripples would look the same, and maybe I could even convince myself the water is, in fact, the same set of hydrogen and oxygen molecules I was watching the day before.

But logic and science tell me they won't be.

213

This moment, Kieran and I sitting together here in Mom's car, is a fleeting collection of seconds in the context of a much larger lifetime. I'm seventeen years old, and barring any unforeseen disasters—which I seem to be more susceptible to since meeting Kieran Lanier—I probably have something like seventy years ahead of me. Hundreds, possibly thousands, of people will pass in and out of my life. Kieran Lanier made his way in. Now, I need to prepare us both for the possibility that he may ripple his way out, just like the molecules of liquid moving past me right now on their way to a wider body of water.

Kieran shifts underneath my hand, and as I glance over, he blinks awake. He looks around a moment and sits up, the continued blinking telling me he's piecing together our conversation from a few minutes ago.

"So," he begins, running his hands through his hair, "I believe you were in the middle of dumping me?"

Sighing, I reach out to take his face in my hands.

"I'm not doing this well."

"Well, this sucks pretty bad from where I'm sitting, so you must be doing *something* right."

His sarcasm wounds me a little, and I drop my hands.

"Okay. Let's rewind here. I said I'm letting you go. I didn't say I'm breaking up with you."

"Not quite seeing the difference," he says, sitting back and folding his arms over his chest.

"Okay." I try again, frustrated with myself that after all these months, I still suck at this relationship stuff—although, my relationship with Kieran isn't exactly average, so I probably deserve some slack. "I love you more than anything, and I love your family. Remember what Gramps said that night your mom came back from

New York? We're all kin even though we're not blood related, and that's not a load of crap to me."

"I feel the same way."

"I promised Jilly I would stand by you and your family no matter what happened with the treatment, and I was serious. Regardless of whether or not you remember me when you wake up— and regardless of whether or not you *ever* remember me—"

The iciness stabs at my heart again—

"Your parents are my neighbors. Your sister is one of my best friends. I can't walk away from those facts any more than I can just walk away from you."

He nods slowly, and I can tell I haven't completely won him over yet.

"So, what's with the 'I'm letting you go' business?" he whispers.

I lean across the center console and put my hand on the back of his neck, pulling him to me until our foreheads touch.

"It's sort of like that old saying about how if you love something, you need to set it free, and if it comes back to you then things were meant to be, you know?"

He gives me a more restrained version of his usual grin.

"I think I've heard that before."

"But I also need you to understand that if you never come back to me, I'll be *fine*. I won't like it, and it'll hurt like hell. But for both our sakes, I'll suck it up go on, and eventually, I'll be okay."

"Zip," he murmurs, his lips inches from mine.

"The decision whether or not to take the treatment is ultimately up to you, but I don't want to spend the rest of my life wondering what your life could have been like if you don't do it. And I don't want you to spend the rest of *your* life wondering, either, and possibly end up resenting me because you didn't take a chance."

215

He brushes his lips against mine, and my resolve nearly crumbles, but I steady myself and continue my argument when we part.

"Being with me isn't worth sacrificing a chance at an incredible life."

"My life won't be incredible unless you're in it," he insists.

I pull back slightly so I can look him in the eye.

"You're not making this easy."

"What? Our non-breakup breakup? That's sort of the plan."

Exhaling, I try again.

"This isn't a breakup. This isn't even a non-breakup. This is me telling you that no matter what happens, I'll always love you." I rake my thumb across his temple. "And I know that somewhere in here, even if you can't consciously remember, you'll always love me, too. But if you don't go through with the treatment, the 'what ifs' will follow us for the rest our lives, Kieran. You know they will. And I don't want our future haunted by that."

I move my hand to his cheek and his eyes shift to the windshield as if watching the river is helping him consider things. Thinking quickly, I shift the conversation to a more positive place.

"Besides, we're talking about the absolute worst case scenario here. You'll probably be just like Cooper—a few weeks of weird for a lifetime of wonderful."

He darts his eyes back to me and laughs a little.

"What?"

"Cooper said that last night, remember?"

Kieran purses his lips.

"Oh, yeah. Rather poetic for our Coop, but, okay." He leans back again, taking my hand in both of his.

"I guess I shouldn't be thinking totally in terms of gloom-and-doom scenarios, so maybe Coop's got a point. After all, he remembered he cared about Maisie, and they're not even together."

"True," I say, another idea occurring to me. "And everyone keeps saying how repeated exposure to familiar stimuli helps. So, maybe there's a way we can raise your odds of coming back more quickly."

He narrows his eyes.

"I'm listening."

"You've got all those journal entries and drawings of your dreams, right? A lot of those dreams came true, so you'll be able to look back through the journals if you lose your memory."

Kieran bobs his head slowly at my suggestion, and his eyes widen.

"And I can make new journals and drawings now that stuff's already happened," he says, his voice edged with excitement. "I can add more details, maybe draw and write about the things I didn't dream beforehand. I can get as much of my life down as possible." His lips form the grin that I love so much. "I'd always thought I'd write my autobiography a lot later in life, but my life never exactly goes according to plan."

I'm relieved his spirits seem to be lifting a little, but I can't help but risk everything by asking, "So, does this mean you're going to undergo the treatment?"

"It means I'm definitely rethinking things," he says, the grin disappearing in favor of a more serious expression. "I still don't like the idea of you being a stranger to me, but—"

I cut him off before he can say anything else that might lead us back down our previous rabbit hole.

"Kieran, I'll never be a stranger to you, no matter what. Your family lives next door to my family. We go to the same school. Even

217

after graduation, we're always going to come back home for holidays and special occasions. As long as your family and my family are living close together, we'll never be too far apart."

"Good point," he says, kissing my forehead. "Maybe we should go back to my house and get to work on my life story. I'm going to need your help remembering all the awesome things that have happened to me over the last few months."

"Like those details aren't burned into your brain every bit as much as they are into mine."

He leans in to brush his lips across mine.

"Of course. It's just easier to draw and write when you've got your main source of inspiration sitting right in front of you."

Smiling, I turn away and start the car, backing up and around so I can drive us up the hill. I stop the back end mere inches from a tree, ensuring I have enough clearance to make a hard left without having to pull too close to the water.

"Careful," Kieran warns, seeing how near I am. "I hear the trees tend to jump out at you down here."

He's grinning, but I roll my eyes at him anyway.

"I seem to remember that, too—smart ass."

Kieran breaks down with laughter, and by the time I've circled us around and have us back on the narrow gravel path, I'm laughing pretty hard, too.

CHAPTER 19

The first basketball practice of the season is the Monday after Halloween, and I couldn't be more ready. Other than the occasional junk food slide, I've stuck to a healthy, high protein diet since the summer, in addition to lifting weights three times a week and shooting whenever I can. The coaching staff weighs and measures us before practice, and while I weigh five pounds more than I did at the end of last season, my body measurements indicate those extra pounds are lean muscle and not body fat, which was my goal with the diet and the workouts. So, now that I'm sure I've met my body composition goals, I'm ready to start tackling my ultimate objective— a state championship.

Since we're getting back into the swing of things and our first game is still two weeks away, practice is pretty light. After the team votes Cassie and me co-captains for the season, we shoot around, run a few line drills, and take some laps—nothing too strenuous, but enough to work up a sweat. On my way out of the gym toward the locker room, Coach Denton trots up behind me and puts a hand on my shoulder.

"You have time to stop by the office after you shower up?" she asks.

"Yeah."

"Okay. Talk to you in a few."

I shower and change back into my school clothes, stopping at the athletic department office and waving goodbye to my teammates as they continue down the hall and on outside. Coach is reviewing paperwork at a battered desk while Coach Murphy, fresh off his first practice with the boys' team, sits in a cracked vinyl easy chair near the back of the office, watching game film on a laptop.

"Zip." Coach nods toward a brown vinyl sofa on the opposite wall that matches the easy chair, both pieces probably having been fixtures in this office since the seventies. I flop down after dropping my backpack and gym bag on the cushion next to me.

"What's up, Coach?"

"Well, I'm impressed with the work you've put in during the off-season," she starts. "Your body composition tests show your effort's paid off."

"Thanks. It's championship or bust this year."

She winks at me.

"Now *that's* the attitude I want out of my co-captains. And how's recruiting going?"

I give her a shrug.

"Okay, I guess. I've talked to a few college coaches, I put game highlights up online…I guess I got started kind of late compared to some people, though."

"Well, the county league games probably got you some attention. You mentioned playing in some showcase tournaments this summer, too?"

"Yeah. I don't really have a good sense of what scouts thought, but…" My voice fades off into nothing. Most girls who are serious about playing college basketball start the recruiting process during their freshman year of high school, something I didn't realize at the time. But with a clueless mother and a busy father—although a busy father who went through the recruiting process himself when he was my age—I haven't had much guidance.

"Mrs. Greenwald tells me you decided not to apply early decision to Northwestern," Coach continues.

Mrs. Greenwald is my guidance counselor. I fiddle with the strap on my gym bag as I think back on my conversations with her.

"Early decision didn't seem like the best idea. If you get in and you decide to accept, then you can't apply anywhere else. She thought keeping my options open for a while in case someone else offers me a basketball scholarship would be the best thing."

"Have you talked to anyone at Northwestern?" Coach asks.

Getting a scholarship to play at Northwestern would be almost beyond my wildest dreams, and although I don't want to go to school anywhere else, I've reluctantly decided to heed both my dad's and Mrs. Greenwald's advice and see if other schools will offer to pay for my education if I play ball for them.

"I've emailed back and forth with one of their coaches, but no invite for an official visit yet. I might take an unofficial visit in January."

An offer for an official visit means a program is interested in you, but recruits can take unofficial visits as well. Both types of visits could result in a scholarship offer. Or not.

I've always understood my chances of getting a basketball scholarship offer from Northwestern aren't good since they're a Division One program, and my odds are better with Division Two schools, or maybe having a Division Three school offer me a full academic scholarship since they don't offer athletic ones. But Northwestern is my dream school, and I've always wanted to go there and major in journalism or communications so I can be a sports broadcaster. And though I'm well aware I may need to choose between going to Northwestern or playing ball, now that the time for making those decisions is almost here, they seem more impossible than ever.

Complicating matters is the fact that Kayla went all in and applied early decision to Northwestern, and so she'll find out by December whether she's in or not. I, on the other hand, won't hear from them until early April and if I decide to go, I'm supposed to make a tuition deposit by the beginning of May. But if other schools offer me basketball scholarships, I don't need to commit until mid May or all the way until August in some cases. The season ends—assuming we get all the way through the playoffs—in March, so hopefully, any school that wants to offer me a basketball scholarship would have done so by then, and I can consider all of my options for a few weeks.

"How about other schools?" Coach asks, dropping the subject of Northwestern for a moment.

"There's interest from a few, but no invites for officials yet."

Coach takes a pencil from her desk and starts tapping the eraser end on her knee.

"What if you don't get any offers? Are you going to be okay with not playing ball?"

"Yeah," I say, mostly meaning it. "I think I can get into Northwestern and get scholarships, and I've always wanted to go there anyway. Not playing ball will be weird, but I guess I'll get over it."

"Well, I know going to school somewhere around Chicago is important to you. I have contacts at a few places—not Northwestern, but other schools. I can give you their names, and feel free to mention me if you contact them, okay?"

"That would be great, Coach," I say, eyes widening with gratitude as she turns to her desk and scrawls some names and school information on a sheet of legal paper. She tears the paper off and gives it to me, and as I'm putting it in my backpack, she says, "I think this might be a big year for you, Zip."

"How so?" I ask, looking up at her.

"Well, you're two-hundred and forty-nine points away from setting the school's all-time scoring record," she says as if this is something I should have already known. And I probably would have if I'd bothered to study the plaques outside the trophy case in the school's main hallway. But my stats nerdiness only extends to my personal numbers, and while I was aware last season was my best ever, I had no idea where I ranked among the school's greats.

"Really?" I mumble.

"Yeah. You scored nearly three-hundred and fifty points last season, so you should break the record easily. You'll probably hold the three-point record by the end of the season, too— for boys' *and* girls'. Not to mention how close you are to the assists record. You're on track to be the greatest basketball player this school has ever seen."

I shift a little on the cracked leather seat. I'm not going to lie—I knew I was a good player by Titusville standards. Really good. I just didn't think I was *that* good.

"But that's only part of my pep talk," Coach continues. "If you play out of your mind this year and we go far into the playoffs, you might get lots of attention from schools that haven't even noticed you yet. A run at state means press and interviews and people watching you, and I'd like nothing more than for you seniors to get the attention you deserve. Trust me, I'm going to be having a version of this talk with Cassie, too, but you're the one I think has an outside shot at Division One."

Once again, I shift around and don't say anything.

"So, are you ready to lead us to glory this year?" Coach asks with a grin.

"Yeah," I respond, still kind of stunned. "Yeah. Definitely."

She waves toward the door.

"Okay, then. Get out of here. See you tomorrow."

I walk out to the parking lot in a fog and drive to the Laniers'—where I'm supposed to be helping Kieran with his college applications—in a blissed-out state. To think I might have the tiniest shot at playing Division One ball somewhere is almost too much to

223

get my mind around. But I come down a bit as the Lanier house comes into view up ahead of me, because playing Division One might mean I'd end up somewhere far away from Kieran. For the briefest second, I wish Kieran were still dreaming the future because maybe he'd have some clue as to how everything's going to work out.

At the Laniers', I duck into the kitchen to say hello to Jim after Carlie lets me in, and then I head upstairs to Kieran's room, where he's at his desk staring at his laptop while Kayla lies on his bed gazing at the ceiling, lost in thought.

"Hey, guys," I say, and they both jump.

"Hey," Kieran says, getting up and crossing the room to hug me.

"You guys seem pretty spaced out," I say, looking at Kayla over his shoulder.

"We're working on the essay for one of his applications," Kayla tells me.

Kieran walks back to his desk as I sink to the corner of the bed.

"What's the topic?" I ask.

He turns to his computer screen and reads, "'How will an art school education help you fulfill your personal and career goals?'"

"Is that on your Sumner application? That question sounds pretty specific for a general liberal arts school essay."

"Nah. It's for the School of the Art Institute of Chicago." He turns in his chair and rests his chin on the backrest. "I should be able to tweak this essay a little bit and use it for my Columbia College-Chicago application, too."

Like the School of the Art Institute, Columbia College has a reputation for good art and design programs. I glance back and forth from Kieran to Kayla, and Kayla's grinning like she knows something I don't.

"It's like you and Gramps said, right?" Kieran continues. "Can't hurt to apply to some places and see whether or not I can get in. I mean, if the treatment works, I'll want some applications out there besides the one to Sumner."

My mouth drops open because I'm not sure I've heard what I think I did.

"What?"

"I said, if the treatment works, I'll want some applications out there."

Kieran gives me that grin as I stare at Kayla.

"Surprise," she whispers, holding her hands in the air, palms out.

"When did you decide this?" I ask him, too freaked out to move. As if he senses my disbelief, he gets up from the desk chair and comes to the bed, sitting down next to me and taking my hands in his.

"About an hour ago," he says through the sliver of a laugh as he glances back at his sister. "I started working on my applications after I got home from school and once I hit the essay, I was totally stumped. I mean, 'How will an art school education help me fulfill my personal and career goals?' I had no idea. My personal goal most days is being able to take a shower without falling asleep and bashing my head open."

"So, we started talking in hypotheticals," Kayla says, crawling down to the end of the bed and sitting on her brother's other side. "Like, what would he want to do with his life if he could do anything he wanted and why?"

"Sort of like what you were talking about with Gramps that day," I remind him.

"Yeah, exactly. And, I mean, art's kind of the only physical thing I've ever been good at. I can't do sports and stuff, and I don't like math and science. But it was more than that—my journals were

225

always the place I made sense of things I dreamed about. Like, back before we knew Morgan wasn't a threat, and I didn't know who he was, I'd always wake up with this vague sense of dread after I'd had a dream about him. But then I'd draw him, and the fear wasn't so bad somehow. Getting him out of my head and onto paper made me feel like I had some control over things in a way, you know?"

I don't, but I nod to get him to continue.

"So, sometimes I think about people who can't make sense of things they're going through. Like, people who go through some trauma, or kids who are just trying to find their way in life, who are trying to find a way to express themselves and make sense of everything. I think I want to help people make sense of the stuff in their lives that doesn't seem to. So, after Kayla and I talked things through, I started writing down what we talked about as my essay." He gazes down at our joined hands. "Well, everything but the dreaming the future part, anyway. I wrote about having bad dreams in general and left it at that. And, I don't know—once I wrote everything down and re-read the essay, I was like, 'Oh, my God. I want this. I really, *really* want this."

I'm smiling so wide my cheeks hurt, and Kieran continues explaining himself.

"When I shut my eyes and try to picture my life after graduation? There's nothing—nothing but a big, blank wall." He glances over at the document over on the computer. "I started working on my autobiography the other day after we were at the river, and I've kept working on it over the last few days, reliving my past, drawing things, making sense of stuff. And then I wrote the essay for my application, and for the first time, there wasn't a big, blank wall where my future should be anymore. I could see a future that wasn't something bizarre in the dreams I used to have, something I didn't have to wait to find out if it was going to happen. I

226

could make this future a reality. And I realized you and Cooper were right. I need to go through with the treatment."

Leaning in, I press my forehead to his.

"You're sure?" I whisper.

"I'm sure. And thank you for convincing me at least part of the way. I'm sorry I was so set against everything the other day, but I guess I needed to write about my future in my own words or something. I needed to kind of imagine things for myself."

I'm not a big crier, especially in happy situations, but a grateful sob is working its way up my throat right now and I swallow it down so I can talk.

"It'll be okay, you know?" I say almost more for my benefit than his. "A few weeks of weird for a lifetime of wonderful, right?"

He raises a hand to my cheek, his thumb stroking across my lips.

"Right."

"Well, while you two sit here and make out," Kayla starts, rising from the bed, "I'm going to go tell Mom and Dad the news, okay?"

Kieran angles his head toward his sister while still not taking his forehead from mine and nods. As soon as Kayla's out of the room, he draws me into a lingering kiss that we only break when we hear footsteps on the stairs.

I shift on the bed to see Carlie and Jim in Kieran's doorway. Carlie takes a few steps inside the room, crouching in front of us, and Jim walks in to stand next to her. Kayla, who must have been behind them in the hallway, leans against the doorframe.

"You're sure about this?" Carlie asks just as I had.

"Absolutely."

"You know, it'll take some time to set this up, and you've got school until Christmas," Jim points out. "So, if you decide at any time you don't want to do this, you don't have to go through with it."

"Thanks, Dad, but I don't think that's going to happen. I want this."

Jim and Carlie exchange looks that seem to be a strange mixture of fear and happiness, but maybe I'm just projecting my own feelings onto them. Carlie reaches over and pats Kieran's hand, which is resting on top of mine above my knee.

"I'll call Ben and make arrangements," she says, the warmth in her eyes melting any icy feelings of fear inside me.

Chapter 20

After Kayla basically kidnapped me from my dad's house in June and dragged me off to North Carolina in search of Kieran, Dad agreed I could return to Titusville for the rest of the month on one condition. In exchange for bailing on my annual summer stay at his house, I had to agree to spend June with him next year, in addition to spending Thanksgiving and Christmas with him this year. And being with him for the holidays is no problem, but my basketball schedule makes things a little challenging. The Brownsville Thanksgiving Invitational starts the day after Thanksgiving, and so after spending the holiday with Dad and his family, I have to get up early Friday morning and take the train back to Titusville, which will give me a few hours to rest at home before I need to catch the bus to the game. So, Dad's going to get his holiday, but he's not going to get much.

The train from Sumner pulls into the shed at Union Station in downtown Chicago, people behind me who have been on board since Mendota or Galesburg or somewhere in Iowa or beyond standing up and strolling towards the exits, where they will continue to stand until we come to a complete stop. Not in the mood to wait in line behind a gaggle of impatient people, I stay in my seat reading *The Awakening* until the crowd thins, and only then do I grab up my backpack and head out.

I'm barely inside the station when I spy Dad just a few feet away, casually clad in an Irish fisherman's sweater and jeans, his hair unsprayed and windblown around his face in full "day-off-don't-care" mode.

"Zipperoo," he booms as I approach, holding out his arms to gather me into a hug.

"Hey, Dad."

I rub my face against the rough wool of his sweater. When we break our embrace, he takes my backpack and keeps his other arm around me, guiding me toward the exit to the parking garage.

"Hope you're ready to eat. Kathy's been up since dawn."

"And I'm sure Olivia's being a *huge* help," I comment, knowing how rambunctious my half-sister can be. I can't imagine trying to cook a full meal with a little kid running around, especially one as spastic as Liv.

"Don't underestimate Liv," Dad says. "When I left, she was actually hand-mashing potatoes. I think Kathy found a productive channel for her energy—for today, anyway."

We find Dad's SUV and he steers us out of the garage so we can make our way to the Kennedy Expressway, which will take us to the suburbs. Once we've cleared some of the traffic—there's always traffic in Chicago, even on a holiday—Dad and I spend of the rest of the drive to his house in Schaumburg talking about the Chicago Bulls and Titusville's undefeated season so far, and he tells me he's planning to come for some games in January.

"Of course, if the team makes the playoffs this year—*when* you make the playoffs, rather—I'll be there, too," he says, pulling into the driveway of the two-story house at the end of a cul-de-sac. "I've already looked up the potential dates on the Internet."

"Impressive, Dad." I nod, anything else I might want to say swallowed up by a shriek from outside the car.

"Zip!"

Olivia, who must have heard us pull up, is outside next to my door, bouncing on the balls of her feet as if she's attached springs to the soles. I get out of the car and her arms are practically around me before I hit the pavement.

"You're so tall," I tell her, and I'm only sort of kidding—the kid seems like she's shot up a good two inches in the last five months. She backs away from me and starts doing pirouettes on the concrete.

"I'm going to get big and tall so I can be a dancer!"

Dad's joined me at the passenger side of the car, and I lean over and whisper, "Are dancers supposed to be tall? I don't know much about this..."

"Me, neither," Dad mutters, as Olivia keeps spinning around, her straight black hair fanning out in the air. "I'm not used to six year-olds who aren't into sports."

I laugh a little at Dad's predicament as Olivia whirls out into the lawn and collapses in a heap, giggling so hard she starts coughing. Dad picks her up and throws her over his shoulder.

"Come on, monkey girl, before your mom gets onto both of us."

Olivia continues giggling as the two of them walk off toward the garage, and I grab my backpack and follow them into the house. Dad opens the door, and the sweet smells of Thanksgiving float out to me—turkey, mashed potatoes, broccoli casserole, cranberries, and apple pie. Stepping inside, I drop my bag next to the fridge so I can hug Kathy, my stepmother, who's setting a casserole fresh from the oven on the kitchen counter as Dad chases Liv into the hallway.

"Hi, Kathy," I say, waiting for her to take her oven mitts off. She gathers me to her, and I raise my hand to touch the ends of her straight black bob, quite a change from the long dark locks I'm used to that matched Olivia's.

"You cut your hair?"

She backs away a little and grimaces, her red lipstick struggling to stand out against her butterscotch skin.

"This was an impulse move from a few days ago. I'm not exactly in love with it."

231

"It looks good on you," I say, being completely honest. I doubt I could pull off short hair, but Kathy's got a round face that makes it work.

"Yeah?"

"Yeah."

"I keep telling her the same thing and she doesn't believe me," Dad says, reentering the kitchen ahead of Olivia. "Liv's all washed up and ready to go, by the way."

"Let's eat!" Liv announces, skirting the breakfast bar and flopping down at the head of the table in the other room.

Kathy turns toward the table, placing her hands on the countertop where the turkey sits waiting to be devoured.

"That's Mommy's chair," she tells Liv. "You know that. You sit in the other chair."

Olivia giggles and takes her rightful place at the table, while Kathy nods toward my bag next to the fridge.

"Mitch, run that upstairs to her room? We'll get the food on the table."

Dad does as he's told, and after I wash my hands in the kitchen sink, I help Kathy set out the food and pour water for me, wine for her and Dad, and milk for Liv. I slide into the chair across from Liv and Kathy sits at one head of the table while my Dad, now back from delivering my bag upstairs, trots to the other end near the French windows, pushing the chair out of the way so he can stand and carve the turkey.

We make small talk about school and basketball, stopping occasionally so Dad and Kathy can remind Olivia not to play with her food, which she mostly does by swirling the mushier dishes around on her plate and making motorboat noises with her lips. Once we're done with the main portion of the meal, Kathy asks, "Apple pie and ice cream now, or is everyone too full?"

232

"Now!" Olivia answers for all of us.

"Well, then." Kathy glances at Dad and me and says, "You guys okay to eat dessert right away? The dictator has spoken."

We both bob our heads in agreement as Olivia asks, "What's a 'dictator'?"

Kathy zooms into the kitchen to leave Dad and me to deal with this one. We look at each other and think, and I arrive at an explanation before Dad does.

"It's someone who always gets whatever she wants."

"Oh." Liv seems pretty pleased with my definition, and so Dad jumps in to salvage things.

"Not always in a good way, though. People…um…people sometimes don't like dictators, so it's not as though you want to walk around school telling people 'Hey, I'm a dictator.' You might worry some folks."

Olivia squints, thinking this one through.

"So, I wouldn't want to be a dictator when I grow up?"

The thought of my adorable baby sister ruling some distant country with an iron fist is almost hysterical enough to make me choke on my water.

"Probably not," Dad confirms. "You might want to choose another job, be someone everyone likes."

"Like a princess." Liv's eyes light up as she turns her attention to me. "When I grow up, I'm going to be a princess like you."

I shrug.

"Might want to set your sights a little higher, kid. Being a princess isn't all it's cracked up to be. You have to wear uncomfortable shoes and you can't wear jeans or sweatpants, like, *ever*, and people tell you where to go and what to do all the time." I lower my voice as if I'm telling her a secret. "It's kind of not a lot of fun. You should maybe want to, I don't know, run a company or something."

Olivia gives my suggestion some consideration.

"Maybe when I grow up, I'll run things where Daddy works."

Considering my dad does something at the Chicago Board of Trade, or whatever it's called, the chances of Olivia someday running that particular operation are pretty slim. But just two seconds ago, I was talking her out of wanting to be a princess when she grows up, so we're not exactly dealing in reality at the moment.

"So, if you end up as my boss someday, do I get to keep my job?" Dad asks.

"Only if you're a good worker," she says, deadly serious, and I bite my lip to keep from laughing out loud. Kathy returns with two plates of apple pie and ice cream for Olivia and me, and then brings two more plates for her and Dad, the two of them exchanging looks as she sits down.

"You know, someone at this table is going to be seven years old on Christmas Eve," Dad points out, glancing from Kathy to Liv.

"Me?" I joke, and Olivia narrows her eyes.

"No. Me," she says, as if I'm the dumbest person on the planet. "You're not seven. You're seven*teen*."

"Thanks. I forgot," I whisper, and she giggles at me.

"And even though it's still a month away, your mom and I have a little surprise for you. And for Zip, too."

I sit up a little straighter in my chair.

"Wait—I'm getting presents for *her* birthday?"

Olivia hunches her shoulders up to her ears because she has no idea what's going on, either. Kathy gets up and grabs two envelopes from underneath the phone book on the counter, handing one to me and one to Liv.

"Careful—don't get food on that," she warns her daughter.

234

"Should Liv open hers first, or what?" I ask my dad.

He smiles, and the suspense is killing me.

"You can open them together."

We tear into the envelopes, but I'm the only one who understands what I pull out.

"Plane tickets?" I look back and forth between Dad and Kathy.

"Where are we going?" Liv asks.

"Keep reading," Dad says, nodding at the documents in my hand.

I examine the ticket to learn I'm flying to New York two days before Christmas. In shock, I stare at my father and wait for an explanation.

"We're all going to New York for Christmas," he says. "I thought we'd sightsee for a few days, and we'll come back the day after Christmas because I know the Sumner Holiday Tournament starts on the twenty-seventh."

"Do we get to see the tree at Rocket Propeller Center?" Liv asks, and we all laugh.

"That's Rock*efeller* Center, and yes," Kathy tells her. "We'll do whatever you guys want."

Olivia grins like crazy and then just as quickly, her mouth slides into a frown.

"But, how will Santa know where to bring our presents?"

It's amazing how her mind works. I put my emotions over our gift aside for a moment to explain, "Dad can write him a note."

"Really?"

"Oh, yeah. Santa gets notes all the time from people who travel at Christmas. He'll find us. I promise."

Liv nods, accepting my explanation, and I turn to Dad, still overwhelmed by his surprise.

"Dad, I—" I begin.

"Eat your dessert," he tells me gently. "We'll talk later."

After dessert, Kathy and Liv tackle the dishes so Dad and I can go down to the family room to watch football and talk. We've barely left the stairs before I throw my arms around him.

"Thanks, Dad. This means everything to me. You have no idea."

"Oh, I have some idea," he says, keeping an arm around me as he walks us to the leather sectional. We sit down and he turns on the Bears-Lions game, but at a low enough volume that we can still talk.

"Your mom told me Kieran's undergoing the treatment the day after Christmas, and she was saying how upset you were that you couldn't be there and how the two of you were going to have to say your goodbyes in person so many days beforehand." He rolls the remote between his hands. "I thought this might be a nice family vacation. The four of us have never travelled anywhere before, and New York's supposed to be amazing at Christmastime. And, this way, you can be with Kieran right up until the day he's treated."

Our Christmas break is almost two weeks long this year, so Carlie had arranged with Ben Halloran for Kieran to undergo the treatment right after the holiday in the hopes he could be brought out of the coma in enough time to avoid missing much school. While I understand the timing, I really hated knowing we would be apart for the last few days before Kieran would undergo the treatment, especially considering he might not remember me when he wakes up.

"In spite of everything," Dad continues, "I like the kid. I like his family. And I know how important he is to you, and I know how important you are to me, so it just made sense. Plus, Liv says something every year about wanting to visit the tree at Rocket Propeller Center, so I figured I'd better get to work on that."

Dad smiles, and I'm overcome with gratitude to the point I feel tears straining at the corners of my eyes.

"Are you crying?" he asks.

"No." I sniffle.

"Well, you'd better man up, McKee. Football's on."

I give him a joke-punch to the shoulder.

"I'll show you who needs to man up," I tease as he turns up the volume and rubs his shoulder. Slumping down, I lean my head against his arm and pull my legs up to me.

"I love you, Dad," I whisper.

"Love you, too, Zip-a-roo," he whispers back.

CHAPTER 21

Much to my immense relief since I'm sitting next to her, Olivia, who has never flown before, spends the majority of our two-hour flight from O'Hare to New York staring out the window, fascinated by being up above the clouds or pointing out interesting things to me below when we're close enough to see the ground. By the time we land at LaGuardia Airport, she's so worn out from excitement Dad has to carry her off the plane and down the passageway leading to our gate.

"Kieran said they're going to meet us at our baggage claim," I tell my family, summarizing the series of text messages I read from him as we were waiting to get off the plane. Since we're leaving the day after Christmas so I can be back for the Sumner Holiday Tournament while the Laniers aren't sure *when* they're coming home, my family and Kieran's had to travel on different schedules. The Laniers should have landed about two hours ago, but rather than the entire Lanier family waiting for us, we're greeted instead by the sight of Kieran, Cooper, and Victor, who's clad in a suit and chauffeur's cap, holding up a sign reading "McKee Family." I run to Kieran and throw my arms around him, giving him a chaste peck on the lips considering my dad and little sister are watching.

"Are your parents and Kayla here somewhere?" I ask, looking around.

"They went ahead to the hotel," Kieran explains. "Although I'm guessing Mom and Kayla are out shopping already. Few things can motivate those two to put their differences aside like a mutual love of designer footwear."

"If world leaders only knew that expensive shoes were the key to world peace."

I press my forehead to his and the two of us hold each other, teetering on the verge of forgetting others are around until Cooper, Victor, and my dad start an exaggerated coughing fit.

"Guess I should make some introductions, huh?" I ask Kieran.

"No kidding. Rude girl." Kieran kisses the top of my head and I set about getting everyone acquainted with everyone else. Upon my introducing them to Olivia, both Cooper and Kieran crouch down to her height.

"Nice to meet you," Kieran says, holding his hand out for her to shake. "Zip's told me a lot about you."

"She has?" Liv gazes up at me with wild eyes as if she can't believe I would ever talk about her to my boyfriend.

"Oh, yeah," he continues. "I can't wait to hang out with you while Cooper shows us around the city. What all are we going to do, Coop?"

"Well, we can check out the Christmas windows at Macy's, and we can visit Santa Claus so he knows you're here in New York instead of Chicago. We don't want him to deliver your presents to the wrong place."

Liv shakes her head.

"Mom and Dad already wrote him a note telling him we were going to be in New York, so we're good."

Kieran stifles a laugh, and if Cooper's confused, he manages to brush it off in favor of tempting Liv with more of his planned activities.

"Well, then, we can go see the tree at Rockefeller Center, and then we can go to this amazing toy store near there," he continues. "Actually, it's pretty close to your hotel. You know the one I'm talking about, right, Kieran? We went when you were here this summer."

"Yeah," Kieran responds, and shifts his eyes to my sister. "Olivia, you would *not* believe this place—floors and floors of nothing but toys. It's awesome."

Liv's eyes grow to teacup saucer-size.

"Wow," she whispers. "Can we go there first?"

"We're in trouble now," Kathy mutters to Dad, her voice low enough Olivia either can't hear or isn't paying enough attention to care.

"We'll do whatever you want," Kieran tells her. "I mean, tomorrow's your birthday, right?" Kieran glances from her to Cooper, who adds "Yeah—just say the word. We'll plan the whole day around you."

Liv's gaze darts back and forth between Kieran and Cooper as if she can't decide which one of them she's more in love with at the moment. Behind us, the conveyor belt beeps and luggage starts appearing, so my dad heads off to retrieve our bags, followed closely by Victor, who says, "Let me help you with those, sir."

"Thanks, Victor. Much appreciated."

Kieran stands up to full height and puts an arm around my shoulder, but Cooper stays crouched in front of Olivia. "Piggy back ride?" he suggests to her before looking up at Kathy. "If it's okay with you. We'll just walk back and forth around here a little bit. Won't leave your sight—I promise."

"I don't see why not," Kathy says, and Liv's practically glued herself to Cooper's back before her mother finishes her sentence. Cooper stands and trots Liv down to the end of the baggage claim area with her giggling the whole way.

"I had no idea Cooper liked kids so much," I whisper to Kieran.

"I don't think *he* knew he liked kids so much," he says as we watch Cooper turn around and start walking them back with a spring in his step that makes Olivia bounce up and down, much to her amusement. "She's a little cutie, though," Kieran continues, loudly enough for Kathy to hear. "In about six or seven more years, she'll be breaking hearts."

"I try to prepare myself for that possibility every day," Kathy replies. "It's not working."

Dad and Victor wheel our bags over to us as Cooper and Olivia stop just outside the group. Victor offers to drive the SUV over from the short-term parking lot and pull up out front, and by the time we've dragged our suitcases to the curb, we only have to wait a few minutes before Victor arrives in a sleek black SUV, much like the ones he and Cooper always rent at O'Hare when they come to Titusville. Kieran and I crawl into the second back seat with Olivia, and, sitting between us, Kieran grabs hold of both my hand and hers.

Taking in the sights as they fly by, Liv and I gasp simultaneously when we approach the Queensboro Bridge, which I've seen only on TV and in movies. It's our first glimpse of Manhattan, the immense skyscrapers looking as though they're going to swallow us up and the sidewalks holding more people in one city block than have ever passed through downtown Titusville. Liv and I spend the few minutes before Victor pulls into the parking garage for our hotel whipping our heads around, trying to look out every window at once as if we're afraid we're going to miss something. By the time we're in our room next to Dad and Kathy's on the eighteenth floor, we're both so hyper we're practically bouncing up and down on the double bed.

We should probably rest before we have to be at the Hallorans' for dinner, but instead, we start talking a million miles a minute as we get up to press our foreheads against the window and stare down at the people passing by on the street who look like tiny marks on an Impressionist painting from this height.

"I want to go to the Statue of Liberty," Liv blurts out.

"And I want to visit the Empire State Building and the Guggenheim," I almost say right over her.

"And the big tree—it's near here, right?"

I nod, continuing with my list.

"And St. Patrick's Cathedral and Rock*efeller* Center and Times Square and—"

"And the big toy store Cooper talked about and—"

"Ladies, you need to calm down before you throw up from all the excitement," Dad says, entering our room from a door connecting our room to his and Kathy's. "We're only here for a few days, and some of those places might not be open on Christmas."

Olivia heaves a dramatic sigh and flops down on the bed.

"Way to kill the buzz, Dad," I grumble, but I'm smiling, and he collapses on his stomach next Liv.

"We'll come back one of these days and do everything we don't get do on this trip, okay? I promise."

Liv perks up a little.

"Next summer?"

Dad grimaces at me as if to say, "Help," and then shifts his eyes back to Liv.

"Well, maybe not *next* summer. But one of these days."

Before Liv can protest, Kathy enters through the connecting door.

"I know a little monkey girl who needs a bath before we leave for dinner," she says. "Let's find your bath stuff."

She crosses the room to dig through Liv's suitcase, and then turns back to me.

"Zip, we'll take her into our room so you can use the bathroom in here to get ready for dinner. Figured you'd appreciate the privacy."

"Thanks," I say, and Kathy grabs some shampoo from Liv's suitcase and steers her into the other room, Dad following and shutting the door behind them. Since I knew I'd probably need to get dressed up while we were here, I'd packed more than just jeans and sweatpants, and so I hang an olive green sweater dress on a hook inside the bathroom door so the steam from my shower can smooth out some of the wrinkles. Once I'm dressed and ready, I check my phone and find I only have ten minutes to spare before we're all supposed to meet up, but I'm too amped to sit and wait.

"Hey, I'm going down to the lobby," I announce after knocking on the door separating my room from Dad and Kathy's. "I'll meet you guys there."

"Okay. See you in a few," Dad calls back, and I grab my black wool dress coat and head downstairs, texting Kieran from the elevator. I've only been sitting in the lobby for about a minute, listening to a guy in a tuxedo play a grand piano and watching hotel guests wander about, when Kieran and Kayla walk up.

"You look amazing," he tells me, offering his hands so he can pull me up.

"And you're wearing a sweater. I don't think I've ever seen you in a sweater before," I say, putting my hands on his shoulders and tilting my head as if I'm trying to examine him completely. He's wearing a navy blue collared sweater with a white t-shirt peeking out, and Kayla chuckles a little, saying, "He left all of his designer hoodies at home."

"I don't look like a complete loser?" Kieran asks me, ignoring his sister. "It was either this or a tie, and I didn't feel like wearing a tie."

"You're the total opposite of a loser. Trust me."

Just then, I glance over Kieran's shoulder at Victor entering the hotel, still clad in the chauffeur's uniform he was wearing when he

243

met us at the airport. As he approaches us from one direction, my parents, Liv and the Laniers walk toward us from the bank of elevators and, our group fully assembled, Victor sweeps his arm out at the revolving glass doors.

"There are two town cars outside to take you to the Hallorans' if everyone's ready," he says.

Everyone nods and follows him out to the hotel's circular drive, where Kieran, Kayla, Liv, and I pile into Victor's town car while the adults get into the car driven by one of the other members of the Hallorans' staff. The cars hardly seem worth it, as we're at the palatial building on Central Park West in minutes, and I barely catch a glimpse of the outside of the residence before we make a left turn onto a side street and enter a parking area underneath the building. Kieran and Kayla, having been to the Hallorans' before, seem completely unfazed by the whole experience, while Liv and I, on the other hand, immediately turn to each other with wide eyes the second we start heading underground.

Victor pulls into a space next to two elevator doors, and we get out and make our way to the elevator without waiting for the other car, which must have gotten stuck behind some traffic on Central Park West as they're nowhere around at the moment. And, regardless, we wouldn't all fit on one car, so I grab Liv's hand and follow the siblings and Victor onto an elevator car lined with mirrors. Victor hits a button and we're whisked up to the second floor, where we walk down an off-white, chandelier-lit hallway to a door with a gold "2" affixed between the top two panels. Slipping ahead of us, Victor opens the door and stands aside so we can pass by him into a mirrored entryway with dark wood panels and a marble floor. I step gingerly into the entry as the floor has been polished to the point the white lights bouncing off the surface from the six foot Christmas tree in the corner give the illusion that the floor is actually wet. A maid—

dressed exactly like a maid from the movies with a black long-sleeved dress, white collar, and matching white apron—takes our coats as Liv and I whip our heads around, trying to take it all in.

"I feel like I just walked into the middle of *The Great Gatsby* or something," I hiss at Kieran, retaking Liv's hand.

Kieran flashes me his grin.

"Just wait—it gets better."

Cooper strides into the entry wearing a white oxford shirt, the sleeves buttoned down over his wrists, and impeccably pressed khaki pants.

"Hey," he says to no one in particular. "Did you guys ditch the adults or something? My dad'll be bummed if he doesn't have anyone to play with."

"They should be right behind us, sir." Victor informs him as Cooper bends down to Olivia, who immediately releases my hand.

"How about a tour? Kieran and Kayla have already seen the place, but they can tag along," he suggests, scooping her up in his arms. He's burly enough that he can hold Liv with ease, something I can no longer do since she's gotten so tall.

We follow Cooper into a hallway that never seems to end, decorated with the same stately dark wood as the entry. "Sitting room," he says, pointing at an open door off to the left. I peek in on a room fit for royalty, its centerpiece a fireplace outlined in marble and topped off with a portrait of a man I don't recognize hanging over a mantle trimmed with pine rope. Couches and chairs upholstered in red velvet that seem too uncomfortable to sit on flank a marble-topped coffee table, and another fully-decorated Christmas tree—this one with mostly red and gold ornaments to match the room as opposed to the white-themed tree of the entry— graces the far end of the room next to a grand piano. I press the toe of my leather boot into an intricate oriental rug that probably costs more than my mom's car,

245

and I'm so busy staring at things I almost don't realize Cooper, Liv, and the siblings have moved on down the hall.

"Dining room, but we'll be in there soon enough." Cooper points at a closed door to our left as I get caught up to the group, sliding my hand into Kieran's. "And there's the kitchen, but it's a mess right now with the staff getting ready for dinner, so I'll show that to you later. There's a breakfast room in there, too, and that's where Dad and I eat when we're not being all formal. And then this is the library…"

Cooper opens a door on the right side of the hall and we step into a room that's straight out of a movie. The Halloran library consists of two floors of built-in bookcases lining the walls, the multi-colored book spines assaulting my senses with a muted rainbow of colors. A spiral staircase snakes down from the second floor, which is essentially a balcony wrapping around the perimeter of the first floor like a track above an indoor gym. In the middle of the first floor are the same uncomfortable couches and chairs from the sitting room, joined by a massive oak desk at the far end of the room. And someone's decked the halls in here as well—pine rope entwined with Christmas lights loops through the railings and bannisters, and yet another tree stands in the far corner of the room near the desk. Considering I still haven't seen most of the rooms in this place, I'm starting to wonder if somewhere in New York City there isn't one very empty Christmas tree lot right about now.

"Does your dad use this as an office?" I ask stupidly, not looking at Cooper but swiveling my head around the room, trying to absorb the entire scene.

"Nah. He's got an office upstairs in his suite." Cooper raises his chin toward a door on the second floor of the library, which I'm assuming must lead to Mr. Halloran's rooms.

I take a breath.

"His *suite*?"

Cooper lowers Olivia to the floor so she can walk around.

"Yeah. Second floor is Dad's suite, my suite, Victor's suite, two guest suites, and a hall bathroom—but each suite also has its own private bathroom." He buries his hands in his pockets and continues listing rooms as if the size of this place is no big deal and everyone lives in a palace contained within an apartment building. "The first floor has five guest suites, but they're smaller than the ones up here, and there's a hall bathroom down there, too. Then we own the entire basement level, where there's a pool, weight room, and a theater."

"Of course," I say, trying to sound unimpressed. "You know, as soon as my mom sells a few more of those earring trees, we're adding an indoor pool at home, so, whatever."

Cooper laughs.

"Well, feel free to wander around," he says. "We've still got a little time before dinner. I'll show you the rest of the place later."

"Okay," I mumble as Cooper trots down toward the other end of the room where Liv is spinning like a top while Kayla leans against the enormous desk, egging her on.

"Want to look around upstairs?" Kieran asks, grabbing my hand.

"Yeah," I say, before pulling him off to the spiral staircase, which curls around twice before depositing us upstairs in front of a section of books that, judging from the author names and my spotty knowledge of literary history, seem to date from the early nineteenth century. I drop Kieran's hand and pick up a weathered volume of Jane's Austin's *Sense and Sensibility*, leafing through its yellowed pages while muttering, "Holy crap, this place is amazing."

"I know, right?" he says, plucking out a book with a green cloth cover whose title and author I can't make out. "Just think about the damage we could do in this room."

I look up from the novel's pages.

"This isn't a room. It's, like, a public library-sized library. It's insane."

Glancing down to the first floor, I watch Cooper swing Liv around, her feet narrowly missing a lamp on a side table near the library door. Kayla cringes at the same time I do, and then she laughs up at me as Kieran shakes his head and places the book he'd been looking at back on the shelf.

"The whole world is Cooper's playground," he says. "Especially now that he doesn't have anything holding him back anymore."

"It'll be that way for you, too," I assure him, touching his arm, and he shoots me his trademark grin.

"Sure—just without the bajillion dollars at my disposal."

"Well, yeah. There's that, I guess."

Kieran shoves his hands in his back pockets and leans in toward the bookshelf, squinting at the titles on the book spines.

"I'm trying to figure out how these books are organized," he says, taking a volume with a red cloth cover off a shelf above his head and leafing through it. "I can't tell if it's by time period or what."

"Me, neither," I say, leaning in to find Kieran's paging through a copy of *Silas Marner*, which I haven't read. He stops on a page and we read together for what only seems like a minute, and I'm so engrossed in the words I don't hear anyone approaching.

"I wish I could get Cooper half as interested in reading as the two of you are right now."

I gasp and turn to discover a man standing in the second floor entry whom I instantly recognize, based on pictures Cooper's shown me and an article I found in one of Dad's financial magazines, as America's tenth richest man and Chief Executive Officer of Halloran Industries—Ben Halloran.

248

CHAPTER 22

Ben Halloran smiles at my surprise on hearing his voice.

"My apologies for startling you, young lady," he says, approaching us. "I didn't expect anyone to be in here. Sometimes I cut through the library to go to down to the main floor instead of walking around to the staircase."

"No...it's...I..."

Kieran saves us from my meaningless babble.

"Hello, sir." He puts *Silas Marner* back on the shelf and steps to Ben Halloran with an outstretched hand. "Nice to see you again."

They shake hands, and the older gentleman insists, "You've been a guest in my home, Kieran—it's *Ben*."

Ben Halloran and Cooper look nothing alike, of course, but the difference is almost jarring now that I'm seeing Cooper's adoptive father in person for the first time. He's wearing a tasteful dark suit and white dress shirt that complement his salt-and-pepper hair, the ensemble topped off by a muted red tie and matching pocket square. Articles I've read all mention that he's forty-nine years old, but his unlined face and clear brown eyes suggest a much younger man, maybe around my mom's age. His narrow nose, pale thin lips, and round cheeks work together to give his face a pleasant, relaxed quality, the exact opposite of the shrewd, calculating corporate warrior portrayed both in the article I read at my dad's over Thanksgiving and in Cooper's descriptions, and I can't help but wonder which Ben Halloran—the one I'm seeing now or the one in the media—is the true man.

Mr. Halloran drops Kieran's hand and reaches for mine. "I'm Zara McKee," I tell him in a small voice before Kieran can introduce us, 'Zip' somehow not seeming formal enough for my first introduction to a billionaire. "It's nice to meet you."

"I had a feeling you must be Kieran's girlfriend." He smiles as he releases my hand, giving me a flash of brilliant white teeth. "And it's nice to meet you, too. But Cooper and Kieran tell me you go by 'Zip' most of the time, correct?"

I try to respond, but my voice catches and I'm forced to clear my throat.

"Yes," I finally eek out.

"Something to do with your athletic abilities?"

"Zip's a star basketball player," Kieran chimes in. "Point guard. Blows right by everyone on the court."

I feel my face getting hot, but Mr. Halloran puts me at ease.

"Ah, yes—I remember the boys mentioning that now. I was a point guard in high school, too. The coaches moved me to shooting guard when I played at Harvard, though."

"Really?" I say, stunned to have anything in common with one of the richest men in the United States, even though logic tells me he's probably done many of the same mundane things most people in this country would have done. But he was doing those mundane things at fancy prep schools and places like Harvard and not in middle-of-nowhere towns such as Titusville.

"Really," he responds. "I still like to take in a game now and then when my schedule allows. I'm a lifelong Knicks fan." He narrows his eyes, but the slight twinkle shining through is anything but menacing. "I'm guessing you must be a Bulls fan?"

"Lifelong." I say with a tiny smile.

"Well, I won't hold it against you." He slips one arm around Kieran and one around me, already putting the lie to the cold businessman persona. "We should go down to dinner, but feel free to explore in here all you want afterwards. This room doesn't get nearly enough use." He glances around wistfully at the rows of books. "I'm usually reading the Wall Street Journal or financial reports, and Cooper's nose is typically glued to his phone screen or his tablet—and I suspect he's not reading."

I can't imagine having a library like this in my house and only using it as a cut-through to the first floor. Kieran and I could probably spend an entire year in here and never leave.

Mr. Halloran takes his arm from my shoulders and sweeps it out toward the spiral staircase.

"After you," he says, and I make my way down ahead of the men, crossing the first floor and opening the door out into the hall, where we find our parents shuffling into the dining room. They pause on seeing us emerge from the library, and Jim introduces Mr. Halloran to Kathy and Dad, who is every bit as humbled and mumbling as I was on meeting a man who's supposedly one of the country's most nimble business minds.

"Jim tells me you work for the Merc?" Mr. Halloran asks as we enter the dining room, immediately taking an interest in my dad. Dad informs him that he's correct and says something about "futures," which is my clue they're about to descend into the kind of stock market-speak I don't understand.

"Mr. Halloran seems nice," I whisper to Kieran as we hang back just inside the door and wait for the adults and Olivia to seat themselves around the twenty-person dining table, set with bone china, silver utensils—real silver, I'm guessing—and crystal goblets reflecting the chandelier light. Everything's resting atop a blinding white tablecloth, the shiny brightness of the room nearly blotting out the city lights visible through the floor-to-ceiling windows on the other side of the room.

"Oh, he's perfectly nice," Cooper begins, sidling up on my other side with Kayla. "Just as long as you don't own a company he's trying to acquire. Or as long as you're not his son."

"Oh, come on." Kayla shakes her head. "He's never been anything other than awesome whenever we've been here."

Cooper gives her a saccharine smile.

"Which is kind of the point. *You'll* never know him as anything other than Ben Halloran, shrewd businessman and benevolent philanthropist. You'll never know him like I do."

"Why don't you kids all sit over here? The soup should be out any second now."

We're interrupted by Ben's voice booming at us from the head of the table, and I turn to find him motioning toward seats on his right next to Jim and Carlie. Kieran, Kayla and I take the long trek to the end of the room so we can round the table to the other side, while Cooper slides into the seat beside his new girlfriend, Olivia, who seems so overwhelmed by the opulence she's seen already tonight that for once, she's speechless. I take my seat between Kieran and Kayla and am shocked by the sheer size of the table—Cooper seems approximately a million miles away, and I couldn't talk to him without yelling even if I wanted.

I spread a linen napkin on my lap while the maids begin serving the food, and it quickly becomes clear I won't want to talk to Cooper or anyone else because I'll be too busy stuffing my face. The meal begins with a sinfully rich tomato bisque, followed by spinach salads. For the main course, the maids serve us beef medallions, thin green beans—when one of the maids asked me if I would like "haricots verts," I looked at her and said, "Um...what?"—and herb roasted potatoes. By the time I put the last forkful of cherry cheesecake in my mouth at the end of the dessert course, I'm convinced I'm so full I won't be able to stand up from the table. But I do, and I drag myself along with everyone else down to the sitting room, where yet another maid enters with crystal tumblers and a decanter of brandy as the adults are busy choosing which uncomfortable-looking piece of furniture to sit on and everyone under the age of twenty-one hangs back by the door.

"You guys want to go upstairs to my room?" Cooper asks, once again picking up Liv as if she's no more than a breadcrumb on the carpet. "Some of the guys at Omega Games sent over a pre-release copy of the new Demon Sport yesterday. They said it's got some bugs, but it should be playable."

Halloran Industries bought Omega Games two years ago, so, naturally, Cooper would be able to get the most anticipated video game releases months before they're due to hit the market—Demon Sport Fifteen isn't supposed to be out until March.

"Oh, cool," I answer for all of us. "Except for...um..." I tilt my head toward Liv, who's nearly asleep on Cooper's shoulder. I don't think Dad and Kathy would appreciate her getting a sneak peek of a video game whose primary objective is to stab winged demons until they turn into skeletons and collapse into ash. And the prospect doesn't thrill me, either, since I'll be sharing a hotel bed with her and her nightmares.

"Oh, yeah," Cooper mumbles, giving her a squeeze. "Luckily, I also own an extensive collection of cartoons."

Liv immediately perks up.

"Cartoons?" she asks, lifting her head from Cooper's shoulder and staring at him dead on.

"Yeah. Let's go find something to watch."

Cooper walks forward toward his father and mine, who are standing in front of the fireplace. He bounces Liv against his hip as he says, "We're going to go upstairs to my room and watch cartoons."

Ben Halloran swirls his brandy around in his glass, his lips twisting on his son's suggestion.

"That sounds incredibly mature, Cooper."

The bite in his voice shocks me a bit, but Cooper isn't the least bit surprised.

"Well, we have a six year-old to entertain. And I'm guessing staying down here won't be much fun for her. I know *I* stopped having fun about five minutes ago."

"I'll be seven tomorrow," Olivia announces at what any other time would be off the subject but, at the moment, seems like the perfect goofy statement to break up the weird tension between Cooper and his father. And while their interaction is uncomfortable, I'm struck with the realization that I've seen something like it before—the biting words, the icy restraint.

It's Kieran and Jim.

"You know, if they want to take Olivia upstairs for a while, it's fine with me," Dad interjects. "Kathy?"

Kathy's a few feet away on one of the stiff-looking red velvet couches, talking to Carlie.

"Did you say something?" she says, jerking around at the sound of Dad's voice.

"The kids were going to take Liv upstairs to watch cartoons."

"Oh, sure, sure." Kathy bobs her head at Dad and Cooper, and I wonder if the brandy's hitting her already because she seems more red-faced and relaxed than usual.

"I'll send one of the staff upstairs for the kids when you're ready to leave," Ben Halloran assures the adults, and Kieran, Kayla, Cooper, and I slip out of the room with Liv still in Cooper's arms.

"You just got a small taste of the usual Cooper and Ben Show," Cooper tells me once we're down the hall enough to be out of earshot of the sitting room. "That's about all Kayla and K-Man ever

254

saw when they were here this summer, too. The full spectacle only happens when no one's around."

I don't bother to ask what "the full spectacle" involves as Cooper sets Liv down and the two of them race up the stairs, leaving Kieran, Kayla, and me in the dust. As the three of us continue making our way to the second floor, I notice Kieran falling about a step behind me once we're almost to the top.

"You okay?" I move to slide my arm around him. He blinks and his eyes stay closed longer than a second, which tells me we're about to lose him. Kayla, her sixth sense when dealing with her brother fully activated, spins around and grabs his arm before his body slackens.

"Long day," Kieran mumbles at me, and I realize the time zone change combined with the general stress of travel has likely thrown Kieran's rhythms off. Kayla and I help him down the hall—of course, Cooper's room *has* to be at the far end of the hall—and as we approach the open bedroom door, Kieran glances at me and says, "Only a few more days, and you'll never have to do this again."

I lean in to kiss his forehead.

"I'd do it forever if we had to."

Kayla and I get Kieran to the couch in Cooper's room, and he tucks his hands under his chin like a little kid and drifts off to a deep sleep. And speaking of little kids, I hear a giggle from across the room and glance up to discover my baby sister—who has evidently forgotten all about watching cartoons—using Cooper's bed as a trampoline.

"Liv!" I shriek, slipping into Big Sister mode and darting toward her so quickly I almost trip up the three steps elevating the sleeping area from the sitting room where I've just left my boyfriend. "Be careful. You'll hit your—"

255

I'm about to say "head," but as I arrive at the end of the bed, I look up at a ceiling so high above us that even Cooper wouldn't be in danger of cracking his skull, assuming the bed could hold his weight if he decided to jump up and down on the mattress.

"Well, be careful," I warn. "You could bounce off and hit the wall or something."

Cooper, who's sitting in a gigantic black bean bag chair next to on the opposite side of the bed, laughs at me.

"I should have known better than to trust you with a little kid," I tell him.

"You should have known better than to trust *me* with anyone," he fires back, standing up. "I think now might be a good time for cartoons."

He holds his arms out and Liv jumps into them so he can carry her down the white carpeted stairs to the couch, which is opposite a fifty-inch flat screen television hanging over a bookcase with an entire electronics store's worth of movies and video games.

Cooper leans over the back of the couch to find Kieran sleeping away. "Well, this puts a damper on things, doesn't it?" he says, looking at Liv in his arms, and he brings one hand to his chin, stroking it as if in deep thought, a motion Liv mimics to the effect of sending both Kayla and me into hysterics.

"Okay, here we go," Cooper says, carrying her around to the front of the couch. "You mind sitting on the floor?"

"I sit on the floor all the time at home," she says.

"Awesome. But first, let's find a video."

He lowers her in front of the bookcase and she takes a minute to pick out a disc. Cooper gets everything set up, and once Liv's all comfy on the floor, he drags the bean bag chair from next to the bed to the area behind the couch and nods at two video game recliners in the corner next to a desk. Kayla and I scoot the chairs over behind the couch as well so the three of us can talk.

"Nice place you have here, Coop," I begin, noticing that this is the first room I've seen today without a Christmas tree. "A little on the small side, but…"

"Don't even get me started on his closet," Kayla says after letting out a snort. "It's bigger than my entire room. Totally not fair."

Cooper shifts in the bean bag chair and surveys the room.

"I spend most of my time here when I'm home. If I could get Big Ben to put in a kitchen up here somewhere, I'd never need to go anywhere else in the house. Dad wouldn't have to see me at all."

I stretch my legs out in front of me and cross my ankles—sitting like a lady in a video game lounger isn't exactly the easiest thing.

"You know, your dad seems okay to me," I point out for the second time this evening. "It's kind of hard to match the person I met tonight with the one you're always talking about."

A dark expression settles over Cooper's face, his eyes seeming more swollen than usual.

"You don't live in this house and disappoint him on a regular basis," he says, picking at some microscopic fuzz on the carpet. "Know how I'm always going on about being the 'new and improved' Cooper all the time? Well, I'm not 'new and improved' in Ben Halloran's eyes. I'm still the same kid who won't grow up, the same kid who doesn't show enough interest in the family business, the same kid who uses *his* money for my personal gain—not that he doesn't do a hell of a lot of that himself." Cooper stops picking at the floor and raises his hand near his face to examine his fingernails. "I think he thought I was going to get my memory back and be a completely different person, and it didn't work that way. Part of me wonders if he didn't like the clueless amnesiac better—he could control me then."

Cooper continues staring at his fingertips as if he doesn't want to meet my eyes or Kayla's.

"This time next year, I'll be coming back from Europe." He drops his hand and looks at us. "I'm tempted not to come back and just disappear—change my name, start over. Screw going to Harvard in the spring, screw taking over Halloran Industries, screw everything. But how do you go off the grid when you're Ben Halloran's son? He has people everywhere." Cooper shakes his head and sighs. "I can finally, *physically*, do whatever I want, but I'm still trapped."

Kayla groans.

"Cry me a river, rich boy. You don't even know what 'Daddy Issues' are. At least *your* dad doesn't conspire with your mom to lie to you on a regular basis."

Cooper raises his eyebrows at her as if to acknowledge her point.

"So, Zip," he starts, folding his arms over his chest and gazing at me. "Want to tell us what things are like with a dad who isn't trying to control your life?"

I match Cooper's posture.

"Sure thing. *My* awesome dad walked out on my mom when I was younger than Liv."

Realizing what I've just blurted out, I clasp my hand over my mouth. Cooper, who's sitting closest to the back of the couch, stands and peers over.

"I don't think she heard you," he hisses as he arranges himself back on the bean bag chair. "She's pretty into that cartoon."

Even so, I lower my voice.

"I see my dad a few times a year and for an entire month in the summer most years. But he's never been to one of my games, and he loves basketball. He's always been too busy. His new family is his life now, and I guess I can't hold that against him. But there were a lot of years between the divorce and—" I point at the couch—"*her* coming along when he could have made more of an effort with me. He's trying now, but I'm almost eighteen. That's a lot of wasted time." I pause, hearing Kieran shifting around. "So, my dad isn't exactly controlling, but that's probably only because he's not in my life on a daily basis," I conclude.

Kieran sits up, only his head visible above the couch cushions.

"What are you guys talking about?" he asks, throwing an arm over the back.

"Crappy fathers," Cooper informs him, and Kieran's mouth shifts into a grin.

"Oh, I can play *this* game. Do you want to hear about my dad who lied to me my entire life, and probably still is most of the time, or should I talk about my other dad, the ex-con who lives down the road?"

"Well, since my ex-con dad isn't alive, I think you win," Cooper tells him. "But, look—" he swivels his head, sweeping both Kieran and Kayla up in his gaze—"All this 'dad' stuff? Just because the treatment makes you a 'new and improved' person doesn't mean your relationships are automatically going to change, too. The sleeping disorder and the dreams are gone, but all that means is Dad doesn't make Victor watch my every move. But I'm still the same me deep down that I was before. And my dad still looks at me and sees Ginny Malsun's bastard son with some lowlife. No treatment in the world can make that go away. No matter how the treatment changes *you*, it isn't going to change your relationships."

259

Kieran rises from the couch and walks over to sit on the floor next to me, taking my hand in his.

"Some relationships, I don't want to change," he tells Cooper.

"Of course. And what I'm saying is that they won't, unless both people involved want things to change. My life is different, but my relationship with my dad is the same as before because neither of us is making an effort, and I'm not sure either of us wants to after all these years." He darts his eyes from Kieran to Kayla and back again. "Once you get your memory back, it's up to both of you to decide what you want—do you want to repair those relationships, or do you want to move on from them?"

None of us says anything for a moment, the only sound in the room a squawking cartoon bird on the TV screen. Kayla locks eyes with Kieran as she responds to Cooper's question.

"I don't think either of us knows if we can trust them again after everything they've put us through."

Kieran nods in agreement with his sister's statement and Cooper shrugs.

"Well, I'm just putting it out there," he begins. "The treatment will fix *you*, but it doesn't fix everything. I've only recently started figuring that out."

Cooper's interrupted by a knock on his bedroom door, and he struggles to his feet since he's wedged into the bean bag chair. Before he can cross the room, Victor opens the door and sticks his head inside.

"The Laniers and McKees are ready to leave, sir," Victor informs Cooper.

Cooper scoops Liv off the floor and tells her, "Time to go, kiddo."

Liv pouts and glances from me to Cooper.

"Do we have to?"

"It's almost your bedtime," I point out. "And we have a big day tomorrow, remember?

She perks up a little at the mention of our planned tourist whirlwind.

"Are you coming with us?" she asks Cooper.

"Wouldn't miss it. Santa doesn't know what I want for Christmas yet."

"Are you coming with us, too?" Liv turns her attention to Kieran.

"Of course," he says, reaching out to tweak her nose.

"I'll be there, too, by the way," Kayla mumbles, and I laugh a little, bumping arms with her.

"I'm sensing we don't matter too much," I mutter.

"You think?"

"Your father has requested that you and I pick the families up from the hotel around ten, sir," Victor says to Cooper, sweeping an arm out in an indication we should exit into the hallway ahead of him. "After consulting with them, he determined that would give them plenty of time to sleep in and eat breakfast while still giving all of you enough time for a full day."

Cooper bounces Liv against him as we start down the hall.

"Dad's not coming with us?" he asks Victor.

"The markets are open until one o'clock tomorrow, so Mr. Halloran plans to go to the office. Then he's going to spend the afternoon ensuring the arrangements are in place for Mr. Lanier's procedure."

"All things a team of well-paid minions could do for him," Cooper mutters, almost under his breath.

"It's okay," Liv tells him as the two of them take the lead down the stairs. "You can share our dads for the day—right, guys?"

Liv looks back at us, and I want to hug her for being such a sweet kid.

"Sure thing," I confirm, and Kayla and Kieran both chime in with "Yeah."

"Thanks," Cooper says sadly as we reach the first floor. At the other end of the hall, the adults are standing around in the entry, Ben and the maids helping our parents into their coats. Ben smiles broadly and roars with laughter at something my dad says, not looking at all like the distant father Cooper portrays him to be. But then again, an outsider watching this scene— or even Victor, for example—would have no idea that any of us has had trouble with our fathers. Our families are what they are to us, but they're something quite different to everyone who's on the outside looking in and can't get past the bright shiny façades we construct to hide the darkness.

We trek down the hall to join our parents, and the entryway becomes a chaotic mess of people slipping into coats and saying "Thank you," and "Dinner was wonderful," and "We look forward to Christmas day." I'm the last one out the door after Kieran, and, my hand locked in his, I glance back at Cooper standing next to his father, both of them giving us tiny waves goodbye. Cooper's probably three inches taller than his father and outweighs him by a good thirty pounds, but right now, with his shoulders hunched forward and one hand buried in the front pocket of his khakis, Cooper seems smaller than I could have ever thought possible, especially with the mirror-filled entryway reflecting every angle of his sad posture back to me. Feeling awful for him, I give them both a wave and direct a tiny smile at Cooper before slipping out the door, leaving the Halloran men alone with their army of staff.

CHAPTER 23

If Olivia's going to do anything when we get back to the hotel, I'll bet she's definitely going to sleep.

Seeing everything New York City has to offer in one day would be impossible, but we've tried our best. We started out on 34th Street at Macy's, where Liv visited with a bewildered Santa Claus who had to pretend he'd received a letter from Dad and Kathy with our hotel address and room number. Next, we worked our way back up to the Empire State Building before heading to a restaurant in Times Square for lunch, complete with a birthday cake Cooper had ordered ahead in Liv's honor. Kieran almost missed Liv's big moment as he was passed out in his chair next to me from sheer exhaustion, only waking up when we all started clapping after Liv blew out her candles.

After walking in and out of stores in Times Square and watching Liv whirl like a tornado through what must be the world's largest toy store, we're all nearly worn out by the time we hit Rockefeller Center. But Liv insists she still has enough energy for ice skating and so Kieran, Kayla, Carlie, Jim, and I watch from the railing above as Dad and Kathy take her around the rink with Cooper tagging along at Liv's insistence. Only the "new and improved" Cooper has never been ice skating before, and right now, we're watching him struggle to keep his balance while Liv attempts to pull him away from the stability of the outer wall.

"Oh, I hope he doesn't fall," Carlie breathes, her expression as tense as if she's watching the end of a particularly suspenseful movie.

Jim slips an arm around her and says, "I don't think Mitch will let him."

Dad and Kathy are following along behind Cooper and Liv as if they're Momma birds watching their little ones fly out of the nest for the first time. Cooper falls—on his butt, thankfully—and Carlie gasps while next to me, Kieran starts to slump into Kayla on his other side.

"You okay?" I ask, although his heavy-lidded expression tells me everything.

"Yeah. Just…the usual." He manages a microscopic version of his typical grin, and Kayla and I turn him around and lower him to the pavement so he can lean up against the concrete.

"I'm surprised you've done as well as you have today," Kayla comments as I slide down next to Kieran and he settles his head on my shoulder. "I'm pretty exhausted myself right now."

"I'm in training," he mumbles. "After the treatment, I'll be able to go all over this city four times without…"

And he's asleep. I glance at the thousands of people moving around us, taking in the sights and sounds of Christmas Eve in Rockefeller Center, not a single one of them noticing the sleeping boy on the ground a few feet away. That's life in New York, I guess.

Kayla stands up and assures her mom Kieran's okay, and I continue to people watch for several minutes until Kieran wakes with a start at the sound of a police siren wailing by out on 5th Avenue. I study his face as he gazes at people pointing up at the giant Christmas tree behind us on the other side of the rink. After a few seconds, his face softens into a calmness that tells me he remembers where we are and what we're doing.

"Are they still skating?" he asks me as I stand and offer my hands in order to pull him to his feet.

"Yeah." I glance over the railing at the swarm of people moving counterclockwise around the rink, and as he pops back up next to me, he drops my hands and looks over the railing as the music stops and the skaters head for the exits.

"Are you able to walk to the hotel, or should we call Victor to pick us up?" Carlie asks Kieran. Poor Victor's been hauling us around the city all day, but he'd dropped us off at Rockefeller Center since it's only a few blocks from our hotel, offering to come back if we wanted to go anywhere else. Otherwise, he'd planned to come back for Cooper once we'd all decided to call it a day.

"I can walk, but I don't want to go back to the hotel yet," Kieran grumbles. "It's still early."

"I'm with Kieran," Kayla chimes in. "Sitting around the hotel with you guys all night sounds pretty boring."

Jim and Carlie brush off Kayla's minor insult.

"I don't know about you, but I'm tired," Jim says to his wife.

"Me, too." She turns to her son. "You're sure you're not too tired?"

Kieran nods down at the pavement where he was sitting a few minutes before.

"Never felt better. I just caught a nap, remember?"

Carlie bites her lip, the frown lines deepening on her forehead, and Kieran reaches out for her arm.

"Cooper, Kayla, and Zip will look out for me. Come on—it's Christmas Eve. I've got two days before my memory gets wiped out for a while. Let me have some fun with these guys while I still remember who they are."

The Laniers exchange glances.

"As long as that's okay with Mitch and Kathy," Carlie says, looking from Kieran to me. Once Dad, Kathy, Cooper and Liv eventually join us from their ice skating misadventures, Dad and Kathy give me their permission to stay out while they take Liv back to the hotel for a bath and bedtime in preparation for Santa's arrival.

"What's your curfew at home now?" Dad asks.

I don't have one—never have, since there's not much trouble to get into in Titusville and, before Kieran, I didn't go out much—but not wanting to risk a snarky comment from Dad over Mom's parenting skills, I decide on "Midnight."

"I'll call Victor and he'll pick us up and bring them back to the hotel well before then," Cooper assures the adults, which satisfies them enough to say their goodbyes and the Laniers head off in the direction of the hotel with Dad, Kathy, and a barely conscious Olivia. We watch as the five of them are swallowed up by the crowd on the other side of the railing surrounding the rink, and then Cooper turns to us.

"So, what do you guys want to do? I might be able to get us into this club in Chelsea if this guy I know is working."

A club probably wouldn't be the best idea for Kieran, but before anyone can object, Kieran squeezes my hand and says, "You know, I'd really appreciate some alone time with my girl if that's okay."

Cooper glances at the sea of humanity rolling around us.

"You're not going to get much 'alone time' out here," he points out.

"I meant 'alone time' away from family and friends. We've barely had a chance to talk without everyone all over us since we got to New York."

Kayla puts a hand to her hip and cocks her head so severely her blue knit beret nearly slides off.

"And what are *we* supposed to do while you two are off by yourselves?" she asks, her eyes darting from her brother to Cooper.

"I don't know." Kieran shrugs inside his coat. "Hang out, I guess?"

266

"I'll behave. I promise." Cooper grins and tugs at the sleeve of Kayla's wool coat. "Let's try to find somewhere to sit around here. I'll even spring for hot chocolate."

"Don't put yourself out," she huffs. "And I'm warning you—I'm going to be on the phone with Brad the whole time, so I won't be great company."

Cooper's grin slides into lizard territory.

"You're *never* great company, Kayla, but I'm willing to make the sacrifice for my friends here."

Kayla whaps Cooper in the shoulder while Cooper, unfazed, starts pulling Kayla off by her coat sleeve.

"Text us when you guys want to meet up," he calls after us.

"Sure thing," Kieran yells back, and as soon as they're gone, he steps to me and takes my face in his gloved hands, giving me a lingering kiss.

"It's been awhile," he mumbles when we part.

"It has," I lean in for another quick kiss. "So, what do you want to do now that we're alone?"

"Well, I can think of several things, all of which would get us arrested for indecent exposure. You might want to handle this one."

I mentally flip through pages of the tourist guides I've read, trying to think of something within easy walking distance.

"Um…St. Patrick's Cathedral?" I suggest, turning around and attempting to get my bearings. From where we are right now, 50th Street should be behind us, and so I point in the direction of what I think would be 5th Avenue.

"Lead the way," Kieran tells me, and we walk through the crush of people to the sidewalk lining 50th Street, where the crowd dissipates somewhat but never quite thins out.

"Sometimes I wonder if I could stand living here," Kieran muses once we've settled into a decent walking speed—which is more like a shuffle—toward 5th Avenue. "Everything seems so busy all the time."

"I get what you mean. It's kind of exciting, but I wonder if I'm not so used to living in a small town that somewhere like this would wear me out." I shrug. "But Chicago's kind of the same way, so if we want to live there, we'd better get used to this."

We wait in a throng about six people deep for the light to change at the intersection of 50th Street and 5th Avenue, and then we shuffle across the street to the steps of St. Patrick's. Before we walk up, Kieran stops and I spring into place next to him, the two of us staring up at the rose window and the spires reaching toward the clouds moving across the nighttime sky. Since mass isn't going on at the moment, we're able to wander around inside without feeling like we're interrupting anything, quietly whispering to each other about the intricate designs of the stained glass windows and the blemished wooden pews that have held countless worshipers. We see people taking pictures and debate whether or not we should, ultimately deciding not to get all touristy in what some consider a sacred place.

"Want to sit outside for a while?" Kieran asks once we've seen everything.

"Yeah. It's not too cold."

We slip past some entering tourists and back out to the steps, finding an out of the way spot on the 51st Street side. We stare for a few seconds directly across 5th Avenue at a giant bronze statue of a buff naked guy with an appropriately placed drape holding up several circles locked together to create an orb.

"So, who's the bodybuilder?" Kieran asks me. I've been our self-appointed tour guide all day, using the web to call up information about any sights around the city Cooper couldn't recall off the top of his head. After a few taps, I pull up the information about Rockefeller Center I'd loaded onto my phone's web browser earlier in the day.

"Atlas. He's holding up the heavens."

"And I thought *my* life sucked." Kieran grins. "Looks pretty painful."

Digging into what little knowledge of mythology I can remember from junior high, I tell him, "If I'm getting this right, Atlas was one of the Titans, and when the Olympians defeated the Titans, Zeus condemned him to hold up the sky for all of eternity." I wrinkle my brow as a thought strikes me. "Figures Titusville would adopt a big bunch of mythological losers as their mascot."

"Yeah. Funny."

Kieran sounds distracted, and I glance away from Atlas to catch him fumbling around inside his coat, eventually pulling out a white box no bigger than his palm.

"So...um...this is why I wanted to get you alone."

"I thought we were all exchanging gifts tomorrow before we go over to Cooper's?" I remind him, but I'm smiling because I'm not upset. "Your present's back at the hotel."

"That's okay," he says, handing me the box. "This is kind of special, so I wanted to give it to you without anyone else around."

I take off my knit gloves and rest them in my lap so I can get a better grip on the lid, which I remove to reveal a tiny silver charm shaped like a key lying on a bed of cotton. After I give him a quick kiss as a thank you, I murmur, "You need to stop giving me jewelry."

"You don't like it?"

"I love it, but—"

Kieran stops me by putting a gloved finger to my lips.

"I've built up years' and years' worth of allowance that I've barely ever been able to leave the house to spend. What else am I going to spend my cash on—video games and fast food?"

"Yes," I say, laughing against his woolen fingertip.

"Well, I'd rather spend my money on you." He kisses me and reaches for my left arm, pulling my coat sleeve back so he can unfasten my charm bracelet.

"So, I'm assuming the key is supposed to mean something?" I ask as he slides the charm onto the bracelet. "Is this the key to your heart?"

I'm joking, but Kieran isn't.

"Sort of." He refastens the bracelet around my wrist. "Cooper said something to me a while back when we were talking about his memory loss that stuck with me. He said when he heard the Maisie Baker song—the one that kind of jarred his memories?"

"Yeah?"

"Well, he said the whole 'wandering period' was kind of like everything he knew had been locked away somewhere and he couldn't get to it. Hearing those lyrics was like a door opening, and things started to come back to him." He fingers the key dangling from my wrist and doesn't meet my eyes. "I don't even want to think about not remembering you when they wake me up, but I know there's a ninety-nine percent chance that's what's going to happen. But I love you more than anything, and I know you'll be what brings me back somehow. Our memories together are too powerful to stay locked inside my mind where I can't get to them." He twists the bracelet around so I can see the key. "And I realize that if they wake me up and I can't remember anything, it'll be hard on you, too. So, I wanted you to have this. If I don't remember you right away, I want you to look at this and know you're the key. Being around you is what's going to bring me back eventually."

I'm too overwhelmed for words, so I grab Kieran's face in my hands and pull him to me for a kiss so intense it seems almost sacrilegious here on the steps of one of America's great cathedrals.

"So, if being around me is what's going to bring you back, what you think it is about me that's going to do the trick?" I ask against his mouth. "My kiss, maybe?"

His tongue darts inside my mouth for a few seconds before he pulls away slightly, giving my suggestion some serious thought.

"I hope so," he murmurs, resting his forehead on mine. "Although the sound of your voice might be enough, too, like Maisie's was for Cooper. I love listening to you talk. I can't imagine not recognizing your voice."

I try to wrap my head around someone loving the sound of my voice because I've never thought of my voice as being particularly interesting—in fact, if anything, it's kind of gravely. But, whatever—if my voice could be the thing to jar Kieran's memory, I'll take it.

"Just don't expect me to sing like Maisie Baker," I warn him.

"Please don't," he says with a little laugh. "She kind of sucks."

"Well, at least she can sort of carry a tune. Hearing me sing might drive you so far inside your head, your memory will never come back."

He gives me the grin that's always my undoing.

"Maybe we should just hope your kisses bring me back."

"Maybe."

"And we should probably kiss at least a few more times, you know? I mean, the more we kiss the easier it's probably going to be for me to remember when I need to."

"No argument here," I whisper, and I press against him so we can smooch until I can no longer ignore something cool tickling my face.

"It's snowing," I say, pulling away from him and looking up at the sky. Kieran joins me in raising his eyes heavenward, and the two of us sit and let the snow hit our faces as if we've never experienced the sensation before.

"Snow on Christmas Eve in New York," Kieran says, smiling at me.

"Yeah. This is pretty much perfect."

"Glad you think so. This was the other part of your Christmas present I didn't tell you about. You have no idea the hoops I had to jump through to pull this one off."

I laugh, reaching for the white box so I can put it in my coat pocket.

"Thanks. The presents I got for you totally suck compared to this, by the way," I tell him. I didn't want to bring a lot of big items with me on the plane, so I bought Kieran some gift cards and some blocks of sculpting clay, things he won't get the chance to use for a while thanks to the treatment—things that kind of seem like crappy gifts in comparison to being handed the metaphorical key to someone's memory.

Kieran puts his gloves back on before resting a hand on my cheek.

"I promise won't get my hopes up."

I roll my eyes and stand, offering my hands to him to pull him up, saying, "You should probably text your sister and tell her we're coming to save her from quality time with Cooper."

"Probably."

Kieran keeps one hand in mine and uses his teeth to strip the glove off the other so he can pull his phone from his coat pocket and text Kayla with his thumb. I pull us past the throngs of people on the sidewalk until we've reached the corner of 5th Avenue and 50th Street as the snow picks up, and, knowing what Kieran's going to go through in less than forty-eight hours, I take one last look back at the cathedral, the spot on the stairs that held our perfect moment of a few minutes ago almost seeming to disappear in the swirling veil of snow.

CHAPTER 24

I let the last essence of chocolate mousse dissolve on my tongue, placing my spoon on the sterling silver plate next to a now-empty dessert goblet, and sit back in my chair, really thankful I decided to wear a dress today and not pants.

"I'm going to be too fat to play ball when I get home," I whisper to Kieran, who's swallowing the final spoonful of his dessert.

"You'll be great," he whispers back. "But, yeah—I kind of feel like all we've done since we've been in New York is stuff our faces. I don't know how Cooper doesn't weigh a thousand pounds with a full staff cooking for him all the time."

On the other side of the table, Cooper, who long ago finished his dessert, appears to be engaged in a serious conversation with Olivia—as serious a conversation as one can have with a seven year-old, anyway.

"Since everyone seems to be finished, I suggest we move into the sitting room," Mr. Halloran booms, standing up at the head of the table. "Surprises for the birthday girl are under the Christmas tree."

Liv hears the word "surprises" and her head spins toward him.

"What kind of surprises?" she asks.

"Well, they wouldn't be surprises if I told you, now would they? Ask your parents if it's okay, and we'll all join you in the sitting room."

Liv turns pleading eyes to Kathy and Dad, who exchange questioning glances before Dad says, "Go on ahead, Liv. We'll be right behind you."

She can't push her chair back and barrel out into the hall fast enough, leaving the rest of us—slow and sluggish from our meal—to amble out after her. Kieran and I enter the sitting room after everyone else to find Liv on the floor in front of the Christmas tree, examining the covers on a stack of books about as half as tall as she is sitting down. Kieran and I join her on the carpet, followed by Cooper and Kayla. The adults hang back near one of the couches, watching us examine Liv's new treasures. Most of the books are ones I remember loving as a kid— titles like *Tales of a Fourth Grade Nothing*, *Ramona the Brave*, and *Harriet the Spy*—that were considered classics even back when Mom was a girl.

"I took a chance on her being a reader," Mr. Halloran explains to Kathy and Dad. "And I wanted to surprise her with something portable, considering you have a flight home the day after tomorrow. But I can certainly arrange for the books to be shipped to you to save room."

"We should be able to make do," Dad says, sliding an arm around Kathy as he keeps a proud gaze on Liv, who's paging through a copy of *Freckle Juice*.

"Olivia, what do you say to Mr. Halloran?" Kathy reminds her.

"Thank you," Liv says, barely looking up.

"My pleasure." He takes a snifter of brandy offered by a uniformed maid and stands over us. "I should apologize if these books aren't what kids are reading these days. I was going by what I remember my late wife reading with Cooper when he was Olivia's age."

Cooper pulls his knees to his chin and wraps his arms around his legs.

"You remember what books Mom and I used to read together?" he asks, his quiet voice not matching his shocked expression.

Mr. Halloran places his brandy on an end table and crouches down in a catcher's stance next to his son, seeming almost comical in doing so as he's dressed in a tailored suit.

"She used to go on and on about how you liked *Where the Wild Things Are*, even long after you should have outgrown it. You'd read to her from it when she'd come to your room to tuck you in at night."

I want to ask where Mr. Halloran was when his wife was putting Cooper to bed but, of course, doing so would be inappropriate. Instead, I study Cooper's expression, which shifts from surprise into some strange mixture of happiness and confusion.

"I had no idea she told you about that stuff," Cooper says.

Mr. Halloran purses his lips into a tight line before answering "She told me everything. Always. She realized I was too busy to be aware of such things myself. She…" He pauses, seemingly on the verge of saying something else, but his eyes dart about at his assembled guests and he changes the subject. "At any rate, I hope these books have stood the test of time so you can enjoy them, too, Olivia."

"Thank you," Liv tells him again. She leans into Kieran, and I can tell she's starting to wind down from presents this morning at the hotel, another visit to the tree in Rockefeller Center this afternoon, and dinner and socializing here at the Hallorans. She closes the cover of *Freckle Juice* and tells Mr. Halloran "I read this one last year. It was really funny."

"But we checked it out from the library, so she doesn't own it," Kathy quickly interjects. "It'll be nice to own a copy for her little library at home."

Mr. Halloran nods, standing up and taking a few steps over to Dad, Kathy, and the Laniers.

"I was thinking," he begins. "I know you need to leave soon to get Olivia to bed, but this is the last night the kids have before Kieran

275

undergoes the treatment. Why not let them stay here? They can use the pool, watch movies…"

I shoot Kieran a hopeful glance. I'd been dreading the moment Dad and Kathy would want to leave, knowing that unless we could talk our parents into letting us go out after we got back to the hotel, this is the last time Kieran and I will be together—together with his full memory intact, anyway—for who knows how long.

My dad's expression, however, shifts into Stern Parent Mode on Mr. Halloran's suggestion.

"I don't know," he starts, looking from Kathy to Jim and Carlie.

"I'll be here to supervise," Mr. Halloran assures him, although I can't help but wonder how he would supervise anyone in an "apartment" this size, unless he plans on following us wherever we go.

"And nobody has to share a room," Cooper says, standing up and speaking directly to my dad as if he's guessing Dad's concern is over the possibility of shared co-ed sleeping arrangements—and he's probably right. "This summer, Carlie had the whole first floor to herself. The girls can sleep down there, and Kieran can take the guest room on the third floor next to mine."

Dad's face relaxes a little with the implication that Kieran and I will have an entire floor separating us when we go to sleep tonight. He scrunches up his mouth and glances at Kathy and the Laniers.

"They don't have any clothes with them," Carlie says, glancing back and forth between Cooper and his father. "And swimsuits? We certainly didn't think to pack those."

Cooper shakes his head and slides his arm around Carlie in a familial way.

"Minor details," he tells her, his voice riding a fine line between condescension and assurance. "We can send Victor to the hotel for their suitcases, and we have swimsuits here if we decide to go swimming. If nothing fits, we'll send out for something."

"It's Christmas," Carlie reminds him gently, which prompts Cooper and his father to exchange smiles.

"Yes, it is." Mr. Halloran nods and strolls across the room to an intercom next to the door, as I marvel at how minor inconveniences such as holiday hours aren't so inconvenient when your last name is Halloran. "Victor?" he says after touching a button under the speaker, and Victor's muffled voice comes to us from somewhere in the house.

"Yes, sir?"

"Could you come down to the sitting room, please?"

"Right away, sir."

Olivia is resting her head against Kieran's shoulder, struggling to keep her eyes open, so our parents will need to decide our fate for the evening soon.

"You know, I'm okay with this if everyone else is," Dad announces. "This is their last night together for a while, after all."

Dad shifts his eyes to me just long enough for me to mouth "Thank you," and Jim chimes in with "I think it's a good idea. There's not much to do at the hotel, and they'll be safer here than out running around the city."

Kathy nods her agreement, and Carlie turns her attention from her children on the floor to Mr. Halloran.

"I guess it's settled, then."

"Victor can bring Zip back to the hotel tomorrow morning in plenty of time for you to catch your flight to Chicago," Mr. Halloran tells my Dad, as Victor enters the room at the far end and belts out a little cough to get Mr. Halloran's attention.

"Ah. Victor. Good—you're here," Mr. Halloran crosses to him and gives instructions to retrieve my suitcase, along with Kayla's and

Kieran's, when he returns our families to the hotel. Those of us still on the floor next to the tree get to our feet, and we follow Mr. Halloran and the other adults into the hall, exchanging goodbyes for the evening as Victor stays behind to gather up Liv's new books. Realizing she won't see Cooper again, Liv throws her arms around him when he crouches down to her.

"Will you come visit me in Chicago sometime?" she asks, her voice tinged with sadness.

He smiles and pushes some dark wisps of hair from her forehead.

"Of course. I love Chicago. But guess what I've never done?"

"What?"

"I've never been to the top of the Sears Tower. The next time I come to Chicago, will you go to the Sears Tower with me?"

Liv beams at him.

"Oh, yeah. I've done that before. It's not scary at all."

Dad and Kathy titter a little and look down at her fondly as she and Cooper embrace one last time. Victor comes into the entryway with a canvas bag full of Liv's books that he hands to Dad, and then he follows our parents and Liv out into the hallway, the silence once the maid shuts the door almost eerie after all the commotion of goodbyes and finding coats. Kayla, Kieran, and I just stand around as if we're waiting for our cue from Cooper as to what we should do next, but Cooper ignores us and instead turns to his father.

"That was really nice what you did for Olivia."

Mr. Halloran's chin tilts forward a bit.

"I wanted to acknowledge her birthday since I wasn't able to join all of you yesterday. She's a wonderful, charming little girl." He glances past Cooper to me. "Your parents must be extremely proud—of both of you."

I hitch up my shoulders on the compliment.

"Thank you. I think they are."

Yet again, I wait for Cooper to suggest our next move, and yet again, he doesn't, choosing instead to continue talking to his father.

"So, Mom really used to tell you all about the books we'd read?"

Mr. Halloran puts an arm on his son's shoulder.

"Almost every day."

Cooper stares at his father, and the silence prompts Mr. Halloran to continue.

"What do you think we talked about all the time, son? Your mother was never interested in business talk, and conversations about our social circle could only go so far. You were always the biggest thing we had in common. After her illness restricted her to the house, you were her whole world."

Standing here watching this father-son moment is beyond awkward, but I don't dare move. And judging by the stock-straight posture of the siblings next to me, I'm guessing they feel somewhat the same.

"I didn't know you..." Cooper pauses, speechless for once in his life. "I didn't know you knew things about me. Or cared."

"I've always cared, Cooper. I'm just not too good with emotions...your mother probably mentioned that to you more than once..." Mr. Halloran's voice fades as he looks past his son to his teenaged guests, and he shakes his head slightly as if he's just remembering we're still here. "Topics for another time. You should entertain your friends." He pats Cooper on the shoulder and turns him around to face us. "Didn't Omega send over a new game a few days ago?"

"Yeah," Cooper confirms. "We were going to try it out the other night, but we didn't want to play it in front of Liv when we went upstairs."

Mr. Halloran nods, seemingly having forgotten his insult over his son wanting to watch cartoons with his friends.

"Well, why don't all of you go up and try that out, and I'll tell Victor to let you know when he's back with everyone's things. And I'll send some of the staff down to check on the pool to make sure everything's ready to go if you decide to swim later."

"Sounds good, Dad," Cooper says, his lips curling into a smile before he turns to the three of us, our stiff postures relaxing as Mr. Halloran heads out into the hallway.

"You guys have fun," he tosses back over his shoulder, his hand on the door to the sitting room. "Call up to my room or tell Victor if you need anything."

Kieran, Kayla, and I mumble responses resembling "Okay," and as Mr. Halloran disappears into the sitting room, we follow Cooper into the hallway.

"Sounds like he's trying, Coop," Kayla points out, bringing us back to our "daddy issues" conversation from the other night.

We pass the sitting room, the sound of the piano filtering out into the hall.

"Yeah. We'll see," Cooper says, glancing at the door and then shaking off the conversation, turning to Kieran as we continue toward the stairs. "Dude, you will not *believe* the graphics in the new Demon Sport. They'll blow you away…"

Up in Cooper's room, we set up a mini tournament, Kieran against Cooper and Kayla against me. Kayla, whose innate aggression serves her well when playing violent video games, eliminates me quickly, and Cooper, who's at an unfair advantage since he's already played the game before, easily handles Kieran. I pull Kieran to the couch, and we sit against each other as Cooper and Kayla sit cross-legged on the floor to do battle, thumbs working feverishly on the controls as Cooper's demon hunter attempts to save the world from the Kayla-controlled winged demons that look like the devil mated with a dragon and had several thousand ugly babies. Cooper's guy has just stuck a sword through the heart of one of Kayla's creatures, sending it to the floor of a medieval-looking castle in a spurt of blood, when Victor's voice comes crackling through the intercom.

"Mr. Halloran, sir?"

Another Kayla-demon descends on Cooper's hero.

"Guys?" he says over his shoulder to us. "Can one of you hit the intercom button? I'm a little busy here."

I stand to cross over to the speaker next to the door.

"It's the button on the bottom left. Ah—nooo! No! Ha—eat it!" he shrieks, and I press the button. "Yeah, Vic?" Cooper calls out.

"I just wanted to tell you I've returned from the hotel with everyone's things, so I'll be setting up their rooms momentarily. And I'll bring the swimsuits to their rooms as well, in the event that you decide to use the pool later."

"Dammit!" Cooper screeches as one of Kayla's demons takes a bite out of his character.

"Sir?"

"Sorry, Vic." Cooper's thumbs tap the controls in desperation. "Kayla's trying to kill me."

"Sir?" Victor's voice sounds mildly horrified.

"In a video game," Kayla calls out, not taking her eyes from the screen as she sends her demon over to whap Cooper's character with a forked tail, sending blood splattering everywhere on the castle floor. "My *character's* trying to kill him."

"Yes, Ms. Lanier." Victor says in his usual unflappable voice. I glance at Kieran and we both try to stifle a laugh.

"Thanks, Victor," Cooper calls out as his hero expels one last gasp and collapses. The intercom goes silent as Kayla clenches her fist and hisses "Yes" before standing up and taunting Cooper with a hip-swiveling victory dance.

"I'll have to tell the guys at Omega they made this game so easy even a girl could win it," he says to Kieran and me as he gets to his feet. Kayla grabs a suede throw pillow from the couch and tries to whack Cooper with it, but he blocks the blow with his arm, so she pouts and clutches the pillow to her instead.

"So, you guys up for some swimming pool action?" Cooper asks, before telling Kieran "I think I had Victor put those trunks you wore the last time you were here back in your room. Check the dresser drawers, and if they're not there, let me know."

"Sounds good," he says, standing up from the couch and, pulling me up with him, leaning in for a quick kiss. "See you downstairs, I guess?"

"Yeah—we can meet the girls on the first floor once we're dressed and then we'll all head down to the pool," Cooper clarifies.

Kieran nods and squeezes my hand before letting go and slipping out into the hall.

"Victor will probably set you up in the same room you were in last time," Cooper tells Kayla. "Zip, you'll be in the one right next to Kayla. If Victor hasn't laid out swimsuits for you, check the dressers."

Kayla and I turn to head for the hall, but Cooper says, "And, Zip?"

"Yeah?"

"The staff leaves the hall lights on at all hours, so that won't be a problem. When you get to the main floor, cut through the library to come up to the third floor. That way, you won't have to pass Dad's suite because the entry from the library opens out right across the hall from Kieran's room."

"What are you talking about?" I dart my eyes from Cooper to Kayla as they both give me knowing smiles.

"I think he's talking about *later*, after everyone's asleep. You know—in case you wanted to pay Kieran a little visit," Kayla fills me in.

"I'll make sure he has party favors," Cooper adds.

"Party favors?"

Cooper sighs and puts an arm around me.

"Zip, I love you like a sister, but you're dense as hell sometimes. Party favors. Protection. Get it?"

I get it because I can feel my cheeks burning. Kayla laughs and saunters out into the hall and I try to join her, but Cooper's grip won't let me.

"You're welcome," he hisses in my ear, and my lips curl slightly upward.

"Thanks, Coop," I whisper back, and I give him a kiss on the cheek before he turns me loose to follow Kayla downstairs.

CHAPTER 25

Only in Cooper Halloran's weird little Upper West Side world would going swimming on Christmas night seem like the most normal thing to do. But when you have unlimited funds and an indoor pool in your own home, your definition of "normal" doesn't quite match everyone else's.

By the time I make it back to my guest room, Victor's already laid out eight different swimsuits, all of them in my size and lined up on the comforter as if they're suspects waiting for me to pick one out of a lineup. I try each one on and, after carefully examining myself eight times in the full-length mirror in my bathroom, I decide on an emerald two-piece with tiny white polka dots. Victor's placed my suitcase on a trunk at the end of the bed, so I open it and dig through to find a pair of sweatpants and a navy Titusville Basketball t-shirt for cover. I'm sliding into my Chucks when Kayla knocks.

"You decent?" she asks.

I open the door. Kayla's wearing a towel over the bottom of her solid royal blue two-piece while Kieran and Cooper are behind her in matching navy board shorts and plain white t-shirts.

"The dork twins and I are here to escort you to the pool," she says, rolling her eyes.

Stepping out of the room, I reach for Kieran's hand and we follow Cooper and Kayla down to the basement, which doesn't look like a basement at all. The floors and walls are lined with a mauve marble, the slickness only broken up by two wood doors on the right side of the hall and two on the left.

"Theater, weight room," Cooper tells me, pointing at the near door and then the far door on the left side of the hall. "And we get to the pool through here." He motions to a door to our right with "Women" stenciled on it in gold letters.

"Is this a locker room?" I ask as Kayla gives me an amused smirk.

"More like a large bathroom." Cooper pushes the door open. "Kieran and I can go through the one down the hall if you're determined to be gender-specific."

I shake my head at his teasing and walk in, pulling Kieran along behind me, before I come to a dead stop and look around. The area reminds me of a bathroom in a fancy restaurant—marble floors and walls that match the hallway, two toilet stalls behind dark cherry wood doors with brass handles and a dual sink on the opposite side of the room. Beyond the sinks and toilets are a shower hidden by a nylon curtain opposite a stainless steel shelving unit piled high with towels. I'm so busy looking around I almost don't notice Cooper and Kayla slipping past, grabbing towels from the shelf.

"The pool's through here," Cooper tells me, opening a door between the shower and the towel shelves. Kieran and I grab towels as Cooper hits a light on the wall, and we follow him inside.

The pool itself is about half the size of an Olympic-sized pool, with a diving board at the deep end and ladders at either end on both sides. The walls in here are the same color as the marble in the bathroom and in the hall, only rather than a solid surface, both the walls and floor are composed of tiny mosaic tiles. After I strip down to my suit and creep closer to the edge of the pool, I notice the tiles get slightly darker, the contrast indicating that I'm getting closer to the water. Just as I'm curling my toes around the edge of the tiles, a hand pushes my back and I can't stop my forward momentum, falling into the pool. Luckily, I'm a few feet from the shallow end so I don't hit bottom, and since the water is just slightly cooler than a bath, I'm not in too much shock when I surface to find Cooper standing where I was a moment ago, his lizard grin on full display.

"You are such a slimeball," I hiss at him.

He puts a hand to his hip.

"Oh, come on. You were getting in anyway, right?"

I shoot him a death glare as Kayla strolls to the other end of the pool, mounts the diving board, and runs forward to complete a perfectly executed dive. She surfaces near me, smoothing her hair back.

"Is there anything you're not good at?" I ask her.

She gives my question a few seconds' thought.

"Physics, I guess?"

"And regular human interaction," Kieran chimes in, sitting down a few feet from the corner at the shallow end and lowering his feet and calves into the water.

"You're not getting in?" I ask.

His mouth twists into a sad smile.

"I can't swim. Never needed to learn how. Mom and Dad were always so afraid I'd have an episode in the water, and I can't say I blame them."

"Well, those days are almost over."

I swivel my head around at the sound of Cooper's voice to see him standing at the end of the diving board.

"In a few days," he continues, "you'll be able to do stuff like this."

He runs to the other end of the diving board and springs high into the air, pulling his knees to his chest so he can cannonball into the water. The force of his body is so great that water laps up into my face, and even Kieran ends up covered with tiny water droplets.

Cooper doggy paddles over to Kayla, who splashes him, and he responds by diving under and yanking on her leg to pull her

286

down. The two of them surface and start laughing, while I glance over my shoulder once again at Kieran who's forcing a smile—the smile of someone who's always left out. I trudge over to him, stopping so close that his toes are grazing my stomach.

"Get in," I tell him. "I'll keep my arms around you."

He meets my suggestion with his usual grin.

"As awesome as that sounds, I don't want to pass out and pull you under."

I have to think this one through.

"Um…how about I hold on to you, and if you feel an episode coming on, let me know. I should be able to help you get on your back so you can float."

Kieran squints as he considers my idea and its probably questionable physics, and I continue.

"As you float, I'll keep my hands underneath your back like swim teachers do when they're teaching people how to float. That way, if you wake up and start moving around, I can grab onto you and keep you steady."

"You're going to put your arms around me *and* you're going to get me on my back?" he asks. "This is sounding better all the time."

I smirk and take a few steps back to give him room.

"Get in, gutter mind."

He laughs and takes off his shirt, sliding from the side of the pool into the water, my hands immediately grasping his sides above the waistband of his trunks. The two of us move together closer to Cooper and Kayla treading water in the deeper end of the pool, stopping when we're still a few feet away from them because the water has started lapping up to our chins.

"Sorry I can't get you any water wings, Bro," Cooper calls out, which elicits a "Shut up," from Kieran.

"Look, I can't really swim, either," Cooper says, his voice apologetic. He's just enough in the deep end he needs to doggy paddle to stay afloat. "Victor used to bring me down here and I'd hang on to the edge of the pool and kick and stuff, but one time, I fell asleep and almost bashed my head on the side, so that was the end of that. Since the treatment, I've learned how to doggy paddle and cannonball and splash around a little, but that's about it."

Kayla, meanwhile, hops toward us and splashes Kieran in the face, droplets of water clinging to his mostly dry strands of hair.

"Have you ever been underwater before?" I ask him, taking a hand from his hip to run my fingers through his hair, trying to distribute the moisture throughout.

"Maybe?" He looks at Kayla as if for confirmation, but she only shrugs. "We went to the beach on Martha's Vineyard a lot when we were little, so maybe Mom or Dad held me and dunked me under once or twice? I don't really remember."

"Me, neither," Kayla says. "That was a long time ago."

"You want to try now?" I ask. "I'll hold you and help pull you back up."

"Might as well get my hair wet like everyone else," he says, and I back the two of us up against the pool wall so we're not out in the middle in case something—though I don't know what—goes wrong. I slide my hands up to his armpits and he allows his feet to go out from under him, slipping beneath the surface with me holding on. My hands pulling him up and his feet pushing off the pool bottom both work together to help him surface, and he comes up sputtering, spitting water out of his mouth like a little kid, his eyes shut so tightly they're little more than wrinkles in his face, and I can't help but giggle at him.

"You okay?"

His eyes pop open, and he raises a hand to wipe away some remaining traces of moisture.

"Yeah. That was kind of wild," he breathes.

Since I can't remember being underwater for the first time, can't recall what I thought or how I felt, it's strange and exciting to watch Kieran experience the sensation for the first time. He laughs, and I half expect him to ask me to dunk him under again, but he doesn't. Instead, he presses against me and places his hands on my shoulders, and I slide my feet out so he can step in even closer.

With Kieran against me like this, I'm about to lose my mind. We've only been close like this in proximity to other people a few times—when we were walking in downtown Asheville this summer, and when were practically making out in the school library the day we went to look up information on Morgan after we first found out about his existence. This time, however, is different—Cooper and Kayla are watching us rather than our risking a reprimand from the school librarian or being stared at by total strangers, and something about having people we know so well observing a borderline intimate moment unnerves me a little. From the corner of my eye, I catch Cooper nudging Kayla at their post on the other side of the pool, and they hop out, wrap up in towels, and gather up their clothes before disappearing into their respective bathrooms almost as if they can read my creeping embarrassment.

Once we're alone, I move my hands back to Kieran's waist and suck in a breath as his lips caress my jaw line, mere inches above the water's surface. My knees feel as though they're about to give way and I'll end up pulling us both under, and, frankly, I'm not sure I care. If I'm going to drown, I can't think of a better way to go at the moment than clinging to Kieran.

His mouth finds mine and I reach around to his back, trying to hold him against me more than is physically possible, wishing for a way we could be even closer than we are now.

And there is a way, of course, but not here—not here where someone might walk in at any second, not here where we're not exactly prepared.

So, for now, I'm content to kiss under the harsh glare of the fluorescent lights bouncing off the water's surface, our bodies moving against each other as if they're independent of our minds. But after what seems like only seconds, Kieran pulls back and raises his hands to cup my face, staring at me with an intensity that steals my breath as if I've slipped underwater.

"What?" I whisper, barely able to get the word out.

"Say the word and I won't go through with it."

I don't need to ask what he means.

"Kieran, no. We've been over this. We decided. All the arrangements have been made."

"I know," he says sadly. "But I keep thinking about waking up and not remembering you, and it hurts so bad."

"It hurts me, too. And I know you're probably scared, and so am I. But I won't be able to live with myself if you don't go through with it, and neither will you. Just concentrate on all the things you're going to be able to do after the treatment."

I raise my left hand above the water's surface and point to my naked wrist, taking the risk of letting him go for a few seconds.

"And you gave me the key, remember? Everything will come back."

He takes my left hand and kisses the inside of my wrist where my charm bracelet—which is upstairs in my room at the moment—would normally be.

"Then I just…I want to study you for a minute, okay?" He takes my face in his hands. "I want to make sure there's no way I can forget your face."

I smile, not only because I love Kieran so much right now but also because if he's trying to commit my face to memory, I definitely don't want that memory to be of me standing here looking like a confused idiot.

"You're so beautiful, and I don't ever want to forget it," he continues, slowly moving my face from side to side. "I want to be able to remember every angle. I want to burn you into my brain so I have no choice but to know who you are when I wake up." His voice drops as he traces my lips with a finger. "I want to memorize every part of you."

My legs nearly give way again.

"What time do you think it is?" he asks.

I struggle to find my voice.

"Not sure. Getting late, I'm guessing."

"Then Mr. Halloran will probably send someone to drag me off to bed if we stay down here too much longer." He presses his forehead to mine, his skin still cold and clammy after his brief dip underwater. "Come to my room later? Please?"

I'm dying right now. Pulling myself together, I nod and touch my lips to his for a brief kiss before bobbing us over to the ladder a few feet to our left. On the pool deck, I grab a large towel and wrap us both in it, the heat from being pressed together almost doing more to dry us off than the terrycloth. Kieran surrenders the towel to me and grabs the remaining one on the deck for himself, taking my hand in one of his as he rubs the towel through his hair with the other.

"So, I'll see you in a while?" he asks.

"You won't be asleep?"

He shrugs.

"I probably will be. Wake me up. There's no need for me to be well rested for what's going to happen tomorrow, and I'm not missing the chance to be alone with you tonight."

I yank my hand in his grip so he has to step to me, and I plant a kiss on his lips when he leans in.

"I'll see you in a few hours, then," I promise when we part. We head off in silence through the women's shower room as if talking any more will ruin the plans we've already made, and once we reach the first floor, Kieran leaves me at my room, his lips grazing mine before he lets go of my hand.

"So, later?" he checks as if he's afraid I've changed my mind in the few minutes since I made my promise.

I nod, and he turns to head to the other end of the hall. Leaning against the doorframe, I watch him until he's disappeared up the stairs and then I slip into my room to get ready for bed. But I don't sleep—I'm too afraid the alarm on my phone won't wake me up, and I'll have to face the morning knowing I didn't keep my promise to him.

Shortly after one in the morning, when I've decided I've waited long enough, I creep out of my room and up the stairs to the main floor which, as Cooper had promised, is still lit. With the smoothness of a spy, I glide diagonally across the hall, pushing open the library door. The city lights through the opaque curtains offer some light, but I activate the home screen on my phone in order to safely make my way up the winding staircase and out into the third floor hallway. I take a second to get my bearings, remembering Cooper's room is the one at the end of the hall, so the door directly across from where I'm standing right now would be to Kieran's room.

Before crossing the hall, I take a minute to steady myself because I'm worried—worried we're putting too much pressure on ourselves, and that even with his help, we're breaking Cooper's commandment about caring more than we should and forcing things to happen.

I hold my breath and cross to Kieran's room, turning the doorknob a millimeter at a time and pushing the door open, bracing for any unintended sounds. But there aren't any, and so I tiptoe across the room, resting my phone on the nightstand, and crawl into the king-sized bed next to him, still worried.

Rolling onto my side, I place a hand on his cheek and kiss him awake, and the trademark grin playing about his lips once he opens his eyes instantly melts my heart and quickens my pulse.

But still, I worry.

"Hey," he whispers, reaching up to tuck some hair behind my ear.

"Hey."

I brush my nose against his, hoping the worry doesn't show on my face. We kiss some more and start moving hands and exploring each other as we have so many times before. But knowing how this always ends, I can't completely block out the nagging fear at the back of my brain.

But we venture further, then further still, and his eyes never close. And once we've made it to the brink, I—*we*—let go of any past or future anxieties and everything we've wanted for so long just happens, exactly as Cooper said it would.

And, as Kieran gives me one last kiss and drifts off to sleep, I realize I'm not worried anymore.

CHAPTER 26

Though I want nothing more than for us to wake up together, I untangle myself from Kieran's arms and leave his room well before dawn so we don't risk anyone discovering us in the same room. Before I go, I spy one of his old dream journals on an antique wooden desk in the corner of the room, and I remember him saying his parents had suggested bringing them along so he could read them once he's awoken from the treatment. I leaf through the notebook on top and, judging by the dates, I determine this notebook was the last one he wrote in before his future dreams disappeared. Thankfully, he's left a blank page at the back, so I grab a pen from the desk and write "I will always remember us. I love you," before placing the notebook on the empty pillow next to him. Leaning across the bed, I plant a kiss on his cheek, but he doesn't move, his breath raspy with sleep, and I sneak out into the empty hallway and tiptoe quickly down to the first floor.

Back in my room, I can't fall asleep even though I don't need to get up for a while. So I go to the bathroom and attempt to examine myself, in my sleep outfit of an Art Institute of Chicago t-shirt and red plaid pajama pants, from every conceivable angle in the full-length mirror attached to the back of the door. I look exactly the same as I've looked for years, but I feel different somehow, a difference that isn't only the slight physical discomfort I'm experiencing from being with Kieran for the first time. I search my face for signs of maturity, wondering if my complexion should be darker or my cheeks should be thinner or *something*. I mean, I didn't expect to be totally transformed into a different person, but I at least thought I'd be able to find some qualities I didn't posses before.

But I appear to be the same old me in every way. I even spend some time walking back and forth across the bathroom floor, angling my head so I can study myself both in the mirror on the door and the one over the sink as I do, convinced that my stride would have changed for some reason after being sexually active for what was probably less than a minute. After one last glance at myself in the full-length mirror, I decide I'm being stupid and stick my tongue out at my reflection before heading off to bed.

My alarm goes off for a second time at eight, and I get up to shower and pack before heading down to the empty dining room, where a maid dusting the sideboard tells me everyone's in the kitchen, and she directs me to a door at the other end of the room. I walk through and find myself in what is essentially a professional restaurant kitchen like the ones my mom and I geek out over when watching cooking shows on TV, even though neither one of us has much desire to cook.

In contrast to the dark woods and marble of the hallway, the kitchen is a blinding explosion of stainless steel appliances and bone white cabinets. There's marble in here as well, but it's a lighter white/gray mix topping the counters and the island in the middle of the room, with stainless steel pans and skillets hanging from a rack suspended from the ceiling. Before I can get lost in mentally recording every detail of the area, Mr. Halloran's voice floats down to me from the breakfast nook at the other end of the room.

"Zip—you're awake. Come join us."

I stroll past the kitchen island to where Mr. Halloran, clad in khaki pants and a blue oxford cloth button down that would look too formal for a day at home on anyone but him, sits at a glass-topped table with his son, Kieran, and Kayla. As soon as I enter the breakfast nook, Kieran rises from the table and puts his arm around me, directing me to the seat next to his with a smile that seems a little too enthusiastic—and it seems so to me probably because I sense mine is a little too broad and goofy as well. I sit down next to him and survey the faces at the table, relieved to find no one is looking at me in a way that seems out of the ordinary.

"Bagel?" Cooper offers, and I take the plate from my place setting and hand it to him.

"Plain, please," I tell him, and Kayla nudges a container of cream cheese in my direction. As I slather my bagel, we all make meaningless small talk—about school, about the snow outside, about the Sumner Holiday Tournament I'll be playing in starting tomorrow night—but the surface level of our conversation tells me we're all probably thinking about Kieran undergoing the treatment this afternoon and we're willing to talk about anything but what we should really be discussing. Kieran eventually slides a hand over mine resting on my thigh, and sitting here blathering on about the strength of Sumner Township's starting five when I really want to be talking to Kieran about last night is totally killing me.

"Does anyone know what time it is?" I ask after I've finished my bagel and washed it down with some orange juice.

Mr. Halloran's the only one at the table wearing a watch.

"Ten after nine. I've told Victor that you'll need to leave for the hotel to pick up your family in about twenty minutes," he tells me, and I find the escape hatch I'm looking for.

"I should probably go downstairs and make sure I packed everything," I say, moving my hand out from under Kieran's and giving his fingers a squeeze I hope he interprets in the way I want him to. "Excuse me?"

"Of course," Mr. Halloran says, and I get up and walk out to the hall, which is thankfully empty. I pace back and forth for about a minute before Kieran comes out and grabs my hand. He pulls me into the dining room, the two of us kissing almost before the door swings shut behind us.

"God, I've wanted to do that forever," he breathes against my mouth, which—even combined with his smile at the breakfast table— isn't enough evidence to dispel a fear I've had since waking up this morning. The first thing on my mind when I opened my eyes, obviously, was what Kieran and I did last night. But before I could start reliving the moment inside my head, I was struck with the horrible thought that due to his blackouts, Kieran might not remember the moment at all.

"Do you…" I start, searching his face for signs one way or the other. "Do you remember? Last night?"

He smiles and kisses my forehead.

"I remember every second. Like, all ten seconds."

I reach my hands up to his cheeks, hoping to soothe the blush taking over his face.

"I don't think we're supposed to have marathon sessions right out of the gate," I tell him. "Maybe it's like training for a sport. You know—maybe we have to build some endurance."

"Good point," he says, wrapping his arms around me. "And just think, next time will be after the treatment. You won't need to worry if I remember or not. I won't need to worry if *I'll* remember or not. Once my memory finally comes back, everything will be different."

Everything will be different.

I think back to Jillian saying those words to me on the couch in the Lanier house back in July, the phrase not as positive coming from her as it is coming from him, and I'm reminded of how when Kieran wakes up, chances are he won't remember me, much less remember us being together last night.

Kieran must be having some of the same thoughts because his happy expression collapses into something darker, and I pull him to me. We don't say anything, but we only hold each other, letting the morning sunlight through the dining room's floor-to-ceiling windows shower us with warmth. I'm nearly asleep against him when the door opens, startling me.

"Ms. McKee. There you are," Victor says as I take two steps away from Kieran. "We'll need to leave for the hotel soon. I just wanted to offer any assistance you may need in packing your things."

"I should be all set—thanks. My suitcase is down in my room." I take a step toward the door, but Victor reads my action and holds up a hand to stop me.

"Not necessary. I'll bring your bag upstairs." He glances back and forth between Kieran and me. "I'm well aware time is of the essence this morning. No need to waste it with unnecessary things."

I meet his smile with a grateful one of my own.

"Thanks," I respond. "We'll be out in a minute."

Victor nods and ducks back out of the room, and Kieran takes my face in his hands.

"Since I won't be able to do this in front of everyone else," he begins, before lowering his lips to mine for a kiss so intense my body tingles all the way down to my toes. "I love you, Zip," he says when we part, and I notice he doesn't say anything about how he won't forget it. I'm about to tell him I love him back when he whispers "Always."

"I love you, too," I whisper. "Always. I promise."

He gives me his usual grin, but it seems forced and unnatural.

"Guess this is it, huh?" he says.

"Guess so."

"I don't know what to say. 'Goodbye' or 'See you soon' don't seem right somehow."

"Yeah." I kick at the floor with my tennis shoe, not meeting his eyes. He grabs my left wrist and lifts it closer to his face, turning it until he can see the key charm.

"It's just for a little while," he says, staring at the key, and he almost seems to be convincing himself more than he's trying to convince me. "Everything will be weird for a little while, and then everything will go back to the way it is now, only better."

I don't know how to respond, so I just lean in and give him one last kiss. When I start to pull away, he puts his hand up under my hair and pulls me to him once more before Victor knocks on the door and we surrender to the inevitable. Taking my hand, Kieran leads us out of the dining room, where we follow Victor down the hall to the entry. Mr. Halloran, Kayla, and Cooper are already waiting for us, and a uniformed maid helps me into my coat. Once I'm buttoned up, Mr. Halloran extends his hand to me.

"It's been a pleasure meeting you, Zip. I hope you know you're welcome in my home anytime. And please tell your family again how much I enjoyed meeting them as well."

"Thank you, Mr. Halloran. I will."

He gives my hand a final pump before Kayla steps over to hug me.

"I'll call when I can, okay?" she says in my ear, and my voice catches in my throat, so I just nod quickly and move on to hug Cooper who, unlike Kayla, has to bend down to whisper in my ear.

"Call me if you need anything, okay?"

Again, my voice fails me and I resort to bobbing my head.

"I mean it," he says.

"Thanks," I whisper before I slide next to him and fall into Kieran's arms, the two of us holding each other for what probably seems like a long time to everyone else but seems like just a few seconds to me. He kisses me on the forehead and backs up, raising his hand in a sad little wave that I return. Feeling a sob working its way up my throat, I turn away and follow Victor out the front door and into the building hallway, taking several measured breaths until the sob dissolves, leaving only emptiness in the pit of my stomach.

Victor and I walk toward the elevator in silence, but once we've reached the doors and he's hit the "down" button, he looks at me and asks "Ms. McKee?"

"Yes?

"You may recall the younger Mr. Halloran mentioning when we were in Titusville that my father was a bricklayer?"

"Yeah," I say, remembering Cooper surprising all of us with his recall of details from Victor's life when he still couldn't bring up many from his own.

"What he left out was that my dad had been in the military before that."

The elevator car arrives, and we step on after the doors open.

"Do you know what *Desert Storm* is?" Victor asks, pressing the "down" button.

I mentally file through history notes.

"Was that the first Iraq War?"

He nods.

"My dad was sent over, and my mother began working for Halloran Industries and I started spending most of my time at my grandmother's. The war itself didn't last very long, but then he was stationed various places overseas for a while afterwards. And we didn't have all the ways people do now to communicate with loved ones in the military—no video chat or anything. Just letters, mostly. So, by the time he came home, he was a virtual stranger to me, and me to him, because I'd changed so much while he was gone. We were happy to see each other, of course, but things were awkward because just enough time had passed, and we hadn't been in communication much while he was gone."

The elevator springs to a stop and the doors open. Victor motions for me to step out, and when I do, I stop and wait for him to fall in next to me as we walk to the car.

"I assume you're telling me all of this for a reason?" I ask, hunching down into my coat against the cold of the garage.

"You and Mr. Lanier—you'll get to know each other again. Mr. Halloran is like a younger brother to me, or a nephew, but I was surprised at how painful it was for me when he was brought out of the coma and didn't remember who I was. But even before his memory came back, he'd accepted that I was supposed to be a part of his life." We approach the back of the SUV and Victor hits a button on his keychain before stepping ahead of me to open the rear passenger door. "I'll never be certain, of course, but I suspect that even if his memory hadn't returned, Mr. Halloran and I would have managed some kind of a relationship resembling what we'd had before the treatment."

He takes my hand and assists me as I step up into the backseat. As I arrange myself, Victor puts his hand on the door handle, but I say "Victor?" and he stops.

"Yes?"

"Thanks. I needed to hear that."

He gives me a slight nod and shuts the door.

CHAPTER 27

I suppose the girlfriend-y thing to do when your boyfriend is in a coma would be to keep vigil by his bed and light candles at a chapel and or something. Or, at the very least, if you aren't physically by his side, you can check your cell phone every ten seconds for any news of a change in his condition.

But in my case, I know Kieran isn't going to wake up from his coma dramatically like something out of a bad movie—the medical team will bring him out when the time is right. And my cell phone's with me at all times anyway when I'm not at practice or in the middle of a game, so if anything changes, I'll find out soon enough. Last but not least, I don't belong to a church and wasn't raised to pray. I don't hold anything against people who do, but praying has never been a part of my lifestyle, not to mention I don't see the point in praying when I already know what's going to happen with Kieran. He'll be brought out of the coma, he won't remember anything for a while, and then he'll be back to normal—or, better than normal, if his storyline follows Cooper's.

So, I could sit around and wait and check my phone every five minutes, but, thankfully, I have things to do to keep me busy— namely, the Sumner Township Holiday Tournament. Kieran's life may be in a state of suspension right now, but my life needs to go on. Explaining my apathy to people outside my family if I *didn't* go on right now would be difficult at best, so getting on with things is all I can do.

In our first tournament game the night after I come back from New York, we blow by the usually hapless River Run Lady Waves. I put up twenty-two points, a season high for me so far, and we remain undefeated.

Our second game, against Tusculum, is a little more of a challenge, as our games against them usually are. They knocked us out of the regionals last year and ended our season, so we're in the mood for some payback. Luckily for us, several of their best players graduated in the spring, and while they're able to hang with us for most of the game, during the middle of the fourth quarter the difference in talent from last year becomes evident. Tusculum's players run out of gas, and we cruise to victory and a spot in the championship game against Sumner Township.

We're the two closest schools to each other distance-wise, so Sumner Township versus Titusville in any sport is always a heated rivalry game, and tonight is no different. We beat them out for the conference title last year, so the Lady Panthers are up for some revenge. With less than a minute left to go in the game and the score tied, it's anyone's guess whether they're going to get that revenge or not.

Anyone's guess, that is, but mine. As the point guard and one of the co-captains, part of my job is to believe we're going to put them away and come out on top. When Sumner's Katie Westerfield fouls Cassie with forty seconds to go, I huddle us up behind the free throw line for a pep talk.

"Cassie makes these, and we've got this. No fouls, play smart, and we've got this. Okay?"

Everyone nods and mumbles as we slap each other on the back. The end of the game is so close, but we're tired and having to dig down into our energy reserves to close this thing out.

Cassie sinks her free throws, and Sumner takes the ball out of bounds. Knowing they're out of time outs, I smother Holly Oxford, Sumner's point guard, in the corner, and Ashley comes over to double team. Holly gets out of our trap by throwing a desperation pass to Brynne Lostrand and they finally get the ball across midcourt, but the team's burned a lot of time off the clock since they couldn't call a time out to reset. Brynne puts up a three-point shot that bounces off the rim, and as Cassie goes up for the rebound, Katie Westerfield fouls her again.

This time, Cassie hits one of two, putting us up by three points. Once again, we press on their inbounds pass, forcing them to waste precious seconds getting the ball up court. They put up a desperation three-pointer that's far off the mark, and Lauren grabs the rebound, dribbling around to run out the clock. For the first time since we've all been in high school, Titusville wins the Sumner Township Holiday Tournament, and my stats over three games are good enough for me to be named the tournament's Most Outstanding Player.

In the locker room, Coach points out our strengths and weaknesses and congratulates us, but she also reminds us of the long season ahead. Our job done for the night, we all shower up so we can go out and watch the boys' game against Sumner.

"So, is Kieran going to be back in time for New Year's?" Cassie asks as we dress near the lockers, as if her shower magically changed her from punishing power forward back into gossipy teenaged girl.

I shake my head. Since Kieran hasn't been brought out of the coma yet and New Year's Eve is two days away, I'm assuming he won't be here in time.

When people ask about my Christmas vacation, I just answer, "Things were good. I was with my dad," and skirt any details, so no one knows I was in New York. Cassie had asked me on the bus yesterday on the way here if Kieran would be at the game, and I mentioned he and his family had gone to New York for the holidays and wouldn't be home.

"Too bad," Cassie continues. "Cody's parents are visiting friends in Chicago, so he's having a big blowout at the farm. Everyone's going to be there. You should come anyway."

304

Winding my damp hair back into a ponytail, I consider her suggestion. I'm not much of a party person, but Cody's sister Candace, who played ball with us, is home from college for winter break, and I wouldn't mind hanging out with her and some of the other people who are back in town until January.

"I'll think about it," I tell her.

Cassie shoves her uniform into her gym bag, saying, "I keep trying to talk Cody into putting some of that bag of money toward stuff for the party, but he's determined to be Mr. Responsible for once and use it all for his car."

"Cody got a *bag* of money for Christmas?" I ask in disbelief.

Cassie heaves an exaggerated sigh, obviously frustrated that—as usual—I'm clueless as to what she's talking about.

"Oh, come on. The news was all over town by Christmas night. I texted you."

"You texted me about Cody getting *some* money for Christmas. You didn't say anything about a *bag* of money." I start, laughing, neglecting to mention I was a little preoccupied with other things on Christmas night, so I wasn't reading her texts too closely. "What—did his parents rob a bank or something?"

Lauren, on my other side, pokes her head out from under a towel.

"She didn't tell you what happened?"

"I was sending a text, Lauren," Cassie snaps. "I didn't have a lot of time to go into details." She turns back to me. "The Hulls got home from church on Christmas Eve and found a paper bag with a wad of cash in it on the front porch with a note saying 'This is for the car.' So, Cody gave a bunch of the money to his grandfather because he made the down payment on the Honda, and then I guess he's going to use the rest on his car payments. I'm surprised nobody in your family said anything to you. I bet your Mom heard about it."

I'll bet she did, too. In fact, I'm guessing she—and my grandparents as well—knew about the mystery money drop and who was responsible long before it happened, if my suspicions are correct.

"Nobody's said anything to me. That's so random, though," I reply, trying to sound as clueless as possible. "Any idea who Cody's Secret Santa might be?"

Cassie shakes her head.

"Mr. Hull was joking around about taking the bag to the county cops next time he's in Sumner so they could dust for prints, but it's not like that would tell us anything."

Struggling to keep the look on my face as even as possible, I bite my lip to avoid saying something I shouldn't. I don't think the Hulls—or anyone else in this town—would be prepared for what they'd learn by matching the fingerprints on that bag to a criminal database.

"Guess we'll never know where the money came from," Cassie continues as Lauren reaches around me to snap her on the leg with her towel.

"Just a Christmas miracle, I guess," Lauren enthuses in a cheesy voice, and Cassie grabs her towel and snaps Lauren back as I yelp and try to get out of the way.

"Children," comes Coach Denton's voice from the end of the row of lockers. "You need to be out of here in ten seconds so the boys can use the locker room."

We quit messing around and pack up the remainder of our stuff, hurrying to follow the rest of the team back out into Sumner's gym so we can sit behind the team bench and watch our boys take on Sumner. I wave behind me in the stands at my mom and my grandparents, my heart catching a little at the thought that Kieran and Kayla would be here, too, if circumstances were different. I notice Brad sitting a few rows behind my family with some Titusville

306

alums—all guys from his class who are back in town for the holidays—and we lock eyes. As I give him a little wave, he holds up his phone, points to it, and shrugs at me, motions I interpret as meaning he hasn't heard from Kayla. Before I sit down, I take my phone from my bag for a quick check, but I don't have any messages, either, and so I shake my head at him and take my seat next to Cassie.

The Titusville boys' team continues their solidly mediocre season by falling to Sumner, and after the boys all shower up, the girls' team boards the team bus with them for the trip back to Sumner. I sit in the back, ignoring the conversations and off-key sing-alongs and teasing of the boys from most of my teammates over how we're having a better season than they are, choosing instead to put in my ear buds and listen to a Radiohead playlist Kieran copied for me. Every few minutes, I look down at my home screen to check if I have any new messages, and every few minutes, I don't.

Back at school, I drag myself off the bus and fall into the waiting arms of my mother.

"You look tired," she tells me.

"Three games in three days will do that to a person. It'll be nice to get a week off before our next one."

She walks me off toward the Cobalt, where I collapse in the backseat next to Gramps, barely able to keep my eyes open as Mom drives us home. The three adults make small talk I don't pay much attention to until Gram swivels in the front seat and glances back at me.

"Guess what I made yesterday?" she sings, pausing for a beat before answering her own question. "Red velvet cake. I figured tonight would be an occasion to celebrate."

"I don't guess you have any big plans for the rest of the evening?" Mom asks, steering the car into the driveway.

"No." I shrug, trying to keep my attitude as light as possible. "I mean, not only is my boyfriend not in town, but he's also in a coma, so my social life is a little limited at the moment."

My mom shirks, but I don't get the chance to ask her why as she parks the car under the carport and the three of them are out of the vehicle and through the side door into the kitchen like a shot. Their combined jitteriness, plus Mom's reaction when I brought up Kieran, tells me something's going on.

"Zip, are you okay?" Gram says to my blank expression as she pulls the aluminum foil off the cake pan on the counter. My eyes focus, and I see my mom and Gramps sitting down at either end of the kitchen table, their eyes trained on me expectantly as if my answer matters a great deal to them.

"No," I tell her, leaning back against the counter. "I get the feeling something's not right here."

Gram stops cutting cake and turns around to look at Gramps, who in turn stares across at Mom and says "April. Now. We're not putting this off any longer."

Before Mom can say anything, I exhale and shoot her a look of disappointment.

"It's Kieran, isn't it? He's awake?"

"This morning," she says quietly.

"This morning?"

"Zip, don't freak out, okay?" she says, walking over to put her arms around me, probably hoping to restrain me as much as comfort me. "I know you'd wanted to know as soon as they brought him out, but you had your game tonight, so I didn't want to upset you. And neither did the Laniers, so they told Kayla to keep quiet."

I press my lips together, surprised Kayla actually obeyed her parents for once.

"And you probably don't feel this way now, but once you've calmed down, you'll understand we didn't tell you for your own good," Mom continues. "Think about how mad you would have been at yourself if you'd been too preoccupied to play as well as you did tonight."

"I need to learn to play through distraction, Mom."

I'm not mad, her preemptive strike at making sure I didn't lose it apparently having the intended effect. And she's got a point— as much as I'll always need practice in blocking things out when I play, and as much as I'm already pretty good at it, any news about Kieran would have been a major distraction, especially if that news is bad.

"His memory?" I ask as Mom steps back, and she shakes her head.

I've been steeling myself for this moment ever since I decided to tell Kieran I was okay with him undergoing the treatment, but I never anticipated quite how bad it would be. Just the slight movement of Mom's head back and forth is like a sucker punch to the gut, and I instantly lose my breath.

"They've told him who you are, shown him pictures," she continues. "He doesn't remember anyone..."

Her voice trails off, and I feel the sting of tears straining at the corners of my eyes. Mom pulls me to her once again, and I start sobbing against her shoulder.

"I know it hurts, baby, so just let it out, okay? Let it all out."

I shut my eyes, choosing to stay in the comforting darkness augmented by my head resting against my mother's shoulder, knowing that when I pull away, I'm going to have to figure out how to cope with this news now that it's real.

"Think about it, though," Mom begins, her voice soft. "They woke him up today. He wasn't under as long as Cooper was. So, maybe that means his memory will come back sooner."

The logic of her statement helps. I step back from her, wiping my eyes.

"It's just so hard to believe the next time I see him, he won't remember who I am. I mean, I *knew* this was going to happen and I thought I'd accepted things, but—"

"I know, but you need to keep in mind that this is a temporary situation."

I bob my head in agreement with her statement, even if my heart isn't quite convinced at the moment.

"Who did you talk to? Carlie?"

"Yeah."

"Did she say when they were coming home?"

"Tomorrow, probably. Kieran's been undergoing tests all day, and if everything comes back okay, he'll be able to come home."

"So, other than the memory loss, he's fine otherwise?"

"So far, yeah."

The kitchen seems especially warm and close, and as much as I love red velvet cake, I don't think my stomach can take eating right now.

"I need to get some air…clear my head," I announce.

Nods all around.

"Can I go for a drive?" I ask my mom.

"You're sure you're not too worked up?"

I shake my head. Her concern is understandable considering I've already wrecked one car this year, but that wreck was due to speed motivated by fear. Driving sad is going to be a completely different situation, I think.

"I'll be fine. I promise to be careful."

310

Mom takes the keys from her purse and hands them to me.

"I'll be back in a bit," I say, my hand clutching the keychain. I shuffle out the door to the driveway and get in the car, checking to make sure my gym bag, which contains my wallet and my license, is still in the backseat. Not wanting to back all the way down to the road, I reverse into the lawn and pull forward into the gravel, gunning the engine and heading for the blacktop with no idea where I'm going. It's almost eleven o'clock, so there isn't anywhere around here *to* go besides the Burger Barn, which is open twenty-four hours a day. But I'm not in the mood to be around people right now, so I make a right out of the driveway and press the gas, driving past the Laniers' house, which is almost totally dark except for a small light shining through a window on the first floor in what would be their living room, a light they probably left on for safety while they're gone.

I keep on driving down the county road until I've reached the Stanley Farm, site of the annual Titusville after-Prom party and the place where Frank Dozier's ill-fated kidnapping attempt on Kieran began. Not wanting to go any further out into the country at such a late hour, I pull into their drive, just barely able to make out the outline of their house and the barn that doubled as a dance club on Prom night. I haven't been back here since that night in May—I wouldn't have had a reason—and the flood of memories about the danger we were in makes me catch my breath as I throw the car into reverse.

I don't need any reminders of how I almost lost Kieran. I'm too busy at the moment wallowing over how he may be lost to me now.

Pulling back onto the county road, I'm at a loss as to where to go. I don't want to go home yet, and I don't want to be around people, so I'm left with only one option. Slowing to a near stop just a

311

few miles from my house, I make the right turn down the familiar gravel path, rumbling down the hill and braking completely so only momentum rolls me over the rut that launched Cody Hull's stolen car into the river. No one's down here right now, of course, but even so, I pull over to the right side of the boat launch and kill the engine.

Spooky as it is, the boat launch at night is almost comforting in its familiarity. Before I met Kieran, I used to come down here once or twice a year with Gramps when he would go fishing; we'd put the tailgate down on the truck and load his tiny battered fishing boat and a couple of paddles in the back, tying the boat down to the bed through four hooks on the truck's side. Once we'd secured the boat, Gramps would attach a red bandana to the end to warn any motorists behind us that our cargo hung a few feet past the truck bed and they shouldn't get to close. Of course, with the boat launch being only a few miles from our house, there usually weren't any motorists to warn, but better safe than sorry.

Once at the river, Gramps would angle the truck so the bed faced the river, and we'd drag the boat out and across a few feet of low gravel and spend the afternoon fishing in a tiny cove just downstream, paddling back to the boat launch a little before sundown. I don't get into fishing at all, but I love Gramps, so spending time with him doing something he loves to do always seemed like a small sacrifice when he would ask me to come down here with him. So, up until a few months ago all of my associations with this place had been pleasant.

Until I met Kieran, I'd never been out here at night. Now, night feels like the only time I *should* come here, the trees making inky black scars against the moonlit sky and the river's frozen surface flat as a white bed sheet seeming more familiar than the time recently when Kieran and I were down here in the afternoon. I stare out my windshield at the opposite river bank and allow myself another cry, realizing that at the moment, Kieran's in New York and can't remember coming down here with me at all.

If Kieran's memory loss is like Cooper's, not only would he not remember the river, but he also wouldn't remember Titusville, or North Carolina. He probably doesn't remember his parents or Kayla, and he's likely forgotten all about his Aunt Jilly.

At this point, he probably doesn't even remember himself. And as sad as I am that he has no idea who I am, the fact that he doesn't know who *he* is right now may be the saddest fact of all.

CHAPTER 28

I'm busy compiling a mental list of all the things Kieran probably doesn't remember at the moment when a rap on my driver's window nearly spooks me out of my skin. I yelp, and then let out a breath when I learn who's banging on the car.

"Morgan," I say to myself, relieved. After I roll down the window, I tell him, "How about using a less threatening way to tell me you were down here?"

"Like what? Shooting off a flare?"

"Or calling me, maybe?"

"I don't have your number," he points out. "And 'threatening' is what I'm good at. I've had lots of practice."

I don't think his joke is as funny as he does, and so I refuse to match his smile.

"I thought prison was supposed to be about reforming your behavior," I remind him.

"Touché."

Glancing past him into the darkness, I can't make out any other cars—Morgan doesn't have a license, so somebody probably dropped him off.

"How did you get down here, anyway?" I ask.

"I walked. Sometimes I walk down here to clear my head."

"This place is, like, *two miles* from my grandparents' house."

"So?" He lights up a cigarette. "Do I look like I'm out of shape?"

After a minute of my staring at him, my eyes hooded with suspicion, he cracks.

"Okay," he says, exhaling a long trail of smoke. "Gramps picked me up from the Diner, and he told me they brought the kid out of the coma and you were pretty upset. I couldn't think of too many places around to drive to, so I had him drop me off at the top of the hill because I had a hunch you might come here. I *was* going to walk back to the house if you weren't here—I wasn't kidding about walking down here and back sometimes."

"Fair enough," I mumble.

He takes a long drag on his cigarette and hunches down into his worn barn jacket.

"So, are you going to let me sit inside the car with you? I'm freezing out here."

"Lose the cancer stick and I'll unlock the doors."

Morgan takes a long final pull on his smoke, the embers burning down almost to his fingertips, before he stubs the butt out underneath the toe of his boot and puts the filter in his coat pocket rather than litter. He rounds the car, and I hit the button on the door to unlock the passenger side. Without a word, he slides into the passenger seat, and the two of us sit and stare out at the river, our breath visible in the cold and fogging up the windows. I really hope no one else comes down here right now because I don't want to have to explain this to people at school Monday morning.

"I'm sorry," Morgan says at last, his gaze still focused on the river.

I glance at him from the corner of my eye.

"For what?"

"This is all my fault—what's going on with Kieran. Trace it all back to the beginning, and everything's my fault." He shifts in the seat so he can face me. "If Jenna and I hadn't stumbled upon that damn drug, if she hadn't done it while she was pregnant, if we hadn't gotten Frank and Ginny hooked, too..." He pauses, and I take a second to remember "Ginny" is Virginia Malsun, Cooper's mother.

"If, if, if. Everything's all my fault, and now you're in pain and I can't do anything to fix it, and I'm sorry."

Rather than convince him he's wrong about causing all this trouble, I choose instead to remind him of the good he's done.

"At least you're trying to put your life back together and make amends," I point out. "You're working and you're trying to form a relationship with Kieran. And you paid back the Hulls for stealing Cody's car."

He sits up and leans an arm on the dashboard.

"What makes you say that?"

"Cassie was blabbing in the locker room about how someone left a bag of cash on the Hulls' front porch on Christmas Eve. And I'm guessing Santa Claus looks a lot like you."

Morgan gives me a sly smile.

"Ho, ho, ho," he mutters.

"So, where'd you get a bag full of money, if you don't mind my asking?"

"I knocked over the First National Bank in Sumner one day on my lunch hour," he says, completely serious.

"Morgan." I'm not amused.

"I'm *kidding*. As you're well aware, my first attempt at armed robbery wasn't exactly a roaring success. Seriously though, once I started working, I talked with your grandparents about wanting to pay the Hulls back somehow. I mean, things will never be completely square because I committed a crime."

"You had to or Frank might have hurt Kieran."

Morgan nods, and I don't think any of us will ever be completely comfortable with the things we've had to do to keep Kieran safe.

"Well, regardless, I wanted to do *something*—something, anyway, that didn't involve confessing to the cops and going back to

316

the joint," he continues. "Obviously, I had to figure out a way to pay the Hulls back without them knowing. Your grandparents agreed to let me stay with them rent-free until I had enough money saved up to pay for the car I stole, plus the probable down payment on Cody's replacement car. You have no idea how lucky you are to have the family you do."

I give him a little smile.

"I've got a pretty good idea."

"Anyway, your grandfather came up with the idea of leaving the bag of cash on their front porch on Christmas Eve. He said the Hulls always went to midnight services at the Methodist church, so we had plenty of time to sneak out to the farm and leave the money."

"See? Like I said, you're trying to set things right."

He shakes his head.

"Doesn't change the fact my past is impacting everyone right now."

"I guess you're right," I tell him, resting my cheek against the seat. "Think about it, though—you were committing crimes when you were younger than I am now. Your parents were totally messed up from what you told me, and some of your foster homes didn't exactly sound like the most loving places in the world. You weren't exactly surrounded by a lot of people influencing you to become a solid citizen."

"Maybe so, but my childhood's a cop-out. I need to take responsibility for the things I've done in my life. I need to own up to the truth of my actions costing me my son—twice."

Morgan's words make me realize that as hard as Kieran's memory loss is and will continue to be on me, things are even more difficult for him as Kieran's birth father. He finally had a shot at setting things right and forming a bond with the son he had to

317

abandon when he went to prison. And now, he's lost his son once again, for who knows how long.

We are quiet for a few moments, both of us swiveling around in our car seats in order to stare out at the opposite river bank. Being with Morgan reminds me something else is gnawing at me besides Kieran, something I've never been able to get a straight answer about from my mom.

"So, speaking of being responsible," I begin, not looking at him. "Mind telling me what your intentions are with my mother?"

I glance at him in my peripheral vision and catch him swallowing hard, clearly uncomfortable.

"What does your mom say?"

"Not much. I asked once if something was going on with you two, and she said you guys just enjoyed spending time together. And I said 'Oh. Is that what the kids are calling it now?' and she got all embarrassed and pretended she needed to clean the bathroom. My mom pretty much *abhors* cleaning the bathroom, so I figured she didn't want to talk and I haven't brought it up since."

"Well, maybe I shouldn't talk, either, then."

I shoot him a grumpy look, and he gives in a little.

"All I'll say is this. You're mom wasn't jerking you around— we do like spending time together *as friends*." He says *as friends* slowly and deliberately so I don't misunderstand his intent. "I'm in no place to want anything more than friendship with anyone for a long time. Trust me—I've got some issues to work out after being locked up for so long. I barely know how to be a good friend to someone, much less anything else, and the only woman who's ever been in my life was Jenna. And I'm not sure if Jenna and I being together was love so much as we were two scared kids clinging to each other because we didn't have anything else. So, there's a pretty good chance I don't understand what real love is."

318

He pauses and looks away out the passenger side window.

"The one thing I do understand is how it's good for me to be around people like your mom—people who are fully aware of what I've been through and what I've done and accept me anyway. I need to be around people like her and your grandparents. Like you said, I haven't exactly had a lot of positive influences in my life, and all of you being in my life helps keep me straight."

"Straight?"

Pursing his lips, he turns back around to face me.

"I'm going to try to explain something here I'm not sure you'll understand. I was in prison for a lot of years, and the nature of the place means there aren't a lot of good people around. And like you said, I've been committing crimes for a long time. In some ways, it's almost all I know. I never held down a real job for long, and although I picked up a few skills while I was locked up, I don't exactly have a wealth of talents. The day I got out, the prison gave me enough money to take a cab to the train station and to buy a ticket to the city, and that was it. I had nothing except the clothes on my back and the phone number of an old friend who was kind enough to take me in. If not for him, I probably would have stolen from someone the minute I got out. I can't tell you how many guys I've heard about who go that way—they get out, but they've been in for so long, they don't know anything else and they commit a crime as soon as they can so they can get sent up again. Prison is prison, but after a while, it's home."

I'm almost too engrossed in Morgan's explanation to exhale, afraid my visible wisps of breath in the cold air will distract him.

"When Frank and I stole Cody's car, I was aware the whole time what we were doing was wrong, but I could justify our actions, of course, because I had to play along with Frank to save the kid." He looks down at his hands resting in his lap. "But stealing was such a rush, just like the drugs shooting through my veins in the old days, just like all those times I stole from someone and never got caught. I had to keep telling myself stealing that car was wrong, that stealing was necessary in this case to help me make amends. But doing it felt right. It felt *normal*."

"But you knew it wasn't normal," I point out. "You said yourself you knew it was wrong."

"I did, but now you get a sense of what I go through on a daily basis. Every damn day, I fight with myself to do the right thing. Dewayne opens the cash register at the Diner, and I wrestle with every bone in my body telling me to do something my brain is telling me I shouldn't do. But when thoughts like that come to me, I remember your mom and your grandparents and you, and I think about the kid and his family. I think about how many people would be disappointed in me now if I slipped up, and those thoughts keep me on the right path. So, I have no idea what, if anything, is going to happen with your mom and me. All I know is I need her in my life. I need *all* of you."

"Okay," I mumble, unsure as to what would be an appropriate response at the moment, but Morgan saves me by shifting the topic slightly.

"You're hurting right now because the kid doesn't remember you," he begins, "and to be honest, it kind of hurts me, too. But you'll never experience being alone without people who love you. Your mom, your grandparents, your dad and his family, even Kayla and Carlie and Jim…"

"And you?" I ask, smiling.

"Sure. Why not?" he says, returning my smile with a sly one of his own. "Since moving here, I'm the luckiest guy in the world with all these people caring about me. So, whatever happens with the kid, I'm good. And so are you."

I slink down in my seat, giving his words some thought.

"And I'm not saying that being without him won't hurt like hell," he continues, "but you've got enough love around you to go on with your life and be okay until he gets his memory back."

"You're right. I know you're right," I tell him, moving my head from side to side.

"But it doesn't completely fill the hole in your heart, does it?"

"Not at all. My head tells me I can get through this, but my heart isn't listening, I guess."

He nods.

"That'll take time, I suppose—a little time, lots of love, and a whole lot of your Gram's red velvet cake."

Laughing, I take the hint and start the car.

"Thanks for the talk," I tell him, putting the car into gear.

"Anytime, kid."

CHAPTER 29

I'm sitting on my bed and staring into my closet, wet hair soaking the back of my long-sleeved t-shirt. Choosing an outfit shouldn't be this difficult, but right now, doing so feels like the most important decision I've made in a long time.

"There's your sweater dress," Mom says from her fashion feedback post on the comforter next to me. "You wore that while you were in New York, right?"

"Yeah."

"So, he might remember."

"Maybe," I say, sighing.

This is the first New Year's Eve I can remember not slipping into a pair of sweatpants and a t-shirt for an evening on the couch, munching on Paulie's pizza and watching a movie marathon with Mom. But this year, I actually need to think about what to wear, even though I'm only going next door to the Laniers' and even though the whole reason I'm carefully choosing my outfit is because I'm hoping to jar my boyfriend's memory by wearing something he's seen before.

Biting my lip in concentration, I step to my closet and start whipping through clothes when I'm struck with the thought that what I'm looking for isn't hanging here at all.

"I've got it," I tell my mom, walking over to my dresser and searching through my drawers until I find a plain navy long sleeve t-shirt, a gray Titusville Titans t-shirt, and a pair of black track pants.

"Really?" Mom says when I drop the component parts of my outfit on the bed.

"I was wearing this the day we met."

I finger the gray t-shirt, and Mom stands up and hugs me from behind.

"Oh, Zip," she says, her voice tinged with sadness. "I'm sorry. I didn't know." She rumples my hair and steps back. "I'll let you get dressed."

Mom leaves and shuts the door behind her, and I set about turning myself into the girl of nearly one year ago, a girl I'm not sure I still am in a lot of ways. I put on my casual outfit and pull my hair back into a low ponytail at the base of my neck. My hair's longer now, so I can't re-create the look perfectly, and I have the charm bracelet now as well—I stare at the silver shining against the surface of the mahogany dresser, and I debate for a moment whether or not to put the bracelet on, but it's such a part of my wardrobe now that I grab it up and fasten it where it belongs. Even though I already look a little different than I did that day back in January, I slide into the same black snow boots I wore then, despite the fact that there's no snow on the ground today. I check myself in the mirror one more time and head out to the living room where my mom is sitting on the couch with her legs tucked up under her watching a news report on New Year's celebrations around the world. On the other side of the globe, tomorrow's already here, which is a good reminder that no matter what happens at Kieran's tonight, tomorrow's still going to come.

"I feel kind of bad about leaving you alone tonight," I say to Mom, shaking off my thoughts about the immediate future and sitting on the arm of the couch.

"And I feel kind of bad that you're about to visit Kieran knowing what's going to happen. I wish I could do something to take the hurt away."

I shrug as if my first meeting with Kieran since he's undergone the treatment will be no big deal.

"I need to get this over with, and the sooner he sees me, the sooner his memory might come back," I explain, relating information that isn't exactly news to either of us. "Plus, it's not like I can avoid

323

him forever, even if I wanted to. We live next door to each other and go to the same school, and even though he can't remember right now, I'm still his girlfriend."

Mom's mouth twists into a grin.

"You always make me proud with how you face things head-on, but this is one time I wish you could hide out here with me and watch movies all night."

"Me, too."

"Anyway, I won't be alone," Mom says in a slight change of topic. "Morgan's coming over once the Diner closes, so he'll be here when midnight strikes."

I bend down so I can slip my arm around her shoulders.

"I'm glad you and Morgan are hanging out," I tell her. I'd mentioned my conversation with Morgan at the river to her, and she basically confirmed what he told me—that they were enjoying each other's friendship for right now and letting the future take care of itself.

"Me, too," she says, angling her head so she can kiss my forehead. "He's got a lot to work through, but he's a good friend. Everyone can use a good friend."

I stand up from the couch, ready to get on with my night, but she reaches for my hand.

"Want me to wait up? You know—in case you need to talk or something?"

I lean down, my hand still in hers, to kiss her on the cheek.

"Thanks, but if you need to go to bed, go to bed. I'll be okay."

She nods, her soft smile instantly comforting.

"Love you, kiddo."

"Love you, too, Mom."

I head outside to the Cobalt for the trip to the Laniers', which, for the first time, is too short. But no length of time is going to seem long enough for me to prepare to meet the stranger my boyfriend has probably become, so once I've parked in the driveway behind Kayla's Jeep, I inhale and get out of the car, walking quickly in the cold up to the front porch.

"Zip," Carlie says on opening the door after I ring the bell, the sorrowful tone in her voice telling me a miracle hasn't occurred since Kayla called this afternoon to tell me they were home. She gathers me into a hug as she closes the door against the cold, and as she takes my coat I ask, "How...how is he?" which seems like a simplistic way to phrase what I'm getting at, but I can't think of anything better at the moment.

"The same. We drove around for a while once we got back to town, but he didn't recognize anything—same for the house. Brad came over a little while ago—nothing." Carlie glances up the stairs. "Jim's beside himself. I don't think any of us—him included—expected him to take things this hard. He's been in his study for hours looking through psychology journals, talking about all sorts of possibilities for memory recovery he never would have thought to suggest when Cooper was like this."

"Things are different when it's family, I guess."

Carlie nods, her eyes not meeting mine.

"At any rate, Kieran's upstairs in his room," she tells me. "He's expecting you."

Words fail me, so I squeeze her shoulder and turn away to head up the stairs. Outside Kieran's room, I count to ten—like *that's* going to help anything—before knocking on the door.

"Come in," he calls out, and my stupid heart flutters with a tiny bit of hope because at least his voice sounds the same. And as I push the door ajar and walk into the room to find him sitting at his desk and reading something on his laptop screen, my stupid heart once again pitters and patters and whatever else it does when it's excited, because he seems just like the same Kieran he always has—*my* Kieran.

And then he turns to face me.

His eyes hold the identical distant, cold glare Cooper's did when I spoke to him at the Homecoming game. They're still Kieran's icy blue eyes, but they're the eyes of a stranger.

"You must be Zip," he says, standing and leaning against the edge of his desk. He doesn't rush to hug me, doesn't hold my face in his hands the way he sometimes does when he's about to kiss me, doesn't even offer to shake hands as if we're starting a business meeting. I stand frozen to the floor next to the foot of his bed and watch as he folds his arms over his torso, closing himself off from me.

"Yeah," I respond, trying to find the confidence to say something else and failing.

He darts his eyes to the floor.

"Zara McKee is your real name. Your dad started calling you 'Zip' when you were a baby because you'd crawl around the house so fast your mom couldn't keep up with you."

Yet again, my stupid heart announces itself to me. *I've done it*, I think. *I really am the key to his memory.*

But before I can rush to kiss him and take a victory lap around the room while pumping my fist, I realize he's staring at me with the same vacant expression he's had since I walked in. He's waiting for me to say something, waiting for me to confirm whether or not his story about my nickname is correct because he must have read it in the notes he took for himself about his life.

"Yeah," I mumble again, and Kieran's probably wondering at this point why he picked such an inarticulate idiot for a girlfriend.

"I've been reading about you since Carlie—my mother—told me you were coming over," he says. "Sounds like we were pretty close."

Pretty close. Now, my heart makes itself known to me in an entirely different way, plunging down to my toes as they grind on the inside of my snow boots. I don't say "yeah," this time, but only bob my head a little.

"I hope you don't mind if I say this, but you're pretty." He avoids my eyes, focusing on some random point on the floor in front of him.

"Thank you."

Like I'd mind him saying that.

He lifts his gaze back to me, his chin jutting out at the bed.

"Would you...would you like to sit down?" he asks.

"Sure."

I sink to the mattress. He doesn't join me.

I. Am. Dying.

After a few seconds of examining me, he finally lands the verbal dagger I'd figured he would at some point—

"I'm so sorry, but I don't remember you."

"Don't apologize. We all expected this."

I sound like a robot.

"I *want* to remember you, if that helps." He points to his computer screen. "I mean, I've been reading all the stuff I wrote about us, and I get the impression we had something worth remembering."

"We did," I confirm, before I realize what I've said and correct myself. "I mean—we *do.*"

The two of us fall into an awkward and excruciating silence. I never thought in a million years I'd be stumbling around for what to say when talking to Kieran. Holding conversations with him has always been as natural as breathing, even when we first met.

"So, do you..." I pause, not sure I should be asking what I want to ask, but in the absence of anything else to talk about at the moment, I go ahead and dive in. "Do you remember anything at all?"

He moves his head slowly from side to side and, his arms still crossed, rubs his hand up and down the sleeves of his gray flannel shirt as if trying to warm himself up.

"No. It's weird. I don't remember that my family's my family, and I don't know all these people I'm supposed to know. As far as I'm concerned, I've never been in this town before…in this house. Nothing seems familiar." He tilts his head toward his computer. "But I knew how to use my laptop. I know that two plus two equals four. I know how to tie my shoes. I can do all kinds of things, and I know all sorts of *facts*." He pauses, his mouth in a tight line. "But I don't know you."

"They said it might take a few weeks. That's how long it took Cooper to return to—" I catch myself. "That's how long it took him to get his memory back."

"Yeah," Kieran mumbles, and I don't even think to ask if he's clear on who Cooper is. I'm assuming they must have met, at least briefly, after Kieran was brought out of his coma, and Kieran doesn't say otherwise.

Another awkward silence descends over us, and I stare down at my hands in my lap in order to avoid gawking at him like some kind of a creep. Less than a week ago, we were as close as two human beings could be. And now…

Nothing.

After about a minute or so, Kieran says, "Um…don't take this the wrong way because I want to get to know you again, but, today's been kind of a long day. I'm pretty tired all of a sudden." Once again, he glances quickly at his computer while I'm busy trying to pull my heart out of the insides of my boots. "I'd like to read a little more before I go to bed," he explains.

"Sure," I say, finding the strength to stand on feet and legs I can't totally feel at the moment—I think my entire body's gone numb, and all the better. If I'm numb, I won't feel any pain.

He doesn't unfold his arms, and doesn't step to me.

"It was nice meeting you," he says, his voice halting as if he's not sure he's said the right thing. And since I don't know how to respond, I just say, "Yeah—you, too," and push my way out into the hall, my eyes not focusing until I'm downstairs and pulling my coat off one of the hooks inside the front door. I don't look around for Carlie or Kayla or anyone.

I just want out of here.

Not even pausing long enough to put my coat on, I open the door and bound out to the porch, where a familiar female voice stops me once I'm almost to the steps.

"Zip."

I turn my head in the direction of the sound and squint into the darkness, finding Kayla and Brad sitting together on the porch swing once my eyes adjust. They stand and walk towards me, each of them holding a plastic cup and Brad carrying what appears to be a champagne bottle.

"Hey," I mumble, slipping into my coat. "You're drinking?"

Not that I disapprove, and not that Kayla and Brad haven't both told me they've had booze before, but I'm surprised they'd be drinking here, on Kayla's front porch, with her parents right inside. On the other hand, nothing seems normal right now, so maybe Carlie gave them both permission to get lit up.

Brad holds the bottle out to me, but I can't make out the label in the dim starlight.

"Sparkling grape juice," he tells me once he realizes I'm struggling to read.

"Ah."

Kayla squeezes my shoulder through my coat.

"I'll get you a cup," she says before disappearing into the house.

"Kay and I were going to watch the Sumner fireworks," Brad explains. "It's a straight shot south from here, and tonight's a pretty clear night, so if they go up high enough, we should be able to see them."

I look off in the direction of Sumner, knowing their parks department shoots off fireworks at midnight every New Year's Eve at Veterans' Park just north of the mall.

Kayla returns with a cup that Brad fills for me, and we sit down on the top porch step.

"So, I'm assuming you've met Kieran 2.0?" she asks, and I grimace.

"Not funny."

"No? Well, maybe we won't go with that nickname, then." Kayla's completely serious. "The other possibility I was thinking of was 'NuKieran'."

"Kayla," I say, sighing.

Brad leans forward so he can look over at me sitting on her other side.

"She's been like this ever since I came over," he grumbles.

"And like I've been telling you ever since you came over, *this* is how you deal with life in Kieran Lanier-Land," she huffs, glancing back and forth between us. "If you don't turn the whole thing into a big freaking joke sometimes, you might go insane. I just keep reminding myself that in a few weeks, I'll hopefully never need to laugh my way through some kind of bizarreness with my brother ever again."

Just a few more weeks. Guess I'm going to have to keep telling myself that, too.

330

"I'm guessing you're so grumpy because your reunion didn't go well?" she asks.

I take a sip of my sparkling grape juice, the sweetness making my lips pucker.

"He's so...empty," I say when my mouth recovers. "I mean, I know how Cooper was when he went through this, but talking with Kieran was just weird. We got along from the moment we met, you know? Talking to him was always so easy. Now it's like, I don't know..."

Kayla takes advantage of my slight pause.

"It's like there's a wall," she finishes for me, her gaze straight ahead into the darkness. "A wall you can't get over or break through, and he's on the other side. And he doesn't even care enough to try to get to you."

Brad takes her hand in his, and I study her, realizing that as hard as Kieran's "wandering" period might be on me, it's going to be a thousand times worse for Kayla, who's short a brother right now.

After setting his cup down on the porch, Brad reaches into his coat pocket for his phone so he can check the time.

"It's almost midnight," he tells us, and we train our eyes on the night sky and watch the initial burst of fireworks above the horizon that from this distance looks like nothing more than multicolored paint spatters against a dark wall.

"Happy New Year," Brad whispers to Kayla, and the two of them share a kiss that goes on long enough for me to start squirming on Kayla's other side. When they part, Brad, perhaps feeling bad that I'm the third wheel, reaches his arm across Kayla and extends his fist out to me.

"Happy New Year, Wallace," I say, bumping knuckles with him.

"You, too, McKee."

Brad turns his attention to his phone, tapping around until *Auld Lang Syne* starts playing, completing the New Year's mood.

"Seriously?" Kayla laughs. "You think of everything, don't you?"

"I try," Brad responds, holding his phone out so we can hear the song. This version is an instrumental, and I'm not completely sure of the lyrics, although I've seen the end to *It's a Wonderful Life* about a billion times and have heard the song on countless TV shows and commercials. And if I'm remembering correctly, the song is about remembering forgotten acquaintances and times past, a sentiment I'm totally on board with at the moment.

I can't help but wonder what Kieran's doing right now. Is he still reading about his past? Is he asleep, experiencing the end of the second full day of his life in which going to sleep when he wants and waking up when he wants is under his control? Is he doing something else?

Whatever he's doing, all I know is that he's not out here kissing me.

Kayla catches me looking back at their front door, and she bumps her shoulder into mine.

"Hey," she says, drawing my eyes to her. "Only a few weeks, right? We'll get through this."

She's smiling broadly enough it's almost as if she's trying to transfer some of her confidence to me.

"Right. Only a few weeks."

Kayla loops her arm through mine and rests her head on my shoulder, and I tilt my head against hers, my ear grazing her hair.

"Happy New Year," she whispers.

"Happy New Year, Kay."

END OF BOOK THREE

ACKNOWLEDGEMENTS

I'd like to thank the friends, family, and fans who have immersed themselves in Zip and Kieran's weird little world. Thanks for going along for the ride—your comments and encouragement keep me moving forward with my writing (mis)adventures.

I also want to thank my attack tabby, Cleo, who sits on my lap and nudges my legs as I write. I'm honored to be your forever human.

A giant "thank you" goes out to Stacey McNamara and Rachel Crites, who read this book when it wasn't fit for public consumption. Your feedback was so valuable (and, Stacey—sorry I made you cry).

And the biggest "thank you" of all goes to Heath Martin, who is an amazing test reader and an even more amazing husband. Everything is better with you by my side.

About the Author

Amy Martin wrote and illustrated her first book at the age of ten and gave it to her fourth grade teacher, who hopefully didn't share it with anyone else. She currently lives in Lexington, Kentucky, with her husband and a ferocious attack tabby. You can find out more about her books and sign up for her mailing list at http://www.theamymartin.com.

Other Books by Amy Martin

In Your Dreams (In Your Dreams 1)
As You Wake (In Your Dreams 2)